# The Mars Doctor

**Author:**

## RM Rotcod

Dedicated to Lorob.

Thanks to editor Krista Matthes.

ISBN: 978-0-09997392-3-5 (print)

Published 2019-8-27


Literary agent; Bosveld books,

2177 Port Talbot place, Coralville, IA 52241, USA

## Preface; to The Mars Doctor

The time setting of this novel is in the very near future. In this fictional story a medical doctor and the space-crew on a journey to Mars and back, experience unimaginable disasters, that need to be handled without usual resources, and within the impossible circumstances of space travel. The entire trip becomes a thrilling survival challenge. The doctor's thought process will be revealed. The medical problems are exciting and how the doctor handles them is innovative and will be fascinating for non-medical readers. Each character's inner mind is revealed. I have a fascination for psychology and the stories of people's lives whom I meet. Graphic descriptions will be given about the doctor's secret and what he hides behind a confidant façade. A doctor is but a human too, and has uncertainties, fears, concerns, and even frailties. It is a challenge for any doctor to project a realistic confidence upon which a patient builds their trust and hopes. Some readers may recognize elements of the story's characters within themselves, or within other persons whom they know.

I have also had a 40-year fascination for extreme medicine. That is when medical care and interventions have to be performed when there are extremely limited facilities, devices and drugs. Extreme medicine also means working in extreme isolation, like in a jungle hospital where patient referral is impossible, as in a space ship. The physicians manage severe patient conditions far beyond their level of training, knowledge and experience. The doctors then have to extrapolate what they know, innovate a treatment, and save a life. As a very young doctor, I unexpectedly once had to deliver a baby in lady's own home without modern drugs and tools. I enjoyed, and needed, the whiskey the husband offered me afterwards, suiting in his lounge. I have also practiced very rural medicine in Africa. I had a colleague once descend for three miles vertical underground in a gold mine, to anesthetize a man in order to amputate his leg trapped under an immovable massive rock, and thus free him to get him back to the surface. The space disasters both medical and other represent the most extreme events I could credibly imagine. I have been making notes and cataloging my thoughts on characters and plots, on extreme space medicine for twenty years, in planning to write this book. Ironically, I won a national essay competition at the age of seventeen years writing about the mind of a male sailing alone across the Atlantic Ocean and how his mind meanders and he gets confused between his fantasies and reality and he comes to imagine that the passing sea life, dolphins and seagulls, speak to him. This book continues that isolated sailor's adventure journey, but as a grown-up reject medical doctor, traveling to Mars in an eclectic group of fourteen astronauts.

There is also stress within the group of fourteen astronauts imprisoned in a space-ship for near three years in a degree of confinement, that would constitute utter cruelty if similarly applied to humans on earth. This claustrophobic physical closeness of these persons, added to unimaginable and never-before space disasters makes for the bringing out of the very worst character traits in persons, and the very best traits as well. The journey of these astronauts travelling to Mars and back, called Marsnauts, is a roller coaster adventure.

The ending is a happy ending that would not be predicted. Don't read it before completing the book, or you will spoil your experience reading the book. When I sat down and finally forced myself to put pen to paper, I wrote the book in four weeks working 10 to 14-hours per day. I had serendipitously discovered a writing competition as I was writing the first chapter, and had to submit my book before a tight dead line. That may have brought out the best in me. The editing, and proof reading took another intense month as well. Thank you, Krista Matthes, for your amazing help.

While writing the book I often cried living my characters' joys, and tragedies. I felt each day that I did not know what lay ahead of me. I had a starting point, but often never knew the story end point, nor the ride in between. The birth process of this book differed little from the natural birth of a baby. The journey is painful and agonizing, and the end is divine beyond humble words. I hope in reading my book you feel the tear moisture in the pages, the stories joys in your heart and the final deeper messages in your soul.

Often, persons burdened with negative character traits involving self-anger or feelings of inadequacy, readily blame or accuse others wrongly, of having the very traits they themselves suffer from. Some of the story's crew have already walked their own personal journey of self-discovery and have embraided their discovered strengths and humility into wisdom. Others of the story's crew are young and naïve and have yet to discover mature wisdom. Often the greatest wisdoms are born from surviving bitter incredible mishaps, setbacks, and injustices. Some of the characters are in denial about their own character flaws. Other characters are innocent enough to be unable to perceive they own inner beauty and strengths. They all have to find friends, and allies. They have to learn to stand together to discover a greater purpose in the Mars mission, beyond what the engineers and politicians envisaged. Each crew member volunteered for this extreme dangerous mission for a secret dark personal reason, but all find the drive to complete the mission for a very different reason. It is an extreme *Big Brother* story. It is an extreme *Survivor* story.

Every human and mechanical disaster that happens on the story's space-flight in the Mars Doctor, has happened on Earth, but never with such remoteness from help, or seeming insolvability. When disaster occurs on an interplanetary space-mission, resolution is found through aspects of humanity that are unexpected. The aspects of humanity that are discovered in the story take a while for all of the crew to understand fully. They each gradually discover those aspects within themselves and then within the others. None of them walk the discovery process alone. They jointly walk the bumpy road of discovery together, to be able to understand what they are discovering. In the story some disasters are unresolvable, yet there are still positives to be extracted from those disasters, as discovered by the crew in the story. The astronauts slowly discover the greatest characterizing feature of the homo sapiens species. They find the human trait most separates homo sapiens from all other life-forms. It is one not usually recognized. Sometimes to find the most beautiful things, one has to first get through that which is hard, ugly and foul. That occurs on the Mars Mission. Beauty often does not lie exposed for instant discovery. It lies concealed and has to be sought. The process of seeking has to be intentional, focused, and systematic. Discovery of things of beauty can be serendipitous. However, more often it is found when one chooses to believe in the seemingly unbelievable, resolutely seeks it, and always move forward. Equally, the very wonderful things discovered are usually not what was remotely conceptualized to be lying ahead on the journey. The discovery of that wonder, only requires one to have an attitude to seek and to believe in a wonder lying ahead, even when one has no concept of what that wonder is. To embark on that journey also requires strength when exhausted, power when depleted, faith when despondent, and an ice-cold calm decision to never yield. That very final element is not inherent in the heart, the body or even the soul. It is a human decision of the brain. The decision is to never be beaten by circumstance down to one's last breath and last beat of the heart. With that decision one is never a loser in life, never.

I wrote from my heart. I could hate some of the story's characters, and I do love some of the others. Every step a reader takes reading this fictional adventure, is a step I have walked in a blur of realities and fantasies. I love discovering the personal life stories of people that I meet. Everyone has a story. In discovering the story of another person, one embraces wisdoms from that story into oneself. In the writing of this book, I had some personal emotional releases.

The story ending is one that no planner of any real manned Mars mission could ever foresee. If a reader, having completed this book, agrees that the exact ending is a feasible ending in a real-life Mars manned mission, then the reader will be a changed person for having read the book.


RM Rotcod

# CHAPTER 1.

## The impossible, and the azure color blue.  (week 124)

*The small white ball subtly seemed to have turned a shade of blue. Was it azure yet? I knew it would eventually become azure blue.*

Rodney Powell, the spaceship-doctor, next reminisced about colors, that he had seen nearly fifty years earlier.

Having completed my first period of military service, I had earned my first week-pass out of the barbed wire enclosure of the infantry battalion base camp. I stood on the platform of a small rural old train station. I was drafted into military service. I am not a natural born-to-be soldier. I was however, I hope, a good soldier. I was suddenly overwhelmed by the colors of the civilian world.  I was overwhelmed by the sight of a few women. I had not seen a female in 20 weeks. I stood in humbled awe of their radiant smiley joyful faces. Their skins were so flawless. They bulged and curved in places I had forgotten humans could bulge and curve in. It was so good. I just wanted to runup to the closest lady and have her scents invade my soul. To have her smile consume me and caress my iron-hard shoulders. I only needed to stand in her aura. I had no idea what else to do, frozen in place watching those pretty talkative civilian ladies. They bounced around in their 1970s colorful skirts on the Grahamstown train platform. I simply was in awe of them. The colors in my preceding 20-weeks consisted of dusky dry grass, dry trees, rocks, sand, men only, and khaki-brown army clothing. That left me longing for pinks, reds, and yes, azure blue. The old train would take me away from this remote drab military base, back to the lively city with a million people, where I had grown up.

After 20 weeks of all-day long physical training, I could run a fast mile wearing a steel combat helmet, a fully packed ammunition belt, and carrying a FN NATO-caliber 7.62 mm semi- automatic combat rifle. That trained soldier ran a mile faster than the boy wearing only shorts and a sports shirt, he had been the year before. At age seventeen, the boy I remembered had been the school and state 400 m sprint champion. He was always an athlete and still a boy. Now at age eighteen after 20 weeks basic infantry training, he stood proudly in his military khaki uniform with a green infantry beret and a Springbok badge. He was no longer a boy. The army had made him into a hardened extra-trim super-fit fighting man, or so he thought. I looked back in my mind, nearly fifty years later, on that young soldier of eighteen, waiting for the steam train and its three passenger coaches to pull up the hill into the station. That train would take him from the drab military landscape to a lively colorful world, and his family and civilization.

Sitting in my spaceship now, I once again waited to return to my lively colorful world; to my family and civilization. This time, my transport was not going to be a tired smoky old steam train beyond its best service years, struggling up a hill at near walking speed. My transport was a futuristic billion-dollar computer-controlled rocket-spaceship hurtling between planets at tens of thousands of miles an hour.

I continued to think of that little 18-year old soldier-boy now, as I studied the white, teasing-to-be-blue ball through a tiny round window. The boy had thought he was a man back then. He was so naive. He was so ignorant about life. He might have shriveled up and died of fear on that train platform, had he known the hardships and set-backs that lay ahead of him in life, were they revealed to him back then. The stars that twinkled before his eyes that far-back day were the bubbling young ladies in their colorful dresses. If while waiting for that very train, his greatest adventure had been revealed, he would have bent forward with his hands on his hips, laughing himself into breathlessness. It would have sounded so funny. That ultimate adventure would then have sounded like fiction, and so far beyond imagination, that it was ludicrous. Science fiction is creative thinking stretching extreme facts and reality, just a pinch further. Suggestion of this greatest adventure, lying ahead of that innocent soldier on the train platform was as inconceivable as science fiction. Even more so, why would it include a person coming from the Southern tip of Africa? It certainly would not include him one day looking at a small white ball in the black sky wanting to become azure.

The distant rumble of the steam locomotive's chugging up the final slope were softly audible. Steam locomotives were ancient technology to the young soldier. The powerful Garrett 2-6-2-2-6-2 double steam engine slowly rumbled into the train station, as if about to totally run out of breath. The enthusiastic young soldier knew modern diesel electric locomotives would be replacing the messy coal burners someday. Those old steam trains could reach thirty kilometers per hour, but only on downhills. He wondered how it felt to ride on a train pulled by modern diesel-electric locomotives that could go as fast as ninety kilometers per hour on level tracks. That boy however never dreamed he would one day have the ultimate high technology ride, fast enough to circle the world in ninety minutes.

*The white ball far away was definitely slightly azure.*

It seems that my life's destiny is to relive so much of my early life's poignant moments again and again. Twenty weeks of color deprivation was an amazing experience at the age of eighteen. This present experience, so far, had been 30 months of color deprivation. My mind seemed burdened by the spaceship black, and white and silver unexciting mechanical colors. Also, the endless Martian landscapes that I had lived in for a year, that were a uniform rusty dirty red color that lay heavy on my mind. I longed to see all the shades of green. The fresh sharp greens of Spring leaves, the mature murky green of shady forest trees. I thought of hot pink. It is the happiest color ever invented. All woman who wear it look fun, happy and cute. Men who tastefully wear a little pink with a tailored suit display a statement of being both appreciative of art and of being sensitive to others. I liked purple with my black suits. If a man wears a dark purple tie with black stripes it suggests he is serious, confident, approachable, but with no need to look powerful. A modestly lighter bold purple striped tie with smaller shrimp-colored stripes in between, always attracts a comment and smile from a woman who is self-confident and has a bold smile. Caribbean coral reef identical fish with luminescent yellow stripes tightly swimming in schools against a mauve blue background create a feeling of unreality. However, it is the color azure that burns my soul the most. I hungered to have it surround me, and be over me, like the warm embrace of a giggling train station girl.

My mind was jumping around like a panicky gold fish. I thought of the color of hot red. I saw the redness of the little bit of blood spurting from Vahini's flesh when I divided it with a pair of scissors. That color was vivid in his brain. I hadn't cut someone's perineal flesh with scissors in the thirty prior years, yet it felt so natural. Vahini, the laboring lady, gave a slight moan, but I knew that she was barely feeling it, as the skin was so tightly stretched out. Two other ladies floated nearby in the spaceship air wanting to help Vahini in her laboring pains. They held Vahini softly but effectively in the makeshift bed-chair. I was tempted to leave the skin and see if it could stretch out enough around the baby's head, without tearing. On the other hand, it might heal better if the cut was clean, neat and well sutured. Suturing a torn perineum was not something I wanted to do. Most of the midwives at the government hospitals, where I had worked forty years earlier, were nifty midwives. They loved to slow down the rate-of-head descent to achieve a real slow skin stretch. I could do that too. I had also caressed many a perineum to stretch that extra little bit, ever so slowly over the doughy edematous head of a baby. The art is in the slowness. The art of midwifery is tens of thousands of years old. I was a doctor however, and I wanted to take things to a modern and better level. I chose to cut Vahini's flesh in a controlled fashion, rather than risk a ragged tear perineum.

If the flesh tears, it is shredded and irregular, and hard to suture it afterwards. Mostly a skin tear was not the midwife's fault. It happens with an uncontrollable screaming wriggling woman who is determined to shout and explode the baby out of herself. The head gets delivered too fast. There are moments, as the head is about to be born, when the mother must bear down, and moments when she must not bear down despite all her instincts to do so. The baby's head's last moments as it stretches the perineum to its maximum, must be as slow and as controlled as is possible. Once the stretched perineum gently shrinks back to lie below the baby's chin, the head is officially delivered. The rest of the delivery is usually easy and no more skin damage can occur My young doctor experience in delivering babies had taught me some lessons in life. When the lady's baby was the fruit of love and her male partner, her noble knight Lancelot, stood beside her, the lady could be so brave during the final moments of delivering her baby. When the lady's baby was the result of unplanned moments, an unwanted tragedy and the fathering-male was not her soulmate and life-companion, then that lady was very different. She would cry loudest, scream loudest, and wriggle most. She was the one who least cooperated with the doctor's instructions, as if trying to get the baby out into the world as traumatic as possible. She was the woman who mostly likely tore her own perineum. There was a correct time to bear down, and a correct time to breathe deeply and not bear down. The midwife, or the obstetric physician conducted those orchestral moments.

Vahini had been born in Agra, India, but had no memory of the place. She had grown up in America, and always loved numbers and challenges. I guess that was part of what bought her life's path to meet my life's path as a doctor. I stood ready to clip the perineum with a pair of scissors. I first met her in my basic crash-course astronaut training. Vahini was my guide and mentor. She was a man at times, and worked me hard on the fitness exercise parts. She was a genius, I guess, and tortured my brain to memorize so much new stuff. I was also rushing to put together my supply list and to brain storm all the medical events I might need to manage as ship-surgeon. NASA gave me a lot of leeway in those decisions.

Vahini had never owned a skirt and she intimidated men, but I liked her. I felt we had a shared wavelength. She may have liked me too, but she never gave a clue about that. I was happy within myself with that. My brain was more befuddled at what I had gotten myself into. I was in no rush to figure out Vahini, and I had all my own astronautical crises to sought out first. My life's journey had shown again and again, those who put on the leatheriest facades, have the softest insides. Sometimes the soft inside is very inadequate and they make for evil people. Sometimes that soft inside makes for an uncomplicated, gentle and so very warm person. Those latter persons could be incredibly loyal and decent, once they trust you. In those early moments of my pre-launch astronaut training by Vahini, I never in a million years could have guessed I would end up stitching Vahini's flesh after she delivered a baby in outer space on a journey over halfway to Mars.

When suturing I could roll my right hand grasping the suture-needle-holder in order to push a suture in a mathematically pure circular curving tract. I had practiced that a lot at Kalafong Hospital on Saturday nights after midnight. That midnight time was when the flow of stab wound patients peaked coming into the emergency room. My medical student buddies and I would party and socialize until 11PM then drive out to Kalafong hospital afterwards, to help out in the emergency room. Once we had each sutured about ten various stab wounds in patients, we would be rewarded with toasted cheese sandwiches and a cup of Coca Cola. After that we went home to bed. I was pretty nifty at suturing skin wounds. Over the years I had mastered the spacing of my sutures, the tautness of my sutures, and how to make three counter-posing wrap knots, which never came loose. I even knew how to bury the knots "underground", for suturing lacerated tongues, so that the knot could not be licked loose.

My training as a doctor had been excellent. I was well taught to treat every patient as if they are the most important person in the world, during the tiny fragment of time they were before me. I also was fully aware every baby ever born is innocent of the sins of their biological progenitors. I was determined to be a best doctor to Vahini in her birthing process as all my great professors, and many wonderful midwives had taught me to be. I never judged, but I sure like to look, perceive and think on everything.

In space, we had forgotten what days and nights were. Our clocks simply ran on a time schedule we called Houston time. The first twelve hours we called up-time, and that was sort of our day. The second twelve hours of the Houston day we called down-time. In space travel when the ship is away from any planet's shadows, the Sun shines all the time on one side of the ship. It is an eternal day. We did follow the usual calendar but Sundays and Wednesdays were identical to us. We just referred to the day of the month, like the 17th and the 23rd.

It was maybe not me who wanted the white ball to become azure, I was thinking. I turned the paradigm around, and convinced myself that the white ball itself was wanting to look azure, just for me. It was beckoning me.

*The white celestial body ahead of the spaceship grew another degree more azure blue and larger each hour and each day.*

There were going to be so many questions to be answered once the mission landed on Earth. I was sure all the NASA leaders, Washington politicians, and the President's men would be hot fighting. They would all be blaming each other for this Manned Mars Mission's failures, and for the astronaut deaths that had occurred. I was sure there would be much acrimony and we, the surviving crew, would likely be each demonized and blamed in some way for something. It would a news media frenzy with all the interviewees, who were not Marsnauts, acting like experts knowing everything. I however, at this point of not having returned to Earth yet, had no idea what was known on Earth, or not known on Earth about the space-mission details.

Well, we the crew survivors, had a lot to say, or maybe very little to say. It would all depend on our moods at the second of being asked a question. It would also depend on the exact tone of the questions. We were not wimps anymore. We will not take bad attitude or nonsense from anyone, not anymore, after what we have endured as castaways into the universe. As billion-dollar test-rats we are fearless. We each felt we are independent universes unto ourselves. We were not arrogant. We only want to give love to all. However, we sure would not tolerate any nonsense. We were lions. We were strong, and could be vociferous. We felt no wish to talk a lot, but we could easily be provoked into some blunt responses. We did not want to play any blame game. Above all, we did not want to take any nonsense from anyone.

This mission was supposed be a career highlight for the President. The mission however, was totally setup to be a disaster from the first day that everything was set to go. I anticipated that we would be politically and economically analyzing the mission's failings for years. We, the crew all just needed to walk on green morning cut grass with their bare feet and feel the crispy sparkle of morning dew on our naked pink toes. We Marsnauts all wanted to hug our dear ones, our spouses, our children, or just another warm gentle human being. We wanted to sit on a beach and leisurely study a sunrise against a blue sky highlighted with gentle fluffy white clouds. When we had done that for a carefree year, rediscovered Mother Earth and the sweetness of humanity, then we would be willing to talk abundantly about the Ares-1 Manned Mars-Mission.

Why do folks describe feeling depressed as being blue, when blue is such a beautiful color? There is no other celestial body that is azure blue like Mother Earth. The most beautiful thing about Earth is the best side of humanity living on Earth. Man can individually be ugly, very ugly. However, if you stand back a bit, and take a broad view and you look deeply you can glimpse the best of humanity. That glimpse is so enigmatic. You can't see it casually. You have to choose to look in a positive way, then the beauty of mankind peeps out, and it is awesome. That best side of humans is how we can cooperatively join with each other in units, teams, societies, nations, and inhabitants of a planet.

We went to Mars to all find it. We in fact, had been to hell to find it. We went beyond hell to find the beauty in humanity. The beauty is when a person becomes selfless, choosing to care for another first. Coming back, we had to re-enter hell from its rear door to be able to walk through hell and come out the other side. We launched from Cape Canaveral as rats, and now we were returning as very beautiful people.

*I studied the azure-blue orb. I felt amazement and contentment. Earth beckoned.*

Of course, errors were made. Of course, things could have been done better. We, the crew, did not actually care about the errors. We have no fight with anyone at NASA, or even in Washington. Our trip should best never have happened. We now realized that they we had to do this trip for mankind, not to discover Mars, but for mankind to discover itself. It is a twisted logic. You leave your home and your life to understand what your home really is and what your life really were. We did it. No need to do it again.

I trust we will not have fame as the first humans to walk on Mars; however, I want us to be remembered as the last humans to ever leave the planet Earth. We, the crew, all share that feeling. The review of the Mars mission, including all the mistakes, the mishaps, and design errors must be an unemotional scientific engineering analysis completed six or twelve months after we land. It must be documented. It must not be manipulated for pre-trial hearings, with all of NASA and the politicians trying to exonerate themselves. The hearing must be closed to the press. The hearing must not be steamed up and inflamed into a reality drama. The review has to be simply a conclusion of the mission, with its interest lying with future engineers getting it right next time. After that, each of us crew wants to get on with our little lives.

The mission that we were given was improbable in so many ways. It was impossible in a thousand more ways. We, the crew, did it. We did the impossible. I guess the engineering and scientific post-flight analysis will conclude in a period of months; however, I will spend the rest of my life seeking words to elucidate how it was the ordinary humanity within us, that made it all possible. The return of the astronauts who survived was less to do with best design and engineering, and more to do with the greatness of human nature. We succeeded not because we were an elite group all with the right stuff. We succeeded because we were ordinary, and somewhat flawed, each in little ways. The crew only had to be humble and embrace each other's flaws for us to bring out our group divine-like strengths and abilities to survive and succeed.

*Coming home the coolness in the azure blue color of Mother Earth, was what most warmed my heart. The azure ball beckoned.*

# CHAPTER 2.

## The broken leg. (Week 1)

The launch had gone as planned. We had separated from the Saturn-8 second-stage rocket on schedule and twelve hours later we approached the Mars-tanker-ISS space-structure group on our Earth orbit. From the first visual sighting it took eight hours to drift close enough to dock. The first seven Marsnauts were on board the International Space Station (ISS) already. They had docked a week earlier. We were the last seven to catch up.  There had also been two cargo ship launches that docked a week apart each with the ISS, before the first crew-ship with seven Marsnauts arrived. Fourteen of us were going to Mars. The ISS also had never had so many people on board at one time. This was a world record for humans in Space all at one time. Once we docked, the total of humans in the ISS would be twenty. The regular number in ISS was 6, with occasional crews overlapping with numbers up to 13 humans on board the ISS. We knew ISS was busting at the seams with astronauts.

The Chinese had tried to go it on their own in Space, but they finally managed to join the ISS operation. The Russians had been unhappy about the Chinese joining the ISS, but since the Americans started to fly their own ships again to the ISS, the Russians could not stop the Americans bringing up Chinese Astronauts.  The ISS had had an extra two extensions added to it to accommodate the Marsnauts during this Mars flight preparatory time.

The Marsnauts, at our last meeting before the first seven launched, were warned to be wary of the Chinese Astronauts. We were told no-one in the ISS other than us official Marsnauts were allowed to enter the Ares-1 Mars-space-ship. We asked why, but only got evasive answers. The muttered answer from General Jen was that it involved preserving medical research hygiene. There were things we were not informed about, to be found out later.

Originally, the Marsnauts were going to be an International group made up of Americans, Russians, and Chinese, the major three space-faring nations. There were also some other nations that contributed just equipment and money. Then twelve months before the start of the Ares-1 Mars-mission the President Announced the Mars mission was going to be a pure American mission. Since I was invited very late, to join the Ares-1 mission to Mars, I was simply overwhelmed by everything and thought little about this political matter. Over the next nearly three years, this matter would come back and haunt us.

There were originally to be two Chinese surgeons, one on the launch Mars mission-team and one on the backup-team. There were a matching two Russian backup mission-team surgeons trained to fly to Mars if needed in the lastminute absence of the Chinese doctors. There were an additional two American physicians as very last backup physicians who could fly airplanes and who were well versed with space medicine. So, the total of possible physicians to originally potentially go on the mission and were fully trained were six, although the actual Ares-1 Manned Mars Mission would only take one doctor to Mars. After the Chinese and Russians were withdrawn, the one American physician crashed his motorbike and fractured his femur a month before the launch dates. The other American physician developed angina also a month before launch and needed coronary stents. That created the gap for me.

There had never been a policy of routinely sending a clinically-skilled practicing-physician on space missions. Some physicians had been astronauts before, but they flew mainly as scientists and played with research critters in lab experiments. For this Mars mission, it was suggested that a clinically-skilled medical doctor should be part of the mission team. NASA management had heard many arguments about what type of physician should accompany the group. There were arguments for it to be a general physician, or a general internal medicine specialist, or even to be family practitioner. Emergency Room physicians were argued by some to have the best package of skills for space travel. Even the various societies of Advanced Registered Nurse Practitioners had argued that an ARNP would be a better care-giver of sick astronauts than a physician could be. They strongly argued that they could do anything with the appropriate help via radio from Houston. They said doctors would be bad nurses and anyone who was sick needed nursing, not a doctor to prescribe drugs only. I laughed upon hearing those things. Politics, and self-interest!

With the final loss of the last of the six assigned space-physicians associated with the Mars Mission only weeks before the launch of the first seven Marsnauts it created a crisis. Some considered the entire mission was poorly planned. The mission was rushed to an earlier date than that initially planned for, for political purposes. So much equipment was under-tested, and even untested. The mission was underfunded, perhaps because the magnitude of this far reaching human endeavor was simply crazy and too massive. Regardless of that, there was no shortage of volunteers to be Marsnauts.

To remedy the financial situation, the President set up a GoFundMe account for the Ares-1 Manned Mars Space-Mission. Fifty million donations came in from around the world averaging $100 per donor. That totaled $5 billion. It strongly indicated the world was very heavily emotionally invested in sending humans to walk on Mars. Maybe that was due to the US President's very effective propaganda. The President took total credit for the huge donor responses.

With the sudden loss of all the assigned mission physicians, NASA management had to reexamine the list of applicants again. There were 4057 mad persons who each thought they had the best credentials to fly to Mars as the mission-physician. I was one of them. I was to be sixty-five years old on launch day and I was a retired anesthesiologist. My curriculum vitae was long, and my publishing and lecturing credits seemed irrelevant to walking on Mars. I was clear in my head that my fifty-page curriculum vitae would never win me this job. The competitive field was too big. It would have to be a crazy sassy hard-punching resume, that stood out dramatically, that would get me the job. It worked.

Yogi Beere had once said that, in a baseball game, you miss the ball on every strike that you don't take. He meant there is nothing lost in taking a swing at a fast low-ball. If you connect it might be a glorious winning home run, and if you miss, nothing is lost. Similarly, it can be said you never get onto the on-stage discussion-panel, if you never raise your own hand when sitting at the back of the school hall. I recall, that when I was a lost teenager, I saw Don Quixote singing in a movie about the Impossible Dream. Don Quixote sang of a broken man scorned and covered in scars who strove with his last once of courage to reach the unreachable stars. He sang that the world would be a better place, if only one man reached for the unreachable stars and strove with his last once of courage.  That echoed through my heart. It helped make me never scared to attempt seemingly impossible tasks. It made me more fearful of having never tried, than being fearful of failing when trying. My personal nature is to contemplate all tasks thoroughly and to generally avoid risks. Sometimes one must throw caution to the winds. I often joked to friends that it is good to reach high and if you fail to touch a star in the night sky, maybe you might only get to rest your hand on the moon, and wouldn't that be amazing in itself.

One day I applied to be an astronaut for a manned Mars mission.

I had actually spent half of my life thinking I was the perfect physician for a manned Mars mission.  When I heard the mission to Mars was to become a reality, I decided to throw my name into the hat.

Two years later I suddenly got an email asking if I was still available, and that an on-site interview in Houston was being offered. My wife thought I would never get the job. She also feared I would die on such a space trip. She could not understand it all. Most of all she said she loved me and supported me.

I got the job. I fully accepted silently in my heart, knowing it was more a certain suicide mission. However, I could never turn it down. My life was lived out and my children were successful adults. I was fresh retired from clinical medicine. I was an oddball and for NASA to choose me was utterly bizarre. Maybe I was perfect, in my imperfections. Maybe they liked my written arguments as to why I was uniquely suitable to be a manned Mars mission physician. I had seven years of experience being a rustic family physician who did a fair bit of surgery and delivering babies. I then worked in private practice with total autonomy of practice, working with top national surgeons in their fields, doing very large and challenging surgeries. I followed that, with a rigid stifling university lecturing career as a professor of anesthesia. My foremost skill was doing regional anesthesia. I knew every nerve block in the book, by both old and modern techniques. The best physician in space would be an anesthesiologist, who never had to use gas anesthesia and who could have awake patients under surgery, who could operate, who knew all medicine in good breadth, and had five diverse medical degrees. My crazy proposal won the day. Inhaled anesthesia cannot be done in a space ship's confines, as the vapors and gasses would cause catastrophic air pollution for everyone.

I confess I was tired of life and the thought of actively ending it all, was a thought I had had to fight out of my head previously. I was not afraid of a naturally-occurring death. Death would be a release for me. If I survived the trip, my life might become a roller coaster ride of paid lecturing afterwards. That would be my reward. I would feel validated in myself. I would feel wanted. Maybe, the platform of being a celebrity lecturer would give me a voice to say so much more about life and the world and about medicine. I might be able to make the world a better place even. How could I turn down this opportunity to be an Astronaut, or more correctly, a Marsnaut? I had nothing to fear and everything to win. With time, I learned that most of the crew the crew had similar motivations, and their own dark thoughts.

---

When we had drifted to within 100 feet of the ISS (International Space Station) a mechanical arm reached out from the ISS to latch onto us. It slowly moved us closer and aligned our berthing hatches. An hour later after berthing and locking and equalizing gas pressures, we could open our side's hatch to enter ISS. The only thing more important than our ship and the ISS successfully docking was to not collide and damage each orbiting space structure. So, there was no rush and the final approach was snail slow. We had a pilot in each structure using small adjusting jets. We tried to minimally make adjustments, so as to save fuel. Fuel was not more important than oxygen. Fuel was as important as oxygen.

Once boarded the ISS greetings were warm. We reached out in handshakes then slowly pulled each other into a hug with a pause followed by gentle push apart. The finger's-grip was relaxed when we each thought we were back in a neutral drift in a gravitation-free float.

I spoke first to a lady Mars-astronaut.

"Hi Vicky." Vicky was a mission engineer, but could backup as IT expert if needed.

"Hi Rodney." She addressed me.

"We missed you folks the last week", I said.

"Yeh!" said Vicky enthusiastically.

I asked, "What has it been like up here?"

Vicky's smile softened a bit. "A little tense. I think there is a lot of jealousy on the side of a few ISS crew. It slips out with little barbed comments occasionally."

"Really?"

"The Russians are great. They love us Marsnauts, but the two Chinese guys are a mystery".

The Russians and Chinese were International Space Station (ISS) crew doing research on the ISS in orbit around the Earth. The Ares-1 Mars spaceship was temporarily attached to the ISS, as the Ares-1 crew and the ship components assembled at the ISA. Soon, the Ares-1 Mars space-mission would separate from the ISS leaving the ISS astronauts behind, and then launch off to Mars

Vicky continued, "The one Wei Zhang was flirtatious with me and also asked me to take him into the Mars ship. I felt awkward. Next, I saw he was being extra charming to Vahini and ignoring me. Vahini is an immaculately polite person, always. Wei Zhang might have over-read that politeness"

That made me curious. "I would guess he asked Vahini as well to take him into the Mars launcher?".

"I asked Vahini that specifically, but she said no. He did not ask. I guess Wei was just curious and maybe he felt awkward that he had asked me, after flirting with me, to see inside the Mars launch ship and I that I declined his request."

"So, what else have you been doing". I chatted on.

"Not much really, we are just checking everything that we can find to check. There are no experiments for now, as you know. This is just a test wait period just for things to go wrong, and then fix, before we launch off to Mars.

I knew this all. I was thinking. Theoretically the Mars mission could still be aborted at this stage. However, once we fired rockets to break out of Earth-orbit and set off on our Trans-Martian-

Injection (TMI) journey, to abort and return to Earth prematurely was considered impossible. There was not even an official protocol how to handle that.

The process of firing the ship thruster rockets to accelerate the space fast enough to escape Earth orbit, in a direction aiming to ultimately be captured into Martian orbit after a long flight, is called TMI (Trans-Martian Injection)

---

The next weeks on the ISS passed in a blink of an eye. We largely all got absorbed into our private routines and spaces. It did not feel like a time to talk deeply on anything. The ISS crew were very mixed in their attitudes to us Ares-1 crew. The two ISS American astronauts were super warm and never ceased asking if there was anything they could help with. The two ISS Russian astronauts were bold brassy fellows who only had loud warm sincere greetings for us with big grins, but minded their own business largely. The mystery was the ISS Chinese astronauts, Wie Zhang and Liu Wang, who were overall cool towards the Ares-1 Mars-mission crew. The only women aboard the ISS at that time were the five ladies going to Mars. The Chinese did treat two of the lady astronauts different to the other Marsnauts. Much later I would learn a lot more about that.

The one biggest task for the Ares-1 Mars-space-mission was to assemble the spaceship to fly to Mars with. It was like taking a train and shuffling the coaches back and forth to get them in a specific order. The train-coaches, or space-modules had launched off Earth, were spread across four Saturn-8 rocket launches. They had all docked at the ISS (International Space Station) in Earth orbit. It took a week to do that final assembly of the rocket-ship to fly to Mars. Some arranging was done while docked to Mars, and some was done after un-docking from the ISS, and prior to blasting out of Earth orbit.

---

When we separated from the ISS it felt exhilarating. We all heard the computer voice of Cecil on the overhead speakers saying, "Pressures fine, doors fine, commence separation". Where I was seated, I did not hear any noises and did not feel any ship movements. We had another six hours of slow drifting apart and realigning our ship for flight. Marjena and Dessa, the Ares-1 two girl pilots were handling this all. The two male Ares-1 pilots were floating besides the seat-strapped-in girls. Per protocol, the guys had to be quiet, but they were encouraged to be present. The four primary pilots would evenly share that task across the three years of the space-flight to Mars and back again. Three years! That time did not make sense to me. I could not grasp it. Three years was a long time to be in a restricted-space journey away from our home planet

It would be another three hours before we all had to get into our seats and be strapped in. We did not need space suites for this rocket launch out of Earth orbit and towards Mars, called a TMI. It was not as dangerous and as powerful as our launch from Earth on top of the Saturn-8 rockets. There were once three Russian astronauts who had died due to unexpected depressurization of their crew-capsule. After that, it became a standard safety precaution to wearing a pressurized space-suits during launch from Earth and descent to Earth. We did not need space-suits now, as the engine-thrust was no so severe as that of the Saturn-8 first stage, so the risk of depressurization was considered minimal.

I had no assigned tasks so I took my cameras and found a window that could see the Earth. The best Earth viewing window changed as the ship slowly turned around into a new orbit alignment so I changed places a few times. I had no hope of taking a photo that had not already been photographed thousands of time from other spaceships. These photos however, would be my own and private photos. A strong sense of things being unreal filled me. My co-flyers later shared that they had had similar feelings as I did.

"This is your captain speaking. Strap into your flight seats please", called out, Captain Chris Bolder. We all liked him as the official mission captain or more correctly the ship-captain. He seemed slightly aloof and a bit strict. We found him however very consistent and predictable. We liked that.

An hour later Houston crackled onto the over-head sound system. "This is the President of the United States of America. We the nation, wish you brave pioneers all success for your mission. Remember you represent the democracy of the United States, and you represent the success of the biggest economic success the world has ever known. We wish you Godspeed."

Another voice came onto the speakers. "We will shortly commence count-down to engine ignition". That was the computer-generated voice officially labeled "Cecil". We came to regard Cecil as another crew member. We often spoke back to him, but he was not programmed to listen to us like gadgets back home, like computer voice "Siri" would listen to people. We had all emptied our bladders and more, if we could, before we strapped in. We all still wore astro-diapers as well. That was a precaution as going to the toilet was not an option for a while. I knew I wore diapers as a baby. I knew I might one day when being super old senile and bed ridden land up in a diaper again. Wearing one now was horrible. I was determined to hold anything in until my eyes exploded, rather than let go into a diaper.

A few seconds later the countdown started. It was not going to produce a dramatic explosive rocket thrust and a monster experience as the Earth launch had been. This was just an acceleration to escape Earth orbit and to get our ship to a speed fast enough to intersect with the Mars planet on its own solar orbit in nine months' time. This blast would only last 60 minutes, then the motors would be switched off and we would then be free to float around the mission ship. The pilots would monitor our flight direction and potentially do some slight adjustments to our direction once a month or so, until we reached Mars.

I heard this soft roar and watched Earth through a nearby window. My arms felt heavier and pushed down onto my lap where I held them. The G-forces from this acceleration were not as intense as the 4G forces we peaked at during Earth ascent on top of a Saturn-8 rocket. Looking out the windows, the Earth slowly started to spin past the window faster and faster, as we saw it. Then it started to lag back in the window and move away from us. This was it. We were leaving Earth's orbit. Very few humans had ever done that. We were going to Mars. No humans had ever done that.

I felt emotional and wiped some tears from my eyes. I don't know why I cried. Possibly, I was realizing that it would be three years before I could stand again on the lawn in front of my humble Iowa home. It would be three years before I could embrace my wife again. I had been totally self-obsessed about this trip, and suddenly I felt guilty. I had once said to my wife that I just wanted to escape life and go sit under Caribbean beach palm tree and be a beach-bum. My wife had instantly said "What about me?". I had replied lamely, "Oh I'll call on cellphone and I'll come back after three years". Yes. What about her? She did not ask me this time, "What about me?", when I announced my chance of flying to Mars if my interview went well. I read the words in her penetrating eyes though.

I was being very selfish becoming a Marsnaut. Loraine, my wife, loved me enough to conceal all her anxieties, fears, and feelings. This was not a career move. I was sixty-five years old already. Was it an ego thing? Was it a life time dream? Was it a suicide thing? I had contemplated all of this for much time preceding our Earth launch, and would continue to do so for a while. I had difficulty analyzing myself. Then I would suddenly stop thinking about those questions.

The dull roar of the rockets made me sleepy and I dozed off in my flight seat.

Suddenly I woke up. It was the silence. The thruster-engines had shut off. I looked at my six colleagues and they had all also fallen asleep. The other seven were on the upper-deck. I didn't hear anyone talking. I suddenly remembered we had escaped Earth orbit. We weren't aiming directly at where Mars was in the heavens at that minute. We were flying tangentially away from the Sun, as well as away from Earth. We were aiming for the further-out solar orbit of Mars. We were also flying much faster than Mar's orbit speed and we would catch up to Mars on its own orbit around the Sun, in nine-months' time. Yahoo!, I thought.

From the closest window I had, I could not see the Sun, nor the Earth, nor the moon. I only saw a patch of the heavens with millions of stars that I could not identify.

Captain Chris Bolder spoke on the overhead. "Crew, unbuckle! Start your post-TMI flight step-one checks."

Then Houston called overhead, "Congratulations Mission Ares-1. You're on your way. All reports fine from our side" I had no experience of space travel but I was surprised how crackly and poor the radio signal voice was. Chris and Houston ran through a quick few standardized flight check-points, that did not relate to me.

"Howzit Babee?" I said to Babee Todd, a lady Marsnaut, with a grin on my face. She was one of two space scientists. I found her a bit withdrawn and maybe aloof. I was working at befriending her.

"Fine." Babee replied unemotionally as she turned to float towards the back of the launch capsule. "I am fine too!" I said back to her too, teasingly, as if she had asked me.

No response.

As the mission physician and an unusually late member of the astronaut program I was the NASA astronaut with the record for having had the least training before doing a space trip, ever. I wasn't the oldest astronaut ever, but I was second in place. Everyone on the mission had a primary task, and a secondary task. Babee was a scientist tasked with a long list of experiments of which I knew nothing. Her second task was IT-communications. She had phenomenal computer programming skills and it was planned that she would be a spare person in case we lost Tyrone and Val, the primary specialists in those fields. I was the only mission specialist without a backup person for my job, nor me having a second job to step into. NASA seemed to not consider my role as very important, and in fact some directors had argued for an extra scientist rather than physician to be on the Ares-1 Mars Mission.  They said any astronaut could inject anything that a Houston ground control doctor could order them to give. So why should a physician accompany this trip?  Man-Oh-Man! Who could ever have dreamed what was still to come? I about half-dreamed it, when I wrote the Astronaut motivation letter, resume and application forms. Even I fell short of envisioning the hell ahead of us.

I floated through the modules to reach my sleep quarter. I was in the med-section, if one can consider a pile of strapped down boxes any form of medical-care space. We called the entire module the sick-bay, but it was much more than that. There was also supposed to be a few more medical supply boxes in the freight wagon.  I had made up a list of drugs, devices, and instruments that I wanted and just met management resistance all the way. I understood space and weight was at a premium on a trip that had to supply food, oxygen and fuel for a three-year space trip

I decided it was maybe a priority to go and check all the med containers. I did not know exactly where they were, as us astronauts had no roles in stocking and packing the non-fuel freight wagons.

An hour later Captain Chris Bolder announced tersely, "Ares-1 crew! We have a problem. The antennas and solar panels are all not deploying".  This was a monster crisis. I knew our batteries were good for about 72 hours and after that everything, like all motors, all pumps, simply everything would die, and us too. "Hell, the trip has barely started. We don't need this", said Chris with his finger still activating the microphone in the command module where he was at that time.

We would die if we lost electrical power. If we attempted a trip-abort now, the process would take us ten days to re-enter Earth-atmosphere. Abort was impossible. The steps to be taken immediately, where we had to send two team members on a space-walk to repair the antennas and panels. They would not be able to denitrogenate much before getting into their low-pressure space suits. So, they would be at risk of getting the bends, better called Decompression Sickness (DCS). I trusted we could do it. The team was made up of incredibly focused, fit and sharp younger persons. I felt I was the only odd fit in the classic "right stuff" image terms of youthfulness, athleticism, seeming calmness and compliance. I was a self-confident human being. I trusted my medical skills and knowledge in very general context. I would challenge any physician to match my total of knowledge and skills. I of course barely knew 1% of all medical knowledge that existed. I just hoped that I could handle whatever came my way. It is strange to be confident and scared at the same time.

Everyone feared an emergency space-walk, or Extra-Vehicular Activity (EVA) as it was called. When outside of a spaceship in space, there is zero atmospheric pressure and zero oxygen. In space, but outside of the spaceship, one would die in 60 seconds, without a space suit. The space-suits worn during an EVA, are pressurized and supply oxygen. The natural Mars atmosphere pressure is too low for a human being to exist, and the Martian atmosphere was nearly zero oxygen to support human life. For a human to walking on the Mars surface the exact same pressurized suit with oxygen is used, as the space-suit used in space-walks. Hence astronauts walking on the surface of Mars also consider it to be an EVA.

There is one difference between a true space-walk and Martian surface walk. Inside Spaceships the air pressure is kept at

100% of Earth sea-level atmospheric pressure, while in Martian surface habitats the pressure is kept at 50% of Earth sea-level atmospheric pressure. A space-suit's pressure is kept at 50% of Earth's sea-level atmospheric pressure. A big problem occurs when one suddenly moves from the spaceship 100% Earth Atmospheric-pressure air pressure to a space-suits 50% Earth Atmospheric-pressure dissolved-nitrogen comes out of solution in one's blood, forming bubbles of nitrogen in the body. That is decompression sickness. Mild decompression sickness is an irritation causing joint pains and burning skin feelings for about three days. If decompression sickness is severe, one can ger brain damage, or die. Treatment for established decompression sickness is to be placed in a pressurized chamber getting 100% oxygen therapy for a day. There was no facility for this hyperbaric therapy in space. For planned EVAs out of a spaceship, an eight-hour preparation is done, called a camp-out. The camp-out produces a gradual washing out of the astronaut's blood nitrogen in a special chamber, while breathing 100% oxygen at stepwise reducing air pressures. That eliminates decompression sickness entirely.  When exiting a Martian surface habitat for an EVA no campout is needed, because one moves from a 50% pressure habitation zone to a 50% pressure space-suit. So Marsnauts, can enter and exit a surface habitat as quick as they can put on or take off a space suit.  The Martian surface-habitats and spaceships all have exit pressure-chambers with a door to inwards, and a door to outwards. This stops the habitat ever losing its air pressure when astronauts enter and exit the habitat.

Chris announced seconds later, "Alan and Larry to the command module. Prepare for space-walk. SM three-b for exit.  All, activate energy economy mode crisis triple-x level."

Forty-minutes later, the hatches on the A-side module of 3 were opened, and out climbed Alan and Larry. They had only ten minutes time to denitrogenate. They were tethered to the ship on 100-foot leashes. The antenna-solar-panel complex that failed to deploy, was off the 7th module.

It wasn't long before Alan reported from outside the ship that the module hatch-door for the antenna-panels unit looked jammed on one side. The panels were so designed so that they opened as pairs on opposite sides of the module. When the one side jammed the opposite side unit couldn't open either, as the two units shared a gear-unit to ensure they were always symmetrical in deployment.

"Larry try to lift the hatch a bit, so that I can peep inside", said Alan

Alan spoke again. "I think I might see the problem. It looks like one of those thin perforate aluminum support bars is buckled. It looks like the weight of the entire solar panel pulled to the side. I guess that happened during Earth blast-off when we hit 4G. The bar looks flimsy. I think we must both simply try lift the hatch door with our hands as hard as we can. I can get a grip under it."

The entire ship-crew was listening to all the dialogue on the loud speakers in each module. They also could all watch on a split screen the head-camera images from each astronaut's space suit, on all module monitors.

Larry, "We can't budge it. We might need an extra few hands out here.

Chris, "God no. We can't have four crew all on EVA. It's too risky".

Alan, "Larry, let's both put our backs really into this thing seriously." Both astronauts adjusted their positions in order to maximize their lifting strength.

We could see from the helmet cameras, that they were both bracing their feet on the module solar-panel and antenna door edge. They had a grip on the door edge with their gloved hands. Larry grunted, "On my count of three. One . .Two ..Three. Aaargh!".

The hatch opened with a jump, then a spring mechanism pushed it further completely open exposing the solar-panel antenna, in its four folded segments. As the hatch door hit fully open both solar-panels unfolded and extended out of their container crates.

"God, God, God" shouted Alan as the antenna unfolded. The far edge of the solar caught him in his waist and pushed him out ahead of it. Alan tried to separate himself from it but his suit was hooked in somehow. Then Alan's tether tangled around Larry's leg and pulled him away from the module. Next Alan felt a great jerk and saw his tether had separated from his waist connector. Only a minute later Alan managed to unhook his suit from the rugged ridge where it had been tagged onto the antenna. "Oh no. Oh no", he shouted as he drifted away from the antenna. He reached out in utter futility to the antenna solar panel. He had already drifted out of reach of it. He looked to his waist for the small hand-jet thruster that astronauts on EVA could use for a few minutes to maneuver in free space. It was gone. In the chaos it had been ripped out of his pocket. "Chris!" shouted Alan. "I 'm adrift. Help!"

"What the hell", uttered Larry about something.

Chris screamed over the radio; "Alan. Alan. Use your hand-jet man!"

A long silence. "Chris, it must have got ripped of my belt. I haven't got it."

A moment of silence followed.

"Can you send someone out with the Jet-back-pack to fetch me?"

"Yes. Yes. Keep calm Alan. We'll fetch you"

"Hey Framingham. Go fetch the Jet-backpack. You're going EVA to fetch Alan." Framingham Milkowski was a pilot and a back-up engineer.

"Chris, it is still stored. It'll take me an hour to get it back here, and to get suited up. You know we can only fuel it outside."

"Just do it man! Rodney, you're spare. Help him don his space-suit."

Vahini now spoke she was out of sight, in another module. Her voice was calm. "Chris. Is Larry OK? We have not heard from him."

Larry replied on the radio. "I am in big trouble. My boot and foot are crushed in the middle joint of the first and second solar-panel sections. I hope I am not leaking gas. It hurts like hell. I can't get loose."

Chris, to himself. "This is unreal. We are like a bunch of amateurs. The mission is failing on day one".

Chris looking rattled.

"Larry we'll get someone up to you. Hang in there, man! Vahini, suit-up and check-out Larry!"

"This is Houston. What is happening there. We are getting red-light signals from Ares-1 spaceship."

There was a moment's silence.

"Houston here. Ares-1, do you hear me?

Chris, "Yes Houston. We have lost a crew member on a Space-walk. We have one crew member trapped in the antenna outside. I have sent a third astronaut out in jet-pack to fetch the lost astronaut, and another out to check on the trapped astronaut."

A moment of silence followed.

"This is General Admiller. Please explain all of that Ares-1-mission."

Chris proceeded to take a long time explaining what had all gone wrong, seemingly all within single minutes.

Alan Jones, the astronaut on an EVA with a severed tether line, interrupted. "Chris I am very far out now, maybe 200 meters away"

"My God", said Chris. "Hang in there Alan. we are working fast."

In about fifty minutes the jet-back-pack was collected, Valborg Schmidt, the IT specialist and back-up engineer, was outside on EVA and the Jet-pack was fueled. Valborg released his tether, rotated himself slowly and set off looking for Alan in space. The jet pack gave Valborg great freedom ability to move about or fly.

Larry said, "Valborg. Alan went in exactly the direction the solar-panel structure is pointing.


It wasn't long before Vahini was also out on EVA. She went to look at Larry. Vahini spoke. "Chris, I think Larry's his foot will be destroyed. It must be severely crushed on the closed side of this big hinge in the panel. We will need to retract the panels to open the hinge to get his boot and foot out.

Chris spoke. "I don't think there is retraction mechanism. Those antennas are for permanent deployment. I am checking the manuals. Yes. Yes. No retraction mechanism. Vahini try and pull on his leg."

Vahini spoke. "It looks like Larry's boot is badly squashed to one third of its width, and that is with Larry's foot in it. I am sure the foot injury is severe. I think we will have to cut his foot off.

"What?", shouted Chris.

Larry just cried. "I don't care. I don't want to die. Do it do it."

Chris turned to me. "Hey Rodney. You're the quack. Can you cut a leg off?"

"The term is to amputate. I can amputate a foot in an operating room.

Chris. "Can you do it out there?".

My mind was ticking at lightning speed. I had never foreseen exactly a scenario like this. This however, is why I wanted to be the Mars Doctor. I am problem solver.

I looked at Chris. "I can do it, but I am not trained in Space-Walking."

"French!" Said Chris. My respect went up for him. He nearly said a close-sounding word to one we that we had all already thought.

"This is Houston **What is happening**."

"We're going to amputate Larry's foot to free him and bring him in."

"What? You **CANNOT** do that. We need the ground med-team to OK that. How are you going to do that out there?" The voice came from Houston Ground control. Usually all communications from ground control to the spaceship went via the one person called the Capcom. This was to avoid having too many people all try to speak at once. This time everybody who was director of something, was trying to say something from ground control. Chris was not sure at any one second who was speaking.

Chris finally found a second to turn to me, standing next to him. "Rodney, if you can don a pressurized space-suit for a rocket launch, then you can do a space-walk"

"Russel, help suit-up Rodney, and guide him through whatever is needed"

I chirped in. "Don't forget Alan."

I then floated to my sick-bay to collect some medical supplies. I put everything in a bag. I had a plan. Because of our unique situation I was going to have to do an ancient Roman medical procedure. Larry would, in a sense, have a double anesthetic to the foot and ankle that was going to be amputated during this space-walk. The extreme coldness would numb the superficial tissues. The deeper tissues, would get ischemic anesthesia from the tourniquet.

"Hell!", shouted out Chris. "Valborg what is happening. Have you reached Alan?  Allan can you hear us. How far out are you?"

Allan replied calmly. "I have rolled around and am facing mother Earth. She is beautiful indeed. She is smaller than the moon now. I can't turn myself back around. I can't see how far from the ship I am. I guess I'll complete this slow roll around in 20 more minutes and then I will maybe see you. I am guessing I am 500 meters out now.  Mother Earth is such a lovely Blue color."

Valborg spoke, "I can't see Alan. I am about 1000 meters from the Ares-1 ship now".

"Val keep moving outwards looking for Alan. Check you view of the ship every thirty seconds. Let me know when you feel you have reached a safe limit before you lose sight of Ares-1."

"Yes, Captain."

"Rodney how far are you?"

"I have my tools and drugs and I am donning my suit. I guess we are bypassing denitrogenation right?"

"Right"

I had six Esmarch bandages, and the usual tear-open antiseptic swabs in my supply bag. I included some surgical instruments. I had a scalpel with a retracting blade. Sterility was impossible, but we would work as clean as feasible. My best kept secret was the Gigli saw. I had never used one on a human. I saw a surgeon once use one for an amputation. I used one once, to cut a branch twenty feet up a tree. I could not climb the tree. The circumstances made using ladder impossible, at least the ladders that I had. I had to throw a metal ball up to the branch a few times. Then I got it right and the metal ball went over the branch I wanted to cut. I had string attached to the metal weight. Next I tied a rope to the string and used the string to hoist a rope up over the branch. Next, I attached a Gigli chain-like hand-saw to one end of the rope. I attached a second rope to the opposite free end of the Gigli saw. The saw was essentially like a bicycle chain but with saw teeth on one side. I then hoisted the saw up to the branch until, about half the chain blade hung on one side of the branch and the other half hung down the other side of the branch. I then attached two six-inch thick wood rods to the two rope halves, to give me a strong grip.

I pulled the one side of the rope down while hanging on the other end. With a regular sawing action pulling alternate sides of the chain saw I managed to cut down this twenty-foot above-ground branch off. Today would be the second time in my life I was using a Gigli saw. This was medical grade saw and was much smaller, and had flexible wire spanned between the handles. The wire was wrapped by another metal wire with sharp irregular sharp edges, resembling barbed wire, and the barbs would cut bone.

I felt good in my Space suit. I was a bit unsure of maneuvering outside of the mission ship, but Vahini was an experienced space walker from an earlier Earth trip to the ISS. She helped clumsy me a lot. She left Larry to fetch me from the EVA hatch. The priority was not to drop or lose control of any medical device or item. We were in a hyper-critical situation that was unimaginable before it happened, and there were no second chances. Maybe, even the first chance was hopeless as well. I was very focused on handling everything with my large thick astronaut space suit gloves. I needed a fine feel that would be very limited.

We reached Larry. He looked pale in his suit. I explained everything that I was going to do. He understood this was all an American Football Hail Mary ball shot that was his only chance to live.

He just said "Let's do it. I got you Doc Rodney. You're the man."

I replied "I love you man. You are my brother. We are in this together." He placed a gloved hand on my padded shoulder. I knew in my soul that that was a tight human hug chest to chest. I thought to myself, what a shift in paradigm. He is the desperate astronaut, facing death; yet he was reassuring me. I was supposed to be the confident one, but I had concerns. A tear fell from my eye.

Larry was well anchored via his trapped foot. I had Vahini get a grip on the antenna so she could hold me steady. She braced one foot on the antenna and pushed the other against me to create a two- point stabilization system with her foot.

I had not discussed my plan with everyone in command as there was little point in it. I knew there were a dozen doctors probably in the Houston control room all watching what they could see via my helmet-camera and Vahini's helmet-camera. I suspected they would each be trying to earn their salaries and instructing me what to do. I was tuning myself out, in anticipation.

I systematically wrapped the Esmarch bandages around Alan's distal lower leg close to the boot but not touching the boot. The bandages are elastic. If you stretch them before wrapping, they are very tight. Each new layer wrapped adds more pressure. I used six bandages because I was unsure how the space-suit garments under the Esmarch bandages would interfere with the compressing effects. I wrapped as tight as was feasible. I finished with an adhesive tape for double security, and a crepe bandage. I knotted the bandage ends. I prayed the total pressure of the bandages was enough to achieve a full tourniquet effect. If it wasn't the leg would bleed uncontrollably during amputation and all of Larry's breathing gasses would leaking out of his space-suit once I had to cut through the suit, before I cut the flesh and bones. If things went wrong Larry would be dead in two minutes.

Next a voice crackled in my ear. "This is Dr. Clark. I am the mission orthopedic surgeon. Why haven't you given him any pain killers or sedatives."

"Yes. I agree, this is Doctor Finkelstein, I am the mission anesthesiologist. I think you need to give him a big dose of ketamine."

I replied tersely. "There is no vascular access for intravenous injections. Please shut up," uttered politely with an end of sentence increased little voice pitch.  That was the last exchange between me and Houston for that event.

Next, I pulled out of my tool bag a heavy grade of medical scissors. In truth they looked like garden shears. Five centimeters below the tourniquet I cut into his space suite. Vahini looked at me with wide eyes, saying nothing. I heard crackly gasps in my ear piece with what sounded like stifled words that the speaker cut himself off from. Cutting like that into any other space suit when space walking would be a death sentence within single minutes from loss of pressure and loss of oxygen.

I held my own breath and spoke casually to Larry. "That tourniquet is not too tight for you?"

"I can handle it." He said direct into my eyes. I covered the exposed flesh within the ten-centimeter circumferential opening that I had made, with a loose cloth to keep it in shade, and cold.  I could not remove cloth and boot more to distal as that part was inaccessible to me within the gap between the metal sheets that crushed the foot. Of note, some blood had tracked up the inside of the boot from the foot, and clotted in the area of skin just above the ankle where the amputation was going to be done. That confirmed the crushing injury that was trapping the foot, was severe enough to have disrupted the skin and let bleeding happen. I did not want to clear more space-suit cloth away higher up the leg. I was aiming at amputating as far distal as feasible. I would be cutting 2 centimeters above his ankle. I knew the exposed flesh would be 250 degrees

Centigrade hot under the Sun, but it would be minus 250 degrees Centigrade under the shade of the loose rag I covered it with. I knew every grain of exposed flesh on EVA would die, and I would need to do a second amputation back on board through the higher living tissues.

Larry would have double anesthetic here while I amputated his foot and ankle on this space-walk. The extreme coldness would numb the superficial tissues. The deeper tissues would get ischemic anesthesia. The ancient Roman surgeons who had to do battle field amputations knew ways of holding an arm tight behind the back so that the blood supply to the distal arm got clamped off. They knew that if the artery clamping hold was held for a long period the distal arm went numb and the amputation was relatively painless during the procedure. This was very esoteric information and no professor ever taught me that. I discovered it doing readings of ancient medicine, surgeries and anesthesia. It is also written about by fellow-followers of rare information in modern printed journals. Just no average doctor knows of it, but then I was not average in many ways. I had to wait at least 30 to 45 minutes from placing the Esmarch bandage tourniquet before ischemic analgesia started to set up well. The time we had to wait after I exposed the leg seemed like an eternity. I asked Larry about his wife and children, I looked at the planet Earth. It was further from us than the moon and a fraction of the size of the moon. The Earth was a beautiful azure color. That color hypnotized me.

The ship crew and Houston ground control saw us through the cameras mounted on Vahini's space-suit helmet and one on me too. They also listened to all our dialogue.

"Dr. Clark here at ground control. When are you going to damn operate, Powell?" Clearly Dr. Clark the ground mission expert surgeon thought he knew more than me, an anesthesiologist astronaut-mission physician, on the subject of a space-walk leg amputation without hospital facilities and anesthesia machines, outside of spaceship. Just who had experience with that?

"Damn shut-up Clark!" I replied. I liked that. He reminded me strongly of another weak character surgeon I once knew who would smile to my face, and speak lies about me behind my back to my boss.

Eventually 45 minutes of tourniquet time had passed. In that time, I had chatted pleasantly to Larry on unrelated trivia. Larry was just amazing. He acted relaxed. His unblinking eyes never looked away from my face.

"I think you will be OK now Larry."

"I trust you Doc."

I was told later that my heart rate was 135 at that time. I knew it about. I remembered feeling this thumping beast in my chest.

The scalpel cut clean. I was able to get down to the two bones with near zero bleeding in a circumferential cut in 20 seconds.

Larry said. "I feel nothing".

Next I placed the Gigli saw around Larry's lower leg onto the exposed bone. Like I cut the branch off the tree, I worked my two hands back and forth as strongly as I could pull, in the awkward zero gravity that we were in. I might never have managed it, if Vahini was not with me to act as a stabilizing strut for me.

It was also very hard to handle anything with those clumsy thick space suit gloves. I soon realized that I could drop things out of my hand, even while thinking I was still grasping it firmly enough. That meant one has to try to keep looking at things in your hand to make sure you don't lose it. Maybe it is easier doing larger scale engineering type jobs where you whole hand hangs onto pole-sized tools, than trying to grasp a fine small-handle scalpel with heavily-gloved finger tips.

Larry never blinked, and said. "I feel nothing." He floated free after he was separated from his trapped crushed foot. He looked back at the solar panel join and said with humor, but mockingly sweetly "Bye-bye foot."

I had to giggle.

Larry still had his tether intact. I said to him, "Can you get yourself back to the space hatch."

"Yes" was his single word reply.

"That's it" I said to Vahini. She said nothing. She had her hand-jet device and used it to position herself behind Larry, and close enough to aid him.

I placed the Gigli saw back in the tote bag that was attached by string to my belt. I saw some drops of blood float off Larry's naked stump. They floated in perfect spheres, then popped into smaller spheres, then popped all each again into smaller spheres. Within about 20 seconds the blood drops had transformed into a vague red mist-like cloud that slowly dispersed into nothing. It was fascinating.

"Larry, that was step one. We will continue in the sick bay." I had already explained everything to him.

Larry spoke into his suit Microphone. "Alan, are you OK friend?"

Alan, who was drifting off into space, responded, "The Earth is so blue and beautiful."

I think the world and Houston had forgotten about Alan drifting off into eternity, their eyes had been so riveted to the surgery.

Valborg in the Jet back-pack said, "I still can't see Alan. The Mission ship seems very far from me. I am guessing it is 1500 meters from me. It is only a tiny silver speck that I might not differentiate from a star soon if I keep moving further outwards. Chris, what must I do?"

There was silence.

Alan spoke. "Valborg, I love you man. Go back. This is my destiny. I wanted this. You all did your best. The mission must go on. Don't risk your life too. The Earth is so blue and beautiful."

Chris spoke again. "Valborg, turn back. Will you make it?

"If all the dials and fuel indicators are right, I am good. This should take me thirty minutes."

Vahini, Larry and I returned to the ship. We got through the EVA airlocks hatch and doffed our space-suits. It was a challenge getting Larry out of his suit as we had to leave the part of the suit under the tourniquet. We could not remove the tourniquet. We made a right mess of the suit cutting it off, but of course the remnants were headed to the spare-parts bin. In space every item is precious and might be usable to repair something else on another crisis day.

---

Once in the sickbay Vahini became my nurse assistant. We set up the operating table and secured it to the floor. We laid Larry back on it and used the Velcro straps to stop him floating away. I place an intravenous cannula into one arm and injected antibiotics. I set up my magnetic instrument tables and prepared for the surgery. This would now be a sterile surgery.

The first step was to anesthetize the same leg, in a region above the tourniquet that was still around the distal lower leg, minus a foot and ankle. We turned Larry on his side with the leg to be operate upon on the down-side, and against the table, and straightened out. The healthy leg was on the upper side and flexed well forward. Following standard safety and sterile procedures we soon injected the sciatic nerve in the popliteal fossa, as well as the saphenous nerve in a position deep to the distal sartorius muscle. We actually did both injections via one skin puncture using an ultrasound to give us an image of the nerves and the deep tissues with our needle. That was concluded in sixty seconds. I gave Larry a concoction of ketamine, midazolam, and alfentanil just before the nerve injections, for his comfort. I had never seen a smiling sedated patient before.

The next step was to lay Larry flat back to the table again. Now I applied a second tourniquet to the upper lower leg just below the knee. When that was secure, we removed the dirty one with the space suit remnants under it, from the very distal remaining leg part. The sedation and analgesia that we had given Larry was just enough to make the nerve injections comfortable. Within ten minutes he recovered from the sedating and pain-relieving drugs. He was alert, and wanting to talk up a storm. He had to be the happiest patient I could recall in decades. Maybe it was from the residual effect of the ketamine drug.

With the high tourniquet in place and the old lower tourniquet removed, we washed the lower leg to sterilize it. Following standard Earth-style surgery technique I did a fresh amputation about mid-tibia and sutured the skin securely covering the bones. This was a surgery of which I had two under my belt from forty years ago, and maybe fifty more under my belt, where I had watched my surgeons closely as they amputated legs during my later career as an anesthesiologist. I hoped none of them would have disapproved of my technique this day. My prime objective was keeping things simple and to not get sepsis following KISS principles. The KISS principle stands for Keep It Simple Stupid. I suspected back on Earth a good surgeon later on, might modify Larry's amputation to be better suit a prosthesis fitting. Those aspects were orbital high above my paygrade and experience at this time.

I gripped the wire Gigli saw in each of my hands and started a saw action, exactly as I once cut down a tree branch. This saw as a virgin saw and a very sharp saw. I cut through both bones in about twenty seconds.

Those of us who had gone on the emergency space walks, without the usual eight-hour preparation to get denitrogenated, for planned EVAs all got symptoms of decompression sickness. Mine was tender skin, and aching hips and knees. Luckily it never got serious enough to damage my brain, that I could tell (ha). I did not get permanent paralysis, but I was miserable for three days.

---

Between antibiotics and daily antiseptic care of the wound with dressings, everything finally settled and when we reached Mars 9 months later, the wound was perfectly healed.

Larry had nearly zero handicap missing a foot. He adapted and mastered all different ways of bracing himself as he floated around, little different to the rest of us.

He took a lot of inspiration from Tyrone. Tyrone Wilson was a paraplegic, but an utter IT-communications genius. Tyrone was not going down to the Mars surface. He was scheduled to orbit Mars and wait for the mission-crew who descended to launch back to the return-shuttle after a year.

My guess is that Tyrone was maybe the only Marsnaut who did not have a wish to die at the time of the Earth launch. However, I could be wrong. Tyrone did have a secret dark side to him.

---

One relaxing time Tyrone asked a me a question out of the blue that confused me.

"Rodney. Imagine you are alone in a spaceship returning to planet Earth. You then find out that the entire human species has been wiped off the face of the Earth. Everyone died. The rest of the planet is green and OK. You are the very last representative of the human species left in the universe. You are the very last human being. Would you want to keep on living? Also, would you want to return back to the planet. A safe landing on a beach is guaranteed, and is not a problem. Would you want to land on planet Earth?"

I later discovered this is variant of a philosophical question going back in Ancient Greek and middle eastern Cultures from hundreds of years before the Christian era. It seems there is no easy answer. The question seems more intended to make one think. Answers are very personal.

I had no immediate answer to Tyrone's question. I did finally decide that I live for being with other humans. Without there being a single other human being I that could ever meet, I had difficulty in finding a reason to want to eat one more meal to keep living. It made more sense to stop eating and then lay back and patiently await a natural cessation of one's heart-beats. That would occur within a very small number of days.

Initially to Tyrone's question, I had wondered how I would react if I did meet other human beings after hypothetically returning alone from space. Does the joy of living concern what other humans in general can do for me, I asked myself? I decided other humans in general only had very limited potential to bring happiness to me. I then wondered about me bringing happiness, to those other humans in general, after I returning alone from space hypothetically. I swiftly realized that I could find humans to whom I could bring a lot of happiness, even if they did not know me. I finally realized it was my primary acts upon others making them happy, that resulted in most happiness within me. The primary good acts of others upon me could make me happy, but in a modest degree. You get most happiness from giving, but you have to be the one to give first. Tyrone's question took me a few months to work though. I had to juggle the secondary questions around and reverse them. I had to relate the questions to close family, to acquaintances, and also to strangers. I realized that I had to survive this crazy human experiment to live on Mars, not for my sake. I had to survive it to be able to make my wife, Loraine happy every day for the rest of her life. I also had to make others happy too, in general. It confirmed we homo sapiens are primarily social animals.

The image I liked in my head, was that somewhere was a humble single lady working two menial jobs and barely making financial ends meet, struggling to raise her five decent little children. Then, if I had the humblest job back on Earth, but managed to have save 100 dollars each month, and that I pushed that 100 dollars anonymously under that poor mother's apartment door each month, to help her financially, then I had good reason to keep living, and working and surviving. Summarizing it all; if there was one other human left on planet Earth, then I had to do everything I could to survive this Mars trip, just to see if I could do a good deed for that other one human being upon my return.

Thinking one layer deeper on this topic, I realized the question that Tyrone asked of me, reflected a glimpse of what went on, within his mind. He had to have a darker and very serious side. His guffawing loud voiced humorous big persona concealed his true inside. His battles to be happy were no less than anyone else's battles to be happy.

Too much thinking can be dangerous I have heard it said. It requires free time to do a lot of deep thinking. Maybe that is why NASA so overburdened the crew with research projects keeping them busy.

# CHAPTER 3.

## Forgetting Alan. (week 3)

I thought it was incredible how soon everyone stopped talking about Alan. His last words were "The Earth is blue and beautiful". No one addressed him again. We assumed he would have been dead after twelve hours in space due to running out of oxygen. Alan never said another word. He must have heard everything that we communicated over the common line, same as all of us did. It felt to me like we just gave up on him or couldn't care about him any more anymore.

I spend days pondering all the conversations that went on over the common-line. Did anyone say anything bad about Alan, that Alan could have heard? I couldn't recall anything. I know I thought non-stop about him. I many times wanted to call out to him, as he drifted alone in space on a solar orbit taking him away from Mother Earth. One of two things could happen to his body. If the gravity of Mars caught him enough, his body would finally smash down onto Mars in nine or so months' time. It was also possible that without being part of our spaceship and getting monthly thruster firings for course correction he had a different orbital-track. His body might then sling-shot past Mars and in a million years' time be beyond the solar system and get sucked down into a big black hole.

Chris was very quiet. He asked me about Larry's progress each day. Other than that, we all seemed to avoid deep conversations, and to busy ourselves in our various scheduled daily tasks.

---------------------------------------------------------------------

---------

Chris came to my sick-bay, one week after we gave up on Alan.

"Rodney," he addressed me. "Do you think we could have saved Alan?"

"I wondered about that too, Chris".

"I think if we could have gotten someone with a jet backpack, get out even quicker, we could have retrieved him in minutes".

'Well, for the little I know about space-flight", I said. "It has never been routine for a Jet back-pack to be part of space-walk gear. I get the idea it is a sort of nice toy to have, but such a lot of bother to set up, fuel up etcetera. We didn't even have it stored for fast access and emergency use.  No one has ever been lost in space before. This was a precedent. Alan's tether was supposed to be his life insurance".

"You're right. But I should have been thinking faster. We did get Valborg out in record time, but those forty-five minutes was life and death difference for Alan. Valborg spoke to me an hour ago and he feels he killed Alan by not finding him."

I was grasping at straws to make Capt. Chris feel less responsible. "Maybe space walkers should have some sort of flare gun or luminous balloon or some way to make themselves visible from a mile away."

"Rodney you have clever ideas. I can see all those things you suggest being small lightweight gadgets we could just add to our belts. I'll shoot that thought down to Houston. Such a simple solution might have helped Valborg aim more specifically towards Alan instead just shooting out in the direction that the solar panels pointed. Maybe Valborg was far out enough, but Alan was possible a kilometer to the side and invisible without illumination.

I was quiet for a moment giving Chris more time to talk. I sensed he was needing to talk out. Maybe because I was not a real military-type trained-astronaut, he saw me as a potential outsider safe-friend. Chris was more used to the artificially stratified ranked military societies.

I said, "I think Alan died happy."

"Do you really think so?" asked Chris.

"Yes, I do. He spoke about the blue Earth being so beautiful from far away. He sounded relaxed. Everybody knows what the Earth looks like, flying over it in the ISS. Very few people have ever seen views of the Earth when it is smaller than the moon. It's different."

"Rodney, would he have suffered?"

"No. Near his ending, he would have felt a calmness come over himself and he would next slowly felt like he was falling asleep. He would become unconscious as the oxygen got depleted."

Chris was studying my face.

"There are people who intentionally asphyxiate themselves to get that great feeling hypoxic drug effect briefly. Sometimes they mess up and don't loosen the strangulating scarf soon enough. They next thing, they get found dead on their beds with a scarf around the necks, and they are often naked. It is called auto erotic pleasuring."

Chris's mouth hung a little.

"I had a related experience once. I was rather overweight at the time and getting lots of gastric juice reflux and heart burn. Sometimes I would find green bile on my pillow in the morning, that I had regurgitated at night. My wife would tell me that I had coughed a lot suddenly at a time in the night. I recall one night waking up coughing, and then I couldn't breathe. I recall standing up and leaning over the bed. My wife sat up and switched the light on and looked at me. She asked if I was OK. I couldn't speak and I couldn't breathe. As, an anesthesiologist I fully understood I was in laryngospasm with my vocal cords closing my throat fully. I had handled that in many anesthesia patients by injecting a fast working muscle relaxant. I also knew most laryngospasms relax just as hypoxia gets severe, around 60% oxygen saturation of arterial blood. I was panicking and recall looking at my wife as I leaned forward on my arms.

The big thing is what happened next for me. I just started to feel calm. I started to feel amazing. It was the best feeling I had ever had in my life. It may have lasted a long twenty seconds then slowly everything went dark.

My wife described me falling back onto the bed and lying dead still. She was half asleep, and in total confusion as to what was happening and as to what to do. She said after about fifteen more seconds I gave a little cough and then gasped making a scratchy sound. She said I coughed and coughed for about 5 minutes and then looked up. I can tell you I went on a serious weight loss program after that to fix my esophageal reflux problem. I knew I had nearly died.

The big thing that fascinated me was that utterly indescribable thrilling, but calm feeling just as the hypoxia got severe and before I passed out. I am sure Alan had a less dramatic hypoxic event than me, with laryngospasm and coughing on gastric juices. His calm feeling would have come in more incrementally and would have continued until everything turned dark for him. It would have been a real mercy death I am sure. I can understand how when people have near death experience, involving hypoxia, that they think they had a brief entrance through the gates of heaven."

"Wow!" said Chris. "I had never heard of such stuff. So, you think Alan had a gentle peaceful death. You make me think that I cannot think of a better way to die in peace and calmness than to slowly have your oxygen levels get depleted."

"Man, these are also dark thoughts!" I replied.

Chris had got me on a thought tangent. "Chris, can you imagine floating in the night sky with the stars being at their twinkling brightest and you are facing the beautiful blue Earth from far and you just get calm and enthralled and the lights slowly fade as you fall asleep. Is there a better way to die?"

"No there isn't," said Chris.

Chris pushed away floating in the air.

"Rodney, thanks for chatting. You have an angle on things that make me feel better."

We two never spoke alone to each other of Alan, ever again.

---

I felt a need to break out of my cocoon a while later. I had been eating alone in my sick bay and avoiding other folks. I floated through to the community module. It was the largest one, and had the fullest frozen and dried foods stashes, it also had the main communication equipment and was effectively the command module. It also had a lot of windows and had the most TV monitors and computers.

"Hi Vahini," I said. "We haven't seen each since that big space-walk." Dessie was there as well as Marjena, Spofford and Babee." Looking around, I said, "We are only missing Vickie. Is this a bachelorette party?"

Barely smiling, Babee said to me "Not funny! Rodney. We were talking about Alan when you drifted in".

I listened as I shook up my meal in a packet to which I had just added water.

Marjena with her neat cut fine Polish features, green eyes and tied back short blonde hair spoke. "I think Alan died happy, and you?"

I agreed. I didn't want to tell the long hypoxia story. "WE were all told before the mission that NASA is planning on, that is willing to risk, 50% of us not returning alive. That is why we have so many duplicate specialists for single tasks, or more sub-specialists on the mission."

Spofford spoke. I never refer to her by her first name of Camilla. I find her a miserable person and had a dislike her for instinctive reasons. She was looking at Marjena. "Do you think NASA meant that 50% of us won't return alive, or that there is 50% chance all of us don't return to Earth alive".

Marjena shrugged her shoulders.

Dessie which is short for her full name of Judessa Weeks spoke, "I was not scared off by that 50% chance of dying line, I have no children or dependents. This mission was my chance to do something for woman."

"Ooh. So, we have a feminist here." I teased. I got five poker-faced dirty-looks and silence.

I decided to be more serious. "I think we should have a memorial service of some sort for Alan tonight. Maybe we could ask Chris if we could do that after the evening daily conference."

"Yes. I agree", said Marjena. "I will talk to the other guys. Rodney, would you OK that with Chris please? I am sure he will agree."

Vicky had some thoughts on this too. "It would be nice if we each got a turn to speak where we recall one nice thing each, about Alan. Something personal, or something we admired about him. Maybe also everyone can select one favorite piece of music that they would like to play while we sit quietly and think about Alan. I suggest email me your thoughts and I'll put together the collection of songs or music pieces that we can play while we meet. Of course, it will have to be music we have in the spaceship computer music folder."

A lot of us routinely compiled a list of favorite music and listened to it all day nearly, on our head-phones while we worked. The ship had ten thousand music numbers in its computer library, and some astronauts had extra personal music on their own computers.

I spoke to Chris, and he enthusiastically agreed with the plan. We needed to honor Alan and also get closure for ourselves.

--------------------------------------------------------------------------------
----------------------

After Dinner that evening Chris started the usual evening conference. Everyone had to make some comment on their research progress, and on any ship-maintenance or repair chores that they had done. It was a mundane administrative task and they kept our reports down to two sentences. Chris entered it in the records. Then, we got to the Alan memorial section. Chris made it an official proceeding and made notes. He asked Vicky to lead this part of the evening meeting, as she had the strongest feelings about it, and she had proposed we do it.

It turned out delightful. There was a lot more to the guy than any of us knew. Nearly everyone knew him in a different way. I guess that applies to all acquaintances. The selection of music in the background was not sad, and it was not funky. It was pleasing, soothing, and tended to make us happy. It worked out perfect. We did not want sad church organ music. We were not holding a funeral.

Alan was a spaceship first engineer. He was also a backup pilot. He had fighter plane landing experience on aircraft carriers. That is considered the highest demanding skill of all pilots. One has to have immense 3-D spatial-perceptions skills and the ability to judge a moving plane's position in two seconds time and twenty seconds time, and how to adjust the flight controls to get it safely onto the ultra-short runway of an aircraft carrier. No one who had only ever been a pilot of slow lumbering freight planes, ever became a NASA astronaut pilot. Astronaut pilots were only ever top-notch fighter jet pilots. There was however, very little conventional flying to do as an astronaut. Astronaut piloting when performed was hyper-critical and challenging. It usually involved controlling jet engine thrust and thrust direction to land a rocket upright and in reverse. It also meant handling a spaceship weighing many tons in a space docking process with another spaceship. It had nothing to do with the skills to fly a humble Cessna-206 plane. To sum up on Alan, he was considered a good astronaut pilot.

Alan however, was on this mission selected primarily as an engineer. From his childhood he played with Lego and Mechano sets. His hobby was amateur radio. He could build both modern and old-fashioned technology radios with bulbs. There was no device in any average home that he had not disassembled and reassembled. While being a pilot he had studied part-time to be micro-electronics engineer. Being a NASA flight engineer largely demanded of one to do in-flight repairs and maintenance, and to be able to be creative. One person, at least on a long space flight, needed to know electronics very well. Alan got onto this Ares-1 Mars mission because of his being so doubled-skilled.

The girls spoke more about Alan as a human. He was married and readily showed people photos of his wife and three small boys. He stated he loved his wife. One person said he had mentioned his marriage was a bit strained, and he had been criticized by his wife for working too hard and not being enough of a doting father at home all the time. Alan was hurt by that because he saw his long hours spent each day at work and at home studying for his engineering degree as a sacrifice that he was making FOR the family. As the main bread winner, he needed to have secure employment. He saw his engineering degree as a backup post-military career. Maybe his wife just wanted more of her husband. This was maybe the marital life as experienced by all woman whose husbands served their country as military personnel. That means they are never at home, as much as a good wife would like them to be.

I knew those thoughts exactly. My first wife had wanted a husband who earned a top physician salary, but who only worked a 35-hour week, never worked nights or weekends, and who never had conferences to attend all the time. All career-focused persons who make it to the top of their professions, pay a price on the home side. It is a special home-spouse who acts out being the good, understanding and supportive role towards the spouse who has the top salaried time-demanding career.

One girl said Alan was depressed about his marriage and saw this three-year Mars mission as a sort of final test for his marriage's survival. He had once confided that if his marriage survived the Mars-mission he was leaving NASA and the military. He would then take a non-demanding civilian job. I suspected that Alan was not too unaccepting of his final destiny when it became apparent, on the space walk. He was happy to be drifting off to peacefulness.

Another male astronaut said he was Alan's exercise partner. They had together figured out how to use the complicated isotonic rowing exerciser as an arm-wrestling device. They each worked together a lot and joked a lot about entering some small-town country-fair arm-wrestling competition one day. They were not focused on trying to be stronger than the other. They were focused on aiding each other to reach higher strength levels. That story triggered a bunch more stories that showed Alan up as being a superb team player.

All the time Chris was entering computer notes. He took trouble to only write best things, and to very sagaciously describe real but less happy things in a way that was respectful of all persons. In the end they unanimously agreed Alan's loss to the mission was a loss to the world, and that Alan was role model human being who had only ever done the best he could in life. We decided to "toast" him. We had no liquor on board so we all gave each other knuckles upwards fist-bumps saying "to Alan". We bumped hands with the front-facing finger tips. In our minds we were holding beer glasses or wine glasses.

Tyrone said at the conclusion that he felt very happy that they had this session to close their hearts about Alan's loss. "Hear, hear", said Valborg. For the rest of the mission, Alan was very rarely spoken of, and then only briefly. He was not written off. The crew just had the mission to have to focus on, and they did not grieve in way that it was hurting anymore.

There was closure.

**CHAPTER 4.**

**Fox TV News Space-exploration rocket-launch special show.
(week 0)**

*(NB. Shift back in time on the story line)*

"This is Brian McMead hosting the Mars Mission Special show. This is the fourth and final launch of the four Saturn-8 rockets, that have been launched each, one week apart. NASA has set never-before imagined records for getting these launches off, so close back to back.

We have three ground reporters out there. Let's cross to Jennifer Beeton at Houston Control. Jennifer how are things looking there?"

Jennifer Beeton, "Hello Brian. It's still dark in Houston, but Mars Mission Control is very alive. We have 150 operators, managers and controllers all working furiously behind me, as you can see. After all the criticism that this immense mission was brought forward to fast and too unprepared, there is euphoria here, because all the launches so far have been flawless. The first two Saturn-8 rocket launches served as test launches for the Saturn-8 upgrade version of the fifty-year old Saturn-V rocket that took man to the moon. Those two launches were unmanned and carried a lot of cargo modules that are now docked to the International Space Station (ISS). As those launches were perfect NASA continued through to the manned Saturn-8 rocket launches. A week ago, the first seven Mars-mission astronauts flew up op the ISS. Today the final seven Mars-mission astronauts launch to join up with everything and everyone at the ISS. Then in two weeks' time, the Mars crew of fourteen astronauts will fly to Mars on the full spaceship after its assembly in Earth orbit.

Now with me, I have General Jones from NASA who is the NASA Manned Missions crew-director. General, thank you for joining us on this special occasion. My first question; how did it come about that a military General should head up NASA's most important mission in decades? Has it not been more of civilian operation for the last 15 years?"

General Jones, "It is correct Ma'am, you may be too young to remember the early years at NASA. Missions were totally dependent on military Air-Force fighter-jet pilots as a source of astronauts, and of course it was a government operation." The General towered over the petit broadcaster, almost foot taller, and twice as broad. He had a stern face as he looked down upon Jennifer, reminding her of her own domineering father.

"As NASA started to use fewer and fewer air-force pilots and involved more civilian scientists as the decades passed after Apollo 11, the NASA operations seemed less military like. One does not need to be fighter-jet pilot to do scientific research aboard the International Space Station (ISS) that orbits Earth. As you remember we finally entered into a phase where we nearly gave NASA over to the private sector to supply and manage all launch and space vehicles. That tended to filter out men and woman who primarily wore military uniforms. We have had non-military NASA directors for decades.

General Jones stood a little taller and smiled slightly, "Then, when our current President of the United States was elected, she immediately strongly demanded that NASA report directly to the Space Force. The Space Force, you know, is a new pure military wing of the USA Defense Force, similar to the Navy and Army, but only dealing with America's defense in Earth orbit and outer space. The president was a former soldier herself and she believes everything functions better under a regimental style of management. She increased the NASA budget ten-fold and discarded our Chinese and Russian partners, and also some other countries from the Mars Mission. I became the new NASA Manned Operations director."

Jennifer remembered she did not like her father much. She digs in, "Thank you for that brief history lesson General. Will you tell me if the first man on Mars be a woman? We all know the President has demanded that."

"Ah yes, the first man on Mars will be a woman, is certainly a catchy phrase. That phrase has driven much of the agenda. I cannot tell you my exact instructions to the Flight-Captain. The Flight-Captain however, has the privilege to override any instruction relating to the first human to step on Mars, if he has justifiable grounds."

"Could you court-martial him after the Mission if the first foot onto Mars, is not that of a woman?"

The General wondered where the questioning was going. He answered hesitantly, "I guess in theory yes, but in combat a leader may make alternate decisions in some circumstances to what standing orders state. In fact, there are rare circumstances where a soldier would be expected to disobey an order. If, just as an example, the Sargent orders a trooper to shoot an unarmed and harmless enemy non-combatant woman who has surrendered, he is expected to disobey. We regard this Mars mission as like a combat mission, in terms of controlling and disciplining the astronauts".

"But General, the majority of the Marsnauts are not American soldiers. How can they be expected to fall under military laws of battle conduct?"

"We regard even un-uniformed civilians receiving military salaries as falling under the UCMJ, that is Uniform Code of Military Justice."

"But general, this is a scientific expedition not a military combat zone. Also, NASA is not a combat unit, even if it is now administered in a sense by the new Division of the United States Defense Forces, the Space Force. Even the Geneva Convention regards contractors accompanying military forces as non-combatants."

The General's face tightens, "Your questions are very argumentative"

"Sorry General, I apologize, I will return to the original question; If the Captain of the mission decided to designate that a man, and not a woman as the President preferred, to take America's first steps on Mars, would this too be swept under the rug like most military issues. The public has a right to know. "

General Jones turns his back, starts to walk away, and finishes the interview with, "The mission plans are simply to have a human step onto the surface of Planet Mars. Male or female."

Jennifer turning to the camera. "I return to you, Brian. I guess we will have to wait about ten months before we know if a woman is the first human being to step onto Mars"

Brian McMead, "Thank you Jennifer. Things were getting heated in Houston there. We now turn to our other reporter on the ground Samantha Newton. Can you hear me Sam?

No reply.

"Can you hear me Sam"

"Yes Brian, I can hear you now," replied Samantha, as she adjusted her ear piece.

"Samantha is in the Launch Control Room at Cape Kennedy. Sam what is the weather there like? We heard there is some risk of the mission-launch being cancelled"

"Brian, that is correct, preparations continue in hopes of a countdown. The winds are within safe limits, currently gusting to 35 knots at launch site ground level, and are gusting to 45 knots at 300 feet high, near the rocket tip. Temperatures are a safe 75 F. The storm clouds are 20 miles off the coast and generating lightening.

Just 23 hours ago. the launch commander, Mr. Albertus Boezaart, came to the decision to load propellant fuel."

"Sam, how are the last seven Marsnauts doing?"

"Yup, the final seven. They are onboard and hatches are closed. We have been speaking to them on intercom and they sound excited. They can't wait to join the first seven on the ISS, the International Space Station. As you know this Saturn-8 rocket carries the last parts or modules of the Mars flight-ship, as well as the last of the Mars-mission crew. It will join the other components of the Mars-vehicle now attached to the ISS. Ten days from today the Mars-vehicle will separate from the ISS and fire rockets to escape from Earth orbit. That will start the nine-month journey to Mars. These pioneering humans will be the first to move beyond both Earth and Moon orbits".

Brian McMead, "Thank you Sam. We will now move to our last reporter on the ground at the Cape Kennedy public viewing site. Fox reporter Lelanie Botha is standing with the crowds. Hello Lelanie"

"Hello Brian, I am standing here at the NASA Mars launch viewing stadium. We are three miles from the launch site. This is the closest the public can get. Tickets had to be booked and cost $200 each. There is a staggered stadium-type seating facing the launch. We are looking from South towards North. It is a temporary scaffolding structure and seats ten-thousand people. It is estimated about five million folks are scattered around various other further-away, non-NASA viewing sites."

Lelanie continues, "The crowd looks like a fun group. It feels like a big football game tail-gate, except the kids are sleepy at this early morning time and everyone is sober. The parking lot has another ten thousand of so folks watching from there. One can smell outdoor-cooking foods. The tail-gaiters, as we call those without formal seating, only paid $20 to be here. About half the people in the stadium have camera tripods and every photo or film hobby enthusiastic in Florida state might be here. I really thought cameras had died off now that cellphones take such good pictures".

Brian continues, "Lelanie, you are South African, correct?"

"Yes, I was born there but I don't remember much. I am a US citizen now. My parents came to the USA in 1994 when I was a little child. My parents later told me how they listened to the whole Apollo 11 moon landing on radio, as there was no television in the country then. Some months later after much public curiosity, people were able to watch films of the landing on TV sets at government-controlled places like public schools. The fact that South Africa was one of few countries in the world then, who never saw Neil Armstrong step onto the moon on July 24th 1969 in real time, triggered public outcry. This started a debate and a political process where the government finally permitted public TV broadcasting in 1976. The public television expanded South Africa's perspective of the rest of the world changed and accelerated the inevitable end of the Apartheid system of racial discrimination in 1994. It is amazing that that "one small step for a man, one big step for mankind" played a tiny, but not irrelevant role in the ending of Apartheid. Standing here today, I wonder if man's first step on Mars will somehow alter world history in another major way".

Brian responds, "Lelanie, thank you for that very personal insight to this great event soon to unfold. I hear you have another South Africa story to tell of".

"Yes, indeed. I was so excited when the rumors surfaced one of the ship's flight-doctor may also be South African by birth. That is an unconfirmed fact. The flight crew's names were only released this morning. It was apparently for security reasons and to protect the privacy of their families. Nearly all the crew are in fact civilians and their families live outside of military bases, so they are much harder to protect. We do know that the President was absolutely adamant that only American citizens can be on this mission, so that Marsnaut will definitely be a naturalized American, if he is foreign born. When the president was elected, she was very clear that this had to be an American space mission, and she excluded the Chinese and Russians, and some other nations, who had been working with us for the last five years towards this mission. Of the current six ISS astronauts two are Chinese, two are Russian and two are American. They are not going to Mars. They have the mission of orbiting the Earth for six months each and doing research. The ISS astronauts are a separate astronaut crew to the Ares-1 Mars-Mission crew. The Chinese were so upset by this exclusion from Ares-1 Mars-Mission that they withdrew their Ambassador from the USA. The President said she wants an American flag, and an American flag only planted in the surface of Mars."

Brian continued, "Thank you Lelanie. I believe you have few members of the public to interview, who have come to Cape Canaveral to watch the final Saturn-8 rocket launch of the Ares-1 mission."

"Yes, indeed," answered Lelanie as she turned towards a gentleman standing to her side. "Hello, you are mister Fred Diederman from California, correct."

"Yes, I am here with my wife, Meg. She is a history professor" replied Fred.

"Fred why are you both here. You have come a long way to see the launch"

"Well we got lucky by getting tickets. My wife and I each think this mission will fail horribly, and that a series of events will happen in domino style, and the world history trajectory will change dramatically. We just wanted to see the start of that historic change.

"Fred that is an odd view. Why you think the launch will fail, or what will go wrong?".

"I am not an engineering type of guy. I am sort of biomedical, you could say. I just think the entire mission has been done too rushed, too cheap, with too many short cuts, and with no profound scientific objectives. My wife and I think we have hit the pinnacle of modern national narcissistic image-driven leaders all over the world. We predict a return to principle-driven and humble, but powerful leaders getting elected.  We might see a second Abe Lincoln, come in as President soon. Except one that will be honored during his life-time. "

"Yes, thank you Fred. We were getting way off-subject there. I did not see those comments coming Brian. Here is someone else I want to speak to."

Hello, your name is Shirley O'Leary, correct?", Said Lelanie turning far to her right, with the close-up camera following

"Yes, Good morning!" Shirley appeared to be wide awake.

"Earlier you told me you had a grandfather who had helped develop and build the Saturn-V rockets that took man to the moon?"

"Yes", said Shirley enthusiastically.

"What else connects you to being here today?"

"Firstly, I am a flight and space engineering student from Albuquerque. This stuff is all I dream about. Secondly, I have a distant cousin who is part of the team the developed the original Saturn-V upgrade to a Saturn-8 launch rocket. However, most of all I feel I have a DNA connection to this Rocket Saturn-8 because a great uncle of mine was in the team of engineers who built the first Saturn-V rocket over 50 years ago. It is like it is family project. Ooh, I am so excited." Shirly pulled her hands tightly closed and to her front and hopped up and down grinning".

Lelanie placed a warm hand on Shirley's forearm, while smiling big, as a thank-you gesture. She stepped slightly forward into the crowd of curious people surrounding her and the camera.

"Brian, if time is OK here is one more interview that I know you will like"

"Time's good Lelanie'" said Brian. "Won't you quickly first ask your guest Shirley who her grandfather on Saturn-V project was?"

"Of course, yes. Shirley, here, Shirley one more question please? Shirley, who was your grandfather who worked on Saturn-V"

"My rocket-engineer grand uncle was Werner von Braun."

Brian spoke. "Thank you, Shirley. Wow! We are touching history here. I am glad we have had the name of Werner von Braun mentioned. He certainly worked well for the USA, and was a giant contributor to the early American space programs and the development of the Saturn-V rocket used to place a man on the moon. The Nazis were the first to develop and fire rockets as military weapons. Werner von Braun was a Nazi officer and worked for Hitler. Von Braun at one stage, while working for Hitler, was developing an intercontinental rocket to bomb the USA. It is amazing how space travel has links to so many other countries' history, and other pivotal events of the far past. Today we launch a Saturn-8 rocket, derived from the Saturn-V. That will launch a spaceship towards Mars, and the Saturn-8 rocket has a developmental link back to the Nazis of World War 2. Back to you Lelanie"

"Hello Father Reynolds, quick tell us what this Mars Mission launch means to you today, and why you are here?"

"Thank you, Miss Boater. Did I say that right?"

"Close enough."

"I am an Irish-born Catholic priest. I have often been asked by my catechism children, "Father where is heaven? Is it up there?" as they point to the sky. When I was younger, I said yes. Now I don't think I can say that anymore. Mankind is about to conquer the heavens and place men and women on the planet Mars. I only recently found out how to spot Mars in the night sky. I look for it every night now, and see it often. So, I am starting to think that heaven although invisible to ordinary sight, is somehow actually all around us and within us. If one believes in a heaven, and you seek to see only the best in fellow mankind, and if you seek your own happiness by simply making other people happy. Then you are enveloping yourself in the heaven to which you will one day enter if you pray for it as well. It is like we don't need to travel to heaven. We can enter right here if we live and worship right.

So, I am here because I want to witness this awesome event. I want to see those monster rocket engine flames disappear into the heavens as it pushes a few tiny people in front of it. Those few people are not even grains of sand in the greater Cosmos. Those tiny grains of sand although so infinitely small in the Cosmos, somehow represent the greatness of men who were made in His image. It is hard to see how something so small can be so large in truth. I am just feeling inspired. God bless the Marsnauts. That is all I have to say."

Lelanie knew she had been upstaged by the priest. How do you follow that?

"Thank you, Father Reynolds. Bless you too. Over to you in the Fox News TV studio Brian."

---

After a commercial break, Brian McMead Fox News studio host spoke, "I have a guest here with me in the studio on this day of the fourth and last Ares-1 mission Saturn-8 rocket launch. Welcome Melanie Jankovitz."

"Thank you. Brian. I am glad to be here."

"Melanie, you are a regular political commentator for Fox news. You have had a big interest in this Ares-1 Mars mission. How do you see the role of politics in driving space exploration?"

"Brian, in this TV launch special you have already touched on some milestones in the evolution of space exploration. It is clear that the biggest forces initiating and driving space exploration have always been political considerations. The first nation to launch a rocket with capability to reach space were the Nazis in 1942. They used the rockets as weapons to bomb the British. After the war, the Americans won over the German rocket scientists to work for them as rocket developers. Next, in the middle of the cold war with Russia, the Russians developed their space rockets and put the Sputnik satellite overhead of the USA going beep-beep as it passed on every orbit in 1957." Melanie actually pointed and looked up as she made her beep-beep noises.

"That frightened the Americans greatly and the great space race began. The Russians kept their lead and four years later placed Yuri Gagarin as the first human, into space in 1961.  That really threw gasoline onto the fire. The gauntlet was down. America finally won the first Space Race and placed a man on the moon only eight years later in 1969. What followed was a relatively peaceful coexistence in the world with little expectation of another world war. Now over fifty years later, the international posturing and rivalry by the major nations is out of control. Each is competing to dominate in international trade, thus setting the market for all goods including the space race!"

Brian interjects, "So you see this purely as political Game of Thrones?"

Melanie continued, "Don't you Brian? The President has demanded it be solo-American achievement. She altered the original plan, for this to be an international collaboration. What else would you call this? Certainly not scientific or altruistic! The scientific goals became secondary to her personal agenda; the first 'man on Mars to be a woman.' Intangible scientific goals are not as glamorous or news worthy as the symbolism of a human footprint beside our nation's flag on the surface of Mars. It has consumed the nation. Buzz Aldrin, one of the men to step on the moon was quoted in saying, that that the failure to follow up placing a man on the moon with a man on Mars for over fifty years was not due to a lack of technology, but due to a lack of political commitment. Ironically, the GoFundMe campaign launched by the President, to fund this Martian project has drawn incredible world-wide support, raising $5 billion towards the costs of the Ares-1 mission. We, however, don't yet know the data breakdown of from which countries the international monies came from."

"Thank you. Melanie, we can always count on your political insight on any category, including space flight. We are down to the final ten minutes before countdown to launch. We have confirmation that this is the biggest viewership Fox TV has ever had. All 4 Saturn-8 launches of the Ares-1 mission have been big news. The first three launches sent up half the Mars crew and large part of the Mars-mission spaceship. Today we launch the final seven astronauts making up the Ares-1 Mar mission of fourteen astronauts. Today's launch also has the last components to be added onto the Ares-1 spaceship. Everything has been parked on the International Space Station (ISS). If today is successful, the fully assembled Ares-1 Manned Mars Mission spaceship will separate from the ISS in about 2 weeks' time and launch off Earth-orbit on a Mars injection that will take nine months to reach Mars. We cross now to our reporter in the Launch Control room for the final count down."

## CHAPTER 5.

## We are the experiment. (week 4)

Everyone gathered in the galley for supper. They were in the fourth week of the flight Earth-to-Mars portion of the mission journey. Everyone counted that as the real Mars mission starting point, when they escaped Earth orbit, even though the Saturn-8 rockets started launching up to the ISS four weeks earlier than that, one week apart each.

Captain Chris spoke. "Update on news. Doc Rodney says Alan's leg is healing well. The radio team still has not made contact with Houston. Everything else seems fine with the ship."

---

The crew carried Larry Rothman safely back on board, and I finished the surgical amputation. Barely an hour and a half later radio-contact with Houston Mission Ground Control was lost. The ship intercom worked. Cell-phones worked within the ship. Every means of communication around the ship worked, including with space suites. They just got no radio contact back from planet Earth. Even the computers which were supposed to be networking with ground control computers indicated the ground half of their network had disappeared. Chris sent voice message and digital files to Earth all the time, but could not tell if Earth was recieving the files or hearing his voice or not.

---

"Capt. Chris" called out Camilla Spofford, the one of the scientists, "Can we not abort the mission and head back to Earth? We need ground control to control the interplanetary navigation".

"There is not a clear answer as to the feasibility of aborting the mission at this point of the journey. I have thus far made it my sole decision to remain on mission. I have been through all the mission guidelines and protocol and nothing is written on when to, or how to abort the Mars mission. It was always considered that once we broke Earth orbit onto a Trans-Martian Injection there was no feasibility of turning back. That would require more fuel to decelerate, turn around and relaunch back to Earth, than what we carry. I have looked into every option I can think of. Vicky, as a flight engineer and Valborg as an IT expert, have conferenced a lot with me on this. What do you say Vicky?"

A Trans-Martian Injection (TMI) is when a space vehicle orbiting the Earth accelerates by firing its thrust rocket motors. If correctly timed, and if the correct speed is reached, the space vehicle will escape Earth orbit and fly towards Mars and be captured by Martian gravity ultimately to be retained in an orbital flight around Mars. If miscalculated and or mistimed timed, the space vehicle will miss Martian capture and continue onwards in outer space likely for eternity.

Vicky responded to Chris, addressing the crew, "In theory we can abort. Unfortunately, we don't have any gravitational body close ahead of us to sling-shot around, and head back. We would have to retro-fire the rockets and come a zero solar orbital speed, re-orientate the ship, and then accelerate again on a new Earth-bound trajectory. No one has ever tried to work that out. We roughly think it will take us a week of continuous engine-burn. We would have to rearrange the modules and dump some first, to save weight and fuel on the burns. It would take us two days to break up the ship and redock the modules we need for Earth return, and each day we take delaying the retrofire the more fuel we need to retrofire. We could retrofire first. Then once we were on an Earth trajectory do the rearranging of the modules and then abandoning of some of the modules. Also, we might have to shift some luggage around the unpressurized modules and shift fuel between tanks. My head is buzzing from trying to work it out. This is not a Star Trek fantasy spaceship. Valborg?"

"Ya" grunted Valborg as everyone looked at him expectantly. "I wrote the navigation programs. We in theory, can fly fully automatically to our Mars destination, land, take off, and return without us needing to do one thing. Me and my ground team, programmed many plan variations, but not a pre-Mars unscheduled return. I am very confident I can semi-manually map the route. We have such clever navigational aids, and I have such an instinctive feel for all of this. It is however, still not a simple stop the Taxi, and catch bus story. I do need to have the exact weights of the re-organized Earth return ship combination before I can finalize the mathematical numbers"

Capt. Chris spoke. "So thus far I have decided to keep on-mission, and I hope we get the radio link sorted out."

Camilla Spofford spoke angrily, "This is unacceptable. How can you be the Captain, the crew leader, and you can't just decide to abort the mission?"

Russel, "Yes I agree, I think Valborg is incompetent in his fuel calculations. I don't think Valborg is getting his numbers right. I simply cannot believe we have too little fuel to do a full deceleration, turn and the re-acceleration back to Earth. Can't Tyrone sort this navigation out?" Russell sounded angry. "And what about you Vicki? Why don't you talk to me on this rerouting-remapping problem? I am also a flight engineer".


"Whoa, whoa" spoke Chris softly. "We mustn't start fighting over this. I am happy with Valborg as a computer guy, working on a backup navigation plan. He is also a back-up engineer, and he has a good grasp of the fuel challenges of a mission abort. I chose to set Vicki aside to figure out how best to re-arrange the flight ship modules and calculate fuel needs etcetera. This is nothing personal. I am always open to discuss anything. I will also listen to any polite criticisms and suggestions anytime. My authority is however absolute."

"Why didn't you choose me. She's a girl" said Russell with sass in his voice.

"Oh! Things are getting sexist now, are they?" spat Babee, into the melee.

"Calm down, calm down please!" said Chris. "My plan is to keep working on the radio issue and hold off on a mission abort action for a few more days"

"Yeh, 'till when Chris?" said Camilla Spofford. "Every day we do not abort, abort becomes more impossible".

I, even though I was only the ship doctor, interjected. "Sorry if I get what I am saying wrong. I know I joined this mission at the last moment and that I have near zero astronaut training. As I think I understand things, if we abort, or had aborted and we suddenly the got radio connection restored, we would never have enough fuel to abort the abort and re-establish a trajectory to Mars. We would not have enough fuel for the mission then. Flying as we are flying now, we should be able to reach mars land, take off and return to Earth in near three years' time, as per plans. I gather from all I have been told since I joined the mission weeks back that we could in theory do the entire mission without mission control. We are the most autonomous space mission ever launched. We even have the scientist who led the navigation-program writing as a core crew member, hey Valborg?

Valborg smiled weakly,

"What the hell do you know?" shouted Russel at me.

"OK meeting closed", said Capt. Chris sounding irritated. We debrief at breakfast tomorrow, as routine and we can talk longer again tomorrow at dinner. Goodnight". Chris kicked off and drifted away to the South inter-module doorway.

The side of the interplanetary ship most close to the retro-engines they called South and the opposite end they called North.

No one spoke in the galley for a minute or two. The angry tones of some crew members had been a surprise to Chris and me. They had not been in any conversations that hinted at the anger.


With the group meeting officially over I turned to Valborg. "Val, did I understand things right?"

The two of them turned and drifted to a window, to make their conversation more private.

"Yes Rodney. We always said it would be impossible to do a sick Marsnaut extraction from the mission once we initiated Trans-Martian Injection. There is no turning back. We always had the concept that we would be locked into this only-return-after-three-years plan, because the planets only align up for the shortest flight once every 2 years. On paper we can do anything, but we would need massive fuel amounts. We are only setup for the shortest flight to Mars using the least fuel. Fuel is still 70% of the weight of our interplanetary-ship. If we mess up and exhaust our fuel stashes before we are in Earth orbit and braking to initiate Earth-entry we would be doomed. That scares me more than completing the mission without radio contact with mission control. I felt you were sticking up for me back there. Thank you"

"You're welcome. I don't know the crew well. The rest of you have been training together for over a year as the first mission crew. I wasn't even a backup crew member. I was in my home in Iowa until 12 weeks ago when I got my call to come in for an interview. Things have been one chaotic rush for me ever since then. I had so much to be trained in. You all trained to be astronauts for ten years or so, it seems. I am the outsider amateur"

"Rodney. Don't undervalue yourself. The way you saved Alan's life will be written into future history books."

"Oh, I don't know. I felt so amateur on the EVA. I had zero spacewalking training. It was all one amateur improvisation for me."

"Rodney, most of the crew see you as hero".

"I doubt it. Did you hear how Russel spoke to me tonight? He calls me stupid"

"Yes. I heard him. He has been going around telling the others that he thinks you are a mission risk."

"Why would he say that?"

"I guess he feels jealous. Rodney, the crew spoke a lot about you in these first days after the disaster, when you cared for Alan and would not leave the sickbay and we had to bring meals to you and Alan".

"What are the stories he is telling about me?"

"He says you flirt too much with the girls."

"What?" I blurted out. "He is crazy?"

There was moment of silence, then Val spoke. "I think I should not have told you."

"It is OK. I would rather know than not know. At least I can now focus a bit on the guy and try to figure out his anger. Val, sometimes in life when people throw knives at others the very knives that they throw are truths about themselves. I'll be watching him and thinking now."

"I hope I did not start a fight between you two now?"

"No" I said calmly. "I have lived through much rubbish in my life. I also see part of my ship-doctor mission as helping retain crew harmony. I will not react to Russel's barbs."

"You are a good man" said Valborg. "I am off to bed now."

"Me too. Goodnight Val. Thanks for the heads-up on Russel"

The two each kicked off, floating out to their respective modules for the night.

---

Four of the girls had their sleep pods in the same module. After they were all cleaned up and zippered up in their sleeping bags, they started to chat before closing their pods.

Vicky said. "I think this mission is falling apart. We are one member down, one member is incapacitated, and we have barely started. We have no communications to ground control, and the men are starting to fight."

Vicky Duploy was primarily a space engineer, but was also a backup IT (Information Technology) expert for the mission. She was easygoing and hyperintelligent.

"I agree", responded Camilla Spofford. "How are we going to get the experiments finished? I am supposed to send my results to ground control every week. They will then instruct me for the next week. Also, Lost-Alan was supposed to work with me on my science project. He has a little project too, but it was associated with mine. Now Alan is dead and gone. What is going to happen to my project".

Camilla was primarily on the Ares-1 mission as a research scientist, but she could stand in as an engineer if needed. She lacked self-confidence but kept that well concealed, behind a façade of negativity.

"I am behind on my science experiment too, since all the chaos of the disaster. Babee, who sleeps with the guys, is also worried about her science project". Said Vahini.

Vahini Baxter was a European descended lady, but had been born in India and given an Indian first name. Her primary Ares-1 Mission responsibility was that of being an Engineer, but she was also a leading microbiology scientist. She liked wearing a very short boy-style haircut.

Marjena said briefly, "Isn't this mission primarily a science project? Aren't we going to make break-throughs in waste recycling and fuel manufacturing? Surely Captain Bolder should be giving us extra resources. My project is a week behind already."

Marjena Lubiski was a primary space mission pilot, but also a leading small-mammal science researcher. She tended to be quiet, but spoke out when she had strong views. She too was hyperintelligent, as so many of the space-crew were on this mission. She was an unmarried crew member and leaned towards keeping to herself.

Vahini oversaw the fuel storage and monitored fuel consumption. Her experiments, which are her secondary job, on the Mars surface would involve methane generation and conversion to fuel. Her flight experiments would be related to energy too. She was a dark horse, others often thought. She spoke little, and one always had a feeling those studious eyes had a lot happening behind them. She almost seemed cool. No one disliked her. Some thought she was shy and some thought she was aloof. The alertness of her eyes however proved she was not shy. She seemed fearless about making eye contact.

Marjena Lubiski's very important job was to fly. She was a pilot. She would make trajectory corrections, re-align the flight ship, fire the thrusters and take over any surface landing if the auto-pilot failed. She could direct and oversea any on-flight changes to the ship module structure. That was a vital part of the mission. They took a few days to assemble the Mars flight-ship while orbiting Earth. Everything had been flown to the Earth orbit International Spaceship (ISS) over 3 weeks, and then spent a week together preparing to separate the Mars-Mission ship from the ISS. They then took a week to shuffle the modules around and set them up for the Ares-Mars injection ship. It was all automatically done by computers, but the pilots all had to standby ready to take control at any second. A module collision causing damage or poor berthing and collision damaging something could have ended the mission, or killed people. Luckily it all went perfect, until the disaster.

Vicky Duploy had no science experiments. She was primarily a pilot and secondly an IT support person. She spent her days studying things on the computer and assuring all was well. She smiled readily at any anyone. No one really understood what she did day to day. It didn't look like she was sneaking in computer games. She could type super-fast. Maybe her tasks were a bit thin, because it looked like she was stretching out her exercise programs a bit long. No one cared about that. She also seemed hyper intelligent and generally only joined conversations with some deep profound thought that others struggled to comprehend.

Camilla Spofford, was a tough cookie. She complained a lot. She was very quick to spot a crumb floating away when others ate, and then chastise them over letting it escape. No one remembered her smiling much. Someone smiled in her family photos that she had shown people. We were not convinced it was her in the picture. Her husband was now looking after her two junior school children, and I am sure that was fine by her. She was definitely the breadwinner and boss of her home. The three girls sharing the sleeping module with her, barely tolerated her. She was not going to find a besty or close friend in this trip. She spent a fair amount of private time with these ladies before they all settled in for the night. She spent most of the time saying bad things about the men. She really hated the doctor, and it was not clear why.

"Did you hear how Rodney sounded tonight?" she asked the group. "His inane comments on aborting the mission? He doesn't even understand what space travel is all about. He has no idea how to do this kind of research. What is he going to contribute or bring back to mankind? He is no astronaut, or Marsnaut as we get called in the press."

"I going to sleep now" said Vahini and closed her pod door.

Vicky did not reply and seemed riveted by her eBook. She slept with her pod door open. The modules lights were dimmed to near total darkness now. The windows were closed to block sunlight. In space travel the Sun shines permanently, when one does not hide on the far side of any planet. There is no day or night, just permanent sunshine on one side of the ship.

Marjena said nothing. Her two arms floated slightly to the front of her, and her head nodded a little bit forward. It floated in the air. She gave a tiny sleep-jerk of her head.   Her pod internal lights were off.

Camilla muttered to herself as she shut down her computer and pod lights. "He could not research the time of day on a mechanical hand watch. He doesn't understand research. He just doesn't get it".


------------------------------------------------------------
----------------


The next day passed routinely. We all gave polite but brief salutations of good morning as we floated down to eat. Breakfast was a rush and chow-it-down affair. Coffee was great except you could not smell it. We had to suck all liquids out of plastic bags via a straw mechanism. Losing the smell of beverage made it taste very bland. The morning captain's briefing was just to ask if anything had gone wrong overnight. Normally we should have been reporting live to ground control at Houston, but now the we reported only to their Flight-Chief Chris, in front of everyone. We zipped off to the research modules or where ever we had to be and everyone kept their heads down. Soon the work sessions, lunch-time where everyone ate alone or privately at different moments, and the afternoon exercise hour all passed. No-one did the paired exercises. Everyone avoided eye contact and conversations. Everyone was thinking. One astronaut dead. One astronaut severely injured with leg amputation. Broken radio contact to Earth. Experiments mostly lagging or not going smoothly. The option of aborting the mission with an early Earth return seemingly unlikely at best, and impossible at worst.

The evening conference started while everyone was eating. All were present. Maybe everyone had something to say, but nobody was actually sure what to say.

"Evening, everyone" said Chris, breaking the silence of plastic crinkling and the soft ever-present hum of motors and fans. "I am going to go down the list asking you each if there is anything the captain needs to know about your work today, and if you have any project or mission problems. This gets entered formally into the mission diary".

"Vahini?"

"No problems" she replied.

"Larry?"

"Very little pain. Rodney says he is signing me back to full duties in two days' time. I don't miss my leg at all". Larry sealed that comment with a smile.

"Russel?"

Russel took a very big breath. "Nothing for the record", he answered.

Chris worked down the full list, and no one had any problems to report.

Chris took a long breath and then spoke another time. "Does anyone want to speak openly and off the record", and he closed his laptop firmly, where he had been typing all the time, as if it symbolized something.

It was hard to tell what Chris was feeling. Was he angry? Was he scared? Was he sad?

Russel Dunaszegi the engineer spoke. "I am not happy?"

Chris did not respond and kept looking at him. Then Camilla spoke. "I am also not happy".

Chris looked around and asked "Who else is not happy?" No one spoke or moved. Then I assume everyone else is happy. That brought no response. Clearly a lot of general emotions were very bottled up.

"Rodney, you are the outsider, the non-astronaut. How are you seeing things?" Chris was thinking that because he had a closer friendship with me, than anyone else on the ship. He thought I might help his position.

I replied. "Chris, thanks for reminding me and everyone that I am a last-minute substitute for this mission. I know some of you have worked and trained at NASA for years. Fram, is it 20 years and you finally got off the planet?" I looked at Framingham Milkoski the pilot and engineer. He was bald and grey in his remaining hair. I was 66-years of age and luckily, I was gray and not bald. I felt a lot of respect for him.

Fram responded, "I have worked for NASA for 25 years. I was chosen as a trainee for the Ares-1 Mars mission when it was announced 30 months ago. I was placed in the first crew 5 months ago. Yup. I have given up my whole adult life virtually, to be in this spaceship today. This is my first space-flight."

I asked him, "What experiment are you involved with?" Fram replied; "I have no experiment. I am a first-choice pilot and backup engineer. My work is to systematically read all safety data tables and check-off on lists hourly and daily. I am also the chief maintenance engineer. Rodney takes blood samples off me every week for his research."

"You are wrong!" I retorted. I got cut off before I could fully explain what I was meaning.

"You are talking junk again", blurted out Russel. He could hardly contain his animosity. Chris raised a hand to draw attention back to himself.

Camilla beat him to the words and shouted, "You are no space-physician Dr. Powell!" with a sarcastic voice tone flip at the end.

Everybody then raised a hand or finger and opened their mouths to say a word.

Chris raised both hands with flat palms moving aside very deliberately he shouted "Hold it!" then continued softly. "Finish what you were saying Rodney."

Everyone looked at directly at me. I took a slow breath, and out again, then I spoke softly.

"You all think you are astronauts because you worked all your lives to be on this trip. Trust me, I worked all of my life to be on this trip too, even if it was not for NASA that I worked. We are all Marsnauts here, by the fact we are in space in a ship pointed towards Mars.

Secondly those of you whose experiments are wobbling and you fear getting back with a failed project. Let me give you all the greater view of this Ares-1 Mars Mission."

He paused and everyone was silent.

"**We** are the research project. **We** are the experiment. **We** are the laboratory rodents. Ironic, don't you think? The whole Mars Mission is an experiment is to see if we just survive. We are nothing more than pawns in these stupid political games, and money games of the private sector enterprises wanting guaranteed incomes from tax payers for contract-work that never benefitted any homeless hungry lady. There are people who say the NASA budget monies would be better spent on homeless and hungry people."

Now I had everyone's undivided attention.

"What is this thing named, the "Right stuff", that all astronauts are supposed to have? It is some sort of courage thing, and toughness thing, and very much a soldier-thing where you jump when told to jump and you have to conform in every way possible and look the same and dress the same. I am not taking away from Buzz Aldrin, and Neil Armstrong the way he got the lander down with only 20 seconds of fuel left. We are not going to cull the human race of all persons who are not of the "Right Stuff" as some managers at the top want. I have seen this same thing in the private institutions where the MBAs in the C-Suite only want lab-rats and moo-cows to do the work and make the money and never wobble and cause a hiccough. The greatness of the human race is its diversity of characters and personalities and individual talents. Even more so, the extreme greatness of humans is how we blend into groups, families, villages, nations and the social structure of the human race of the entire planet Earth. Everyone is important however large or small their task is in life, or on this mission.

We must be united. We are stronger in the summation of us individuals, when we hold hands. This Ares-1 Mars mission does not go around how we test the technologies to recycle feces and eat it again. It does not go around anyone's changes in stress hormones. It does not go around how the bugs grow in the Petrie dish. It does not go around the rocks and soil sample we are supposed to take back to Earth.

The Ares-1 Mars Mission experiment only has one end-measurement point. It is to see if we ever get home to Earth again. It is focused on how we all survive as a joined unit. They want to see whether we just survive at all.

**We are the experiment.**"

## CHAPTER 6.

## Something hot to chew on - A peritonsillar abscess. (week 5)

Ship-captain Chris Bolder and I had our sleep-pods in the last habitable module of the Mars-mission ship. That is farthest from the ascent module that formed the front or North end of the ship. The module had some limited exercise options, a toilet, a wash facility, and two modified patient-pods called beds. Medical research could be carried out in there, as well as surgery. A large amount of space was given up for storage of medical related items, including a limited supply of food.

Chris also had his own experiments set up in the sickbay, next to mine. This meant we saw a fair amount of each other through the day.

"You know" said Chris. "I have thought a lot about the deeper reasons for this manned mission to Mars. I guess any of one hundred persons involved could offer a different argument for one reason or another reason. Some think the mission's job is to drive technological development for things that will benefit mankind. Others say we are doing this to develop a road to Mars for the Human species to relocate itself. Some feel we are doing this for military reasons to stay ahead of the enemy, whoever the enemy is in any given decade. I totally can see that politicians also want a legacy item for themselves.

I can see this trip is obviously highly experimental. I like your view that we are the experiment, as you said last night. The more I think about that, the more it sounds just right. If we all die and never get back to planet Earth, the mission will be a failure of the human species to relocate across the solar system. It will be more than just a failure of 14 individuals who names will be forgotten. We will just be bunched under a name Ares- 1.

"Rodney, why did you want to come on this mission? We all had to sign those horrible contracts that quoted a 50% mortality likelihood."

I sighed and then replied. "I can't really answer that question. My answer is complex and it will change with the hour of the day, and my mood. There are a lot of reasons. I guess it is very selfish. I did not ask my wife's permission. I am not doing it for her. In truth I am neglecting her a lot. I could leave her as a widow. I see myself on talk-shows on radio and TV after the mission. I see myself lecturing afterwards. Maybe it will be the platform for me to air my quirky life philosophies. There is money to be earned in that too. There are books to be written. There is fame. That all sounds very narcissistic. I ask myself if I am narcissistic? I don't think so. I care about people and I don't spend time and effort on my appearance and on vanity aspects.

The trip is in so many ways the ultimate adventure. It is a racing motorcycle ride. It is a jet plane ride sitting in the cockpit. It is summiting the highest mountain on the continent. There is story telling in that. I like that. Maybe I most want to be with people after the mission and to enthrall them with stories.    Part of me also wants to be clinical doctor and to help people. I get joy in that, and fulfillment in that. I hear myself saying *me* a lot. Am I denying my narcissism, I ask myself?  Why did you want to be Mars-mission astronaut Chris?"

Chris responds, "Hmm. I guess I simply saw it as career peak to aim at. I always wanted to be a pilot. Then a fighter-jet pilot. I just kept wanting a higher bar to climb. This is the ultimate bar. Maybe for me, it is just in me to strive to be dutiful, and excellent. This is an ultimate challenge."

I spoke again. "Do you fear dying Chris?". Although Chris had a military title and rank, he preferred all of us to address him by his first name.

Chris. "No. Not all. That is not a worry at all. I will work hard at not dying, but I do not fear death, should it be inevitable."

"Hmm" I said while thinking. "Forgive me asking this. Have you ever been suicidal in your life?"

Chris took a few moments to reply and he moved his lips a few times as if he was about to speak and the changed his mind. "Yes, I have had my dark moments"

"Have you ever serious contemplated actually taking your own life?"

"Man!!" Objected Chris. "This is getting very personal. Have you ever thought of taking your own life?"

" Yes."

Silence.

I spoke again. "Chris, did you want this mission as a sort of suicide wish?"

"I can't truly answer that. I can only say; I fear nothing and I am driven to do my best for the mission and for everyone. Let me throw your dirt back at you Rodney. Are you suicidal here on this mission?"

"I definitely am not suicidal. I will definitely not add to my death on this trip. I will fight like a lion to get back home. However, if I die it will be with a smile on my face. I am 100 % not afraid of death. What lies beyond death, whatever it is, only seems peaceful and good to me. If I look back on my whole life, there are sad moments when death seemed like an attractive escape from the burden of hopelessness and sadness that smothered me. It is incredible that one human can make another human feel so low.

I got through that. It was as if I was at a place beyond hell. I had to enter the back-door of hell and walk a full journey across hell to come out of its front door. When you have done that and found a way to get your mind through it all, then you are strong. It is as if your soul dies and becomes born again in new world where it is unbreakable. It is only your body that still lingers in this crappy world.  Your soul cannot die twice. You become utterly fearless of death after such low points. It is such a fearlessness that you almost want death, of your body at least. However, you are not suicidal. You are determined to fight off the tigers. You determined to stand up straight every time you are punched down. You have no fear of continuing. You want to be like a lion to the last."

"Wow! Rodney", said Chris. "You sure opened up there. You have a way with words. Maybe all your words could apply to me too. Rodney, one thing always puzzled me all my early life, especially being a military man.  How does a soldier engage in military combat knowing there is a half chance he will die that same day? How did a soldier climb out of a trench in the first world war, and run into machine gun fire? How did the men, in the American Civil war, be part of Pickett's charge and run up a hill into certain death? I finally figured it out for myself. They accepted death beforehand. In a sense, they had already died within their souls. The final conclusion of a bodily death seemed trivial. This allowed them to become divinely unselfish, and not think twice about charging ahead. In some way, they assumed a child, or a woman, or someone else far away would benefit from their death. The brave soldiers in the famous Civil War Pickett's charge, performed unselfish deeds sacrificing their own life for another's survival. Sadly, if they survived certain death, they are often bewildered about it. They ask, '*Why did they die and not me.*' They have survivor's guilt, walking around feeling like ghosts, while their fellow soldiers died."

Chris continued, "Rodney, I have no fears about the dangers of this mission. I only fear failing this mission."

I drifted across the module to Chris opening my arms to hug him. Chris hugged me back.

As we drifted back apart, I said, "We are brothers."

Chris affirmed, "We are brothers."

I then changed subjects completely and we never spoke of such dark matters ever again.

"I never ever thought of being an astronaut myself, "I said. "I saw Nel Armstrong step onto the moon when I was a young teenage boy, but I never aspired to be an astronaut. It was not until very late in life, and after I was already an American citizen for over ten years, when I was trying to find some final missions to add some extra purpose to my maturing life, when it dawned on me that my package of life skills would be useful on a trip Earth to Mars. I could see myself doing a nerve block and doing the surgery too, while floating around. That was a clear vision. About 3 years back, I did some searching and found an application site to be an astronaut. I completed all the forms, and attached all my documents, including a sassy braggadocious resume. I got an automated reply and forgot about the application. I always had a fascination for extreme medicine and steadily read a lot about space medicine. It became my hobby going-to-bed reading matters before I turned the lights off. Then 12 weeks back I got this phone call, and......... here I am on my way to Mars in a broken spaceship. It is crazy."

"Life is crazy," said Chris.

"Yup. Indeed," I replied.

"Work time now."

The two men stopped talking, and turned to the computers, on their research station table-tops.

"Doctor Powell", greeted Tyrone Wilson as he drifted into the sick bay.

"Rodney! Please!"

"OK. Rodney. My mama taught me a lot about respect".

"What can I do for you?"

"My throat has been very painful for about 5 days now, and today it got a lot worse"

"Point to where it is sore."

Tyrone pointed to under the angle of the jaw, on the left side.

"Let me feel you neck please," I asked. I felt and caressed both sides simultaneously comparing for swelling, tenderness and the presence of swollen lymph nodes. I grabbed a small flash light and wooden spatula. "Open your mouth Tyrone".

I then adjusted my position so as to peer into the back of Tyrone's mouth, as I pushed the tongue flat with the spatula and shone the flashlight into his mouth. I peered over the small flashlight trying to look along its beam, and I sniffed his breath.

It was difficult with both of us floating around. The second I pushed Tyrone's tongue down, at that same second I started to float to above Tyrone.

I spoke. "I caught a glimpse there for a second. It's enough for me to work with though. You still have your tonsils, right?"

"Yeah".

"And you couldn't open your mouth much".

"Yeah. It was hard to brush my teeth last night. I couldn't open my mouth much. I also haven't eaten since yesterday morning. I feel thirsty".

"Tyrone, your left tonsil is swollen, and covered in a white thick paste. That is what smells. Also, your tongue, in the middle has this a thick white plaque that is part causing your bad breath. It comes from dried saliva and you not swallowing and drinking. Your breath smells pretty bad. You have trismus, that is spasm of your jaw muscles, and that is why you are having difficulty brushing your teeth and eating and swallowing. I also see your left tonsil is very enlarged, with a near certain abscess in it.

I am going to give you a liter of fluid IV with your first antibiotics. That will take an hour. I will disconnect the fluid line, but leave the IV cannular in your hand. I'll cover it with a sticky bandage I will give you some acetaminophen capsules to swallow every six hours as well as antibiotic tablets. I want to see you after 24 hours again. Unless you have had dramatic improvement, I will also need to drain the abscess, that I am sure you have."

Tyrone; "What do you mean drain it? Are you going to operate?"

"Yes. I will cut into the abscess to let the pus inside it drain away. The swelling will go down and it will heal fast then".

"Operate? Here in space? What about an anesthetic?"

"Well, you do not need a full general anesthetic. It is in fact safer to do this awake. If any pus ran into your lungs you would have your cough reflexes to protect yourself and you would cough the pus out. I will use topical and local anesthesia"

"Aargh! I don't like the sound of this. Are you going to cut here?" Asked Tyrone pointing to his left jaw angle.

"No. I'll work inside your mouth. I'll inject some local anesthetic drug into the wall of the abscess, which is part of that tonsil. When that is working, I'll insert a scalpel into it until it reaches the pus cavity, that I am sure is there".

"Do you have to do that? Are you sure you are right? Aren't you just an anesthesiologist?"

I replied, trying to sound confident and reassuring. "I am an anesthesiologist, but I have drained two of these peritonsillar abscesses before in my general practice career, when I was a rural doctor forty-years ago. The experiences of doing that is still vivid in my memory."

"Are you definitely going to drain it? Can the antibiotics be enough on their own?"

"If it were a pure unilateral tonsillitis, antibiotics alone would be enough. The fact you have trismus, that is jaw spasm, and the fact it is so swollen it pushing your uvula to the right points to it being an abscess. The uvula is that tiny little tongue at the back of your palate. At the least you have severe unilateral tonsil infection, and likely also the development of an abscess in that tonsil. I am going to give antibiotics a chance to work first. If things do not improve dramatically within 24 hours, I will have to operate. If we did nothing you could eventually get so much airway swelling that you would choke and die. Also, if that ruptures and you inhale some of the pus you could develop a bacterial pneumonia as well, and die."

"Die!" Screeched Tyrone. "Let's do the IV. I hate needles".

"Yup, you are the same as my wife. Don't worry now Tyrone, you can do this, and I am super good at this. I just need a few moments first".

As I prepared the IV fluid and the needles and antibiotics, Tyrone looked around nervously. I tied a three-centimeter-wide elastic band around Tyrone's left mid-forearm. Tyrone winced.

"Tyrone, I want you to look away. Imagine you are walking along a sandy tropical beach towards the setting Sun, holding hands with the most beautiful girl in the world".

Tyrone flipped his head around and looked at me in the face from inches away, as if he could not believe what I had just said. "I can't walk."

"Ah, stupid me!" I Replied. "I was talking in my doctor autopilot mode. I have only done this a million times before. Tyrone, let's do it different. Imagine you are steering you motorized wheel chair down the sidewalk of the Champs Elysees in Paris. It is a beautiful day and you can see the Arc De Triomph ahead. Holding your free-hand is the most beautiful girl in the world".

"OK that works better".

"Now I am scratching your hand and tapping you hand", I said as I wiped the skin with a cotton wool clump wet with anti-septic fluid. I next stuck the used wool clump onto a Velcro face on my work-table.

"Now here comes a mosquito from Mexico and he is dancing," I said, as I gently tapped the flesh behind the back of Tyrone's hand. I firmly held his hand's fingers firmly in my other hand. The tapping broke the spasm of the skin veins, and one started to swell up proudly. "Ah! We have a dancing partner here. The mosquito is scratching the dance floor. Can you see the Parisian City lights blooming in the early twilight Tyrone? Think what you would say to this lovely lady".

Tyrone just said, "Ahh" softly. I continued, now saying "scratchy mosquito, scratchy mosquito. scratchy mosquito", as he scratched the skin over the vein with the hub of the needle.

I then swiftly flipped the needle around and inserted the sharp needle end into the vein, while holding the needle nearly parallel to the vein. As soon as I saw a flush of blood in the clear rear-hub of the inner steel needle, I lowered the hub a degree further, and advanced the needle cannula a further centimeter within the vein's lumen. Then, I calmly straightened my bent index finger to advance the cannula off the steel core introducer, while my other fingers of that hand held the needle steady. It was like pushing the plastic cannula hat was over the steel needle, gently away with my finger as I straightened it. "It's in, relax now"

"What?" said Tyrone". "I felt nothing".

"Keep your hand still," I said as I connected the IV fluid system and tubes to the cannula in Tyrone's vein. I flipped the on-switch on the fluid pump, and grabbed the adhesive dressing that was loosely attached to the working area surface. All the time, my left-hand held Tyrone's left-hand in a rigid position and my left thumb held the IV cannula in place. I next wrapped a short pink elastic bandage lightly around Tyrone's hand for added IV security.

"Why pink?" Asked Tyrone?

"It's the happiest color I know", I replied grinning.

"Rodney, I have to hand it to you. That was the most amazing injection I ever had; I can't believe I never felt it go it. Did you anesthetize he skin somehow?"

"Tyrone I just used basic procedural hypnosis. If one understands the pain physiology it is very easy. When a needle gets pushed into the flesh it cuts a track through a little bit of tissue. The microscopic cut cells release potassium that instantly induces pain signals to run along the nerves to the spinal cord. At the spinal cord those signals get re-transmitted up to the brain, or not. There is a gateway mechanism for the re-transmission of peripheral pain signals, up the brain. Only when the signals reach the brain, does the person gain awareness of the pain and the tissue injury. Knowing how to manipulate those gate-way control mechanisms is all about pain control. The gateways are heavily under mental control from the brain. The brain can open the hiway for pain signals to come up to the brain and consciousness, or the brain can close the gateway down entirely, and I mean entirely. All I did was manipulate your brain to do that with hypnosis".

"Hey now, Rodney! You didn't hypnotize me. You didn't swing an old-fashioned waist-coat chain watch before my eyes," said a very relieved smiling Tyrone.

"No. You are half correct. I didn't swing a watch before your eyes, but I did talk to you and control your mind. I used the power of cognitive suggestion. It is the same as when someone yawns, a bunch of other people in the same room yawn too."

"NOBODY controls my mind. I am the boss of myself!", said Tyrone firmly.

I replied. "If the person looks at their hand studiously and fearfully, as the needle is inserted the gateways are wide open. If they are fully anticipating the pain and studiously observing their hand to see the needle penetrate the skin, it will hurt a fair bit. I have seen folks jump up, or rip their hand away from me.

On the other hand, figuratively speaking, when I use a double hypnotic technique, I can eliminate the pain experience 100%. When one is adrenalized as you were, and I have their attention and the rest is easy. The adrenaline makes them focus and all I have to do is point the focus where ever I want it to go. The first technique is called Transform the Anticipated Sensation. I say TAS. I cannot lie and say that *you will feel nothing*. So, I tell the truth and twist it a bit, and I say *here is a mosquito*. No one is scared of a mosquito. Well that is a tiny white lie, but I am sure you forgive me. Next, I say *he is scratching you*. I then scratch the skin point where I plan to insert the needle and get into a rhythm. I keep saying *scratch* as I scratch. You start to anticipate just a scratch. You are not scared of the scratch. Then without breaking the rhythm I swop the thing I am scratching with, for the actual needle. No-one even notices, and the needle is already in. I can do this on toddlers. I get the mother to hold them and comfort them. I then play with their hand behind their backs. I don't talk intelligently to the kid. I do talk in reassuring tones like I am singing and I say *scratch-scratch-scratch,* and then swop the scratch for the needle tip and push it in. The kid does not understand, but does not flinch. I was amazed when I discovered this technique for myself.

Anyway, back to adults like you. I also used Dissociate-From-Procedure for you. I call that DFP. I got you thinking about some pleasing place and image far removed from this doctor's sick-bay. It is simply the power of suggestion. When your brain gets distracted and dissociated from the needle it eliminates all thoughts of needle anticipation. The brain totally shuts down the signal hiway from the spinal cord to the brain. The brain has nerve cables that go down the spinal cord and physiologically inhibit the transfer of the pain signals upwards. It is so simple, yet so elegant. There are hundreds of stories of soldiers who during the heat of battle do not feel a limb get blown off and they kept trying to fight they because were so distracted, being so focused on their fighting roles. I remember from my youth, from when playing rugby. I would take a shower after the game and feel pain. I then discovered I had skin scraped off my knees or elbows, where I had fallen onto the ground at full speed sprint. I never felt it during the game. It was only when the cool shower water washed onto the raw flesh that I discovered my injuries. I guess I was fired-up and focused on playing the hard game of rugby, and distracted from injuries.

So, Tyrone I hypnotized you using the power of suggestion, and you just got a lecture for free.

Tyrone then asked, "Rodney, do you play chess?". Tyrone was clearly very content as a patient, and he wanted to change subjects and get to know me better. We each from that day found fascination in exploring each other's minds on diverse topics, and we became very best friends.

---

Tyrone came back to the sick bay the next day.

I asked, "How are you feeling? Any better?"

"I am not sure, maybe the pain tablets helped a bit. It is as hard as hell to swallow, but I worked at it. I haven't eaten anything, but I at the least don't feel thirsty. I worked at getting tiny sips down a lot. Swallowing the tablets hurt like hell, but I got them down. I am sure I was not a pretty sight when swallowing, with all the noises I made."

I instructed, "Open your mouth as wide as you can?   Is that your best? It's not worse, but I definitely am going to drain the certain abscess. I'll only know I was right, if we get puss out".

"What if we are wrong?" asked Tyrone sounding nervous.

"Well then you get cut for nothing, and provided I only incised the tonsil, no harm will be done other than me causing some trivial bleeding. We just can't afford to be wrong in not draining an actual abscess."

"I am not going to like this".

"You can do it Tyrone Wilson. You were a noble brave Knight yesterday with the IV needle. I am sure you will be knighted today and become Lord Wilson".

"He he", giggled Tyrone. "Lord Wilson", he said grinning. I found he loved being called "Lord Wilson". It always made him grin and laugh with pride.

"Tyrone, I want to Velcro you onto this table. I am putting this band across your legs. You can stay sitting We both need to be steady. I'll stabilize my feet under these floor straps".

I set up my procedure tray next to Tyrone. Everything was either secured onto Velcro, or lightly secured by magnets.

"Open your mouth. I am going to place this local-anesthetic soaked swab gently onto your tonsil".

At the second the swab touched the tonsil, Tyrone closed his mouth and flinched back a little. I was expecting that and had my hand resting secure against Tyrone's chin, so that my hand moved with Tyrone.

After a minute I said, "Tyrone open wide again". I had a tiny headlamp that was neatly sitting between his eyes. I adjusted my view-point angle so that I could see deep into Tyrone's mouth, that was only 3 cm wide at the front teeth. I saw the bulging peritonsillar abscess. I sprayed a few drops of local anesthetic drug onto the mucosa where I planned to incise. I waited a minute and touched the mucosa with the fine needle point of his syringe of local anesthetic. Tyrone was breathing slowly and deeply, mainly through his nose. I pushed Tyrone's tongue down very slightly and gently with the spatula in my other hand that was braced against the chin.

"Here comes some of the finest Tequila from Guadalajara. I lectured there once. The tequila burns a bit like fine tequila should, burning, burning, . . . so fine." I made my voice soft and slow trying to sound reassuring. I injected a tenth of a milliliter. Tyrone did not flinch. I kept advancing the needle in tiny steps while making tiny injections. I have found using this technique most patients do not feel the injection at all.  When the needle was about four millimeters deep, I very slowly injected one and a half milliliters of local anesthetic drug. The mucosa blanched and the blanching spread sideways.  Tyrone was unflinching. I thought to himself, that this was a miracle. I always was in awe of the art and science of medicine whenever I applied it to a patient with an intervention. There were very many things that I had learned not from text books, but from my mentors, and watching them be masterful in caring for their patients. There are so many study courses one can do on line these days and get a doctorate and all sorts of degrees. Good medical learning can never be that. There is so much art in medical care that can only be passed direct from physician to physician.

I picked up my scalpel. It had a small number 15c blade on it. "Open wide" I said gently and patiently. I placed the scalpel against the bulging tonsil and secured my hand so that the scalpel would move with Tyrone's head, if Tyrone flinched severely. I pushed it a half centimeter in and saw pus appear. Then I sliced one centimeter upwards. Tyrone uttered a soft "Ugh" but did not flinch.

I extracted the scalpel from Tyrone's mouth and gave him a gauze swab. "Spit into that". Tyrone had a lot of blood and pus on his tongue and was glad to be rid of it.

"One more look," I said and Tyrone opened his mouth. I inserted a long handle hemostat into the abscess cavity. The hemostat resembled a long stainless-steel skinny pair of pliers. I opened the hemostat jaws about 2 centimeters wide to stretch the abscess incision wider.

Tyrone pulled back with a mellow "Arrgh". I admired his self-control. He made my job easier.

"Sorry for that", he said.

I already had the instrument out. I had just needed to stretch the little pockets of pus in his tonsil, that I had not drained wide enough with the incision. The surgery was finished. "How are you feeling".

"Wow! It is so much better! You are a wizard Rodney, truly a wizard."

I smiled and felt happy. I knew Tyrone would do well.

"Gargle with this 4-hourly for 24 hours. Spit the gargle stuff into the bathroom vacuum collector. Only drink fluids for 36 hours, and if you feel brave trying eating semi-soft-food and if that goes well you have full license to do what you like. Use those acetaminophen tablets as you feel a need for pain relief, but only six-hourly. Absolutely finish your 5-day supply of antibiotics no matter how well you are. Check in with me after 24 hours. I'll will take out your IV port then."

I was feeling very relieved. I knew I would catch up on my own missing sleep that evening. I had been nervous about draining Tyrone's peritonsillar abscess. I had learned how to do that from an old Polish doctor who had trained in the time of Communist Poland. That however was over 30-yers ago. Some folks spoke down about the Old Polish doctor who taught me to drain a peritonsillar abscess during my internship, or housemanship, as we called it back then. They looked down upon him because he never had a so-called proper Western Medicine training. I can only say he was very intelligent, incredibly experienced, and magnificently skilled. Tyrone would not understand it but that old Communist system trained Polish doctor had drained Tyrone's peritonsillar abscess this day, via my hands.

One is tempted to think that the best medical care only comes from a doctor who graduated from some big name western famous university. I know that is untrue. I have met doctors trained in India who were among the best I had ever met. What India gave them, with its maybe less than most expensive resources than rich countries medical schools, was a massive clinical experience more than triple what a student and trainee doctor could get in Western university. Then the final things Westerners overlook, is that information travels very well in the form of books and the internet. All third world trained doctors can write and pass all western medical exams because they studied the same books and information sources. The third world trained doctors have a unique advantage of having much more hands-on experience and skills very early in their training and early practice. Where in Boston or London does one find an anesthesiologist who has drained peritonsillar abscesses during his career?

I had been a medical teacher all of my life. Every now and again I would get a seasonal greeting card from a former trainee or we would cross paths at a university. They greet me with warm glow and often relate to me some wisdom I had spoken to them or some skill I had taught them, and how they had applied it and thought of me at that time. There is no monetary value for the good feeling such words give a teacher. More often than not the skill or wisdom that resonated with my former trainee was not something I had invented. It was wisdom and a skill that one of my former mentors and teachers had passed onto to me.

Whilst on-line learning and book studying is a major part of learning and advancing as a physician, the golden facts and diamond skills are learned in face-to-face interactions with medical teachers where one can ask a dumb question. As a teacher I always enjoyed the student who asked dumb questions, over a student who asked a question only to show off what they thought was their own top-notch knowledge. I love dumb questions, because they nearly always lead to some poignant very important point being made. Also, dumb questions lead to fascinating tangential discussions that otherwise never would have arisen. One of my sayings is that there, truthfully, is no such thing as a dumb question.

---

"Tyrone. There is something I was wanting to ask you?"

"Yeh"

"When did you become a paraplegic? What is that all about"

"My injury happened four years ago. I am so excited to be the first paraplegic astronaut. I applied and someone wrote to me saying it was ridiculous that I was applying to be an astronaut. He asked how do I expect to use a wheelchair in a spaceship? He also added some insult. I wrote back and managed to get my letter presented to the head of NASA. Basically, I said legs are a near useless pair of appendages in microgravity, and that we function with only our brains and hands. I don't need a wheelchair in space. My IQ is 160, making me an official genius, and I co-wrote the dammed navigation software for the mission. I already worked for NASA. Just who can do the job better than me. Also, I am a degree electronics engineer, with an honors degree in micromechanics from Oxford."

"Whoopee" I said wanting to show how impressed I was. "Good for you? How did your paraplegia start?"

"I already had all of my degrees and I was working for NASA when a truck hit me on my Moto Guzzi motor bike. I got a T1-2 fracture with spinal cord wipe-out. This was only four years ago. I was only off work for 7 weeks, and I got commendations on every annual review in my job since. I started to realize about two years back that I will function better in space than on the ground, because I could discard my wheel chair. Here I am." He grinned.

"Hey man! I also ride a Moto Guzzi motor bike. It a small solar system indeed"

"Yeh it's a small solar system indeed. Who would ever expect two Guzzi riders would meet up halfway between Earth and Mars?"

# CHAPTER 7.

## Skabenga the Sphynx cat. (week 6)

Everyone was present in the galley module. It was dinner time and everyone had something to chew on, or suck from. Some Marsnauts were making small talk, and the others were quiet and listening to anything they could hear. Captain Chris ate in a rush, caught a floating crumb, and discarded his plastic trash into the recycle-bin.

Every disposable form of plastic on the ship was made of PVC resin type 4, or low-density polyethylene also called LDPE. Mixed plastic types don't recycle well. When mixed types are melted together phase-separation tends to occur. The reprocessed plastic blends usually get downcycled into some limited-utility low-grade coarse plastic-objects, like a brick. NASA decided that all space travel disposable plastic will be of one plastic type. This would lend itself to simpler re-cycling processes and more utility of the products. The recycled plastic would have close to virgin-plastic quality. The recycling would start during the ground-phase of this Mars mission.

I was feeding Skabenga. I squirted a drop of water into the cat's mouth, followed by another and another. The cat got her meals in the form of paste smeared into a board. She had to lick it off the board. Skabenga ate three times per day, like everyone else. A lot of the Marsnauts liked Skabenga and took turns feeding the cat. The cat technically belonged to me, as I had medical research plans for the cat much later on. His research was going to be done on the return-to Earth flight. Until then, the cat was just going to be the ship-cat, and everyone's pet. I had noticed there were two Marsnauts who never played with or fed the cat.

"Gather around everyone" called out Chris. "We are 6 weeks into this mission now. I think we are beyond any realistic option of aborting the mission with an early Earth return. I sense everyone understands that. We have had zero contact with ground control. We cannot tell if they can hear us. We are still sending out all our data, and a daily summary statement from us, in case they can hear us. I have worked hard with the engineers and IT persons and we have no reason to think that we cannot do this mission entirely autonomously without ground control. Everything was designed for that, as a principle, from the start. However, no one thought for one second, that we would ever actually be out of contact with ground control.

We just cannot explain this lack of contact with ground control. Dessie and Vicky could not spot a single suspicious damage point or anything else suspicious during their inspection EVAs (extra vehicular activities). They have now totaled sixteen hours inspecting outside, and have found nothing. Inside we have tested everything, stripped down and opened about every radio-related device or computer. We won't stop looking and trying to fix the problem, but I think we cannot devote two astronauts fulltime indefinitely to this task. It will become a distraction to the fuller mission purpose, if we just focus on trying to repair the radio links much more. It is not a life or death situation for us, I am starting to realize. We have enough in-built automation, enough control to override all automation if needed, and enough expertise amongst the astronauts to complete the mission without ground control communications. Doing this is not something we specifically planned for before launching the mission, but after thinking a lot and talking to all of you in your various fields of expertise, I believe we can function without ground control communications. So, I will soon stop this fruitless and increasingly pointless search to solve the Earth radio problem."

Chris continued, "When NASA sent Alan Shepard in 1961, the first American, into space around Earth, he had no windows, no tasks and no responsibilities. He just had to sit out the ride and keep talking so that NASA knew he was alive. He was just an expensive test rat. We as the first Americans to visit Mars, unlike Alan Shepard, we have vast capability to manage the flight, set directions, change and adapt, and repair things. Although, this loss of communications with Ground-Control, is unprecedented, and was unplanned for, but I do believe we can survive it.

The radio frequencies sent from Earth to us are definitely blocked. Our short-range radios seem to be fine. We can communicate by hand radios, our on-ship cell-phones, and mobile radios with our Marsnauts when they spacewalk. We can communicate with ourselves. Our ship is so large, we are the first astronauts to have on-ship cell-phones. We also have overhead communications and our computer intranet system. Thus, our internal communications are working 100% as designed. I like the cell-phones. I can have private conversations with anyone I need to talk to, at any time and wherever they are. I can't yet say if we will have Mars-orbit to Mars-ground communication. We will only find that out once we land on Mars."

Russel intervened, "Chris, what if we have no Mars-ground to ship coms? How will we launch back to Mars-orbit and dock back with the Mars-orbiter modules? The automatic pilot system won't work. We can do a manual docking but we need to be talking to the Mars-orbiter when we do that?"

"Very good question Russel. We will have to be very clever and innovative at that time."

"That's is a crappy answer. I think we are all going to die," snapped Russel back. "We cannot risk that, doing the surface landing part of the mission. I think we must simply orbit Mars for that year, and then return to Earth at the set time, when the planets are best aligned for the shortest Earth-return distance for us"

"Russel, as ship-captain I have final say on these questions, but I will listen very hard to the group's viewpoints when we reach that big descend or not decision time. The Mars-landing is still over seven months away"

"I am an engineer and you have hardly consulted me on all of this. Why not?" Russel sounded angry.

"You are a first assigned engineer on this mission, as well a backup pilot, Russel. That is true. You are however, exaggerating. You know I have spoken to you for hours on this". Chris sounded a bit irritated with Russel. "I have had Tyrone and Vicky working mostly on this matter because they were each working for 2 years on the software and hard ware of the ship communication systems before take-off. They know it best. They were in the development team"

Russel snarled. "I think, this is all their screw-up. It's their fault"

"Hold it!" there interjected Tyrone. "You have nothing to base that insult on".

I spoke up in the moments pause as everyone gasped and wanted to start speaking their minds too. "The great Chinese advisor to the kings and generals of 600 BC had an approach to this sort of problem. His name was Sun Tzu. He said to always to keep the grand view of the plan in mind. Don't be distracted from the end goal. He has been translated as saying in modern-speak, do not sweat the small stuff. Only be forward looking. Don't waste time looking back. Let's not break the team down trying to assign blame, when we have no basis to blame anyone. We must just focus on completing the mission. We must just be forward facing all the time."

Apparently, Russel did not care for anecdotes and blurted out, as he looked at me, "You are always putting me down!"

Chris spoke now to everyone, but glancing at me. "Thanks Rodney. I agree. Let's stand together and be forward looking".

Camilla Spofford cut Chris off, "Rodney has nothing to say about these scientific and technical matters. He is only a medical-doctor, and doesn't have a PhD. I have a PhD."

I made a bowing gesture with a gracious hand gesture to Spofford and smiled. I felt it wiser to remain quiet, and act gracious.

Chris took up talking again, somewhat tersely, "Everyone please sleep well. I will be visiting each of you during work times tomorrow and I want face-to-face reports and demonstrations of your research work and how it is going." With those comments completed he picked up the cat and headed back off to her sleep module far South along the spaceship. I followed him as second person out of the galley.

---

Skabenga was a research cat. Part of the project was to see if a pet served any useful purpose in the Marsnaut relationships. It was also the first free-roaming animal in space travel. Free roaming takes on other meanings in a float-only environment. One is utterly stranded if you float stationary in the middle of a module, and cannot reach to some side structure. No one had any idea how the cat would adapt, or even could live in a gravity free environment. I did have one experiment to do on the cat. If the cat tolerated gravity existence well, the experiment would be done late on the mission trip in the gravity-free environment. If the cat did poorly, it would be caged and experimented on very early before Mars was reached. The experiment called for the cat to be euthanized at the end of the study, and have its lungs preserved for analysis back on Earth.

Skabenga was the name the breeder gave the cat. The word meant a lot of naughty things. Because cats can shed a lot of hair that could mess with the spaceship instruments, NASA decided not to use a hairy cat. Skabenga was a Sphynx cat. She had narrow sloping evil looking blue eyes. Her skin on very close examination had a very fine fur needing a magnifying glass to be observed. The skin, at a glance resembled Chamois leather. However, it looked hairless from two feet away and Skabenga was considered a true sphynx hairless breed. She had massive ears, colored black like a Persian cat, and a black face. She was a year old when the Ares-1 Mars mission launched.

Skabenga was used to having water injected into her mouth by now, and was used to licking her food-paste off a board. She also was fairly good at dropping her stools onto an absorbent diaper like paper-rag, and to urinating onto to it too. This would be offered to her and held against her rear end about 5 minutes after eating. It took a while before she got accustomed to having a human so close to her, to do this. The rag got disposed of. She always made instinctive attempts at walking around her poopie spot and scratching it. Her legs twitched oddly in free floating mode. Obviously, that was an instinct deeply buried in her DNA. It was hilarious to watch this, if she was floating in the air.

In space I was her main custodian, but very soon most of the Marsnauts were asking if they could care for Skabenga for the day. That took a big burden off of me. Skabenga being really hairless, got cold easily. She had a couple of knitted woolen pullovers that could be positioned over her chest and tummy. There were no sleeves. It was just a tube. It fitted her like a strapless boob-tube on a lady.

Skabenga, like any cat, just wanted to relax and snooze for most of each day. She had a leopard skin patterned thick blanket bed. In essence it was a tube. She could crawl in one side and disappear entirely. One could see that she was in the tube by seeing her shape under the blanket. The cat-bed also had a Velcro strip on one side giving it 100 places to attach to in every module.

The other wonder thing that Skabenga had, was a magnetic launch-pad. Basically, it was a black matt colored square metal plate of about twenty by ten centimeters size. It was lightly magnetic and had a Velcro strip under it. The spaceship had a hundred of them. They were useful for astronauts when working on something, to hold items. If the item was not itself magnetic, tiny magnets could be taped onto the item.

Skabenga had magnetic boots. They looked like thin cotton socks. She also had magnetic sleeves. The routine was to have a magnetic boot on the left front-paw, and one on the rear right-paw. The magnetic sleeve was placed on the other limbs, just above the foot. The boots and sleeves were finely knitted and had very weak tiny coin-looking plate-magnets stitched into pockets on the sock undersides, and onto the sleeve outer-sides. The boot magnets were on the sole of her feet, and the sleeve magnets were on the outer-sides of her forelimbs. Skabenga had it all figured out within ten days.

The magnetic grip was just enough to stop the cat floating away into the air, but not so strong that it stopped the cat lifting a foot and breaking magnet contact.  Soon the cat was able to leap off her launch pad and glide through the air to another launch pad that she had seen. She was clever enough to reach out with a booted paw to grab the magnetic pad if she was floating close by, but about to miss it.

Her masterful trick was to first stand on the launch pad and lift the two paws with socks, to break that magnetic contact. Then she gave a tiny kick with the two feet with no magnetic sock and she drifted away in a direction she learned how to control. The sleeves with magnets were enough to hold her onto the magnet-plate if she was relaxing on her side. When lying down on her side she looked like she was just off floating above the launch pad. Looking closer one could see one sleeved limb flat against the magnetic plate.

Occasionally Skabenga would get things wrong and land up floating aimlessly in the center of module. She would give a soft meeow to call attention to herself. Whoever was closest would grab her and give her a little cuddle, a kiss and an ear scratch and place her on the closest magnetic launch pad. Sometimes, if they were busy, they would just reach out and give Skabenga a tiny nudge so that she would float over to another magnetic launch pad.

Sphynxes are incredibly ugly, but it was amazing how quickly Skabenga seduced herself into everyone's heart. I was getting a suspicion that I would never be able to do my experiment on Skabenga. The experiment required her being euthanized in the end. In the experiment I would have to sedate and paralyze her, before placing a tube into her lung pipes and connecting her to a ventilator that would breath automatically for Skabenga for a week. After that Skabenga would be euthanized, and her lungs preserved in chemicals for analysis back on planet Earth. As an anesthesiologist, I knew a lot about ventilating lungs. The study was not my own idea but that a famed researcher, also a fellow anesthesiologist I had worked with, called Dave Kalia. Dave had an office adjacent to mine before I retired, and he was mainly a laboratory researcher for 80% of his work time. Dave loved hearing about my clinical experiences and thoughts. I had many ideas for animal research, but my patient care and teaching responsibilities left me no time to do laboratory research. I loved hearing Dave's amazing knowledge of things that had not yet been developed enough to be introduced in human patient care. In another life, the us two-men might have made a very productive research team of physician-scientists complimenting each other's different skills and knowledge.

Suddenly Skabenga pushed her head up through the collar of my shirt just below my chin. "Oh hello! Are you awake now?" I asked. I lifted his shirt up from my waist to back over Skabenga's head. Skabenga pushed and drifted away into the module center. I pulled his shirt down and went back to working on the computer in front of me. Skabenga had been sleeping on my chest and tummy inside my golfer's shirt. All the astronauts wore those kind of stretchy loose fitting very comfortable shirts. The collars only opened downwards for two button's length. The shirts all had Velcro fastening pockets. There were two chest pockets in the front, and one pocket on each sleeve. Every astronaut had something in nearly each pocket. Everyone had a Swiss army pocket-knife. The red-handle pocket-knife was a sort of astronaut badge-of-honor, that was very handy when we were forever fixing and adapting things to some purpose.

Sleeping inside my shirt was a day-time treat that Skabenga liked in the mid-morning.

---

Chris looked up from his research desk. We two men each had their own personal research desks in the sick-bay module. "Rodney, what are you making of Russel's and Camilla's clear dislike of you?"

I turned to look at Chris face to face. "Chief, my only worry is what you make of it. It is probably irrelevant, but they are also the only two persons on the ship who never fuss the cat."

"I don't understand it. In the military it is easy to sort out. I would just issue a brusque command to whoever I considered the guilty party. I could also demand the parties stand before me at attention and answer my questions. They are effectively under oath, being under military command, and they dare not speak untruths. I may not resolve their private problems, but I certainly could solve the problem as the unit was experiencing it. Here on this space-mission although everyone is employed by NASA they are not exactly under military command. Certainly, the civilian astronauts don't have a yes-sir no-sir culture of answering the officer in charge. Another problem I feel strongly, is that I am missing ground control to speak to, and I am missing having their greater authority to back me up. I feel like I am slowly losing control here. I shouldn't really speak about a crew morale problem to one member of the crew. Sharing this module with you though, and having watched you a lot, I feel I trust you"

"Captain. "

"Please Rodney, don't call me Captain, or Chief or anything. Please call me Chris. Technically I am a Colonel, although my responsible position is being the Ship-Captain. You are not military so it means nothing to you. Call me Chris."

"OK Chris. I might still address you as *Chief,* if we are having our twice daily crew debriefings, just to show I have respect for you, before the others. I just feel more comfortable that way. But thank you for being so respectful of me Chris. I had my own package of anxieties about this mission for twenty different reasons, one of which was I was not sure how well I would be accepted into the team being so untrained, and being such a late-comer."

"Rodney let me put this straight. You are amazing. The way you fixed up Tyrone's throat abscess so fast and so well, was amazing. Tyrone is your biggest devoted fan in this ship now.  Some times when you are not around, he sings your praises. You don't even know it, but I am telling you now. Russel and Camilla always mutter a negative a side-comment against Tyrone too, if he mentions your name."

"Maybe those two dislike Tyrone for his boisterous loud personality", I replied.

"Maybe", responded Chris. "However, what I was wanting to get onto saying is, that the way you performed an amputation of Larry's foot during an EVA (Extra-Vehicular Activity), is a new world record. The way you completed the surgery so efficiently back inside the ship and the way you just grabbed persons to help you and gave them on the spot training and instructions to help you do the second clean-up amputation is beyond my imagination. I would never ever believe such things were possible, in space, and more so, done by an anesthesiologist!".

I blushed and opened my mouth, raising a finger slightly, and wanted to speak, but I could not find a word.

"Rodney, after that we became so distracted in the loss of communications to ground control. Life was moving fast. I was thinking non-stop about whether we should try to abort the mission, and wondering how to even do it.  I think we over-looked thanking you for saving Larry's life."

Chris continued. "I also feel guilty that we never gave much thought to Alan Jones after we lost him. It was like we just had to move on. I feel a bit of a failure as the ship-captain that we were not faster getting someone out to chase after Alan."

I spoke. "Don't beat yourself up Chris. Alan's severed tether, and Larry's crushed trapped foot was a double whammy. Who could have foreseen such catastrophes? You did your best."

"No! This talk is turning back on to me. I meant to be talking about you Rodney. There has never been surgery done is space before. Then suddenly you do the first two space surgeries in history, when the mission has barely started.  Those stories will be retold in your honor for a million years."

"Chris, if we never get back no-one will ever know anything. We must all just survive and return. We are the experiment. Returning will be the ultimate great achievement and it will be everyone's to share. If all computers, machines and devices function as they are programmed to do, we should get back. We just have to eat and sleep and do our simple chores, and we will get back nearly on auto-pilot alone."

"Rodney, what do you make of Russel's and Camilla's negativity towards you?"

"Chris, I have had that sort of junk intermittently happen to me all my life. I have survived and my very private vision looks far beyond them, and far above them. I am unphased by them. I have thought out some plans. I must be honest to you too. I have been just observing them a lot and figuring them each out. I think I have a good estimate of what their inner secrets are, more or less. I trust I can handle them. I, in fact, have some plans. I was in no rush to start them, but since you told me some extra stuff, I think I will initiate my plans sooner".

"What are you planning to do Rodney?"

"I don't really want to say. It will be nothing dramatic and nothing in a hurry. I will give you a report in four weeks' time, if you like?"

"Meeow" said Skabenga softly. She was floating with her legs trying to run, and she was going nowhere. Chris leaned forward and gave Skabenga a shove towards the module door so that Skabenga would drift into the next module. Someone there could sort him out. Chris felt burned out.

---

Skabenga floated through the inter-module door with her four legs spread wide apart. She eventually collided with the side of the next module. She pushed away and drifted onto an opposite side. There she kicked off again, but had more grip on the structure this time, and could aim herself better. She reached a magnetic-board. She turned on her side and one sleeve on her leg stuck to the board. Like any domesticated Earth cat, she liked to lick herself all over, before curling up tight to stay warm and fell asleep. In a minute one could hear soft little breathing snorts like a feline type-of-snoring. Her body hovered above the board except for the closest leg sleeve with a sown-in tiny flat magnet. That was flat against the magnet plate launch pad. The sleeve magnet was smaller than an American cent, but it stopped the cat floating away. The metal plate was just a working tool to everyone else on the ship. There were dozens spread every module. To Skabenga the cat wearing her magnetic boots and sleeves, the magnetic boards were either nesting places, or launchpads.

# CHAPTER 8.

## Vahini's morning sickness. (week 10)

After breakfast on the first Monday of the tenth week in flight, Chris called everyone's attention for the first meeting of the day.

"Good morning all you wonderful Marsnauts," said Chris brightly with a smile.

Tyrone first said sharply "Team!" to get everyone's attention, then slowly in theatrical style, as he looked about him at the other Marsnauts, and raised his widespread arms with up-turned hands in gesture implying "say loudly with me". All but two of the other astronauts immediately understood and took the cue.

"Goo-oo-oo-d morning, Mr. Bolder!" they said in chorus style like a bunch of junior school kids greeting their teacher. All the cooperating team members smiled with silly expressions at flight-captain Chris Bolder.

"Hot shot Tyrone!" smiled Chris back at everyone. "I am glad to say I have no problems to report from overnight. Our flight seems to be smoothing out these recent weeks. Anyone have anything to report from overnight, or any challenges expected in your work today?" He then looked direct at each astronaut, in turn addressing them on their first names. Chris typed their answers into a computer

We had no negatives to raise, or report. We were slowly recovering from all the initial disasters. This is typical on all spaceship or orbiter flights. The initial launch adrenaline in everyone settles. They stop overthinking things and settle into hard work routines.

Vicky the fourth flight engineer and a backup IT person added in, "After lunch today I could use a helping hand. One of my chemistry projects is looking at lithium-quartzite crystal growth in the absence of full gravity. I call it my Dilithium project after the Star Trek movie story on Dilithium. I just need a third hand as I look under the microscope at the growth in the current crystal brews".

Valborg jumped in first. Valborg Schmidt was a main IT-astronaut and a backup engineer. Vicky Duploy was an engineer first and second job IT person. That paired Valborg easily with Vicky whom he could guide if she was needed for her second job. She could in turn guide him for his second job if ever needed. Many of the astronauts were casually finding one other astronaut as a close friend, and often it was boy-girl pairing. These best-friend parings were considered very good for overall team spirit. Val and Vicky were both married. It seemed a healthy mutually respectful friendship.

"I can cram my morning work a bit, and free up my afternoon. I can help you Vicky", said Valborg."

Vahini made a little noise like she was burping, and Chris asked, "Anything Vahini? Are you OK?"

"No." she said. "Fine". Her cheeks seemed red. Maybe she blushed. No one seemed to notice, but I did. It was out of his mind in a second, though.

"Have a great flying day!" said Chris to everyone, as his push-off flew him straight through the South end port of the galley module. He tucked his arms in. Skabenga was not to be seen. He has skipped breakfast. I would fix her a meal in the sick-bay if I found Skabenga there, when I got back there.

I was still working on eating a very chewy health bar and needed an extra coffee to flush it down. I found a coffee tube marked "cream, 2 brown sugar", and injected a mix of hot and cold water to get the brew to the exact warmness that I liked. Waiting behind me for the water gun for her beverage, was Camilla. She said nothing when we made eye contact.

I hung out there feeling lazy, as all the other astronauts took their turn to go through the South port to their own workplaces.

I spoke to Camilla once she turned after preparing her tea in a tube, and she seemed surprised. "How is your project going?"

She stuttered, "uh. OK"

"What is your project?" I asked. "I've never had much chance to chat to you".

"I do microbiology experiments. They are complex." It sounded like she did not want to talk much more.

"Sure thing." I replied. "It is a long trip. I would like to learn from you about that stuff. Can I visit your research lab sometime?".

"I guess so." She replied hesitantly.

"How about in the half hour before afternoon exercise?"

"OK", she said. She had not smiled once. Her demeanor seemed surprised and maybe suspicious.

"Ciao" I said as I pulled himself through the South Port. I had to travers a lot of other modules to reach my sick-bay module. It was the last habitable one on the South end.

---

At exactly 30 minutes before exercise time, I launched himself into Camilla's research module. We referred to each other's work spaces as laboratories, which was ironic, because on Earth a small laboratory might be as small as a room, but the whole room. A large laboratory would occupy be the entire floor of a building, if not being the entire building. Our spaceship laboratories were four feet by four feet, with masses of filled storage spaces above and below. The table was crowded with a computer, often a microscope, and more boxes. Some storage containers were aerated, temperature controlled and many have filtered air in them. It depended whether the research involved living organism like bacteria, or was chemical research. The list of experiments done in space is endless, and sound bizarre to ordinary people, but what they all had in common was the utter lack of space. The only spacious thing associated with a spaceship, was the space of the universe outside of the spaceship. It was such an opposing contradiction. One side of a spaceship window there is barely a corner to hide a tooth pick, and on the other side of the window is emptiness to infinity; hence the term "space".


"Hi Camilla, have you got time for me?" I was trying to be polite and respectful. "I can come back another day."

"It is OK", once again she didn't smile. She looked like she was wondering why I was there. She probably was suspicious. She was either the most suspicious and unfriendly person I had ever met, or a repeat patient for Botox.

"OK. Camilla, tell me in simple term, what you are researching. Remember I don't know your world".

She relaxed a little and proceeded to explain everything. Lithium is an amazingly reactive element. It is involved in so many things already in commercial industries. Think of lithium batteries. Some naturally occurring large jewelry crystals of amazing colors are complex, but the color is very related to the lithium portion of the crystal molecules. In her research she was investigating to see if crystals of lithium could be seeded in microgravity and even have their growth accelerated electronically. She was initially studying very simple bi-element crystals, and then going to experiment with three element crystals. They hoped if she got some promising results, the seed microcrystal could be grown further on Earth onto macro-sizes suitable for jewelry. There was also hope for use in ultra-micro-electronics. Camilla explained all of that in many more words.

"You know Camilla, I have an interest in Lithium too".

"I have over the years periodically had a patient whose peripheral nerves, when I stimulated them electronically either would barely produce a muscle contraction and others, where I got massive contractions from almost zero electrical current. This difference puzzled me a lot. I kept records of all of these patient's names and got a hair sample from each of them. One can measure body lithium levels in a hair sample. I also noticed some people, had nerves that were very slow to nerve block during epidural blocks, but did block fully eventually. I could not propose a technical reason to explain that. I also started to notice as the cases numbers accumulated, that the persons with the slowest setting-up epidural blocks would be the most dynamic intelligent and driven persons. With the epidurals I am talking mainly about woman, as it was for laboring woman or where I have done the most epidurals. I read up a lot on basic science and soon discovered both lithium excess and lithium deficiency have potent effects on peripheral nerve functioning and health, as well as brain effects with things like depression and psychosis. I had always hoped that someday I could get someone to measure the lithium content in the hair of each patient and we could see if a low or a high lithium level correlated with any of the phenomena that I had observed. I still have all those records, the hair samples, and of course signed patient consent for the research."

"That is sure one highly technical bunch of stuff you spoke about." Coming from Spofford who usually acted like she knew everything, that was a big concession. She seemed interested in my field of dealing with lithium.

She continued, "I think I could find a lab that will measure all those hair samples for you, and do it cheap for me. I also have research funding to cover those costs. I could help you write up the results, if you let me be second author. I can't believe the conversations we just had!"

"I agree. Who would have known that an obscure meaningless mineral to ordinary folks, like lithium would bring us together? I had no idea you were doing lithium crystal research."

"Well, I do not mean to sound insulting, but I never thought an anesthesiologist could have such an inquiring mind and know rare information about lithium and nerves.

"Did you know Camilla, that there is theory that too many Americans drink only bottled highly filtered water. After filtration It has no minerals and the manufacturers then add back some selected salts in controlled amounts just to give a taste. They do not add back lithium. So those people who drink exclusively filtered bottle water get zero lithium in their diet as solid food contains practically zero lithium too. So, it ends up that half the nation is lithium deficient and that is why half the nation is on antidepressant medication. No one knows that ordinary tap water that at some point has bubbled out of the ground or out of rocks in the mountains is the besty source of dietary lithium"

"Yup, that makes total sense to me. Rodney, can I call you Rodney? Can I check out your research some time?"

"Sure, come on by any time. I have the original scientific articles scanned as PDFs on an external drive. I'll explain a lot to you. I am going to my exercise session. What do you do mainly, bungee running or pseudo-weights?"

"I do a little bit of weights. It does not feel like real weights, but I was never an exercise or sports person. I spend all of my time in the laboratory."

"Hmm, have you tried the partner rowing machine?"

"No, I usually rely just on myself."

"Camilla, I am just asking? Do you know your own IQ?"

"No."

"How clever do you think you are?"

She was silent for a moment before speaking. "My dad always told me I am stupid. He hit me if my school marks were on the low side. I got bullied at school for being chunky and I hated school. At university I always made my grades, but it was very hard work. I finally got a PhD but no-one calls me doctor. I keep to myself and I work hard."

I spoke now, "Well, let me tell you the first thing about intelligence. It does not get you to pass exams. You still have to work hard. You just cannot know anything unless you nail that butt to the chair and spend hours studying the books. A super bright person who does not read the books cannot pass an exam. Good brains help, but you still have to spend that time doing hard work. No-one is born with knowledge. No dumb person can get a full-time study PhD, like you did. I am not talking about all those doctorate degrees every gets on line these days. I mean a real PhD takes real good brains. The BIG factor in success, more than anything else is hard work. A modestly intelligent person can achieve mega-success, if they are wise and work hard enough. A lazy clever person will only ever be a laborer. I am not speaking bad of laborers. The world needs people at the top, but needs even more people at the bottom. No society can survive without assembly line workers and street cleaners. In a perfect world all people are hard workers and all are honest, no matter how clever they are or not. That makes YOU, Camilla a very important person in the world.

"My dad doesn't think that of me. He wanted me to be medical doctor. He tells me my PhD does not make me a doctor."

"Camilla, thanks for sharing your story. I can believe you are on this Mars mission because you are top of your field. Your work is interesting to me. Come visit my lab sometime."

"I will", said Camilla, and she smiled. That was the first time I had seen her smile in ten weeks.

---

At supper that evening it seemed like any other night. I noticed that Vahini only drank fruit juice, and ate nothing. It wasn't real juice. It was the typical dehydrated one in a tube that an astronaut had to add water to, and reconstitute it.

I floated innocuously closer to her making like I was trying to sneak up on Skabenga the cat. I asked softly below the ever-humming noises on the spaceship. "Are you OK Vahini?"

She replied, "I am just not hungry. You know that space-flight sickness that everyone gets in their first 36 hours of being in a weightless environment. I never got it, so I think it has caught up to me. I'll be OK."

Babee Todd, who shared the same module as Vahini was close enough to overhear this quiet verbal exchange. She leaned in and said in front of Vahini, "Rodney maybe you should check her over. The last week she has had a little vomit each time she gets out of bed in the mornings. Maybe she has a bug. I hope we don't get it."

I agreed, nodding. "Come see me after exercise time, Vahini, and I'll check you out a bit. No harm doing it. It's my job to make sure everyone is well". He smiled.

---

Back at the sickbay module Chris and I joined together in the partner rowing-machine. This was a new development of NASA. There were two types of movements. Either the two persons held the two upright bars on front of each in a locked state, and pushed the foot pedals back and forth a bit like riding a bicycle. They were strapped down to sitting as if on the floor. The pair faced each other. Their feet were strapped into the peddles and they had to push forward with one foot while simultaneously pulling the other foot back towards themselves. That last movement of pulling upwards with foot was an unusual exercise movement, and was very tiring.  If they flicked a button, the foot pedals locked and the hand bars unlocked. They could then push the one hand bar away while they pulled on the other. Each person held onto the same bars as they sat facing each other. Their feet nearly touched and their hands nearly touched, except they had their own grip handles and own foot pieces to strap into. Although it looked like they were pushing the hand-bar against the other person's efforts, it was actually a machine against which they pushed. The other person when opposing the bar or foot piece coming back to them it felt like it was their own effort stopping the other person it was actually the machine. The real clever bit was a weak person and a strong person could work together and set the resistance. If they were of identical strength, they could set the machine 1-to-1. If it was a little lady rowing against a jock of a guy, they could set the machine 5-to-1 favoring the girl. It was possible for very unequal people to share the exercise. They could agree to do the arms ten times, then the legs ten times and then the arms ten times again. The goal was to try to keep going. The most amazing thing each person could be made to sweat and struggle identical to the other. As they faced each other, they could encourage each other. It swiftly helped develop a feeling of sharing and a feeling of helping each other. Also, it did not exhaust folks too quickly. It achieved a balance between aerobic and anaerobic exercise. They can keep at it for 30 minutes if they so set that as their goal.

Chris said to me. "I have been doing fives lately. Is that good for you?" I agreed. They started working out and every five foot-push-and-pulls they switched up to hand exercises. After every five hand-push-and-pulls they switched back down the feet exercises. It definitely took effort by both parties at the same time. The machine would not work if only one person sat in it. It was electronically controlled. Most people once they found the right partner, loved this as a work out.   It also never felt like the two persons were competing with each other. It felt more like they were helping each other.

After 15 minutes of working out I suggested to Chris. "Let's try runs of tens, but we go a fraction easier". Chris agreed. It was good to mix up the exercise, and with the rowing, it was good to mix up the partners too. No one seemed lazy. It seemed all the astronauts needed two hours of exercise per day as much as they needed food each day. Some did more exercise, but no one did less. These were all top character people.

---

When the hour was up, I cleaned up and dressed back into normal clothes. A few moments later Vahini arrived. I pulled the curtain to divide off the sick-bay end of the module from anyone else's sight, who might enter the module. I checked her usual vital signs like blood pressure, heart rate etcetera. While I worked, I asked her the usual questions. I casually worked down the routine list and asked when her last period had been. She gave a date that preceded the Trans-Martian-Injection (TMI) space launch by three weeks. (That is blasting out of Earth orbit to aim at Mars.) That period date would have been two weeks before Vahini's launch on the huge Saturn-8 rocket. She thus had a late period now. Vahini was only 28 so this was not menopause. I asked if her periods were regular. She said yes, but blinked. I asked if she had had the mandatory sterilization that all the women long trip astronauts were supposed to have had. She said yes, and that matched the computer medical record in front of me. I was bit puzzled. Her tummy was nowhere tender and her bowel sounds were normal. I got my ultrasound out and connected the tummy, curved transducer. I was startled by what I saw.

"Vahini, are you sure you had a sterilization?". Vahini's rosy cheeks glowed a bit more. She looked down and said, "No. I got a false certificate. I am young and still want babies when I get back to Earth".

"Oh brother, this is a challenge," I said. "Look at this ultrasound image. That is a baby there. You likely fell pregnant while orbiting Earth after your Saturn-8 launch to the ISS. Who is the dad of your baby?"

"Rodney, it is Alan the dead astronaut, it happened when we were in the ISS waiting for your launch vehicle to link up to us."

NASA had a list of illness and medical conditions that that would, if one was positive for the condition, it would exclude one being a long-trip astronaut. There was also a list of surgeries that the astronauts had to have before being allowed onto the very long Mars mission. Everyone had to have had the appendixes removed. Woman astronauts, in addition had to have been sterilized. There had been a very contentious argument for men to also be sterilized and for everyone to have had a tonsillectomy, and cholecystectomy as well. It was finally decided to back off from that last list of surgeries. It finally transpired that many false certificates of health had been submitted by astronauts determined to fly to Mars, no matter what lie was needed.

I thought a bit. "Vahini, being pregnant is not an illness. You have been having morning sickness of pregnancy. I was thinking recently that your cheeks had become rosier, and being pregnant explains that. As I look at you now, I now realize your breasts look fuller than when I first met you during mu astronaut training. I didn't realize this fact until now when I was examining you. Those are all signs of pregnancy. I guess I must say congratulations. If you go to full term, your baby will be born just before we land on Mars.

At dinner everyone was talking about that there was going to be a baby born in the spaceship. Vahini had told everyone. I kept quiet, and was deep in my own thoughts. I just listened to everyone else suggesting baby names.

# CHAPTER 9.

## Mutiny on the Bounty. (week 37)

When looking out the spaceship windows, Mars looked big in the black sky. It was clear this leg of the journey would be ending soon, in a couple of weeks. Mars was not so big that the Marsnauts thought they were orbiting her, but she was still the largest eye-catching object in the sky. The Sun was as bright as ever, but fascinatingly it was less than half its former size as seen from Earth. The Marsnauts could tell that planet Mars orbited the Sun further out than planet Earth did.

Vahini with her bulging tummy, had been quiet at breakfast and she had grimaced silently once or twice. I couldn't help observing her all the time and wondering whether delivery contractions were starting. I was planning to talk to Vahini privately during her routine visit to me, that was happening after breakfast. I had looked regularly at the fetus with the ultrasound, and it seemed like the baby was doing well. I was very glad that they were now beyond the premature-baby phase of her pregnancy. Vahini seemed to have had a flawless pregnancy so far, other a little morning sickness early in her pregnancy. That also subsided once the news was out about her pregnancy.

---

Camilla and I fell into a routine of exercising together on the paired row-machine on every other day. I was amazed how much she opened up, once she saw me as an equal. We spoke about her a lot on her scientific world and about her life. I volunteered very little about himself, but answered any very specific question she asked honestly. I sensed Camilla had strengthened both physically and emotionally a lot since we started to exercise together. She seemed to look forward to our dates.

Camilla had a very negative self-image and subtly verbalized a lot of anger against her father. Once she let me into her head, I saw deeper into her words than what she realized I would. Camilla started to speak a lot about Russel. I saw where this was headed and chose to just listen and not ask or say anything.

I have to admit, I was shocked when she revealed Russel nagged her for sex all the time. I wondered how on Earth, I should say in an orbiting spaceship, Vahini had found a secluded space in a space vehicle, much less a private moment to fall pregnant with, now dead, Alan Jones. I wondered how Russel and Camilla would have found an intimate space and time if they had wanted to have sex together. There was very limited privacy on a spaceship. Sex also seemed technically impossible in space, especially for the guy, and there was no evidence that any woman and guy had ever done it ever before in space. Vahini's pregnancy is a first space event in multiple ways

It also was revealed that Russel was becoming increasingly critical of Chris. His complaints targeted others too. Camilla confessed Russell's paranoia that Chris and I, while sharing a module were holding themselves above the rest of the crew and were conspiring against everyone. Russel's pet grievance above all, was that he wanted to abort the mission.

Russel argued that he had done the calculations. We only needed to orbit Mars once before firing the thrust rocket-engines to break out of Mars orbit to return to Earth. Our return flight would be four times longer than our out-flight as the two planets orbits then would be near maximum distance apart for a return flight. Russel argued that saving fuel not distance, could save our lives. We could save a lot of fuel by not landing on Mars, and by not needing to launch off from Mars again. He argued that with that saved extra fuel, we would be able to fire the rockets for longer to accelerate to a greater speed for our Earth return flight and cancel out the greater distance we would have to travel back to Earth with an early return. He estimated we could shorten their trip by 18 months. We would still be the first humans to orbit Mars.

This contradicted everything that Chris had been told by Vahini and Tyrone based on their calculations, a sling-shot around mars with a special accelerated-return formula, they calculated there would leave insufficient fuel to decelerate as we made final approach to Earth. We would then fail to be captured in an Earth orbit, simply shoot past Earth into the eternity of the Cosmos, and die when supplies ran out.

Russel was constantly trying to convince other team members, to back him up. Of course, I had not heard anything about this before I managed to win Camilla's friendship. Russell miscalculated Camilla's friendship and support for him, not understanding she seldom formed friendships. I thought I might have Camilla's friendship now, but I was enough experienced in life, to be open minded to me being wrong on that. Chris definitely had not indicated even hearing a whiff of this brewing rebellion. It was also clear that Russel was avoiding me as well. I decided to keep quiet about Russel's arguing for now, for a speedier Earth return.

---

At the next evening after-dinner meeting Chris called for everyone's attention. Then just as he was about to start with the routine business matters, Russel spoke out.

"I am announcing, that by POPULAR vote, we have decided to abandon the Mars ground mission, and to return direct to Earth after one Mars orbit."

Chris barked in irritation at Russell, "Thanks for the update Russell Dunaszegi. It's too bad this is not a debate matter. That is not a matter up to crew vote. I may seek crew input on big decisions, but I am the ship captain and have final authority. I have said we are going to complete the full mission, as originally set out. That is final."

"Well, in that case I am relieving you of your command and I will be ship-captain. Hold him Fram".

Fram had been floating at the ready, directly behind Chris. Before Chris could blink, his arms were held behind his back. Russel was in like a bullet and slapped hand-cuffs onto Chris. Ten seconds later he placed ankle-cuffs on him too. Chris stopped wriggling.

"You are in on this too?" I was absolutely bewildered as I spoke to Framingham.

Framingham Milkowski, a space pilot, just nodded his head affirmatively.

Larry, the amputee, explained. "We knew every ISS mission has the means to restrain an aberrant astronaut, so we were sure there were restraints on this mission. We broke into Chris' module personal storage and found them amongst his private materials."

"You're in on this too?" I also asked Val in my astonishment.

"Yes".

Russel spoke. "Some of you have not made a commitment to me yet. Rodney are you with us or not".

"Hell no! This a mutiny. You'll all do jail time for this".

"OK Dr. Powell. You gave exactly the answer we expected of you. We need you for Vahini's baby delivery. You have two choices. You can join Chris in cuffs, or you can swear to not interfere, then I will give you conditional freedom."

"I am a doctor sworn to look after people. By the Geneva convention you have to leave me be to do my work."

"There ain't no Geneva convention in this territory" said Russel sardonically, as if enjoying himself.

"This is a NASA USA vehicle and we are bound by both American military law and American federal law, with the State of Texas law where ground control is based", I replied.

"OK, the three others of you, who voted against me taking over command, I remind you that you agreed to not obstruct the new mission and you agreed to continue with all your functions".

"Take Chris to the first pressurized storage module. Cuff him by ankle to the long chain we have set up there. There is a toilet there. We will bring you food and water ex-captain. That is all."

A group of the rebels took the shackled Chris out of the module.

-----------------------------------------------------------------------------------
--------------------

I had a sleepless night. The module felt so dead without Chris the captain sharing it with him. Early the next morning I got out of bed an hour early and went into the first pressurized storage module. It was in fact the immediately South of the sick-bay module.

"Chris!" I called out."

"Yeh" replied Chris. I switched on the lights. The storage module had no windows but could be an emergency habitat, as it had a toilet. There was not much space to move in as the walls were full of shelves all deeply packed with secured boxes of supplies.

"Are you OK?"

"Yeh, and you?"

"I never saw this mutiny coming."

"Neither did I."

"I see your hands are free. Do you have your cell-phone?"

"Yes."

"Are you able to charge it? Yes."

"OK. Then contact me for anything, and we have a private communication line. What are we going to do about Russel?"

"Rodney, there are many options. I have authority and power to execute a severe disruptive person whom I consider a danger to us all and or to the mission. That is stated in my mission contract. I am requested to do that preferably after we set up a tribunal, who should vote on his guilt and on his punishment. I can however also take a fast decision in a *heat-of-battle-moment* and execute him without a tribunal hearing. I last heard of such things being done in the first world war. I would hate to do it. I know my duties however. As I am handcuffed, I obviously cannot do a thing. We have no astronaut weapons on board. All luggage was X-rayed to may sure of that. What no one knows, is that we do have 4 combat rifles modified to be capable of being fired by an astronaut with large EVA gloves on. This is a top secret, that I am sharing with you. We may under no circumstances fire it on board a spaceship, lest we puncture the hull with a bullet. We can posture with them with no one else knowing they are unloaded. Only I know which container the guns are in and only I know the key code for the lock on the inside of the outer box. My instinct is we should just observe the situation for a bit. You can be my spying eye. Russel does not know I have my phone. He is no regular military man, nor a real leader."

All I needed to do was nod affirmatively to Chris. He understood my compliance and loyalty to him and the mission.

"Chris, I am going now. Text my phone anytime. I'll come see you in the evening again."

"Rodney, you are one super gentleman. Go well."

I returned to my module and prepared for the day's routines. I wondered who were the three who voted against Russell's mutiny. I hoped I would find out. Maybe they would identify themselves to me.

---

After an extremely quiet breakfast, Camilla joined me for the paired rowing exercises.

As soon as we were into the movements, I asked, "You voted yes?"

"I did, but I am not sure I did the right thing. Last night Russel came into my module, and he smelled of alcohol. He was very flirtatious with Marjena. I heard giggling. I thought alcohol was banned on the mission."

"He must have smuggled it in his two allowed-personal-luggage bags."

"Dessie told me he tried to seduce her, and Vahini told me he also tried to seduce her before we found out she was pregnant. I told you that he tried me too. What I did not tell you was after I gave him a very blunt no, he started to cry like a baby. He stammered through a lot of stuff saying his dad had been a womanizer and had abused him and his mom. After the crying episode he stayed a mile away from me. I feel very sorry for him and really wanted to hug him but didn't."

We switched the exercise machine from arm-pushes to leg-pushes and kept talking. When working with guys, I liked this exerciser to be adjusted to be pretty strenuous like we were near sprinting, but with Camilla I set the energy levels lower to like that of a slow jog and we chatted a lot as we faced each other.

"Rodney, what are you going to do about Russell's usurping command."

"I do not know what to do at this moment. I am sure however to have any chance of surviving this entire trip, we need every person of the crew to do their best, and we need to work as a perfect team. I also think Chris was chosen as ship-captain because he has lots of space travel and command experience. He also had supplementary training to be the captain. What are Russel's skills are for leading this mission?" I wanted to tread this matter lightly with Camilla.

Camilla explained. "I know him well. We were in training for the last year together. He is definitely clever. He is also a never-ending soft flirt, when other men are not around. He is a double qualified as a mechanical and an electrical engineer. He switched to the air force and became a fighter pilot, but his flying hours are few. He is employed mainly by NASA as a flight engineer, and I think he is mighty good at that. He trained on simulators to fly the spaceship and do the retro-thrust landings on simulators. He never had actual real retro-thrust flying experiences outside of the simulators. He is just a backup pilot, beyond being primarily an engineer. My guess is that it was his double skills of engineering and flying that got him into this mission. As a pure engineer astronaut his emotional ups and down might have kept him off the Mars mission."

"Do you fancy him Camilla?"

"I feel protective towards him, like I want to cuddle him like a child."

"But you didn't want sex with him".

"Three things Rodney: first his approach was blunt and crude and a surprise ambush to me. Secondly, I am married. Thirdly you are asking very personal questions."

"OK. I understand. I am sorry for trying to understand him and you more. It was you who told me of his making a pass at you first. So, you like him now?"

"Well it is a bit of a compliment when someone wants you physically, and I felt so sorry for him. As hairy and muscular as he is, a fragile delicate person cries inside him like a baby. I felt protective towards him then."

"You sound confused Camilla. The bigger issue is we have to get this crew all working together, or I fear we are all doomed."

"To be honest Rodney, I felt we were doomed before we even flew"

"So why are you even on this Mars mission?"

"I wanted the fame and glory very much, but I just didn't care if we never made it back alive."

"Do you know who were the three that voted against mutiny?"

"Yes. It was Vahini Baxter, Babee Todd and Tyrone Wilson"

I gave a silent squeal of delight when he heard Tyrone's name. He was a very strong character to have on the side of good. I tried to stay poker faced.

We kept working out until the hour was up, but remained quiet.

---

That evening after supper Russel said slightly flamboyantly. "Attention everyone. It is time for daily reports. My experiment is progressing satisfactorily. I have no problems related to the overall ship to announce. Rodney what is your report?"

"I guess the mission is aborted effectively, so do my little experiments even matter?"

"The mission is not aborted. It is just modified in the light of our loss of communication with ground control. We are all going to be heroes. What is your report please? I don't want nonsense now."

"I see you have not even opened the computer to enter our reports in the captain's logbook, or anywhere else for that matter."

"Colonel Chris Bolder won't give me the password, so I can't enter into his logbook. I will make my own notes afterwards."

"You don't know anything about my research projects while Ship-captain Colonel Bolder did. He was briefed and studied on everyone's scientific projects before the launch. That is part of being the ship-captain. I am not going to waste my time briefing you. You are not the ship-captain. You are a usurper."

"What's an oosurfer?"

A few Marsnauts giggled.

"I am your commanding officer and I order you to give your report to me, Powell"

"It is Doctor Powell to you Mr. Dunaszegi".

"Aaaargh" screeched Russel and he turned and flew through the South port, out of the Galley. A sound followed like he had burst into tears.

I looked at Camilla and said, "I think you should go after him and make sure he is OK."

Camilla floated into the next module. It was the spaceship control module.

Screaming was heard, "No! No! No!" Then smashing breaking sounds followed. All the Marsnauts crushed forward to the port. Valborg was first through the portal between the two modules, I followed, then Babee and Marjena came through as a pair hugging each other.

Camilla wrestled with Russel who had a hammer in his hand and was trying to smash one electronic control panel. Camilla gripped the hammer with both of her hands, but it hardly made a difference. Russel still hit the electronics board. Val and I grabbed the hammer head and tried to wrestle it from his grip. Everyone flew wildly around in the air.

Babee wrapped her arm around Russel's neck in a wrestling choke hold and shouted "Stop Russel, stop Russel". I held onto one arm, while Valborg freed the hammer from Russel's other hand. Instinctively Russel smashed his free elbow back into Babee's face. Blood spurted from her nose. Babee let out such a scream everyone else slackened their grips for a second and Russel ripped himself loose of everyone and flew free across the breadth of the module wriggling like crazy. His head smashed into metal support beam, then jerked forward violently. He moaned and rebounded slowly, before going completely limp.

Everyone turned to Babee, already holding handkerchief to her nose. She pinched her nostrils correctly, to stop the bleeding. "I'm OK. I'm OK" she said with nasal high-pitched voice.

Russel gave a low moan and his limbs fell flaccid. I drifted over to him and shook his shoulder shouting, "Have you gone mad?". Russel did not respond and only moaned softly.

We immediately turned to the control panel. Marjena recognized what was left of the pressure monitoring system. "Luckily we have duplicate panels in two other modules. I can bypass this one and check it out in the morning. She opened the front hatch, flipped a switch and all the lights on the instrument panel went out.

"I suspect I will need to replace a bunch of LEDs, but there should be nothing major to repair. This is not a big problem. It is likely a half a day's work."

Now everyone looked back to Russel. He was looking bad. He was limp, his head hung backwards, and his eyes were closed.

I said, "Let's take him to the sick bay. I need to check him out. I think these are the handcuff keys in his pocket. I opened one sleeve pocket and gave them to Camilla.

Camilla knew what to do and pushed off with her feet to be the first heading South out of the control module

As we escorted Russel into the sick bay, Chris now just freed from his restraints, was waiting in the sickbay. Having heard about the scrap from Camilla, Chris had already unfolded the sick-bay procedure table and locked it down. We immediately aligned Russel with the table, and Chris attached the Velcro straps to hold him onto the table and keep his limbs from floating outwards.

I applied ECG stickers, and put an oxygen probe on one finger and activated the automatic blood pressure cuff that someone had already wrapped around Russel's one biceps. Everyone was silent, jostled for a view, but stayed out of my way. I shone a light into Russel's eyes, then closed the eye lids, waited ten seconds and opened then and shone the light again. I picked up each arm and everyone noticed one was limp and the other not. The only sounds one could hear was the beep of Russel's heart from the vital sign monitor, and the ever humming of ship fans.

I could feel everyone's gaze while I thought, before looking up at everyone.

"Russel has a serious problem. He has lost consciousness. His body is flaccid on the right side. His left pupil is fixed dilated. That suggests he has something happening in the head. I am going to guess he has a subdural hematoma. He needs an urgent CT scan to exclude that or to make the diagnosis, or any other related diagnosis. We do not have a CT-scanner in the spaceship. I am therefor going to have to make a diagnosis purely on the clinical grounds of my physical neurological examination. I am going to have to make a hole in his skull to drain blood. I think I can do that, but if that does not help, I have not the skills, nor have the equipment to do anything more. If I operate on him, it will be a football Hail-Mary pass. He wins or he loses, but it is his best chance. Without a CT scan we cannot think of conservative treatment and observation. If we are wrong, he is finished. If I operated, maybe unnecessarily and this is just severe concussion, we lose nothing other than risking brain sepsis. I will need a tool to make a burr hole in the bone. Dessie, I saw you had a battery Dremel rotary tool. Do you have grinding bits for it?"

"Yes, I have four sizes and types, and spares of each."

"OK. I need them all now. I must sterilize the grinding bits immediately. Camilla will you assist me. I need you to put on a sterile and put a sterile outfit? You can be my surgical assistant. Chris, I need you as my scrub nurse. This is all not too complicated. Bebee and Marjena I need you each to make sure he does not move his hands away from his sides. You will have to hang onto to them. The legs should be OK with the Velcro bands holding them down. You might also need to hold his head steady"


A few minutes later the Dremel rotary drill arrived with the grinding bits. I placed them in sterile paper packets inside the microwave sterilizer lying on the anti-arcing sheet. Camilla was garbed in sterile gowns gloves and masks. I sealed Russel's closed eyes under adhesive tapes to protect them. Next I shaved and sterilized Russel's head. I showed Camilla how to lay down the sterile adhesive sheets. The grinding bits were ready and he passed with no touch technique to Chris. One had to be meticulous with all the instruments for the surgery not floating away. Most things had an iron part able to attached to a magnet and could stay stuck to the surgical trays. A fact that always fascinated me from my childhood physics lessons, was that a magnet attracted iron but not steel. You could thus use a magnet to determine if a chrome covered metal object was made of cheap iron or higher quality steel. Most surgical instruments were made of the finest steel. For our space travel, a small extra iron cuff had been attached, to help the instrument stay on a magnetic tray.  Other non-magnetic things had to be retained in closed sterile boxes and only handled direct hand to hand at all times. Chris was familiar with this and was my right-hand man by now. The Dremel rotary tool got inserted into a sterile plastic bag and got handled through the plastic bag. The rotary bit was itself sterile and projected out of a hole in the bag.

As I washed-up and put on all his sterile gear. Bebee asked, "Does Russel get an anesthetic?"

"Only local," I replied.

I injected an eight-centimeter-wide circle of scalp skin on the left fronto-parietal side with local anesthetic solution.

Camilla asked, "Why are you injecting only one side, and why chose the left side?"

"A subdural hematoma is nearly always on one side only. It is highly likely on the same side as the dilated pupil that I saw, and on the opposite side to that of the paralyzed arm." I became deeply focused on what I was doing, and felt tense.

Scalp skin is very tough and thick. It is hard to inject into and injections usually hurt. The secret to minimize discomfort is to inject very slowly and to advance the needle very slowly. There was adrenaline with the local anesthetic and Camilla observed the injected skin blanching. Russel moaned, and squirmed slightly. Bebee and Marjena stopped him from disrupting the sterile covers around the surgical field, and from moving his head too much. Ten minutes later I cut the skin down to bone and clipped all the bleeding points and cauterized a few too. Russel's heart-beat, blood pressure and oxygen saturations were fine. There was an IV-line (intravenous live) in place and drugs ready to be injected by Bebee into the IV line, if I gave the order.

I took the Dremel grinder and handled it carefully, not letting any unsterilized part get out of the sterile plastic cover. Squeezing the button, it made a high-pitched whirring sound. I proceeded to grind bone away. Once I got through the bone, there appeared to be a membrane under the bone. I ground the bone opening about 2 cm wide making sure not to break the deeper membrane. Next, cutting through the membrane, dark blood poured out. Camilla assisting me, had to be sharp sucking at up the blood and swabbing it so that the blood did not float out across the flying module.

I said, "I guess this about 100 milliliters. That confirms the diagnosis of a subdural hematoma. I am glad we operated."

I placed a very soft rubber tube against the brain, and I could see that all the hematoma blood was removed. I stitched up the skin around the rubber drain tube so that it poked out through the skin. Finally, I placed a gauze dressing over that, and secured everything with a bandage around Russel's head. Antibiotics had been given.

I pulled my face mask off signaling the surgery was finished.

Chris asked, "How many of those have you ever done Rodney?"

"None before today. I have watched plenty, when doing the anesthetic for the case. Forty years ago, when I was a rural doctor, I read my books on how to do one, if such an emergency ever came my way, but it never did. Let's hold thumbs that this is enough surgery to solve Russell's problem. I do not know what else to do if this does not work."

Russel just lay breathing quietly on the table with closed eyes, as if nothing had ever happened.

The next morning, I re-did Russel's skin dressing. As very little blood had drained through the night, I decided to pull out the drain pipe. I redid the dressing with fresh sterile gauze. Russel moved a bit. His pupils were now equal and he had some movements on his right side now. By lunch time he was trying to sit and was following simple commands.

By that evening, Russel made efforts to talk but was incomprehensible. He did manage to suck some fruit juice out of a plastic tube. The next day he spoke coherently and fully obeyed instructions. By the second day he started to ask what had happened. I told him everything. An hour later he asked the same question again.

The wound looked good, so I fully removed all the gauze and bandages and covered the suture line with a clear medical epoxy glue to keep it sealed. I told Russel that he was free to move around the ship, as long as he was with me or Chris at all times.

---------------------------------------------------------------------------------

------------------------

Seven days after surgery Chris and I came to talk to Russel. Russel's IV was out.

I started gently, "We know you are struggling to remember everything. We have printed out everything that we are about to say to you, for you to read again, whenever you want to. You led a mutiny against the ship-captain. You physically sought to destroy the spaceship, and that amounts to a murder attempt against the entire crew. You smashed you own head against a metal bar, causing a lethal bleeding onto the brain. I quickly recognized exactly what the problem was, and got it drained about 40 minutes after you injured yourself. Without surgery you may have died. Had you lived without surgery, you would have been mentally retarded and paralyzed on one side of your body. You owe your life to the entire crew who all played a role in saving you. We need you. Every person in this spaceship is critical to every other person in this space ship. In a week's time we will subject you to cognitive tests and if you pass, we will then expect you to return to all your chores, responsibilities, and research. All your pass words are blocked until we can see you are 100% functional and behaving well. Your hand implanted microchip is also blocked.

Chris spoke next, "We want you to focus on mentally relaxing. Watch movies, listen to music and do three hours of exercises per day. That is all we want from you now." He then muttered under his breath, "If we all make it back to Earth it is going to be a miracle."

Realizing what he had said, Chris' voice became more serious discussing the ultimate heart of the sit-down with Russell. "I have ruled that if we find you being a threat or a risk to our survival at any time, and in any way, we will summarily execute you and discard your body to space. I hope that was stated bluntly enough".

I thought I should remind everyone of our common goal, after such a bleak statement from Chris. "We are the experiment, remember! The Mars-Mission study is to see whether as human beings we can function together and handle big challenges. Hell, someone could write a book about this mission! It would be a best seller, and we have not even reached Mars yet! All joking aside, the other crew have all agreed that we will stand together 'til death do us part'. Just like a spouse can't testify against the other, no one will testify against you. and the study outcome is to see whether as human beings can function together, can handle the certain big challenges we do not yet know of, and manage to get back to Earth. If ever the story of the mutiny gets discovered, or written about, your actions will not be prosecutable without a complaining witness. This is the outcome we all unanimously choose. You have an opportunity for your own redemption. You have an opportunity to be a value to other people."

Chris followed, "Are you going to be a team member?"

"Yes." Russel nodded as he spoke.

"Good. Let's us all shake hands and close this deal." We each shook Russel's right hand. His grip was not tight, but his hand was definitely not slack.


"Now Russel, I want to talk to you as ship-surgeon," I said. "I am speaking in front of the ship-captain and you have no privilege of medical confidentiality. I have a few points to make. One, you can speak to me any time about anything. I want to know every week how happy you are, how sad are, and how your memory is doing? I am willing to listen to anything want to talk about. My objective in all of this, is to be of help to you. I am not the disciplinarian. That is a captains' job. I am a helper. I only want to help you. I can work on your physical health and I can work on your mental health. Second point, please stop making sexual passes at every female on the ship. It is disruptive. This is a simple request only. You can trust me to act in your favor. Got it?"

"Yes."

"OK. let's take you to the entertainment module. You will have the big screen all to yourself. Vahini is taking things easy and will be there as your observer until we fetch you for supper. I suggest you work out on exercises while watching movies. Physical health leads mental health."

"Follow me", said Chris.

An intercom message came in overhead. It was Bebee's voice.

"Hey Rodney, Vahini is having severe tummy pains. We are bringing her to the sickbay."

## CHAPTER 10.

### It's a girl. (week 39)

I set up the procedure table, flexed it slightly like it was a relaxing chair, and secured it to the floor. Then I attached the leg holders for lithotomy position and lay them downwards. Although I had a very familiar feeling for delivering a baby from forty years ago, this was not a familiar setting at all: in outer space with virtually zero resources. I hoped it would be an experience like riding a bicycle, and muscle memory would take over.

NASA require all the woman astronauts to have had their fallopian tubes ligated. Everyone should have had their appendixes removed, and there was even discussion whether gallbladders and tonsils should be removed. In the end the NASA surgeon-general decided not to mandate that. I wondered why the women were forced to have their fallopian tubes ligated, but the men were not equally obliged to have vasectomies done too. It felt sexist to only force sterilization onto one gender. The surgeon argued that only women fall pregnant. A feminist could counter argue, that it takes two genders to make a pregnancy. I thought back to my first marriage. After our two children were born, my wife had insisted, I should be sterilized. I did it reluctantly. How ironic life is. My wife eventually divorced me and after I had remarried a younger wife, we could not have children, because of a vasectomy that I never wanted. As a couple, we decided not to follow the burdensome route of vasectomy-reversal and assisted fertility treatments. We accepted our guaranteed childlessness; all because of my first wife. I never speak criticisms of my first wife for this. At fifty, when we divorced, she was beyond having children in any new marriage she entered. On the other hand, at fifty years old however, I would have been able to consider fathering another child in a new marriage. Ironically, my dad had fathered me at the age of 58, when he married his third wife, my mom.

If you think too hard about everything in one's life's journey and try to add up all the unfairness's that befell one, it becomes too overwhelming. I have a dear guy friend who always said, "Life is a bitch, and then you die!" Then, my friend would grin. My friend always projected a happy face, although I knew his true deep dark inner mind. I took some wisdom and inspiration from that friend. He tried to focus on being positive every day, and only seeing the full half of a half-full glass. Yup, my first wife had given him the best two children on the planet, in my own biased daddy-mind at the least. Also, life had given me my second wife who is my best-friend and soul-mate. It was like it was all separate parts of some great plan.

"We are here." A woman's voice cut my trip down memory lane. In floated Babee Todd and Judessa Weeks, two lady Marsnauts, with Vahini Baxter and her bulging tummy. Babee and Judessa were Vahini's closest friends on this flight.

"Hi Vahini. Are you having contractions?".

"Yes. Yes", she said breathing deeply between words. "They have been coming every 3 minutes for the last half hour.

"Vahini we spoke before, and you said you wanted Babee and Dessie as your companions when you labored, right?"

"Yes!"

And, you also said you want no one else present, especially a male, but that I could call in Ship-Captain Chris, if things got complicated. You know he knows a good amount of where everything is stored in the sick bay and that he is my best helper.

"Yes, but only if very necessary, please?"

I replied, "Yes, only if very necessary". He added, "I am so glad we reached full term forty weeks with your pregnancy. That will give the baby it's best chances at survival."

We secured Vahini, in a semi-sitting position onto the sick-bay table, setup to be a birthing bed. She was so positioned that she was semi sitting. She was lightly tied down by Velcro bands across her chest, but she was able to wriggle onto her side if she wished to. She had an Intra-venous (IV) cannula in her one hand but no fluids running. The IV cannula was injecting emergency drugs, if needed.

"The baby's heart rate sounds great. Its beating happily at one hundred and forty beats per minute and not slowing badly with contractions. Vahini I need to do an internal examination now. Just focus on relaxing with slow breathing.

Dessie and Babee were alternately swabbing Vahini's face with a cool damp cloth. I looked at them and smiled. "I am so glad you are both here. You can be my assisting nurses too. I want you to also relax and not swab Vahini's forehead like you are trying to polish it. Gentle dabbing is good.

That broke the ice a bit, and Babee and Dessie laughed loudly. "Sure, we will chill out a bit."

I felt the baby's head from outside the tummy, using my spread-out fingers and thumb of one hand. It seemed firm and engaged in the pelvis. Palpating a bit higher, I felt the curve of the babies back under the tummy skin, and estimated which way the baby was facing. It all came back to me now. I made sure all my hand touching was controlled, and never rough or snappy.

"I am feeling inside now," I said inserting my right-hand gloved index and third finger into the birth-canal. My left hand stayed on the abdomen lightly feeling the baby's head.

"Your cervix feels about seven centimeters dilated. Your waters are not broken and I feel the membranes bulging. I can't feel any suggestion that the cord is in front. I am going to rupture the membranes. That is, do an amniotomy". I reached for an amnion hook that I had in my procedure tray and pulled it out from under its securing Velcro strip. I had previously cut the amnion hook from a sheet of thick plastic

Looking at Dessie and Babee I said, "Please hold those suction funnels here to the side of my right hand and try to capture all the fluid coming out". He inserted the amnion hook into the vagina, between my two fingers, hooked the membrane and tore it. A lot of amnion fluid gushed. "Your waters are broken."

Dessie and Babee were by now expert in free fluid management in micro-gravity environments and nothing got away. The fetal heart slowed a bit with each of the next two contractions. I thought they were slightly slow to accelerate again, but did not verbalize my concerns. The Internal examination was OK, but I lingered on the examination, unsure about how the head was aligned in the vaginal birth canal

"You are sure you do not want an epidural?"

"Yes."

I moved away to my research station and loaded some music from my computer and loaded it to play on the space-module overhead-speakers. I set the volume to medium soft.

"Tel me if you want something different." I Said. "This is just my favorite chill-out music."

Vahini said nothing. Babee said "Thanks", as if she was speaking for the three sisters.

The first song was "Oxygene". By Jean-Michel Jarre. I obsessed about the song and played it ten times every day. In my head I called it the Astronaut song. The next song was the old British group, the Communards singing "Don't leave me this way". I loved the beat and the falsetto voice. I found my own personal harmless happy meaning in the words

Over the next hour, I kept an eye on Vahini, and caught up on computer work at the same time. I wanted to keep Vahini calm as she labored, and Babee and Dessie did just that engaged in soft trivial chatter involving Vahini who managed to grin or giggle sometimes between contractions. As the hour finished Vahini said that she wanted to bear down.

"Hold it there, breathe deeply, let me check first". I grabbed a pair of gloves and shot across to the bottom of the bed. Vahini spread her legs and bent her knees in the lithotomy poles. I lowered the foot end of the bed so I could move closer to Vahini, from the beds' foot end.

"I want to push".

"OK. Ten centimeters! You are fully dilated. Caput is very little. Place your hands around your thighs like this, and pull your legs up. Push your hardest and pull on your legs during contractions. Between contractions relax, gather your strength and breath slowly, but deeply."

Caput is the edematous swelling a baby gets at the presenting part of its head in the birth canal, especially in long difficult delivery.

"You can do it girl!" said Dessie. Standing beside Vahini, each friend placed an arm around her shoulders for support when she bent forward during contractions.

At the start of each contraction Vahini gave a loud scream then pushed as hard as she could.

"It's crowning. I see black hair!" I said. No one seemed to think about that fact.

"Wow, this is only two and half hours of labor. You're amazing Vahini." I 'm sure everyone could hear the relief in my voice.

As the crowning of the head stretched the perineum vaginal opening to about seven centimeters, I decided to do an episiotomy. With the next contraction I snipped the perineum starting in the six-o-clock position. I cut to medio-lateral into the stretched-out blanched skin and tissues. I timed the snip to be done during mid-contraction. Vahini seemed unaware of being snipped. Bleeding was minimal from the taught stretched skin. The episiotomy made it easier for the head of the baby to deliver. Also, it was far easier to suture a neat cut episiotomy, than ragged torn perineum overstretched by a large baby head. If the perineum is stretched very slowly it is less likely to tear at all, but not tearing is never guaranteed.

With the next contraction the head advanced another two centimeters and I was able to push the perineum to below the babies chin. "Nearly home," I thought, willing it to be true.

The head advanced another centimeter with the next contraction. Three more contractions went by and the head seemed to retreat. The perineum folded up like a heavy woolen turtle neck shirt around the baby's neck. The baby's nose barely peeped out the vaginal entrance and the head started to look a slightly dusky red shad, seeming congested.

I palpated the abdomen again, just above the pubic bone. I looked at the head at the perineum. Vahini's baby still hadn't done any external rotation. "Oh my God" I thought to myself. I knew there was shoulder dystocia present. I began digging deep into my memories. I recalled Professor Labuschagne's student lectures on this topic, and one case I had managed over 30 years ago.

With shoulder dystocia, the baby's shoulders being the widest part of the baby fails to rotate into a left-right plane to enter the pelvic bony brim, thus aligning with the brim's widest diameter also being left-right. The shoulders instead align themselves front to back and get stuck at the pelvic brim in its narrowest front to back diameter. The shoulders usually enter the pelvic brim as the head completes to delivery to outside of the birth canal. One can tell the shoulders have rotate correctly into the bony pelvic brim, by seeing the head give quarter turn just after it is delivers to beyond the perineum.

I looked up with my mind whirling, and six eyes were looking anxiously at him. My job now was to rotate the shoulders correctly, and time was of the essence.

"Dessie, I want you to push hard up here continuously", speaking very, very clear and very firm. I placed her hand firmly on the abdominal wall cupping the fundus of the top end of the uterus.

"Vahini, **now** I want your best pushing when you feel a contraction. Babee help Vahini pull her legs up as much as possible towards her tummy". The girls jumped to their tasks without a second's hesitation or a sound.

The baby' head was facing to my left between Vahini's legs. With my feet firmly wedged under the Velcro straps on the floor, and waist hitch pole connected to my belt. I reached back grabbing the release clamp to allow me to lean forward another inch. The back of the pole was in a securing-wall-notch. When a doctor has to operate in a gravity free situation, he needs to be anchored at three points to stop him or her floating around, when pushing and pulling on something. The sick bay had forty anchor points spread around it depending on where the surgeon wished to stand. An adjustable aluminum pole clicked into the wall end and latched onto the firm leather belt that the surgeon had around his waist. The length of the pole could easily be adjusted by the surgeon so he could vary how much he wanted to lean in or out. Each foot had a number of floor position options to be anchored at will, a bit more to the left or a bit more to the right, or a bit more forward and also even a bit more backwards. I was going to be standing firmly anchored, to manipulate this baby in the birth canal.

Describing this is challenging as the mother's and the doctor's left and right sides are opposite, and the baby's left and right sides are rotating around in the birth canal. I was however crystal clear in my head, what I was doing.

Left hand into vagina, two fingers extended. Push on the anterior aspect of the baby's posterior shoulder from my left towards my right. Dig two fingers of the right hand into the birth-mother's abdomen just above to her pubis and left of midline. Push the abdominal fingers towards the mother's right, imagining the baby's anterior shoulder is being pushed. The baby's head can thus be rotated 180 degrees to the opposite side, with the face passing posterior. "Keep pushing downwards" I said to Dessie without looking up.

I sensed the baby had descended perhaps a centimeter or two. I slid a finger within the birth canal again, up the baby's chest and found I could sweep its upper arm, being the left one, forward across its face and deliver it to lie above the baby's head outside of the birth canal. With the next contraction I reversed hands and pushed on the posterior baby shoulder, being the baby's left one now, so as to rotate the baby's head back 180 degrees, with the face passing the mother's posterior direction again. The objective was not actually turning the head, but rather rotating the baby's shoulders that were aligned front to back within the pelvis entrance instead of transverse across the pelvis entrance as occurs in normal births. The baby seemed to descend another centimeter or two. I was able to pass the other baby's arm across its chest and deliver it to outside of the birth canal. I next held both the baby's arms in one hand and I cupped the head in his other hand, applying very gentle traction. "Big push now everyone".

The baby was delivered and I held it upside down by its feet. I grabbed a clean sterile gauze surgical towel to wipe the bay's face, mouth and nose clean. The baby's body was starkly pale, contrasting the with the very plethoric looking head. It let out a little cough, and a bigger cough and suddenly the baby let out a wail. It cried louder. I choked and tears blurred my vision and overflowed my eye lids. I could not wipe them and the drops drifted into the module air. I couldn't blink them away fast enough.

The two assisting girls were sniffing a lot. Vahini reached her arms up. Her loose patient gown had slid down her arms exposing her chest. I lay the baby on Vahini's swollen breasts. Vahini snuggled the baby and kissed its head saying softly, "I love, I love, I love you," to the baby.

I cut the umbilical cord and clamped each end in a hemostat instrument. I gathering my breath, I gently felt the top end of the uterus fundus through the tummy wall. Because a space pregnancy was never in the wildest imagination considered when planning for this Mars Mission's medical supply needs, I had no oxytocic drugs to make the uterus tighten up and stop bleeding. I would have to be patient and wait for the uterus to contract and do a fully natural delivery of the placenta. I had never performed one before, but after the last half hour's experiences, I felt confident things would go OK. My experience was with doing assisted third-stage placenta deliveries after injection of drugs to make the uterus contract.

About five minutes later, a gush of blood came out the vagina. Babee was there with the cone vacuum and some extra swabs to catch everything. I felt the uterus get taller under his hand resting on Vahini's lower abdomen. The protruding umbilical cord lengthened at the vagina. I applied very gentle traction and asked Vahini to bear down. Her bearing down was probably ineffective as her tummy was so flaccid now without a baby in it. A fully intact placenta was delivered. I massaged and squeezed the fundus to encourages its contracting, before injecting some local anesthetic into the skin incision, and suturing the episiotomy. Vahini was so relaxed that she just did not care what I was doing. I cleaned up all the mess and packed instruments packed away for later sterilizing.

Surprisingly, the sick bay looked remarkably neat and clean after all of that. The baby's umbilical cord had been cut shorter and tied it off with a surgical suture thread. The baby wore a gown on that the crew members had sown-up by hand in the preceding months. They even had made some ingenious workable diapers, held on with an ultra-low-technology safety pin.

I shifted across to Vahini's side and I hugged her. She hugged me tightly and said "Thank you". I said nothing. What words could live up to that moment? I did blink a lot, still pumping away tears of relief. My two birth-assistants were on a natural high and talking of drinking wine, even though there was none on board. I was feeling inside like the good Lord could take me now. I had served my good life in the world now. I had delivered many babies before, and long ago. I, however, never ever had had such a feeling of fulfilment and gratification ever before. In those far away days, as a busy general doctor, one savored such a moment briefly, and then moved onto the next patient waiting.

Chris and I had found a very large stash of whisky in Russel's personal luggage and we told everyone that we disposed of it, which was a little white lie. Chris said that on this mission nothing should be discarded, and that I mentioned I use whisky as an alcohol-based disinfectant if I needed to. The whiskey was locked in a secured medical storage container.

"Doc, can we call in visitors?" asked Dessie.

"Of course, yes." I replied. I warmed inside, having not been called "Doc" or anything like that in good while.

Dessie grabbed the intercom system and flipped the button title to the "Full ship" position.

Speaking into the hand-microphone she flamboyantly announced. "Attention Ares-1 Mars Mission Nation. We have a very big announcement. The crew numbers just went up by one. A beautiful little girl just entered the world of interplanetary travel. Mother and child are doing well. Please join us for celebratory drinks and frivolities in the sick bay"

Seconds later the entire crew floated in, one immediately behind the other. They had all been waiting close by in the next module and on emotional tenterhooks. Lots of joyful squeals were heard. Lots of hugs, and kisses on cheeks were exchanged. Everyone babbled an about the details of the birth. Some held the swaddled baby who was sleeping all pink and happily.

Grinning non-stop, I floated far to the back of the module to leave extra space for the visitors. I was feeling a blend of exhaustion and exhilaration. Chris came by and asked "Celebratory drinks?"

"No real drinks. Dessie was just being theatrical and wishing"

"Everything go well?" Asked Chris.

Not wishing to be technical, I replied, "Just another day at the office. Everything is fine".

Had I not resolved the problems speedily, I knew we were just minutes away from having a dead baby, because of the shoulder dystocia. I wondered how many other anesthesiologists on the Earth planet could have handled that. Thank God I had the best medical training and an opportunity to live it out in rural medicine, before studying anesthesia. What science fiction writer could ever have a man who was supposed to be small town family doctor, end up delivering a baby with its shoulder obstructed in a lady's pelvis 50 million kilometers into outer space. Reality is a very strange story writer. I teared up again.

---

The *espirit-de-corps* of all the Marsnauts was on its biggest high since the launches from Cape Canaveral. In a way, we had forgotten about the planet Earth. The lack of communications with ground control had made us more invested in our group identity. They were a little universe unto themselves within their spaceship.

Russel had been quiet, but compliant and dutiful in the preceding times. He came to me the day after Vahini's baby was born and said to me, "I heard how complicated the delivery was and how unflinchingly you sorted it all out with a perfect ending. You saved more than a baby's life there. Well done man!" He shook my hand. I briefly grasped Russel's forearm as we shook hands.

"Thanks man. I needed that", I replied.  Russel, I am sure, wondered what I meant by "needed that". Russell had initially hated me because he saw me as a cheap astronaut who had been thrust onto the real astronauts as a last-minute crew addition. Also, I might also have seemed arrogant to him, in my own efforts to project confidence, that likely challenged his own inner insecurities. That would be my fault. I also tend to speak my mind and speak straight. That trait has caused me grief a few times in life. I am generally unrepentant about that though. I have learned over the years to phrase things a bit better though.

I think Russel envied me, because of my ability to adapt so quickly. I think it made him feel more inadequate, which led to his being such a cheap flirt. He felt good whom he won the attention of a woman, but the next day when the high wore off, he always hated himself for it. He was acting like the evil cad of his father.

I am sure I understood a lot of what inside of him, and made him who he was. Maybe the truth was that Russel envied me for all that he had initially perceived me to be. Even if all Russel's perceptions were in realty off the mark, Russel's very real envy of me had led to his own feelings of inadequacy getting worse. Russel also felt self-anger and hated himself for being such a cheap flirt. He felt good when he won a dalliance with lady, but the next day he always hated himself for it.  He was just being like his evil father. The more he hated himself the more he had felt a hate for me. Then Chris and I gave him a chance. It likely, did not make easy sense to Russel.

What I had meant saying "I needed that" was that I was glad to see Russel normalizing and seeming to be really trusting of others, probably for the first time in his life. Chris and I had given him another chance, and at first Russel couldn't understand why. It was all his negative self-image that led him to mistrust others, and ultimately the mutiny. With the crew's support, Russel finally wanted to make a real effort aboard the ship; Ultimately this change in attitude made me feel like our investment in his recovery was worth it. me now.

When the esprit-de-corps is high, it hardly matters how you got there, only that you are there. There is only one way to face in life, and that is forward. Looking back is for academic historians. There is little to be gained from being a historian of your own life. Another useless concept is "legacy". A person should never dwell upon their own legacy That just leads to ego issues and degrades their humanity. Legacy is what you see in the lives of others that you wish to embrace into your own life. Promoting Legacy is something what you refer to in honoring others, and providing inspiration for future generations. Don't dwell on personal legacy.

The Mars doctor slept well that night after Vahini's baby was born.

---

On the day after her giving birth to the baby I decided that Vahini would sleep best with the other woman Marsnauts in their own module.

At dinner that evening, we wrapped up quickly with the debriefing and formalities. Everyone wanted a turn holding the new Marsnaut.

"How much does she weigh?" asked someone.

"We can't measure weight in the absence of gravity," I replied. "However, I would guess she is a perfect, Earth gravity, seven and half pounds."

"Vahini has she got name yet?" asked someone else.

"I am still thinking" replied Vahini.

"Why don't you name her something that reminds her of daddy, Alan. Maybe Alana." Suggested Dessie.

"Yeh. Alan was such a handsome blonde man. It's tragic he died," chipped in Marjena.

"Hmm. The baby has quite a bunch of black hair. Do you think it could turn blonde when he is older?" pondered Camilla.

Slowly coming out of his post-surgery quietness, Russel asked. "Vahini you have brown hair. How could you and a blonde guy have a black-haired baby?"

Framingham Milkowski the quiet engineer leaned forward. "Those baby eyes look a little bit like they are hooded like oriental eyes. Alan was a pure Anglo-Saxon as much as anyone could be. Vahini do you have Asian blood?"

"No. I have an Indian first name, and I was born in India, but I am not genetically Indian. My parents were there doing missionary work for a few years, when they had me. They are Scottish, as is my last name Baxter."

Camilla, who lacked delicacy blurted out, "So Vahini, tell us who the real papa is of your baby?"

Vahini gasped, looked down and sniffed. Dessie and Babee immediately drifted to her side and put their arms around her. Babee said, "I think maybe we shouldn't be asking these questions."

An embarrassed silence followed.

Vahini spoke. "It is Wei Zhang, the Chinese Astronaut on the ISS". (International Space Station).

Silence.

"He was pestering me to take him into the parts of the Ares-1 space mission ship that was docked with the ISS while we waited for the last seven Marsnauts to launch and join us."

"I told him it was against the strict orders that we had. One day he told me he had some best Baijiu with him and it was better than any drink the West had. He said it was a secret, but he would share a glass with me. I eventually said yes. We each had a drink. It made me giggle. He convinced me to have another and he said we were not on a mission yet as our mission only started when we undocked from the ISS. The second drink tasted different, maybe slightly salty. I vaguely remember going with him into the Ares-1 spaceship. He wanted to see my sleeping-pod. My next memory was having a headache and being in my pod missing some lower garments. I have had a strong idea that is where I fell pregnant. I couldn't tell anyone because it would have terminated the mission. Also, I had broken a NASA command. I never saw Wei again before the undocking. I couldn't find the garments so I guess he took them afterwards. I felt shame and I felt dirty after being violated. I did not want to talk about it.

"Oh God! Vahini" cried Dessie and hugged Dessie crying herself.

I spoke. "Vahini, we are all your family. We are all your brothers and sisters. We are here for you. The baby is innocent and we must not let one thing get in the way of loving that innocent little soul. We are all your family and we are all here for you."

"Agreed" said a voice and then a number of others called out in agreement.

Vahini sobbed softly looking down. Vicky had been holding the Baby.

She floated over and said "I think we should call this little miracle and blessing Aresha. That is from the Greek name for the planet Mars, Ares." She placed the baby against Vahini's chest.

Two days later Vahini told everyone that she thought the suggested name of Aresha was just perfect, and that would be her baby's Greek derived first name. She thanked Vicky for coming up with the idea. Everyone clapped joyfully.

---

During the next evening's debriefing, Valborg said he wanted to share some information. He reminded everyone that the Mars Mission, in its early concept was planned to be an International project. The Chinese government had strongly wanted to be the front leading partner. Their biggest goal was to use their computer systems, which are world leading in capacity on board the ship. The chief manufacturer of Chinese computer motherboards had a major share-holder and board director, who wanted his son to be on the mission. This director donated $50 billion to the project as a way to guarantee his son a place on the crew. That was Wei Zhang.

Unexpectedly, The American president decided the mission would be a solo-American project, and the $50 million was refunded. Wei Xhang was then sent to the ISS as part of the Chinese mission piggy backed on the Russian flight modules. Officially all the nations accepted this change in the Mars-mission plans. In fact, most space faring countries who would have been partners seemed almost relieved as the projected costs were astronomical enough to make a bad joke. Everyone knew that once they committed to putting a man to Mars, a monster blank check had been written. The trillion word was whispered by some journalists. Wei Zhang's dad, who seemed to have the deepest pockets, was very angry and threatened to sue the Chinese government for giving in. No one took him seriously and most folks barely know this story now.

Valborg kept talking. Everyone was listening, riveted to whatever structure they were holding onto to keep their floating positions in the cabin. "I think this Wei Zhang story is tied to our loss of communications. I think he somehow sabotaged the ship after he was done with Vahini".

Mouths hung open. I spoke next. "Is this information a possible clue to finding the sabotage and fixing the coms problem?" I asked, hoping this was the missing link to our problems.

Chris spoke. "OK. In the light of this profound new information all IT and engineer specialists meet me in the recreation room after morning exercise tomorrow. We will brainstorm the loss of our coms until lunch time". I also remind everyone that we are only a couple of weeks away from entering Martian orbit. As you know we will be doing a lot flight module re-arranging to finally separate into three descent vehicles. As Sir Winston Churchill once said, *"Now this is not the end. It is not even the beginning of the end. But it is, perhaps, the end of the beginning."* So please think of that in terms of wrapping up experiments for a while until we are settled on the surface.

"Speak for yourself", shouted out Tyrone with a grin. No one responded.

Tyrone was speaking only to himself for the next year. Tyrone would remain alone in the part of the mission ship that was going to orbit Mars for a year, while we descended to Mars surface. No human had ever spent that much time in space alone. Tyrone underwent very intense psychological assessments before the NASA chief flight-surgeon would give his permission for Tyrone to join the mission, in this role. There had been a lot of planning discussions on whether two astronauts should remain in the Mars orbiter. The decision was that the primacy of the Mars surface projects was too large considering the costs of the entire mission. Every possible Marsnaut had to be on the surface.

The orbiter just needed someone to oversee the periodic flight corrections, to retain orbital altitude and direction, and do general maintenance of all the systems. In theory orbital corrections would be automatic. One Marsnaut still had to be on the Mars orbing part of the mission to manage those tasks and maintain the ship.

I had an interesting thought.

# CHAPTER 11.

## NBS News NASA disaster analysis. (week 4)

*(NB. Back in time to the fourth week of the Mars Mission)*

"Good evening. Welcome to the NBS TV NASA-Disaster analysis special program, and I am Dan Alister, your host. It is now four weeks since the NASA Mars mission disaster. The fourth launch of Ares-1 Manned Mars-Mission was the most watched television event in human history. It was to be the legacy American event of the United States of America's first woman president. It certainly was an unprecedented expensive project. The Ares-1 budget exceeded the gross domestic product (GDP) of 90% of the nations of the planet. It was riddled with controversy from the start. I have some regular NBS commentators with me. Joan DeBakey, independent journalist and commentator on woman's rights. Welcome Joan."

"Hello" smiled Joan Debakey with subtleness, looking directly at the camera.

"Next we have Mario Monmachio, an associate Professor in Space Engineering, from Caltech"

"Buon Giorno", he smiled with glistening teeth, looking towards Dan, then glancing sideways at the camera with his endearing grin.

"Next we have Salimoni Simmington, a political economist, former Professor at Harvard, and now a free-lance consultant working in Washington DC. Hi Salimoni"

"Good day to you Dan. Thank you for inviting me here". She said stiffly and formally looking with her penetrating dark eyes at the camera."

"And completing our team is Minnie Lucas, an attorney specialized in industrial liability."

"Hello".

"Joan, you were a big supporter of this outer-space manned mission at the start, but you have reservations now. Is that correct?"

"Yes Dan. As you know, I am a fairly militant feminist. I lobbied through all the channels open to me, that the first person to step onto Mars, <u>had</u> to be a woman. NASA leadership would never give me straight and unequivocal affirmation on that. They led with the phrase that a woman *could* be the first person to step onto Mars. They never conceded more than that. I was also upset with there being only six female Marsnauts out of the crew of fourteen. I argued this could be an all-female crew. I argued the ship captain had to be female too.

"All my life I have fought against sexual abuse of woman. I argued for capital punishment for the crime of female intimate assault."

Dan interjected, "There were some pretty prominent pre-twenty-twenties slogan-driven feminist movements. Do you think they changed anything for woman?"

Joan replied unsmiling, "Well they might have improved things slightly, but men just seemed to withdraw into themselves like they were afraid to socialize with woman. Woman never get invited to the pub after work with the guys anymore. That is where so many business relationships develop that lead to closed management teams, with only token woman co-directors or mid-level managers"

"I was wanting . . . ..." Dan tried to say.

Joan raged on. "I look at NASA. It is a total old boys club. They are so military in their structure. Woman leaders are there only as tokens, and only in a few places." Joan seemed to have run out of breath, after having gotten those meaty comments off of her chest.

Dan tried to speak again. "Ms. Debakey, to be a bit formal, I was wanting to focus on a different aspect. NASA received criticism from other persons, saying that the crew quarters were far too cramped to have men and woman be expected to share those spaces for near three years. Some critics argued that mixed-gender crews would lead to romantic relationship and jealousies and conflicts during such an unprecedented long space trip."

"Dan, I do partially agree with that. In fact, that was one of my arguments for why the crew should have been all- female. I would have however yielded in my argument, to a balanced ratio of seven woman to seven men. That crew of six woman and eight men, just used those six females as symbolic equals to the men. Also, why were only the woman mandated to be sterilized before the mission, but the men were not? Were the woman meant to be concubines for the men?"

"Joan, Joan, Joan!" interrupted Mario Monmachio. He smiled all the time. It was a very disarming smile.

"I know I am only a space-flight engineer, but I unavoidably in my career deal with far more matters than just engineering. It is a scientifically studied and well-documented, therefore a verified observation fact that woman members in a large team dampen down male alpha-male behavior patterns. This has been observed on all Mars mission simulations in Hawaii and underwater and in other Earth studies of psychological behavior patterns. The potentially worst dysfunctional group is two men alone together, for a long time. There is no scientific question that in groups larger than four and more, a mix of genders produces the most cohesion. The Mars group had to have women in it for this serious reason. It is also seen on larger groups in confined work spaces, the astronauts tend to form pairs of best friends. Those pairs strongly tend to be a male-female paring that is platonic. That is very healthy and positive for total group cohesiveness. I also want to say, that although it has not been studied, I am certain that an all-female large space crew would be very dysfunctional. It would have been just like an open-office full of hen-fighting female secretaries. I must also add, that in all the bi-gender space travel so far not one incident of sexual intercourse has ever happened, to all best knowledge. There are also medical theories that men once acclimatized to microgravity and all the fluid shifts from the legs to the head have happened in the first two days, that men can't do "it" anymore"

Joan screamed back. "You are such a misogynist. It's your Italian machismo-driven biased views."

"Panel members", spoke Dan Atkins. "I know this Mars mission disaster has been heart breaking for the world, but please let's keep this discussion at a higher dignified level for the viewers", said Dan Atkins.

"Yes, the viewers", said Salimoni Simmington

Joan looking at Mario, "You don't respect woman"

"My dear Joan, I love woman very much", replied Mario with his ever-glittering smile. He lowered his head a fraction as if wanting to indicate respectfulness, and continued. "I respect your right to have views of your own, and speak views that I do not share with you. I however, strongly believe that humanity is at its best and highest point in social evolution when men and woman hold hands and work together." He gave a theatrical pause, and still smiling disarmingly continued, "and I mean hold hands symbolically, more than necessarily literally.

One could easily see that Mario Monmachio could charm any human on the planet.

The cameras shifted back to Dan Atkins the chief presenter, and missed Joan's blushes.

"Mario, was this mission an engineering disaster?" asked Dan bluntly.

"Well, we first have to approach this question academically and unemotionally. We do not know exactly what went wrong, so it is pure speculation from this point onwards.  On the second day after the Ares-1 space-mission had left Earth orbit on a Martian injection, we lost total radio contact. We had no verbal contact with the Marsnauts. We lost all technical communications direct between spaceship machinery and Earth-bound computers. There were dozens of transmission channels that shot-off at exactly the same second. The last second of audio received sound like an explosion, in some opinions. That second of recording has been enhanced digitally and studied by the world. No one has a concrete solid opinion what that sound was. Journalists have liked to drive the one opinion that it was the start of an explosion.

The few days preceding the loss of communications was a farcical series of disaster following disaster following a disaster. First the Ares-1 Mars-Mission spaceship solar panels failed to deploy after they blasted out of Earth orbit. A theory is that components of the solar panels were under-designed to be flimsy, and they buckled during the Earth launch on top of over-powered Saturn-8 rockets. Then, of the two astronauts sent to repair the solar panels in an emergency space-walk, one got lost and died, and other was an inch from dying and had his leg amputated during a space-walk, to save his life. Then the three astronauts who had to space-walk in the emergency rescue actions all got decompression sickness because of a failure to be denitrogenated before going on their EVAs. Can anyone not call that part of the mission a farce?

In my opinion, as we have spent a month now working on the loss of contact with no success, I agree with what most people is saying. The spaceship is critically damaged or totally destroyed. The crew is dead and the mission is lost. I however zero opinion as to how it happened. So, your question is asking, did we design something wrongly or construct something badly? My answer, is probably yes. I just do not know what exactly. To speculate on every possibility would take a life time. This was a massive engineering project of unprecedented size and complexity. The number of parts is billions; a billion screws, washers, bolts and computer motherboard soldering. There was more energy in all the fuel used in the four Saturn-8 launch rockets, and that was sent to Mars, than that needed to power industrial size city-generators to make enough electricity to supply every household, factory, street light and everything else in Great Britain for three years. It is hard to understand those numbers.

The decision to build the exact Saturn-V rockets that launched the Apollo series of missions over 50 years ago, and the decision to build those same old F-1 engines of the Saturn-V rocker first segment except use eight motors per rocket instead of five per rocket, I personally thought was brilliant. The upgraded Saturn-V Rocket is now called the Saturn-8 because of the three extra engines on the first stage. The designs were old, that does not mean bad. We tend to incorrectly always think something new is better. The Saturn-V were the most successful large space rockets ever built. There are many modern small and medium rockets that are finally getting things right. But for large rockets, I am a believer in the Saturn-8 rockets that we used and closely derived from the Saturn-V. I think that in that part of the mission the best choices were made. All of the components of the F-1 motors and the Saturn-V rocket was designed by an iterative process. That means each component was tested as an isolated-component and redesigned and retested until it was flawless and perfect as a component. Then finally the fully assembled engine or rockets were tested. Modern trends are to excessively rely on artificial intelligence and computer design and computer testing and limit physical testing to late in the development process. So, only final assembled structures are physically tested for the first time. That means it is a sort of hit or miss process and small subtle defects may not be uncovered until far down the phase of actually using the device. This modern design industrial process is economical and works up to a modest threshold of complexity. A space rocket-cum-spaceship is too large and complex for this design procedure. Clearly these recent four launches from Earth were superb, using the upgraded Saturn-8 rockets. The first two unmanned launches carrying equipment effectively served as test launches, for the following manned last two launches. So, if this disaster was an engineering defect, the defect it was of the Mars-mission spaceship and its systems, and not the launch rockets. This entire venture was computer controlled to a very high level of complexity. Therefore, it was excellent that there were two onboard-computer-engineers and two back up engineers in the flight crew, as well as two IT experts. Also, the fact both primary engineers in the flight crew were in the development team was very good. This meant they had a chance to sort out any design or function aberrations, that might have been discovered after launch."

"Thanks Mario. I guess that is a big mouth-full of high-tech-talk for our average viewer to grasp", Said Dan Atkins. "Do you think the last-minute decision that the President forced onto NASA to leave the Chinese, Russian and others out of developing and providing crew for this mission was a bad thing?"

Mario replied, "It was bad in that we were very dependent on the Chinese for computer mother boards. That crammed our development needs into a very tight schedule. We certainly used American motherboards, but these days we use components from suppliers who source subcomponents from other suppliers who in turn source even lesser sub-components from other suppliers. It is a burdensome useless process to track all those component chains. The entire computer world these days is a universal blend of components. One chip on a large complex computer board could come from Peru and the one next to it from Norway. I think that we were close enough in using mainly American technology, for the President to rightfully brag the Ares-1 mission was a pure American venture. That is what she wanted."

Dan, "Did the Chinese have grounds to be aggrieved by being left out of the Ares-1 project?"

"Well they should not complain too much because three other space-faring nations were left out too. In fact, some were relieved to be left out. Those not sending astronauts were supplying components and lots of cash. The project just got too big and expensive. I think the Chinese were hoping to have their status as a high technology supplier to the world, to be endorsed."

Dan. "Some have suggested that it was a Chinese computer component that malfunctioned that caused the disaster.

Mario, "I doubt it. The Chinese are just in the position that the Japanese were once they recovered from World War two. Made in Japan was at first a label for rubbish and soon it was a label for excellence. Same for Korea. Anything made in Korea is now similarly rated as excellent. I think anything made in China is has also reached a deserved reputation for being of excellent quality".

Dan, "Salimoni Simmonds, thank you for being so patient. You are a Harvard Professor in Political Economics."

Salimoni, "Sorry I am not at Harvard anymore. I now consult in Washington DC"

"Ah yes. Forgive my space-brain mistake. You also have a total of seven degrees including two PhDs from Oxford University. I once visited Oxford to give some lectures and had such a magnificent time walking along the River Cherwell in Oxford and I picnicked where the River Thames canal joined the River Cherwell."

"Ah yes" said Salimoni. "An English summer day besides the Cherwell River in Oxford has to be one of my life time's high points. It is hard to absorb all the history of the University City of Oxford, and comprehend how many world-famous scientists, teachers, even a few politicians cut their intellectual teeth in Oxford. I recall the greenness, the grand shady trees, the peacefulness and abundance of ducks and garden birds all calling each other charmingly."

"Salimoni, if you look at the photos we have of the harsh red desert-like oxygen-deprived waterless desert features of Mars devoid of life forms for billions of years, if not forever. Is it madness to send humans to Mars?" Asked Dan.

"Utter total economic madness. It is indefensible theft of public resources for the egos of politicians. The exact bill for this mission is being withheld from those very persons who pay chunks of their salaries to the government as taxes. The government is supposed to be wise, elected and caring custodians of that money. How can it be justified to send humans to Mats when the bill could reach a trillion dollars? I quote Nobel Prize winner Steven Weinberg, who is famously known for saying that humans serve no useful purpose in space. All of that money could be better spent invested in education of our citizens, in educating and feeding millions of poor children around the world. I could list endless better ways to have improved our planet and its citizens, if not our own American citizens."

"Professor Salli Symington, we knew those are your views and we wanted to air them as part of an open democratic discussion. You are a rare person studied in Political economics. It is said that political economics is an also a study of governing ethics. Thank you. We will come back to you. I have a video link with Jonathon McMuche a former advisor to the President. I know he thinks different on this subject.

Did you hear what Salli said Jonathon?"

On the video screen behind the panel Jonathon McMuche adjusted his ear-piece. "Hi Dan. It's great to be back with you. Yes, I heard everything Salli said. I have to disagree with her.

If there was a professor of political economics in Africa hundreds of thousands of years ago, Homo Sapiens would never have walk out of Africa and explored the world. Every single human being would still be an African, if we did not have the courage to walk to the other side of a mountain, or swim to the other side of a river. Without that courage in human beings, all human beings would all exclusively be Africans living in Africa. We humans would not have explored and spread across the entire planet. Europe would have no roads, and would just have bearded slow-talking hairy men struggling to exist in caves. Asia and the entire two Americas continents would not have one human being on them. The Pacific islands would not have native populations, had not their forbears been courageous enough to row canoes out to sea and beyond the sight of land. We humans are explorers. As Europe developed technology and culture, can you imagine the Spanish and Portuguese explorers never sailing off into the unknown beyond the sea horizons. Humans are explorers. We test hypotheses. We try out new recipes. We also evolved into uniting in complex civilized societal structures. We have taken technology and knowledge to levels that could never have been conceived twenty thousand years ago. We humans test the limits and the horizons We were born to do that.

How can someone even suggest investigating Mars direct with humans on the surface, is not worth it when we haven't even tried it?"

Salimoni interrupted. "You sound very cavalier Jonathon. You seem to be able to justify any madness or bestiality of humans".

"No, I am not. What I am saying is that it is a human trait to ask questions, to explore and to experiment".

Salimoni cut Jonathon off. "This is the point Jonathon. Why do humans have to go to Mars? We can send unmanned orbital satellites and unmanned surface Rovers at a fraction of the cost. Collect more information, and not risk one life. We just shot fourteen humans into space like they were expendable lab-rats. Here is the punch line. If the Ares-1 mission had to get ethical approval as a science investigation at any Western Medical school it would never have gotten ethical clearance. There is insufficient clarity of good outcome to be assessed, there is no evidence that the risk to the astronauts is less that horrendous, maybe even certain death.  What do you say to that?"

"My dear Salimoni!", replied an irritated Jonathon McMuche, former presidential advisor. "It is a human trait to reach for the unreachable and to sail to the horizon not even knowing the world is round. You are inhuman in trying to reduce everything to some politically-correct, arbitrary, and never-risky action. How do you personally, have the courage to pull your head out from under the darkness of your blanket and face the world in daylight each day?"

Dan nodded his head to some technician off camera, and spoke as the two previous angry speakers were removed from viewer screens and their microphones cut.  "Ladies and gentleman, as we can see the loss of the Mars mission has brought a lot of very opposing views to the fore. At NBS we try to be journalistic and present all views in a democratic style. We will be a little cooler and more relaxed I hope now.

"Minnie Lucas is our legal contributor today. Minnie my question to you is, does NASA have any liability here to the families of the lost fourteen?"

Minnie. "Thank you, Jonathon. I certainly learned from all the previous commentators. They gave me much to think about. I must say that I represent no party, or potential party in this question. I will just approach answering this a very generalized academic fashion.  This is simply my opinion based on available information to the public. I reserve the right to change my opinions, should more information ever become available.

It is my understanding that all the Marsnauts, as the press likes to call the fourteen astronauts on the Ares-1 Mars mission, signed indemnities and contracts that have wording about dying. NASA estimated that the chance of dying on such an extreme and un-precedented mission, as fifty percent. The Marsnauts all have a modest supplementary life insurance cover. NASA pays the premiums. I have read in the lay-press, that the fourteen families all now have one attorney who is saying that NASA mislead the Marsnauts into trusting that half of them, at least would manage to return to Earth. Also, the quoted fifty percent survival rate was a thumb-suck number. The say NASA had no statistics to base the quoted mortality risk on, therefore the signed indemnities are invalid. Therefore, the families of the deceased are owed more than the hundred-thousand-dollar life insurance that each Marsnaut had. NASA is also contesting that the Marsnauts are not proven dead and says it will not concede on that until four years have passed. They say that together with regenerated oxygen the Marsnauts could have enough oxygen for four years survival. My guess is that this is just the two sides rattling sabers at each other, and a confidential resolution will eventually be reached."

"Minnie" said Dan. "I have an actuary who is specialized in assessing flying risks, military risks and research risks. We are speaking to him via video-link. Benjamin Hindman."

"Hello Dan"

"Benjamin, what do you estimate the death risk for the Ares-1 mission Astronauts to be?"

"Hi Dan. It is simple really. The statistics we have, show twenty-one Brazilian ground workers were killed in an incident related to a rocket explosion. We know that at least twenty-two astronauts have been killed in the launch pad while in the rocket, during launch, in space, or on return from space. We recall with sadness the Challenger and Columbia space shuttle- disasters, and the Apollo-1 American deaths that totaled seventeen deaths alone in only three incidents. We suspect some non-Western nation space-faring countries have concealed some fatalities. We can also look at the large number very near-death disasters that could have caused more deaths. We should add those near-deaths into our calculations. My personal estimate of death risk on this Ares-1 Mars surface mission is 100%. I think the Marsnauts were simply expendable test-rats in a wild take-a-chance experiment."

"Thank you, Benjamin, our space-flight death insurance actuary, for your estimate on the danger of dying when flying to a Mars landing." Spoke Dan. "My director is saying to me on my ear piece that we should break for some advertising. I am told our NBS TV News land-phones are overwhelmed by all the incoming calls from viewers. Clearly this discussion is inflaming a very contentious subject. I shall return to the panel for their closing comments after the commercial break. I ask them to cool down a bit please. Let us be respectful of the feelings of the surviving families of the fourteen deceased Marsnauts. Let us be dignified. We will also have some of the families on video links speaking out their heart aches during the second hour of the show. We will be back shortly. This is Dan Alister of NBC TV News, and the Areas-1 disaster special two-hour program.

## CHAPTER 12.

### The end of the beginning. (week 44)

"Captain Sir, I have an extra thing that I would like to talk about".

Chris and I were by now very close friends and on a definite first name basis. Because I was using his title and not being humorous or sarcastic, he knew something was up. Chris respected me in turn so much, that he often consulted me privately on challenging non-medical decisions. I had also played a tiny role in helping us survive the mutiny. By intentionally choosing to raise this matter publicly before the crew, and formally after our dinner meeting, made it harder for Chris to deny my request. I was sure Chris also knew me well, by now and understood my game. Machiavelli could have learned political strategy from me, maybe.

"Yes, Rodney", answered Chris, with some private apprehension about what was coming next.

"I am worried about how Larry is going to function with only one leg in gravity, on the Mars surface soon. We don't have any crutches for him, although we could easily manufacture a make-shift pair. He will certainly still be unsuitable for surface work in a space suit. All entry and exits from the descent modules, is by ladder and in a space suit. That is mighty tough and risky for a one-legged gentleman. A fall from the ladder can be fatal.

I also think for Tyrone to be alone for one year on the orbiter Ares-1 ship is not cool. That will be a new world record. I think Larry must stay with Tyrone on the orbiter".

Silence.

Chris caressed his chin, as if he had a beard. He blew air out of pursed lips slowly with bulging cheeks. Then he asked, "Larry are you good with this proposal?"

Larry inhaled deep and said, "Yes"

"Tyrone are you good with this proposal?"

Tyrone grinned and replied, "Ya betcha, my Captain!"

"Done!" Chris picked up some papers and closed the computer that he had been entering notes into.

Chris then turned back to face everyone, smiled and said, "Someone I admire greatly once said *"We will be lions to the last"*. Let's make that our mission motto. We will never give up on a critical challenge or a problem because we think it is insoluble. We will fight to the end, and with devotion, diligence and positivity. I see a magnificent lion with a proud mane standing on high rock and roaring. I see a lion fighting to his last breath. The main mission is about to start. "

As Chris drifted off back to his sleep module for the night, he glanced sideways to me. I was in fact watching to see if Chris would make eye contact. Neither of us said a thing nor made a single facial movement. The brief duration of eye contact said a million words between the two us. Chris realized there was little to discuss, He knew I had already worked out my suggestion thoroughly with Tyrone and Larry. More than that; it was the right plan and Chris had been too wrapped up in other pre-Mars-orbit matters to get near thinking about Larry's amputation challenges. Tyrone as a paraplegic, and Larry as a one-legged man, were 100% functional Marsnauts in a weightless environment. On the Mars-surface, either one of them would be an additional problem for the mission and a big distraction.

Chris seemed to be thinking silently, as he locked eyes briefly with me, and had a hint of a smile. I am sure his eyes said, "Rodney, you were very right. Good work Doc." It is wonderful when two people can trust and deeply understand each other.

---

After discovering their communications break down with Earth ground-control was the work of one crazy Chinese man's sabotage, the crew had tried again to solve the problem. That saboteur gained access to the Ares-1 Mars mission ship by subterfuge. The drugging, and assault of one of their female Marsnauts was like it was an extra insult, further revealing the evil nature of the individual. It was hard to say which crime was worse; what he did to Vahini or what he did to the communications system of a manned outer space mission ship. Some crimes reach such a level of abhorrence that the punishment for each cannot be less than whatever is maximum for a society. There is no subtle grading between those crimes.

A lot of scientific research time was postponed. The IT and engineering experts had searched the ship inside and out again. They had explored all software and used NASA secret security software. No damage was found, and no recognizable added hardware stood out. No functioning software indicated any problems or aberrations.  Simply put, we received zero auditory signals from Earth, and no explanation why. It was as if Earth did not exist. Various spaceship machinery was expected to be fully automate regular communication with duplicate Earth-based computers. There was nothing. On board systems were in a mode of functioning independently and autonomously without Earth-control input. In theory the mission should be able to function perfect and all Earth communications were simply a triplication of back-up and safety mechanisms. Fortunately, the entire mission was designed for autonomous functionality. Once the Marsnauts saw the large picture, the loss of ground communications was on the smaller side of mishaps that they could face. Certainly, they lacked access to some of the engineering and computer experts. Also, they lost advice from the various expert specialty physicians at Earth-control. On the other hand, they had the largest most comprehensive team of experts ever sent into outer space. THAT is what reduced the magnitude of the problem. Everyone on board felt more confident for the mission.

---

For the deceleration retro-firing of the engines, everyone had to be strapped into the ascent-descent modules at the very North end of the ship. The firing of the motors was designed for G-forces not to exceed 4G. The new Marsnaut baby Aresha was an easy problem to sort out. There was a spare space cat container into which they could strap her. The astronauts, cat and baby, would be in closed space suits getting independent oxygen supplies. Everything was designed to be protective in case a sudden loss of cabin atmospheric pressure happened.

I couldn't predict the effect 4G deceleration would have on a baby barely a month old. We had no other option, and no real expectation of damage to the baby. Vahini breast fed her just before securing her. They also managed to get a diaper change done. Every single member of the crew had had the privilege of changing a diaper a bunch of times. They found it an honor in cleaning a poopie diaper. Who would have imagined that?

In orbit around Mars the planet looked massive. The computers were in control. The engineers calculated their journey by Sun, Earth and star sightings, aligning laser pointers with their centers, and making final adjustments. The Ships navigation system made minor flight and orientation corrections. Manual take-over was possible at any time if needed. An automatic computer voice countered down to ignition. The crew called the computer voice Cecil.

Cecil said, "Final ten seconds to retro-engine deceleration firing. Ten seconds, nine seconds, eight seconds, seven seconds, six seconds, five seconds, four seconds, three seconds, two seconds, one second, ignition. Engines firing. Estimated G-forces one point five, two, three, four-G. thrust adjustment." Everyone watched the speed dial back in tens of thousands of kilometers per hour. The larger numeric display expressed the speed in meters per second.

For the retro-firing to decelerate, the spaceship had turned around so that the engines faced the direction they were moving in. The astronauts had spent three days checking everything was secure and that nothing would fly at 4G speed across a module. A lot of small items got lost over time and the odd pen did appear from somewhere and hurtle across a module and bounce hard on the wall on the other side of the space-module.  The roar of the jet-engines finally ceased and within seconds everyone could lift their arms easily. Gravity was zero, and back to the normal that they had lived with for the preceding nine months. They were in orbit around Mars. There was to be another half hour of automatic computer checking of the orbit's altitude etcetera, before the Marsnauts unstrapped themselves from their seats.

A very delicate process now commenced. It was maybe the most dangerous, precise and unforgiving part of the entire mission. All the space-modules that were now hooked together had to be disassembled into four units with the astronauts splitting into two teams. Tyrone and Larry were staying in orbit for one year in one ship. The rest of the crew were descending onto Mars in another ship. The two other unmanned cargo space-ships would have to make automated landings on Mars. All port or doors had to be 100% perfectly sealed with no crumbs on the rubber parts during descent.

After four days, things looked good. We discovered was that the cell-phones still worked and ship-to-ship UHF radio worked for both computer and oral communications, while all the four ships were within a half mile of each other in Mars orbit.  Whether there would be Mars-orbit to Mars -ground communications were still unknown.

Tyrone Wilson, the paraplegic, and Larry Rothman, the amputee, seemed euphorically happy as waved goodbye before the hatches were closed and their ship separated.  They would live in a pressurized module in for a year, which was relatively spacious for just two guys. They also had a pressurized cargo ship-module which they could enter with minimal space. That contained all of their food supply, as well as the food needed for the full crew on the missions final reunited flight back to Earth on the third and final part of the full operation. The last element of their orbiter-space ship was the orbiter fuel-thruster section. It had single thruster engine. It could be fired to accelerate or reverse thrust and decelerate the orbiter to adjust its orbit altitude. Without it there was risk that the orbiter would suffer eventual orbital decay and fall down to crash onto the surface.  The orbiter also had smaller maneuvering motors on the side of the fuel module.

The three descent rockets left for Mars, one at a time. One had all of the crew. One had all the pressurized storage modules. One had all of the unpressurized modules and the macro-items. Those were the surface habitat materials, and the vehicles and drones, etcetera. All the ships would retro-thrust with their engine to decelerate and fall out of orbit. The first part of the fiery descent would be in sideways flight position like a sky diver. There was a heat resistant material covering the ground facing side of the ships. After the initial fiery descent within the uppermost Martian atmosphere, a series of parachutes would open to slow the ship down more, and allow its nose to point upwards and the retro-thrust engine downwards. Finally, the parachutes would separate and the retro-thrusters would fire. The final descent of the ship would be fine controlled and three legs would project out from the ship. It would land standing upright. Everything was under automatic control. This form of reverse flight upright landing was a well-developed rocket landing technique. Mishaps still happened with explosion or crashes, with an incidence of about 1%. If the ship landed, and then toppled over it was considered a half success, and there was potential to rescue the situation, but with no guarantees. The unpressurized cargo ship would land first, while the other two stayed in orbit. If that went well the next cargo ship would land, followed later by Marsnauts. It was critical that radio links existed between the ships in order for the mission ship captain to know each ship's landing status, and initiate the next landing.

The first ship landing had commenced, but with no radio contact, Chris gambled and initiated the second cargo-ship landing. Again, no radio signals were detected after what should have been adequate time. Chris knew full mission abandonment at this stage was near impossible as they had insufficient food and fuel to join the two still orbiting ship units now and survive near two more years in space. This had been a suicide mission from the very start. The Marsnauts wrestled with their own private dark thoughts from before they had launched from Earth. Only few had shared their perceptions of this with close crew-friend, but everyone understood they were the human experiment. The test was not to turn back. The test was to keep moving forward and resolve every problem. The mission motto that we embraced was to fight and roar like lions until the last.

In the Marsnaut descent-ship seven crew were seated in the front tier, and the others, with baby and cat, sat in the lower tier. They could not all see each other between tier levels. Ship-Captain Chris Bolder looked around him and gave a thumbs up sign. The other six Marsnauts he could see gave him an approving thumbs-up back. Chris flipped the descent button. Everything was automated. Marjena Lubiski was given the important task of being descent pilot. She could activate manual take-over of controls. She would then manage everything and even fly the ship to the ground. The controls were about her. In all likelihood Marjena would do nothing other than read all the data, and watch the outside camera views. Data included ship altitude, ship attitude, ship speed, fuel amounts, engine thrust, etcetera. The three motors were gimbal mounted and she could steer the direction of their thrush as well as the amount of thrust.

Cecil the computer spoke. "Count-down to descent warning. Ten seconds and counting, nine seconds, eight seconds, seven seconds, six seconds, five seconds, four seconds, three seconds, two seconds, one second, ignite engines, full thrust."

The astronauts had had many lighthearted discussions as to who Cecil was. Even though it was not exactly a recording of a human voice, one could tell someone had donated their voice for Cecil. That person had made a ton of voice recordings and a computer algorithm then fabricated a replica of his voice. NASA no doubt owned the voice and had a copyright. The original human version of Cecil was paid, and was under a life-time contract not to sell his voice again. He couldn't even read audio books commercially. Who he was, was a mystery? It became an astronaut joke to say to each other, "So! Who is Cecil?" and smile as they passed each other. It was a casual greeting not dissimilar to say "hi" in passing, when there wasn't time for any small chat. It was a bonding thing between all astronauts in recent years. A response to the greeting could be one of smiles, or a hand wave without looking up from a task, or a verbal reply of "Yes. Who is Cecil?" If someone who was not an astronaut and tried the greeting, they would not get a response. There were unwritten rules understood by most folks who worked with astronauts. The question was a bit like a secret Freemason greeting. The only difference was that the membership of the astronaut club was not secret, and that it was all a light hearted joke. Popular theory was that Cecil was an Iowan. He had a definite Midwest American accent, or lack of accent as Americans would say. He was not a cowboy, or a hippy. He was also not a Bawston or Joisy guy. He didn't have that slurred Southern Iowa style of speaking. He didn't have the subtly heavy guttural "Ts' and "Ds" of Northern Iowans. I had guessed he was a Central Iowa liberal arts professor living in Riverside Iowa, on the English River. Riverside was where Captain Kirk from Star Trek was going to be born in the future one day, according to fiction.

As the thrust engine's first roar was felt, Marjena turned her head to the others and spoke.

"Just who is Cecil?"

For her to say this at this moment meant she was on an adrenaline and dopamine high. Marjena was generally a quiet and serious person. Her family fled Poland were post World-War II refugees to New York and were subjected to ethnic prejudice in their early years. After losing their accents, the second-generation Poles managed to achieve all their individual career full potential, but not without still hearing a few polish jokes. Marjena's childhood was filled with Polish jokes, which were never meant to be vulgar, but rather clever. Marjena told Polish jokes herself, once she relaxed with a vodka drink. She proud of her Polish-America identity. It has been humorously said that to own a hyphenated identifier you are required to speak two languages, or at the least be able to speak in two accents. So truthfully Marjena identified herself purely as American, unless she drank Vodka. She was incredibly proud of her Polish-American identity.

"How do you recognize a polish astronaut? Answer: She is the one watching the rocket launch."

"Why are there no Polish last-name woman astronauts? Answer: They all married Irish-Americans."

Everyone on board the Ares-1 Mars Mission liked Marjena. She was a formidable lady. She seemed shy but was very clever, an expert in her astronaut specialties. I especially like her green eyes offset by her blonde hair and fine pointed features with a slight long nose. I had read those were Celtic features that some Poles whose village origins were close to the Baltic carried. The Celts were far more than just Irish, Scots and Welch.

A red-orange color glowed outside the descent ship windows. We were burning through the outer Martian atmosphere. I could feel the deceleration by how heavy my arms felt. Then the ship jerked violently to one side. I strained to the side to look into the cat carriers. Skabenga looked OK, but she was wide eyed and crouching as much as the straps allowed. In the other cage-box. Aresha, the baby, was fast asleep. Babies can really sleep though everything.

The descent ship cameras switched on. They were about 10 000 feet above the Mars surface. At 2000 feet the canopies separated and the retro motors fired. Marjena, with her hands on the controls closely studied the approaching terrain. No one spoke. Our heartrate monitors all showed numbers over 100 beats per minute.

My heart jumped. On one of the camera screens I saw the other two cargo-landers, intact and upright. That meant we would survive too. They were 200 meters apart, at a guess. We were landing in a pretty wide level plain.

"I am doing the Armstrong", said Marjena calmly over the intercom. I knew what she meant by that phrase. Neil Armstrong also took over final control of Apollo-11s landing. He touched down with only 20 seconds of fuel left, his heart rate was 150 beats per minute. His move saved his and Buzz Aldrin's lives, and the entire mission.

Marjena flipped a switch. She increased thrust to slow down descent even more. That give her more flying options. With a tall rocket falling in its long axis, she was not able to fly it like an airplane with wings on Earth. I heard a subtle difference in the motor thrust. My arms felt heavier, as she slowed descent down. The closer we got to touch-down, the smaller the radius of optional landing points became. Her hands each made flicking movements on the control sticks. The G-forces felt really heavy. There was a slight jar and the engines ceased firing. A mountain of dust billowed up passing the ship windows. The standard cameras lost their view. Marjena still had a 3-D simulated image derived from a scanning high fidelity radar device. It was designed up from a type of pre-clinical ultrasound imaging device used on rats, where the sensor flickers back and forth emitting and sensing sound waves in flesh. This Ares-1 device worked similarly, but used radio waves passing through the dust cloud. It recorded and image point, and then moved a degree and shot another radar beam. It completed a 200-point sweep at a rate a rate of 10 times per second. Each sweep generated a new full image. The screen showed a 3-D picture of the landing terrain. Compared to the video camera 60 frames per second images, it was slow, but vastly better than having zero image in the middle of a dust cloud.

Marjena sensed things before she even saw them on the 3-D radar picture and she made a perfect landing despite the despite losing the video images.

"I thought the computer chose a landing spot had soft soils so I chose 100 meters towards Martian north that I felt had a more solid rock base. Both sites looked equally flat though."

The entire time she was flying Chris spoke out vital data, keeping Marjena's eyes on the image screens. He said steadily. "Fuel plenty, 1200 feet. Fuel plenty 1100 feet, fuel plenty 1000 feet. ............" until he finally said, "Ground contact at zero feet. Motors off. No problems".

Marjena said to that, "Thank you Captain Bolder."

We discovered Marjena was precisely right in her assessment of the ground on which the two other two ships landed. The one tilted, due to the softness of the soil letting one of the rocket legs dig in two feet deep. The astronaut rocket was on very firm soil resting on solid rock base just inches deep. She based this judgment purely on seeing a subtle difference in surface color and observing the one cargo rocket had a few degrees of tilt after it landed. The three rockets were also situated in a near perfect triangle being each 200 meters from the others. The ground engineers in Houston could not have designed a better automated landing for the three rockets. Her alterations moved the landing point about 100 meters, from what the auto pilot was planning and the crew ship was on solid ground.

"My God, Marjena do you have underground radar in your head," I said later at the crew debriefing meeting, speaking about technical aspects of the landing.  ".

"No," she replied, "I saw the cargo-1-rocket had a slight tilt on the ground and the surface was 100% smooth. I saw the cargo-2-rocket stood perfectly vertical, and from the surface color I guessed the were tiny rocks on its surface. I guessed that meant the subsurface structure had rocky solid structure to it. I worried the more plain-looking surface consisted of old river bed sandy soil. Pure granular sand would not hold our ship weight."

"You can see tiny pebbles at 1500 feet altitude?" I asked still incredulous.

"No. It was more that the shadows of the little stones that gave the surface a darker hue as seen from far away. It also looked more matte colored as we got closer. I decided at 1000 feet to act and take over the landing. I just aimed for soil of the same color as that under the upright cargo rocket ship".

Chris said, "I guess we can say we have reached the end of the beginning. Now the real mission starts."

## CHAPTER 13.

### The President's announcement. (week 12)

In the White House press-briefing room, journalists sat excitedly, waiting for the first female president to make an announcement. Since the Ares-1 disaster there had been a news block-out from all official government sources. Rumors flourished. Theories explaining the events ranged from plausible to bizarre. All the worlds' major TV News broad casters had bought rights to relay this meeting live as breaking news. The rumors about what happened after the start of the Ares-1 Mars mission disaster, and what caused it were infinite. The world knew of the disaster, but had never had any explanations from officials. Having drawn names forma hat to determine the order in which they could ask questions, Madame President would take questions, relying on her staff for help on technical questions.

What was known about the disaster was that only single hours after the Ares-1 Mars spaceship mission had fired its thrusters to leave Earth orbit on a Trans-Martian-injection (TMI) that an explosive like sound was received by the ground antennae positioned around the world. That was followed by total radio silence. The most common opinion was that the ship had exploded.

NASA announced two months after the disaster that it was closing. Its director was fired. A new satellite exploration body was forming and would be a non-military-based government body. About a third of the former technical and scientific staff of NASA would be offered jobs in the new organization. It was notable that they were all the youngest who had not yet earned management level positions.

Even more bizarre than the disaster rumors, NASA announced two months later that it was closing. Congress had defunded it. Its director was fired. A new satellite exploration agency was forming, and would be a non-military-based government body. About a third of the former scientific and technical staff of NASA would be offered jobs in the new organization. It was notable that they were all the youngest who had not yet earned management level positions.

The nation mourned the loss of life, and Ares-1 had had an effect on its value systems. manded this ending of NASA. Congress demanded the ending of NASA, through a bipartisan agreement, arguing the that humans do not belong in space; all future space launches would be unmanned and purely for well-justified scientific-research. The military was going to also have its own space program but would be restricted to Earth orbit work, and financed from the standard military budget. The great space era was ended. Future space related budgets would be minuscule compared to the previous 30 months expenditure of billions approaching trillions of dollars that was spent. The country would take ten years to recover from Ares-1 Mars-Mission debt.

People coined the term the Great Space Era, but cynics added up all the persons who had died on the launch pad or in space across all the space faring nations, and pointed out that there was nothing great about it. Over fifty humans had died on the launch pad or in space across all the space-faring nations. People spoke of the big three disasters, that is Challenger with seven human deaths, Columbia with seven human deaths and now the Ares-1 mission to Mars with fourteen human deaths. American was by far the leader in killing astronauts.

---

"Please stand for the President of the United States," announced the press secretary into the podium microphone. Everyone stood as the President, dressed mournfully in a black one-piece dress with jacket and a red pocket handkerchief and the obligatory US flag badge on the left jacket lapel entered the room. Four men accompanied her standing two to each side. The room became uneasy.  A flock of underlings stood at the stage sides carrying recorders, folders, and brief cases.  Camera shutters clicked everywhere.

"No flashes please" said an unknown voice over the speaker.


She looked up and at the center of the group of journalists.

"I want to thank you for all being here today. I have a few announcements, concerning two matters. The first concerns the lost Ares-1 mission."

She looked down, planning to read from the typed notes in her hand and not the teleprompter.  All the journalist held poised pens and note pads. They subconsciously moved slightly to the front of their chairs.

"I have had much communication with the President of China during our meetings Hawaii." The simultaneous inhalation of all the journalists was audible in the otherwise silent of the room.

"We now know that the end of the Ares-1 mission was due to sabotage by a foreign astronaut employed on International Space Station, the ISS. This occurred in the days before the final Ares-1 mission astronauts arrived at the ISS. The saboteur drugged one of the Marsnauts, after she had opened the security hatch and let him into the ship. She was unconscious and unable to stop his tyranny.

The saboteur is Wei Zhang. He is a Chinese astronaut and his father donated $50 billion to the Ares-1 project, before I removed outside foreign influences. This made it impossible for the Chinese astronaut's father's computer company products to be part of the mission equipment anymore. Mr. Zwang, the father, then bought his son an ISS flight, that coincided with Ares-1 being docked to the ISS.  the Chinese part of the ISS at that time. When the Ares-1 mission was in its concept development he was going to have a bought place on the mission paid for by his father. We are told this action of sabotage was purely conceived by the young man. His father had no knowledge of the planned sabotage, nor anyone else in the computer company who lost the contract, and nor did the Chinese government. I met both the Chinese president and the father of Wei Zhang in Hawaii. They offered profound condolences to the surviving families of the deceased Marsnauts. The Chinese president agreed to match the sums. On behalf of the nation and the 14 Marsnauts surviving I accepted the sympathy donations, and agreed to convey their condolences. I plan to meet with the families next week. I will take some limited questions before I make my second announcement.

She waved to the first journalist selected to ask his question.

"Yes."

"I am Matt Michaels. Madame President, how did the Chinese discover this explanation?"

"Wei Zhang had a fellow Chinese astronaut with him on the ISS. Apparently, they did not get on well. After returning to Earth 2 months later, an intoxicated Wei Zhang revealed to his fellow astronaut how he drugged the lady to get into the Ares-1 spaceship. He said he planted a device there, without giving more technical information. The second Chinese astronaut immediately reported this to senior officials. The Chinese reviewed all ISS video recordings made in the Chinese Government modules on the ISS. They found clips that showed Wei Zhang prepare two alcohol beverages for a lady Ares astronaut which she drank. It also appeared that he added a second component to the lady's second drink, which we assume was a sedation drug. These videos have been given to us. The lady was far from the camera with her back turned away. We do not know her identity, although she clearly wore NASA garments."

"Sheila Wong. Madame President. Where is Wei Zhang at this time, and where will he face prosecution?"

"Wei Zhang is dead. The Chinese government arrested him immediately. He recorded a full confession on tape, which will not be released. He died of medical problems. His body has been incinerated.   The CIA never had a chance to interview him or finger print him."

"John Bollinger, Madame President. Do we know anything about what the exact sabotage was? Was it an explosive?"

"The Chinese Government with the assistance of the Wei Zhang's could not determine that. The detainee refused to speak regarding technical specifics and died before his interrogation could be completed.  Wei Zhang was a prominent leader computer and software development in his father's company. This company spent a month investigating all of Wei Zhang's computers, notes, records and colleagues as to what he could have done to the spaceship. They insist they have no hint or clue as to what Wei Zhang could have done to the spaceship. That is all the information I can give you at this moment.

My final announcement is that I am resigning as President, for personal reasons. I spent the day in meeting with the leaders of the House and the Senate. Upon their advice of Congress, and counsel I am resigning effective this minute. I wish to express my appreciation to the wonderful people of the United States. It was a privilege to have served you. I wish to express my very sincere and personal condolences, to the families of the fourteen Marsnauts who have died. I am glad we know what happened now and I hope there can be closure. I wish to emphasize the Chinese government is very regretful that an aberrant citizen of theirs did this deed. They want Americans to know the Chinese feel our pain, hope to remain cooperative allies moving forward."

The president immediately turned, walked swiftly out of the room, and hung her head. The press secretary grasped the microphone and announced. "The meeting is finished thank you ladies and gentleman".

All bedlam broke loose. Those left in their seats grabbed their cellphones and started screaming over the din, to news producers around the world.

--------------------------------------------------------------------------------
-----

In the days following the stunning Presidential announcement, more about the saboteur surfaced. He has earned a master's degree and PhD in computer programing at Oxford university in Britain, in addition to other multiple Chinese certifications. He was very wealthy and drove the most expensive sports cars in town. His dad's company paid for everything. He liked to drink a lot, which usually sparked a temper. He was an absolute mathematical genius. He always dreamed of living in California, and many friends believed he could start up a computer company there, and even surpass his father's success. Some friends were not too surprised to hear the sad ending of Wei Zhang; everyone was very saddened about the whole story.

As far as the world was concerned after the Ares-1 disaster, and the big Presidential announcement, human space travel had reached its natural end. Life moved on for all nations. Space research became a low publicity venture for scientists all launching their own small low-budget shoe-box-size satellites by thousands, into the growing litter in low and high Earth Orbit. The volume of orbiting metallic debris in orbit around Earth space had already been an accumulating problem over many decades. Being hit be a piece of steel flyting at 30 000 kilometers per hour is a very serious concern for manned spaceships. For small unmanned satellites metallic debris damage in orbit is a budgeted expense, and an inconvenience. The satellite can be replaced within months. That didn't change life on the green planet with blue skies and endless water.

The red planet was still visible in the early evening sky. A couple could sit on a hillside and watch the most beautiful sunset to be seen on any planet on the entire cosmos. No other planet was exactly this close to the Sun with such dense atmosphere, to produce a large golden large golden orb against a stunning azure blue sky. If the young couple was in Iowa, the pure clarity of the air left the sky a pale magnificent pastel blue, but produced a silvery gold Sun. If the hill with a young couple was on an Africa grassy plain, the natural dust in the sky made the sky that framed the golden orb into burnt fiery red Sun in an azure blue sky. It is not possible to agree on which Sunset is more beautiful.

After the Sunset the sky would steadily darken and the planets become more prominent, especially before the stars could really twinkle in the sky. That was the best time for a young man wanting to impress a young lady with his astronomical knowledge, to point out cool Venus, and Mercury and Jupiter.

Then there was red Mars. On an exceptional night with exceptional eyes, you could even see the two moons of Mars, Phobos and Deimos.

To the ancient Greeks the God of War was Ares. To the ancient Romans the god of war was Mars. Modern people thus sometimes associate the name of Ares with the planet of Mars.

The first human space trip to the planet Mars was called the Ares-1 mission. It had a doctor on board who had seen Mars twice from Earth, while sitting on a hill. Once watching an African sunset and once watching a Midwestern Iowa sunset.

## CHAPTER 14.

## The first step, and the crushing job of unpacking. (week 45)

It was utterly bizarre to have such a perfect landing of three rockets, but most strange was that something actually went right. We were grateful to have this one day, during one week, to have something go well. There was no place for dark thoughts. Place the burden over your shoulders, lean forward, and walk.

No one spoken about who would place their boots onto Martian dust first. It had been a big challenge getting around the manned ship over the last two days, as they acclimatized to the mild Martian gravity. The ship was designed to floated around in, not climbed, around in.

At the first evening post-dinner conference on Mars, Chris voiced what we all had been thinking. He started by saying, "I want everyone to write on a piece of paper who should be first out the ship, to step onto Martian Soil".

"You, as Captain" should be first said someone. Another agreed. "It is the captain's prerogative"

"I'll do it, Gimme gimme," shouted out Russel Dunaszegi.

He paused and then said. "I was just joking."

Chris said again. "Write your suggestions" and he passed around torn paper strips. "You can add a reason for your proposal too, if you want"

No one rushed to write anything, but eventually, they each returned a folded piece of paper which Chris placed in zip-lock plastic bag.

"I am going to look at all of them and see if there is any clear majority vote winner. I'll make the final decision, but I just want help with my own thoughts."

Ten minutes later Chris spoke. "One name cropped up six-times, and another five times. I like the suggestions very much and they actually matched my own thoughts."

"I don't want to snatch that privilege for myself. I want the first step onto Mats to belong more to the team, to the crew. Before we left Earth, NASA commanders called me into a private meeting. They said they were giving me a very firm command. The first person to step onto the Martian surface had to be best representative of NASA's 'right stuff'. They said the person had to be military pilot first, have a university degree, be married, have children, not be a heavy drinker, and be a compliant and cooperative soldier while under command. They also wanted it to be a male, tall and good looking. This was important for all the publicity afterwards and the image of the nation. It sounded to me like they were casting a character for movie hero. A

"So, who is it, Chris?", interrupted Tyrone.

"Alan! He never knew and is dead now. I never got further instructions what to do in such situation, so I am free to give any orders on this that I like. Marjena your name was the six-vote one. Your *Armstrong maneuver* in taking over the landing from the automated computer to optimize the crew- ship landing might have actually saved the mission. If we had landed in soft soil and the ship toppled over it would have been a monumental problem to fix. So, I think the lady who did the *Armstrong maneuver* to take over last-second flight-control so brilliantly, also deserves to take the *Armstrong first step*, onto Martin soil.

"Yay", I said, applauding.

Everyone approved, applauded and said something sweet. Marjena blushed, just further making her the perfect choice.

"Now", said Chris, "the five-vote person I think also deserves to be the special second person to step onto Martian soil. You all know that is Rodney."

"Yeh", shouted the crew and all applauded.

"I will take third place", said Chris. "and after that, ranking does not matter. Just do your best, as your time comes. We will try to make sure we get photographs of everyone's personal first step onto Mars."

"We first three will walk at lunchtime tomorrow. We must do an inspection of the other two rockets. We will be testing communications as we get further from the ship."

That night the three Marsnauts scheduled for a surface walk, to avoid decompression sickness. Lt was cramped, but we were too exhilarated to care

---

Opening the outer hatch, I saw a 100foot long ladder, reaching to the ground. Even after this much time in space, I felt clumsy wearing a space suit. That together with wearing heavy boots, and having restricted vision out of the space suit head piece made climbing down the tall ladder intimidating. It was incongruously low technology to descend such a tall ladder. It required patience and a systematic way of taking one slow step at a time. Marjena went first. I went second and was official photographer. I had a video camera mounted on a film-stick and strapped to my space suit. All three of us Marsnauts descended together, close to each other.

When Marjena was ready to put her boot down and touch Martian soils she waited for me to give her final instructions. I had to be ready with the camera held out to the side on the stick. I saw the image in tiny side screen close to my eye in my helmet. In the ship, everyone was watching on their computers' screen. In the original plan Ares-1 space mission plan, the entire population on planet Earth's population was going to be watching too an ultra-high definition 4K video of this moment. It wasn't going to be grainy poor black and white TV show like they had of Neil Armstrong.  The irony was, as far as we Ares-1 crew knew, the Earth may well have been watching us. At that time, we had no idea if Earth received communications from us. Marjena waited as I optimized the image composition and adjusted how I held the camera at the end of the stick.

We previously chatted about what words would be appropriate to say when a human first stepped onto the surface of planet Mars. Marjena was very noncommittal, and no one pushed her for her thoughts. Some joked, and said the rest of the crew should over shout her and sing happy birthday to her. Yes. it was Marjena's birthday and was in fact her 40th. Someone suggested she copy Neil Armstrong's moon landing words and say *"One small step for a WOMAN, one giant leap for mankind"*. No one could be serious. It was like no words could ever supersede Neil Armstrong's words, let alone surpass them. The first words of the following got less serious and finally silly. Marjena finally got it figured it out. She must speak from her heart. She must say what feels comfortable for her. She must not try sound overly profound or wise. She knew no matter what she said, the world would immediately judge her with approval, or not via social media. You can't win either way.

I said, "OK I'm Ready. Action!"

Marjena bent her one knee and placed her other leg down onto the Martian soil. A brief silence followed, and then she spoke unemotionally.

"Mankind, we are all like lions to the last."

No one dared to speak next. These moments felt almost holy. Marjena placed her second foot on the soil and reached up to take the camera from me, so she could take over filming. I loosened the hitch, gave her the camera-stick and camera. She gave her a big thumbs up. I stepped down onto the Martian soil.

Standing with both feet on the red soil, making sure my boot prints were separate from those of Marjena's I looked at the camera and said lightheartedly; "What's up Doc?" in tribute to Bugs Bunny. I was not sure if the Camera caught my grin behind my space suit visor. I couldn't take myself too seriously.

Chris next hopped down also making sure his boot prints would stand unique and separate.

He looked at Marjena and I, and said his own special line.

"Now begins the real part of the toughest thing that mankind has ever done, and will ever do". Chris was being very serious.

The crew back up in the spaceship were listening in and watching on the four camera views available to them. There was a camera on each of the three astronaut's head, as well as the high-fidelity camera that I handled.

Babee spoke "Enough nonsense now gals and guys. Let's get serious, sing with me. One two three! Happy birthday to you. Happy birthday to you . . . ." and, they all sang to Marjena on her 40th birthday.

---

The two cargo ships seemed intact. The leaning one concerned us, because it could lean more if the one foot sank further into the soil. We did have equipment to reinforce the foot hold of the legs on the soil. Once that was done, the legs could be hydraulically adjusted to move the rocket back to a dead perpendicular position.

Within two days the leaning ship was upright and secured with widened footholds on the soil. External ship control-panels in the legs were opened. Ladders were sent down. We astronauts could enter the storage modules. Everything was unloaded and stored in an unpressurized tented storage barn within another 3 days. All that remained to unload were the Rovers. The rovers were boxed and heavy. Unloading them was to be was to be the very last task.

We moved onto the second ship which contained pressurized storage modules. It was more complex but soon we had built a second tent barn that was pressurized and that had an EVA chamber to enter and exit the barn via. We got the ship fully unloaded in another week. The pressurized barn was stocked to its roof with stuff from the ship. We laid the second spaceship down onto its side. It stood fifty meters tall. Extra leg struts were projected towards the side it was going to be laid down towards. They came down from higher up the ship. Slowly the ship tilted towards the side the extra legs were on. The positions of the supporting legs were controlled by hydraulics. When it was finished the ship lay on its side on the ground and the struts acted as braces to stop it rolling in any direction. That took one day. This horizontal ship on the ground, ground station or ground habitat, when we built the second pressurized habitat connected to the ship nodules on the ground. The manned descent ship would not be used through the year at all. We would only enter it again when we rocket off the Mars surface.

All communications between the three ships computers functioned; however, there was yet no contact with the orbiter ship carrying Larry and Tyrone. I had to build a new sick bay in the main pressurized barn. It was really just a job of assembling a bunch of shelves, cupboards and furnishings. It was like IKEA mail-order furniture. Everything was easy to assemble with minimal effort, if you followed the paper instructions and had one spanner and one star-screw-driver. A priority design feature of everything was to have no sharp edges. A fear was that a furniture item falling onto a pressurizing material wall of the habitat could puncture it. I had been nervous about living in an inflatable tent on Mars, but now that I saw the structure in its reality, I felt relaxed. The habitat was so strong and sturdy, made of Kevlar and metal fibers, with 50-foot deep ground anchors. I was sure it was hurricane proof.  I was sure it would survive a hurricane, if it was well anchored. It was definitely secure. I had helped bore the fifty-foot deep pegs into the ground. Every action served a double purpose. The soil and rock that they drilled out, got sent to testing.

---

After supper, Chris announced that all the ground-mission-station assembly work had gone perfect and was near complete. Only the surface manned Rovers needed off-loading and assembly. Once complete, we could officially start the Mars surface projects, which comprised three facets. The green house with plant growing was the first project. Collecting soil and rock samples from drilled hole was major second part of the Ares-1 mission. The third project involved research into self-sustenance and recycling. The Carbon dioxide extracted from the waste breathing air would be oxidized to produce water and methane. The methane would be added to bacteria that used it for nutrition. The bacteria would grow into a colony that was a gooey substance. The bacterial gooey substance would be pure protein and could be dried into food pellet for pets, or humans too. Waste plastic get re-manufactured into bricks. Human waste entered a bio-system for reprocessing, using bacteria, and there were many options. In essence a mini contained and controlled eco-system was set up. All considered, all food on the planet follows a cycle from feces to plants and bugs and then into a food chain until human eats the final corn-cob and slice of beef again. On another Mars mission they could bring chickens and feed them the bacterial produced recycled feces derived protein, then eat the chickens. For this mission we made the food pellets, simply as a scientific feasibility exercise, and as back-up.

Eight astronauts donned their EVA suits preparing to go outside of the pressurized habitat. Two crew members had climbed the ladders up eighty feet to enter the storage module of the cargo ship holding the Rover containers. Additional cables had been set and anchored to deep bolts bored ten feet into ground opposite from the swivel-hoists. We were concerned the sideways pulling weight of the crate containing a Rover when it was out on the hoist, would cause the ship to topple over. That would not happen if the ship was standing on solid thick concrete. The Earth engineers who designed everything had not factored in a soft soil landing. Using ship anchor cables on the side of the ship, opposite to the side with the hoist, was the idea of engineer Vicky Duploy. It was engineer Russel Dunaszegi's idea to bolt 8-foot long bars to the feet of the rocket to widen their contact with the ground soil and reduce the chance the rocket landing feet sink deeper into the soft soil. He bragged about his good idea. The first crate was lowered to the ground perfectly, and we moved it aside on a flat cart with powered-wheels.

As the motors started to winch out cable and lower the second crate, Chris held onto a loose rope that hung down to the ground to stop the dangling crate from rotating. The ship tilted slightly as the one foot had dug three inches deeper into the soil. Marjena was maneuvering the second flat cart to receive the crate when it reached ground.

With the rocket tilting again, the hoist was angled slightly to one side of the rocket and started to buckle. Everything on this trip was designed to the limit, barely sufficient in strength, and nearly everything was made of aluminum, because the overwhelming priority was weight saving. Bars were thin, narrow and had large perforations to save weight. Due to the rush to launch the mission tests of designs were minimal too.

When the rocket tilted again, hoist angled slightly to one side of the rocket and buckled. With the change in direction that the cables lowering the crate puller off perpendicular from one cable-wheel's bracket, which then bent as well. The angle of the wheel changed enough for the cable to jump and snap the wheel axil out of its bracket.  That gave an extra eight feet length to the cable and the crate fell downwards until the eight feet of cable slack was taken up. That the heavy crate to halt with such a jerk on the cable, that winch motor winch gearing got smashed and the crate descended in free fall. Chris ran backwards still holding the rope. The Crate hit the ground and flipped over onto its side. It ripped the stabilizing rope that Chris was holding around the box, and yanked his back backwards and up above his head. The Crate just missed Marjena but a wooden beam of the box sprung loose hitting her like a swinging baseball bat, of the side of her chest. Both Marjena and Chris lay on the ground moaning.

The other four Marsnauts in the ground, ran over to them, as fast as is possible in an EVA suits. The two astronauts who in the storage rocket came down the 80-foot ladder.

Chris was moaning say "My shoulder. I think it's broken." Marjena was also lying on the ground, and on her side and moaning. She did not respond to any questions.

We carried the injured astronauts about 150 meters to the "dome", as the habitat was called. Marjena was fortunately petit, and even with the space-suits added weight, two men could carry her using cloth handles on the outside of her EVA suit. Marjena was in a semi- sitting position as she was carried. It took four astronauts to carry Chris as he was big man. He weighed 50-lilograms than Marjena. Although Martian Gravity is a third of that of Earth gravity, the Marsnauts were very weakened from their preceding nine months living without any gravity. They were not weak in resolve and had enough adrenaline that they would move a mountain for a fellow astronaut.

Within twenty minutes, we were all out of our suits and in the Dome sickbay. I ignored Chris with his injured shoulder. Marjena had lost consciousness. The pulse oximeter read blood oxygen saturation of 65%. It should have been 95% to 100%. I did not have an X-ray machine. So, I placed my stethoscope on her left chest in front below the collar bone. I barely heard breath sounds. She was breathing very shallow and I could not get her to take big breaths. Vicky and Babee held her forward and I heard normal breath-sounds at the back of her left chest side too, although rather soft. Normal breath sounds are called vesicular sounds, and resemble the soft rustling of autumn leaves being crinkled between two fingers. When I listened to her right-side front and back, I heard lonely abnormal irregular wet noises. The automated blood pressure cuff machine on her left arm gave a warning sound that it was unable to measure a blood pressure. That implied the blood pressure was very low. Marjena's face was not blue, but she looked as white as a sheet. Her eyes were closed and she did not to stimuli. I opened her mouth and saw her tongue was blue. I next palpated her trachea, her air-pipe from her throat into her chest, in the suprasternal notch. It seemed to deviated to the left when I palpated as deep down the suprasternal notch as I could. This indicated that the usually central lying trachea, was being pushed to the left by something wrong on the right side. Next I placed my left-hand index finger flat onto her right chest ten-centimeters below her clavicle bone and resting on a rib. I thumped this resting finger with the tip of my right-hand middle finger. I repeated this percussion test on the other side. The left chest percussion gave a dull sound whilst the right-side percussions made a resonating sound, a bit like a drum, suggesting the right chest was filled with air and the lung was compressed to the center like a sponge squeezed in a hand. Also, the heart was being pushed to the left together with the trachea, and the heart was compressing the good left lung. The situation was critical and Marjena could die within minutes.

I immediate grabbed a 20-milliliter syringe, filled it with saline solution out of an ampule, and connected it to a 14 Gauge intravenous cannula. I ripped Marjena's shirt top at the neck to fully expose her right upper chest. About four finger breadth below the center of her clavicle, I identified a space between her ribs, and inserted the needle perpendicular to the chest after wiping the skin with a cleaning solution. With very firm and stable hands I advanced the needle deeper, while simultaneously pulling back on the syringe plunger so that the syringe was aspirating. Marjena was motionless and her oximeter was still showing 65%, with an erratic pulse. The syringe and needle suddenly gave a tiny little snap, as it penetrated the chest cavity. Experience is needed to recognize that feeling. Normally, if the needle was inserted into a healthy lung a few tiny bubbles would be aspirated, or none at all. From Marjena's right chest I aspirated abundant free air that bubbled vigorously through the saline in the syringe. This indicated to me that the needle tip was in the cavity of Marjena's right chest, and her right chest was filled with free air, and the lung was compressed out of reach of the needle. That is a pneumothorax. I stopped advancing the syringe and slipped the outer white plastic cannula forward and off the inner steel needle that had cut the path into the chest. After I withdrew and removed the inner steel needle, leaving the cannula in the chest, I heard the hissing sound of air escaping via the cannula. The compressing pressure on that right lung was diminishing. I knew the pressure on the left lung, would be relieved as well, as the heart would also not be pushed so tightly to the left anymore. In seconds Marjena turned pink, her saturation jumped immediately to 85% then slowly climbed to 89%. The blood pressure cuff read 85 over 65 mmHg. Her heart rate read 105. Things had improved a lot.

I said to no-one in particular, "Better to have an open-to-air pneumothorax than a tension pneumothorax".

It took me four minutes to prepare for my next step. Marjena needed a larger, more durable chest-air drain than the temporary emergency IV cannula that was in her chest. I injected local anesthetic into the skin, with a sterile technique, and made a

1-centimeter skin incision with a scalpel. I adapted a sterile large-bore urine-catheter for the task of being an intercostal-drain tube. I inserted it with the help of fine point hemostat clamped firmly holding the tip of the catheter. I forced the catheter tip about 6 centimeters into Marjena's chest cavity, and released the hemostat and removed it. I had made a simple one-way valve mechanism, using the cut-off finger of a disposable sterile rubber glove with a hole in its tip to pass the catheter through. I next removed the intravenous cannula that had been in the chest as temporary air drain. The gas could escape better through the much wider valved-intercostal-drain. As Marjena breathed more deeply in and out now. Escaping air could be seen rippling through the cut-off plastic glove finger on the catheter, the homemade one-way valve. When Marjena inhaled the sides to the glove finger simply collapsed and sealed off the urine catheter. I cleaned up and it secured the intercostal drain very well, with skin-sutures and adhesive dressings.

I said, "She will need a more efficient underwater drain connected to this chest tube, instead of the rubber glove finger valve, but I will sort that out later".

I turned to Chris and tried to sound reassuring.

"Chris. Marjena is fine. You will be fine too. I am just going to examine your arm".

Chris was on the second sick bay bed, and his left arm was at his side. I gently palpated his left-hand fingers, then the wrist, and next the forearm. My palpating fingers steadily worked up the arm, while studying Chris's face for any blinks indicating I had touched a tender point. His elbow was fine. His lower and mid humerus was fine. With one finger gentle probing the upper humerus I determined it was also fine. I felt relieved. A fracture site would have been exquisitely tender.

"No long bone fractures" I said quietly.

I then identified the shoulder's acromion bone feeling from above the shoulder. I tried to determine if the ball of the humerus was immediately lateral to that. Chris had a lot of muscle in that region, and his body cues and blinks showed me it was tender when touched. The acromion itself was not tender; therefore, not fractured either, but the ball of the humerus was not exactly where it should have been. I tried to move the arm outward a bit and palpate deep and high in the axilla. I could not palpate the ball of the humerus and was only causing Chris immense discomfort. I palpated the outer shoulder again, gently. I was not seeking signs of pains and injury, but rather trying locate the ball of the proximal humerus. The whole time I spoke soothingly to distract Chris.

"Chris just imagine you are sitting under a shady tree on the bank of the Mississippi river, on a grass patch. You are fishing for catfish and having a relaxing day with your wife and you are each sipping a cool beer on a hot Missouri day".

I became convinced that there was a dislocation of the shoulder- joint to posterior and upwards.

"I am going to give you a small injection in your neck".

I first placed an intravenous catheter into Chris' right hand for emergency drugs, if needed later. I connected all the standard vital sign monitors to measure blood pressure, heart rate and oxygen levels in the blood. This is a routine precaution before injecting very large doses of local anesthetic drug.

Deciding speed and efficiency was the priority, I did not want to dig out, unpack and set-up the ultrasound machine, as that would take me an hour. I grabbed the close at hand nerve stimulator and attached one lead to Chris. The second lead got attached to the nerve block needle, that I was about to use. I got Chris to look to his right side and I marked a first line across the sternocleidomastoid muscle that was two fingers breadth above the clavicle bone, and a second intersecting line along the posterior margin of that sternocleidomastoid muscle. I disinfect ted the skin at intersection of the lines, and injected some local anesthetic drug subcutaneous. Next, I inserted a 50mm long nerve stimulating needle to seek the nerves to the shoulder.

"Chris you may feel your arm moving and twitching. It will hurt a bit, but I will be quick."

I felt very confident about being able to find the nerves to the shoulder, because was my career primary medical skill, and I was well practiced in all classic and modern technique variations. An old-fashioned technique suited this moment. For today, I just wanted immediate analgesia of any degree, and without delays. Within 2 seconds Chris blinked and his deltoid muscle over his shoulder joint was twitching. I switched off the stimulator, did routine safety actions and injected a long acting local anesthetic.

Not even 30 seconds had passed, and Chris said "Ahhh, it's feeling better!".

About ten minutes later Chris was 100% pain free. We made lie on the floor. I placed my socked left foot into Chris' axilla. I took his left hand and pulled it 45-degrees towards the front and 45-degrees towards the leg. Chris grunted slightly. I steadily increased the traction on the arm and adjusted the position of my foot. I used my foot to give me both something to push against as I applied traction to the arm, and to push the ball of humerus outwards with my toes. There was a very soft thud sound as the ball of the humerus popped back into its socket.

Chris spoke "I think you got it". I next moved the arm around and it seemed the shoulder was capable of free movement again. I was certain the shoulder joint dislocation was fixed. On Earth I would have taken an X-Ray to confirm the shoulder joint reduction, but I felt confident about success regardless.

"Let's get you back on the bed now".

We helped Chris stand up and I held onto the now lame arm from the nerve block, keeping it in front of Chris across his chest. I did not want it to dislocate again. I fashioned a collar-and-cuff bandage to hold his limp and numb arm. It would stay asleep for five hours.

"I reckon we can say you are on light duty now".

Chris laughed.

"You must keep this collar-and-cuff on for two weeks. I will help you with safe exercises. I reckon you will be nearly normal and able to try anything in about 6-weeks."

Marjena spoke for the first time since her accident.

"Hey Rodney! Come tell me what all this is and what happened."

I looked at her and she looked great. I moved the monitors back to her, saw her oxygen saturation was a perfect 98% and her blood pressure was normal.

I was feeling more relaxed and tried to continue with humor.

"Just another working day on Mars, I guess".

I then explained everything to Marjena. I removed her chest drain was removed three days later, because it hadn't bubbled any air out for 36 hours. Marjena was resilient and pushed herself in her exercises to comfort tolerance limits. She ceased taking pain tablets after one week and rated her pain as 99% gone by three weeks after the accident.

Chris was a perfect obedient and diligent patient. He rehabilitated so quickly I signed him off for normal duties. Chris spent nearly all his free time bending with his head against a cupboard side, with his arm hanging forward from his body towards the ground. He lifted hand weights and squeezed forearm and hand-exercise devices for hours continuously each day with both arms. He swiveled his injured arm like a hanging pendulum as widely as he could within his comfort limits. After six weeks I let raise his arm to above his head and progressively do more strenuous things.

---

Eventually the Mars mission returned to "normal."

Chris and Russel went out on the unpressurized manned Rover, noting general observations, taking five-meter deep soil and rock samples.

Framingham and Judessa took the pressurized Rover vehicle out doing geographical exploration and collecting and testing surface samples. They did exactly what previous *unmanned* Martian Rovers did only 1000 times faster, and they would take the samples back to Earth for examination

The Rovers managed to retain radio contact with the Martian Ground base even if twenty kilometers away, as long as they were in line of sight, and not down a Valley or around a mountain. There was no contact with Tyrone and Larry in the orbiting spaceship, and that would be problem when they had to re-dock at the end of the Mars mission.

---

Due to the fact that the Ares-surface-habitat was only pressurized to the same pressure as the space suits, meant when preparing for walking outside the habits, they did not need any 8-hours of acclimatizing.

While living on Mars, the Marsnauts adjusted their life cycles to that of a Martian day which is thirty-nine minutes longer than an Earth day. Those extra minutes were automatically adjusted for by the electronic clocks, at midnight during our sleep. Days seemed otherwise normal. We however had to still track the real

Earth calendar based on the time and date in Houston, at Mission ground control. So, if someone asked what was the date, the answer was Houston date. If they asked what was the time then it was Martian time. That meant that sometimes the date changed at any hour of the Martian day. It was no bother. We only thought about the present Martian day and the next Martian day. We never thought of Earth.

One day I asked Camilla if she would join me for a sunset walk. She agreed to join me. Martian twilights last much longer than twilight does on planet Earth due to the dust high in the Martian atmosphere. I wanted to take some photos so I had my camera and tripod. To protect the camera from the extreme of temperature between sunlight and shadow the cameras were all in casings very similar to those used for underwater cameras. The entire contraption was also enclosed in a multilayered knitted casing. It was possible to operate all critical camera buttons and to also view the digital screen. A protective front window could be opened like a hatch door to let the camera lens shoot through a second high-fidelity polished glass window that still sealed the container. The inside of the casing was air-tight and contained air. I was a camera hobbyist and had the best camera set-up of everyone in the mission. I had a couple of different lenses, but I had to change them before I went outdoors with his cameras if I wanted to use one specific lens. Today I used a mild telephoto-lens. About four hundred meters away, there was small easy-to-climb hill. I was hoping to get sunset photos with the ascent-ship silhouetted in the images. The setting Sun on Mars was tiny when compared to the Sun seen from planet Earth, which is much closer to the Sun than Planet Mars. The Sun was still as bright as on Earth

The major thing that I wanted to capture was the color of the sunset sky. I already had some great fisheye lens photos showing the butterscotch yellow-brown day sky overhead that flawlessly transitioned into a blue sky on the far horizon surrounding the brilliant setting Sun. With a fish eye lens, the setting Sun looked as small, but very bright, star. Today the telephoto lens would make the Sun a lot larger in the image. The most exciting thing was however that the day time had produced an uncommon violet sky. That happened when very high-altitude clouds carried ice particles. I expected if the ice particles would make the sky on the horizon at sunset a purple color.

When I was talking enthusiastically about my camera, lenses, and aspects of photographs that I took, Camilla listened patiently. She however had not one creative or artistic grain within her. She wasn't bored to listen. She just had nothing to say, and she enjoyed the outing. Also, she was developing a girly fancy for me, I suspected. I make a specific effort to be extremely non-flirtatious. I did find over my life, that in casual situations that I was usually more at ease with woman than with men. On the other hand, the men who I came to be close friends with, I am sure would give their lives for me. It seemed when I had a serious male friend, it was a very special close friend. I attributed these features within myself, to having grown up in a home without a male role model, as my dad had died early in my life. At this time on the mission everyone was getting along very harmoniously. Who would believe that this general all-around comradery could now, when only months earlier there had been a mutiny and that the ship-captain was willing to execute the lead-mutineer?

While we waited for the Sun to get lower in the sky we chatted.

"Camilla, how old will your children be when you get home?"

"One will be thirteen and the other one fifteen years old."

"The older one is the girl, right?"

"Don't you feel bad taking yourself out of their lives for nearly three years?"

"Not really. They are closer to their dad than to me. I was always the professional mom, with the better job. I tend to work longest and hardest. My husband was more of a mom to the kids than me. I made the money."

"Hmmm", I was thinking. "How close are you and your husband?"

"We have been married sixteen years, since I was nineteen"

"You didn't exactly answer my question. That sounds like you had a honeymoon baby. "

"What does it matter?"

"Did you have a big family style wedding?"

"We got married before a justice of the peace, with one friend each as witnesses."

"Would you say you and your husband love each other still?"

"Rodney you ask the most personal questions, of anyone on the planet, and I mean Earth. That still sounds odd."

"I am guessing you wanted this Mars-Mission job to get away from your home Camilla?"

"Isn't that everyone's story on this space-mission, hey Rodney?"

"I think everyone has a story in life. I don't know the story of every individual on this mission. I do know they are all top qualified for their technical or scientific roles. I think I am an oddity myself. I applied for the job, nearing retirement as a gray-haired anesthesiologist. It was a wild-shot. I wrote an outrageous bragging resume thinking I had nothing to lose. Here I am now."

"Rodney do your love your wife? "

"I love her with all of my heart and my soul."

"So how does she feel about you leaving her for three years on an ultra-dangerous trip?"

"I never asked her permission, and she never volunteered to tell me. I am sure she hates it and didn't want me to go. I know she will be very proud of me if I make it back. She is the most loyal human who ever lived. We both tolerate each other's eccentricities. I guess my coming on this trip is simply madness on my side. I could never imagine anything more exciting to do, that I could have done in my life. Maybe I was also seeking some validation in my life."

Camilla was surprised.

"You needed validation?"

"As I said, everyone has a story".

I stepped forward to my camera on the tripod and started taking photos.

"I hope a pelican flies past the setting Sun." I said.

"Are you crazy?" said a strange voice in the earphones.

"Is that Babee?" asked Camilla in surprise.

"Yeah. We have all been listening to you two"

"Aaah Dammit! I forgot one never has privacy if a microphone is on in front of one. We will be back in about an hour.'

Babee asked, "What is this thing about a pelican Rodney?"

"Standing on the Mexican Baja Peninsula, I photographing a magical beach sunrise, as a pelican glided by and dipped a wing onto the water reflecting the first sunrays. A tiny ripple followed the wing tip on the mirror smooth water behind the wave as it washed back. The pelican was in perfect silhouette against the bright background. I stopped taking photos that morning knowing I had just captured the perfect one. I knew I had to sit on the sand and absorb the rest on those peaceful beautiful moments into my soul. How can a day be bad that starts like that? How can life be all bad if you have had one morning like that? Now I stand looking at a Martian sunset against a luminous bright purple sky with a silhouetted Spaceship from another planet. It reminded me of my Mexican beach pelican moment. "

Babee replied. "Rodney, we all can't wait to see your sunset photos."

We sat silently chewing on our private thoughts. A relationship is matured when you and a partner can enjoy silent time together. I longed for my wife. We had such harmony in our marriage. As Camilla and I walked back to the habitat, it took us half an hour because we dawdled and looked at pebbles and things along the way. This whole setting and time of watching a Martian sunset had an incomprehensible unreality to it. We could never have imagined it, yet we were in it.

# CHAPTER 15.

## Design protocol failure – A Boeing moment. (week 60)

As the crew felt more disconnected from Earth, living on the surface of Mars steadily became mundane and routine. Saturday night, or Family-Night, as we now called it, was the highlight of the week. Everyone contributed in some way. Playing musical instruments was most popular and we took advantage of the more spacious ground habitat. We plugged the instruments into the habitat speaker system for all to hear. Russel Dunaszegi played an electronic piano which was nothing more than a simple keyboard that fit into his personal luggage suit case. Over the speakers it sounded surprisingly real. Vicky Duploy played her ukulele which she had played throughout the mission; however, no one knew due not seeing it, nor hearing it over the constant hum of spaceship noise. When Vicky first played the ukulele in the habitat it was a welcome surprise to everyone. In total we brought five instruments on board. Fram the quiet pilot/engineer had an electronic keyboard, that mimicked any musical instrument imaginable, including percussion. Marjena played an electronic fiddle. I brought an electronic cello, and everyone chimed in, I am not surprised." My teammates all thought my liking a cello was offbeat and fitted my general quirkiness. I took that as a compliment. All the musicians initially used their own music as mental relaxation therapy.

I began my first performance, by apologizing that I was very unmusical, and was self-taught from books and videos. The number I chose to play was a pure instrumental version of Leonard Cohen's "Hallelujah". I refused to sing the song. Judessa said she could sing it and the two of us promised they would perform together in a month, after we had worked out the mixed vocal and instrumental arrangement. The full cello version was not bad, but everyone politely said that with more practice I might have a winner.

Russel's big piano number was Billy Joel's *'Piano Man'*. He had no other song worth playing and everyone just loved to hear that song every time that Russel got a turn to perform. A few months later Fram figured out how to play an accompanying harmonica on his electronic keyboard. That ensured that song of Russel, "Piano man" was a permanent favorite.

Marjena was a virtuoso on the fiddle with endless genres and numbers she could play. The crew liked it best when she played Blue-grass, clapping their hands and stomping feet in accompanying rhythm.

Fram a beautiful, melodic, never off-key voice and keen ear for any rhythm section of any song. He could replicate drums and other instruments simultaneously on his electronic keyboard. The phrase "let's try this" became a standard phrase on Saturday nights. Our unanimous favorite song Fram sang was 'A horse with no name.' We liked the lyric references to the sand, the hills, the deserts and the loneliness. We lived on our own desolate red dry planet. The Ares-1 music festival evolved and developed throughout these jam sessions. There were sing-alongs too, with no-one caring who sang off-key or had a lousy voice. It felt like a drunken family Christmas sing along, but sober on another planet.

The early twentieth century psychologist Maslow wrote that after the basic needs of survival were satisfied, humans had higher needs, that had to be fulfilled in order to enjoy psychological well-being. The foremost higher needs included friendship, intimacy and creative outlets. Friendships formed and our overall sense of team work prevailed. Fulfilling intimacy needs in this cramped environment seemed ridiculous, so we banked that for our return to Earth. This void placed extra emphasis on the third higher need, being creative. For a poor mother of large poor family, might find her creative outlet in managing to cook up a humble meal that the family found palatable. On this spaceship, every Marsnaut found their individual creative outlets in their own personal, unique, often quirky and private way. That was an important basis for psychological well-being during this crazy Mars human experiment.

---

Beyond music, I had another creative outlet. I loved sketching odd things on paper, and painting with water colors. All my sketches shared one style. They were of strange imaginary creatures, maybe even imaginary Martians. If you looked closely little clues surface identifying the animal as a giraffe, a monkey, a policeman or even a doctor. The doctor was a give-away, because there was a realistic looking stethoscope hanging around my creature's neck. These creatures had holes in their arms, legs and body. Some body parts like, an arm would pass through a body hole from back to the front. The eyes would bud off the side of the head and then curve back suspended on a long stalk to float in a wide hollow space, where normal eyes would usually be.   I called these critters Doogels. Bored of a lecturer's slow exposition, I developed these sketches to stop myself going crazy or going to sleep. My doodling grew for drawing circles and squares, then shading them to give perception of depth. Finally adding shapes together to get more complex over the years, until I developed the doodle creatures. I called my creatures Doogles.

My other hobby is watercolor painting. I never wanted to show anyone my paintings. They were just for self-entertainment. My dad was a painter too, but he used oils. I framed some of his nature scenes and foot paths. I love the wet-on-wet technique, when watery colors ran into each other and mingle. I see water color painting, wet-on-wet style, as like "trying to control the uncontrollable". I disregarded oil and acrylic techniques because one could paint over anything, to correcting it. I preferred the commitment a watercolorist has to make. Once it was on the paper it was on the paper. I could add second dry layer to any dry layer, but you could never eliminate that first layer with its edges. It took an element of courage the commit a brush to paper. There was also a great art in deciding how wet a brush had to be before committing to paper. There was art in choosing how hard to touch it to the paper, and how fast to move and how large to crush the brush against the paper. Some of my favorite paintings that I owned were nineteenth century Japanese water-colors of high heeled Geisha ladies holding colorful umbrellas. They strolled walking a path, surrounded by blossoming cherry trees reflecting in the pools of water on the ground. I had inherited those paintings from his father, born in 1894 and had fought in World War One for Britain. My father died when I was only six years old. The paintings tethered me to memories of someone I could barely recall. When I painted now, my mind connected to very long-lost stories.

One crazy Martian day I sketched the Doogle-doctor with a ball point pen and colorized it with water color paint. Next, I used digital graphic-editing and my electronic drawing-pad to inserted a photo of a real stethoscope into a scan of the original sketch. I then printed this combined image. Marjena saw this bizarre multicolored Doogle-doctor pinned to a board over my desk, and asked, "Rodney, is that a self-portrait?"

I gave it some thought, and replied "Maybe. I never thought of it that way."

"I want a copy, please."

I gave Marjena a printed color copy.

"Please sign it," she asked. "I want this as a souvenir of Mars."

I laughed. "That must be the first ever silly pen-doodling signed in history. Doodling isn't art".

"I like it," Replied Marjena, with a subtle smile.

As time moved by, we began pushing the Rovers to the limits of their motoring ranges, and the EVA time limits for oxygen supplies. Chris expressed concerns that we were maybe even being reckless at times. The crew also made sure that everyone got to travel on one or two far-out trips, even if the experiments on that day did not relate to the person. I also went out a few times and always took my best cameras with me. I loved my fish-eye lens camera. I soon realized that a plain photo of Mars with only Mars in the picture was close to meaningless. There were no recognizable objects to give the image perspective, size, and meaning. I tried to also always place a Marsnaut in the image, but that soon got very stale. They were just inanimate, white colored dolls who looked all the same. Through the tinted polarized visors of the head masks, you couldn't even see any human face or expressions. Also, the Marsnauts always posed the same, feet apart, and arms hanging to the side and angling slightly outwards. If I placed a rock-feature close in the foreground, it was hard to see in the image later on, whether the rock was ten feet high or only a one-inch wide pebble.

I photographed the Rover a lot. That seemed a better representation of humanity, more than a Marsnaut posing the same way every time. I tried photographing the Rover tracks in the dirt. I crafted some great views using the fisheye lens that kept everything in focus from close to far. I would hold the camera low, nearly touching the ground. I loved these low-view shots. It was very tough getting down that low, and standing up again, when in a space suit. I adapted an aluminum rod into a walking stick, with both ends were well-rounded and a heavily duct-taped over to tennis ball size, both to hold onto and avoid any sharp ends, that could damage a space suit if I stumbled. He could stand up much easier using this modified support stick.

This reminded me about a joke about duct-tape. A man walks down the coach of a train. He asks each passenger, "Are you from Alaska?". When he finally finds an Alaskan gentleman, he says, "Can I borrow your duct-tape?". By popular Legend many Alaskans who live in places were no roads go, and have to use boats or planes to get back to civilization, all use duct-tape to repair everything. In one famous photo, a man who had in a remote area had his one-seater airplane's wing chewed up by a grizzly bear. It was an old light-weight plane, and the wings were covered in coated canvas. Luckily, he had a crate of duct-tape in the remote fishing hut that he was visiting. He wrapped the entire length of ripped wing with duct-tape, and managed to fly back home.  Who would believe a story that duct tape was put to use on Mars during the highest technology and most expensive scientific project ever conceived by twenty-first century modern humanity? Only a bunch of Alaskan outdoorsmen over beer.

Another photographic trick I tried was placing ordinary objects from the Martian-surface habitat on the ground, as if they had fallen there by some strange chance. In the photo, the object would be large and in the foreground. The background was usually an endless flat desert-like terrain stretching out to the horizon. Sometimes it was a mountain or a gulley. The found object, such as a pencil, a Bic pen, or a pocket knife in the foreground, gave a sense of size, and contrast, being such an unlikely item to be lying on the ground on Mars in the photograph.

I especially enjoyed incorporating person items, like a photo of himself as a baby child fishing with my dad, and a fluffy chubby ten-centimeter woolly teddy bear. It helped me feel my family was involved in this mission somehow. My daughter had given me the teddy. I wondered if Loraine had yet noticed I had sneaked the baby teddy bear out of our bedroom. Nearly every Marsnaut had brought some secret sentimental item from Earth, that they related to.

Framingham drilled four-meter-deep holes into the ground and collected rock and soil samples, which he sealed into bags very carefully. Our time limit on the trip was ten hours. Their space suites had an eleven-hour supply of oxygen. The Rover had additional separate individual safety oxygen supplies. The Rovers, we jokingly called Teslas, ran mainly on electric batteries, that charged overnight back at the ground-habitat and also had some solar panels to supplement the batteries, but it was really a safety feature. Some argued it was over-design. The motors of the Rover could produce a speed of 2 kilometers per hour when using just solar power. When using the batteries, the Rover speed could be taken up to thirty-five kilometers per hour. We decided to only ride at full speed on formal designated safe-roads. A designated safe-road showed the tracks of a prior Rover trip. Being safe meant there were no unexpected holes, dips, pits or rocks. Dangerous ground features were marked with red flags fifty meters before they were reached. Designating roads as safe and marking the risk-features slowed down only the first few months of exploration. It was a mission goal to have one venture reach the 100 kilometers from base record. The Rovers designed only for fifty-kilometer round trips needed a design upgrade. The mission-engineers found ways to increase the Rover's battery loads and solar panel capacity even. They also hooked in RTG nuclear units. The RTG nuclear units could give a continuous output for 15 years, but its output was low. The RTG units worked best with tiny unmanned rovers that moved at a crawling pace. We believed we would achieve a 100-kilometer trip sometime as we steadily mapped out the longest safe roads and the engineers made steady Rover performance improvements.

---

One late afternoon Chris called on the habitat intercom, "Everyone to the control module please".

We raced in a flash.

Chris spoke. "We lost radio contact with Vicky and Russel on the open Rover at about 11AM today. They were going to descend into the Dragon's gorge. We worried that as they got deeper into the gorge, we would lose radio contact. They were supposed to drop a booster radio-beacon at the apex of their ride. When we lost radio contact, I checked a few things and discovered they had forgotten to take the radio booster-beacon with them. Per protocol, they were supposed to abort the mission and return if radio breakdown occurred. I have found Russel is sometimes sloppy on protocols and on check-lists. I have spoken to him a few times, but I wanted to keep him feeling positive and motivated. He is a ferocious worker as long as he feels validated, which I want him to feel all the time. I has also been working on Russel's mind and mental health, perhaps without Russel realizing why I sought him out for exercise or leisure-activities. With loss of radio contact, I had a discretionary option to launch rescue action or not. As the Rovers have been functioning so well, I decided to wait and see.

But now, with only one hour of oxygen left, I want volunteers to go rescue them. It will be challenging. We only have the pressurized Rover, with no EVA exit facility. So, I am thinking we must have one person be the driver on the inside. He or she will not be able to get out the vehicle if and when we find Vicky and Russel. So, I want two space-suited volunteers on the open back storage portion of the pressurized Rover. They will have to take auxiliary space-suit units with them, for spare oxygen which we can connect to Russel and Vicky. We may also have to tow the other Rover back."

Almost in unison everyone volunteered.

"Fine!" said Chris. "I will be the driver on the inside. Rodney, you and Valborg are the space-suited pair on the back of the Rover. Let's move".

Vahini added in. "I can send out the drone helicopter. It is faster than the Rover and can get a high-altitude view."

"Good idea, Vahini". Chris felt extremely proud of his team.

The Earth's atmosphere is much more dense than Martian atmosphere, but special designed drone-helicopters can fly on Mars. They need about ten times more rotary blade surface than matching Earth helicopters. Luckily, as the blades only meet a very reduced air resistance when rotating, small electric motors to drive the propellers can perform very well. Another advantage on Mars is that the weight to be flown is only about 38% of Earth weight. The helicopter thus flies very well and has a long range for a given amount of battery weight. Vahini would be able to stay in the Mars-surface-habitat, and fly the drone remote using its multiple cameras. We would receive immediate updates in the Rover as to where to go.

The one great advantage of running the habitat at the same sub-full Earth atmospheric pressure as the EVA suites was the lack of a need to decompress to a lower atmospheric pressure for 8-hours. Here everyone was ready to go on EVA in thirty minutes, the time it took to don a space-suit. No one needed specific instructions, the worked in its organic and maximally efficient way. Everyone jumped to a task and if they were beaten to it, they simply grabbed the next task. Everyone knew everything that needed to be done. We were dealing with a problem that they had never before rehearsed. A lost Rover beyond its oxygen supplies required a very innovative plan. We would have to work together as one organism. Chris was happy to have me as one of the outside astronauts on the rescue Rover. Valborg was a superb primary engineer. He would be the strongest force to fix the lost Rover, on the fly. Knowing the lost crew might need medical attention, I grabbed a crate of medical supplies and placed in the outside storage half of the Rover, behind the closer driver cabin. Valborg placed his kit of tools alongside my box. Chris knew we were thinking ahead and strategizing.

Vahini asked Chris innocently, just before he exited the habitat, "Why are you taking Rodney?"

Chris explained, "Rodney had shown indescribably good ability to think fast, analyze correctly in seconds, and then make and execute a perfect plan. He was the guy for the back. He is our roadside paramedic, just in case if Vicky and Russel are unwell."

We separated the pressurized Rover from the habitat. Chris was inside. He rode the Rover forward.  Valborg and I had already exited the habitat via another hatch. We hopped into the back of the Rover. The back was not primarily designed for passengers to ride more than very short distances, let alone twenty kilometers at speed on rough terrains. This could get interesting.

Chris accelerated. The Rover motors hummed sweetly. Speed was governed to a limit of thirty-five kilometers per hour. That was flying in a sense, and every now and again, the wheels bounced into the air. We took the Red road number ten because it was designated as safe for forty kilometers, with only a few slow sections. Valborg and I held onto a cross beam above the cabin. We knew that if the second Rover even had a small crash, but enough to become un-drivable, there were no more Rovers left for the Mission. It would mean the loss of five astronaut lives. Those left at the ground habitat could complete the mission and get back to Mars orbit, but it would be a big challenge with so few of the team left. Luckily a very large amount of redundancy was built into the mission-team make up. The bottom-line critical-skill was that of pilot. They only needed one pilot to get back to planet Earth. They started with five. They still had three left in the habitat. The mission's most grand goal was not to get everyone back to planet Earth. It was to get ANYONE back to planet Earth. That was the big experiment. We were a cohesive team and everyone would be working unselfishly to get us back. No-one put themselves ahead of the others. These magnificent humans were working together, even after a ship mutiny, which only four crew out of fourteen opposed. How these humans had changed and turned around into a maximally cohesive unit was impressive.

After about twenty minutes of flight, Vahini said she saw on the drone cameras Russel and Vicky driving up out of the Dragon's Gorge on the drone cameras. Their vehicle was moving, but they were very far away, and unlikely to make it back, guessing the time needed to reach the habitat with their oxygen supplies. Chris realized he had called the rescue rather late. He drove a bit faster, thus taking more risk crashing the Rover.

----------------------------------------------------------------------------------

--------------------------------------

An hour and a half later, we reached the apex of the gentle climb, before the descent into Dragon gorge. We were 40 kilometers from the base. Chris stopped and Valborg hopped off the Rover and placed the first radio re-transmitter that Russel should have placed. We had good contact with the base-habitat, but had not managed any contact with Rover number one with Russel and Vicky even at this high ground point. From here we would have to ride at a safe speed of 5 kilometers per hour. We would follow the other Rover's tracks. It was late-afternoon and the Sun was moving towards the horizon.

Five kilometers further, heading down the winding track Valborg suddenly slapped on the roof of the Rover cabin. "There they are, there they are!"

Looking ahead about a quarter kilometer further stood the open Rover. It was upright, but with no sign of dust from driving, moving, or of anyone. Getting closer, it became clear the Rover was stationary facing the return direction to the base habitat.

As we pulled up next to it, we saw the two astronauts each sitting in their seats lying low, and slumped forwards. Valborg and I stepped off the second Rover as Chris came to a stop. Valborg pulled the first astronaut so that he leaned back. It was Russel. I had a wide electronic wand in my hand that looked like a fat ruler, with a tiny computer screen and a set of operating buttons. The underside had a round metal plate. I placed it against a matching round circle printed on the chest of Russel's space suit. Valborg had never that printed circle noticed before and immediately spotted I had one on my suit too.

I said ice cold, "No heart beat for an hour. He is dead."

Valborg pulled Vicky back who had been the one driving the rover. I placed the wand against the same round circle on Vicky's space suit. Two seconds later I pronounced happily, "Heartbeat, she has got a heart-beat, oxygen saturation IS 70%. Suit carbon dioxide is 20%."

Valborg fetched the auxiliary vital support system in the back of the second Rover. He clipped the two gas-pipes to the red and blue large connectors in front of Vicky's space suit after disconnecting the auxiliary pack behind Vicky that had run dead. He crossed a power electric wire over to the life support module on the back of Vicky's space suit. Instantly, lights popped on in front of Vicky's visor.

Chris said. "Base we found them. Russel is dead. Vicky is barely alive. We are working on her".

The few astronauts left at the base were all sitting around the radio-receiver, waiting to hear news. They did not speak back, because they did not want to distract the rescuers. They just listened to the dialogues among the three rescuers.

Vicky's microphone became active as her suit regained power. She was grunting and jerking lightly as if choking.

I updated the vital sign values, "Suit $CO_2$ is down to 10%, oxygen saturation is up to 81%".

I leaned Vicky back more, trying to get her head to fall backwards. A perfect suit gas $CO_2$ would be zero or one or two percent. I shook her by the shoulders as violently as I could, while wearing my own heavy space suit, with its large power and life support unit on the back. Wearing a space suit in zero gravity is one thing. Wearing it in the presence of gravity, even only one third of that on planet Earth, was burdensome. Added to that, everyone was physically under-conditioned compared to what they had been before the Cape Canaveral launch.

Slowly, Vicky's oxygen saturation climbed until it reached 90%. I had no means to measure Vicky's blood carbon dioxide. I knew that the person, invented a device that could be strapped onto a finger, just like a pulse oximeter, and that gave 100% accurate real time measure of arterial CO2 concentrations would win the Nobel Prize for medicine. I guessed her arterial CO2 was about 70 mmHg. 35 mmHg was normal in arterial blood. An acute high arterial CO2 concentration of 70 mmHg is enough to sedate some nearly to anesthesia levels. At an acute blood CO2 of 60 mmHg depressed the heart dropping the blood pressure by half. As things improved Vicky groaned a bit louder, and when I shook her, she opened her eyes briefly but without focusing on anything. If we had only reached Vicky 5minutes later she would likely have been dead and unsavable.

Chris said, "I am going to pull our Rover around. Will you guys hook up the towing hitch please?"

We carried Russel's body to the open back of the pressurized Rover. Valborg climbed on the back of the Rover too. I took the seat next to Vicky in the fully open unpressurized Rover towed behind. I wanted to tend to her. We started the return journey. Chris drove more slowly this time to reduce the big bumps, and the return took four hours.

Once we had docked the pressurized Rover, we entered the EVA chambers. Next, we helped Vicky to the sick bay where we all at looked at each other. Vicky responded to simple verbal inputs with a nod or a grunt. We could figure out yes and no answers from her, to simple clear questions.

I had a private chat to Chis. I suggested that we store Russel's body frozen and plan to take it back to Earth. I also wanted to take the bowels out and store them separate. Chris did not know exactly what I had in mind, but responded yes.

By the next evening, the open Rover had been examined by engineer guys, and Vicky had recovered enough to tell the whole story.

---

The fact Russel and Vicky omitted to take the booster beacon radios with had been a simple oversight. Vicky had overslept, and they had rushed. At the bottom of the Dragon gorge they also collected all their planned drilling rock and soil samples. Returning up the Gorge their vehicle started overheating and a battery pack exploded. The climb back was 5 kilometers long and steeper than anything they had seen yet on this trip. They were one kilometer from the top of the Ridge when the Rover broke down. They still had solar panel power and also the IGB unit power; however, that only enough to move them at a half kilometer per hour going uphill. They were hoping that once they reached the ridge summit and re-established radio-communications they would be able to call for help.

Then their suit oxygen started to run out. Russel's ran out first. They hooked up to their spare auxiliary life support. Vicky was driving, and her oxygen ran out next. Russel hooked Vicky into the single life-support system. Every 5 minutes Russel hooked himself back for 30 seconds to blast fresh gases through the inside of his suit, and then hooked up Vicky again. This worked for another hour as they creeped up the hill. Russel got too weak to hook himself up and refresh his gasses again. He died, sacrificing his life to let Vicky hang on the longest. The auxiliary system oxygen was near finished and the $CO_2$ washer was long saturated and no longer removing the $CO_2$ from the system when we found Vicky. She nearly died.

Valborg became uneasy and relayed to us that he had been part of the NASA team coordinating with NASA design ground engineers for the design of the human occupant Rovers. They had concerns that their attempts to re-design for better for performance put the lithium battery in jeopardy. Heating problems happened under strain, like climbing hills fast. The batteries were one of few items source fully from outside of NASA internal engineering and construction resources.

There was a suggestion to make layered batteries with a different battery type in between lithium battery layers, which would use the discharged heat to benefit. The second battery type when heated generated electricity from heat, as would be released by the lithium batteries. That secondary generated electricity could be stored and then released periodically, when resting the lithium batteries to cool. The concept was brilliant. It did need more development and refinement though. It would have been a hyper-efficient battery system, but there was nothing commercially available yet.

The outside company hoped to market the Rover's specific lithium battery system for commercial citizen road vehicle use after the Mars mission, claiming the Mars usage proved their battery. NASA leaders also strongly resisted a late change in the Martian manned Rover power systems and they proposed a computer override system "safety system" rather, that would cut lithium battery power if the lithium batteries reached a safety temperature limit. The engineers then gave the driver the ability to bypass the safety-system if they released and fully depressed the foot control twice in a row. Vicky said that had happened riding up the ridge. Russell kept bypassing the power cut back, to keep their speed up as he was worried that they might not have enough oxygen for the whole trip if they rode too slowly. At one point the batteries, due to Russel's persistent bypassing the safety feature, overheated and exploded.

Russel didn't factor in that they used low energy descending into the gorge, but consumed massive battery energy climb out of the gorge. With the batteries were over-heating and the safety mechanism kept cutting their speed to half Russell realized they would run of oxygen before reaching the habitat. That was why he persisted in bypassing the safety power cut. He also could not radio for help, like extra oxygen supplies be brought to them. He panicked.

Valborg continued. "Our friends are not to blame for the debacle. It is tragic summation of so many small, some trivial factors. I most want to blame the senior NASA management who gave in to the Rover battery supplier's pressures. It is the Boeing Max story again that occurred far back in the pre-twenty-twenties. Two airplanes crashed in late 2018 and early 2019. Sales targets down the end of the line overruled the influence of good Boeing engineers working at lower ranks, than financial managers. The minimum the NASA design engineers should have done, was not allow that overheating cutback-system to be overrun by the driver, and the Rovers should not have been rated so high for maximum travel distances. We astronauts should also have been better trained in understand the phenomenon of overheating lithium batteries."

I surmised, "I think this is all one amazing story. We will all die one day, as natural human beings. Sometimes, we die prematurely because we are frail humans. Yet sometimes we survive, because we dig into our two biggest human features. We combine our intelligences and share like no other creatures in the cosmos. We are standing on the surface of Mars surviving and dying, because we are human. Space travel is brutally unforgiving of errors".

Chris said. "We will honor Russel for giving his life to save Vicky. We will get through the challenges of the rest of this mission. We will be Lions to the Last."

# CHAPTER 16.

## Preparing to return, and saving the cat. (week 82)

As the weeks went by the astronauts stopped speaking about Russel. It was not that everyone had forgotten Russel who died after running out of oxygen during an EVA, or even forgotten how Alan who floated off into eternity when his space-suit tether got cut. They just had nothing to say that they all had not already said so many times. They recalled the best of the two men. They recalled the quirks and shortcomings of the two men. When they recalled their short comings, it was not meant critically. It was discussed in a process of recognizing their own shortcomings and that maybe they deserved to have died in their dead men's places. This was seen a lot amongst men who survived the horrors of trench warfare. Death was so arbitrary, and when they could not figure why someone else did die and why oneself did not, they developed what became known as survivor's guilt. As much part on the psychological reasons for these discussions going silent, was that they all recognized it could have been any of them who had died instead, and more so they realized that any of them could still die.

When they reached that final point of thinking, they all started to recover and find smiles and humor again. They had all thought through dying on a Mars mission before they even applied for a Marsnaut position. They all were in fact not afraid to die. Death was not a bad thing, for in many ways, death can be a release from the ghosts that nagged them in daily life. In other ways all these Marsnauts were strong. None wanted take their own lives. They were all determined the fight like lions to the last. That phrase was branded deep into their flesh, by this time.

Aresha cried. Everyone close by to the baby and whose hands were free, ran across to her home-made crib. She was thriving on her mother's breast milk. Vahini almost never changed a diaper. Someone always wanted to do it. One Marsnaut was getting to do it much more than the others. It was Framingham Milkowski one of the chief pilots, and a backup engineer too. He was Mr. Quiet, but also a strong character if one dug into his mind a bit with conversations. He liked the baby so much that if some folks had already not loosened the diaper, they would offer the diaper-change opportunity to Fram if he also arrived and stood close by. Fram was athletic and his arms showed it. Maybe he had the tightest arm sleeves on the mission because of having chunky biceps. Everyone else's legs on the mission had become very thin. It was common therefor to refer to astronaut's legs as chicken legs, meaning they were long and thin. Fram did not have chicken legs. Fram just found an hour of time a day extra that no-one else could find, and really worked his legs as hard as he could on whatever exercise device was available. His daily exercise total was three hours per day. Chris had told me that all Fram's research projects were up to date, or completed and he even at times ran two projects side by side. He, in his extreme diligence was doing some of the projects of the dead astronauts. So, seeing Fram be all soft and gentle with the baby, was a contradiction in images. His first image was being a physically iron hard man, whose work ethic was that of an unemotional automaton that never slacks off. He was the best Marsnaut to get the baby asleep after her breast feeding and diaper change. His hummed soft melodies with a soothing voice, that balanced against his syncopated-beat rocking-rhythm and slow tapping foot. It was lethal if one sat close by leaned back in the chair and relaxed. Lethal, meant humorously, that Fram's baby sleep method put adults to sleep too, if they sat close by and leaned back and closed their eyes.

Aresha was old enough to sit on her own, by now. She just grinned all the time and at anyone, but none more than she did for Fram.

I studied these baby dynamics. He always jokingly said I was a student of life. Everyone on board the ship would have labeled Framingham Milkowski a gentleman. I was thinking, that maybe the foremost feature of being a gentleman, was to be gentle. If that was true, then Fram was definitely a gentleman. No-one saw Fram's gentleness before Vahini's baby was born. The baby brought a special side out of Fram.

I was also studying Vahini and her reactions towards Fram. I, based upon my general observations, once thought Vahini could be lesbian. When I first met the other crew in training in the four weeks before the spaceship launch, I noticed that Vahini, always were Levi jeans with a loose boyish cut, and a button up plain shirt. Her hair was also short and boyish in style. She never wore make-up. Of course, that style does not mean a girl is a lesbian, although some lesbian girls might like that style. My deepest instincts felt a bit different. I thought that were I a free and unattached male of younger age I might try to find the courage to ask Vahini out for coffee. I could not explain this disagreement between what my eyes saw and my subtle instincts. This question did not burn long in my mind. It was all just a passing thought, at that time. I was now sitting in a human habitat dome on the planet Mars, and studying a beautiful baby and the people around the baby.

A month later Vahini announced to everyone at one evenings conference, that she and Fram were engaged. Fram sat and smiled and blushed. Hunky masculine Fram blushed. Vahini did the talking. Fram stood next to Vahini and put his arm around her. It was almost as if the couple were needing the approval of everyone. Everyone jumped up and hugged Vahini and some hugged Fram too or alternatively shook his hand. Girls like it when guys hug, but not all guys can hug. Certainly, everyone seemed very happy for the couple.

What a story! Can one imagine in ten-years' time some persons saying to Vahini and Fram at a social party asking, "So tell us where you two met each other?" Imagine the expression on the faces when the answer came back, "Mars"

I smiled inwards to myself. He thought "I *knew* she was a regular girl". Vahini really opened up after she became engaged. She shared the story that she had been violated as a child, and it scared her off men entirely. She intentionally cultivated the image that she believed would fall most far from the descriptor of being sexy looking to men.  It was a defense mechanism. The circumstances under which she has become pregnant was a disaster in her life beyond her worst nightmare. By bizarre design of destiny, that baby was her blessing. It led Fram to revel in his natural gentleness. It led Vahini to look upon one male as being less than a beast. The baby Aresha in a strange way, introduced Vahini and Fram to each other. They were the best couple match imaginable for each other.

I thought how sometimes you see a newly engaged or newly-wed couple and you take a bet with a friend that the marriage won't last ten years. Then one meets a couple like Vahini and Fram and you sense they such a such deep love for each and such deep commitment to each other and such respect for each other, that you see a hundred-year marriage before your eyes. I thought back to my own wife waiting for me on Earth. My instincts were that we had our own hundred-year marriage in our own dorky style. I let out a laugh to myself, so happy.

---

Skabenga the cat, loved this Mars habitat. She could walk normal. The baby had stolen a lot of attention away from Skabenga. However, Skabenga was happy enough that folks still gave her a scratch behind the ears if she rubbed up against their legs. I looked at her now and again and felt sad that she would be euthanized in an experiment once they were back to a gravity free environment. As Houston ground control was utterly out of their lives, now that there was no radio contact, that I already was working the idea through my head to tell Houston to go away. I guess that attitude made me a rebel. I was just not going to sacrifice Skabenga. I felt that was my privilege to decide, under the circumstances. The only real problem was we had no contact with NASA mission control based in Houston. Maybe that was not a problem. It is strange in life how in a differing perspective something bad, can be something good. I would argue that Skabenga had become a therapy cat for the crew. I did not yet know what was going to happen before the week was done.

In the afternoon of the next day Babee was working on her project. She was analyzing rock samples, and treating them with chemicals and studying them under microscope with ultraviolet lighting. She was actually seeking evidence of gold metal being present and was using an unusual technique. She was deeply concentrating on her microscope and she reached out with her hand to grab her plastic bag of reconstituted orange juice, to suck some up via the straw. She inadvertently picked up a container of liquid chlorine squeezed the bag because she was not looking and placed her mouth over the straw like spout. She got a mouth full of chlorine. The potent chemical smell slammed her like a sledge hammer. It burned and hurt terribly she jumped up and inhaled in order to yell. The sounds she made were actually nearly nothing as she went into severe laryngospasm. Camilla was working at a table next to her. She looked at Babee in surprise. Babee's eyes were wide, she was silent. Then slowly her legs buckled and she fell to the ground, a half minute later she started with little coughs, as the laryngospasm broke. The coughs got bigger and bigger. She lay on her back coughing and coughing. Camilla had screamed for me. I was at Babee's side in a flash. Looking at the things on Babee's desk and smelling the chlorine smell on her we swiftly realized she had drunk liquid chlorine, and choked on it.

Babee's arterial blood oxygen saturation would not rise above 80% despite her getting a 100% pure oxygen therapy via a face-mask. Listening with my stethoscope, I heard crackles in all of her lungs front and back, left and right. I was sure she had aspirated a lot of the liquid chlorine. I predicted this was going to rapidly deteriorate into a case of severe ARDS (Acute Respiratory Distress Syndrome). I also thought that even if she was on Planet-Earth in the best private hospital intensive care unit in a top 1st world country she would likely still die. My options were to do absolutely nothing and save sparse resources for the other Marsnauts. It would a triage decision. Maybe I could pretend to do something modest, save precious medical supplies quietly, so it did not upset the other Marsnauts who would not understand triage. Maybe I could pull out all stops and do everything I could think of.

Triage is a technique of selecting patients for medical care when there are more critically injured patients than what the health care resources can cope with. Triage is done on the military battle field. Triage is done in a hospital when 20 critical patients all arrive at once. Generally, they choose the young over the old. Females are chosen as potential future mothers, over males. Also, the most critically injured are left to die because they consume too much time or too many healthcare-providers. They consume drugs and other resources that might become unavailable to other victims who would more likely have benefited from them. It is simply the rationing of healthcare. It is a sinking ship saving woman and children first. It is trying to save those who can still serve the community, over those who only depend on the community. Being a triage officer requires a resilience, and maybe even heartlessness. The goal is to rather save a few lives than to end up saving no lives. This broad philosophical concept of triage even applies to normal non-emergency health care. If you correctly look at health insurance, nearly all of one person's expensive healthcare is paid for by a hundred other healthy persons monthly insurance premiums that went unused. To claim maximum possible healthcare for all individuals is to impose the cost of that onto your neighbors. For this reason, esthetic surgery is not covered by insurance for 85-year old men, as liver transplants won't be paid for, for an eighty-five-year lady. I looked at Babee certain she was going to die, without getting serious big medical care. She was critically ill.

The easiest decision is always to treat a patient maximally. The hardest decision is to not treat a patient, in some special circumstance. Weak character doctors just prescribe and treat everyone maximally and also do endless costly tests. The ends with immense wastage, and massive costs out of proportion to the benefits the population pays for.

The decision to treat Babee was mine alone, and I wished to treat her. If success was feasible on the Martian planet, I would find that success.

I placed an IV (intravenous) cannula into Babee's vein on her fore-arm, and set a fluid pump running. Next, I passed a tube through her nose and down into her stomach to be able to feed her. She barely responded and offered no resistance to me doing that very uncomfortable procedure. I saw her throat was very red, but not swollen. That was encouraging. I knew chlorine is a highly potent chemical and can nearly instantly forms acid on contact with water.

Babee's lungs were the biggest challenge to treat. I injected antibiotics and large doses of corticosteroids to limit lung inflammation. We never set up the medical side of the space mission to be an intensive care unit. If I ever had to operate someone and stop their breathing, the plan was for one astronaut to ventilate them manually for the duration of the surgery. We had no human ventilator with us. To sustain Babee with manual ventilation for maybe ten days and more, seemed like a real mission impossible. My brain was churning.

He did have an automated ventilator for the cat. That was to be his major medical experiment for the mission. I unpacked the ventilator out of a small box. It was very basic. I looked at the setting options. There was no way this machine could provide a breath large enough for 70 kg human as opposed to the 5 kg cat it was designed for. His mind whirled around as thoughts came and went.

The problem with giving an adult human a cat-size breath of only 30 to 100 milliliters as opposed to human breath of 500 to 800 milliliters was that so little gas would be breathed out, it would not clear the end of the airway piping. It would simply be pushed back again as the same stale gas, with the next incoming breath. The old stale air just gets shuffled back and forth with no fresh gas reaches the deep lung tissues where gas exchange takes place, if the breath size is too small. For fresh gasses to reach the depths of the lungs, the separation point of where the fresh gas entering the system via one pipe, and the stale gasses exited the system via another has to be close enough to the patient's deep lung tissues to effectively remove old stage gas. That airway space between the deep lung tissues and the in and out gas mixing point is called the lung dead space. The breath size must exceed the lung dead space size by a lot to be well effective. Best efficient gas exchange happens with small dead spaces and big breaths. In a normal person the gas separation point is at the mouth and nose. That gas separation point determines the dead space size.

My brain was flying through ideas now. His big problem was he could only ventilate Babee with cat-size breaths. I therefore had to reduce the as much as possible to help those tiny breaths achieve any effect. How could he reduce the dead space more? He remembered once reading about an airway tube design called the ZEDS tube, which stood for Zero Dead Space. The ZEDS tube was a double-channel, endotracheal tube, or a one could say lung breathing tube. In gas went via one channel and out gas went out via the other channel. This shifted the start of the patient's airway dead space to the tip of the lung breathing tube. The ZEDS tube thus eliminated most of the dead space and made using small breaths possible while retaining good gas exchange. I instantly realized I could replicate a ZEDS tube simply two slightly small tubes side by side down into Babee's lungs. He jumped to the task. I opened Babee's mouth with a laryngoscope. She did not resist at all. I inserted two slightly smaller than standard size tubes through her larynx deep down her big airway pipe called a trachea. They were number 5.5 size tubes. The tubes in the larynx aligned easiest one behind the other within the larynx. He softly inflated the sealing cuffs. I switched on the ventilator to its maximum breath size of 100 milliliters, and set the breaths at a very fast rate of eighty breaths per minute to offset the tiny breath volumes. I almost saw no movement in Babee's chest because the cat-size breaths were so small. Babee's saturations slowly climbed from 80% to 85%. At the least, that was in a positive direction. He also set the Positive End Expiratory Pressure high on the ventilator.

Now came a miracle coincidence. I had been planning on doing something called partial fluid ventilation on the cat. Single months before this flight, my brilliant anesthesia research friend Dave Kalia in a corridor conversation told me about a technique under research for treating ARDS. We once had adjacent offices when we both shared an employer. We love to talk intellectual things when we met in the corridors, on any day. David flooded the lungs of a research animal with perfluorocarbon liquid. That perfluorocarbon liquid was a very good carrier of oxygen into the lungs and remover of carbon dioxide ($CO_2$) from the lungs. Research suggested this fluid ventilation could be very good for treating ARDS, for two reasons. Firstly, it delivered life-saving oxygen very effectively as well as removed the waste $CO_2$. Secondly, the fluids had a soothing effect on the damaged lung tissues and helped them heal faster. I convinced the NASA science directors of the merits of studying this. They wanted to see how fluid ventilation worked in zero gravity conditions. On Earth gravity tends to cause air from lung ventilation to go to the uppermost long parts preferentially and relatively little to the dependent parts of the lungs. There was therefore much curiosity how perfluorocarbon fluid distributed in the lungs in the absence of gravity. The cat was going to be the research subject, and we going to preserve the lungs in chemicals after the study, for analysis back on the Earth.

I hooked up the extra attachment needed, and flooded Babee's lungs with perfluorocarbon fluid. Her saturations improved to 90% within ten minutes. I would have loved to have had an X-ray of her lung, but we had no X-ray machine. He listened to the lungs with his stethoscope and only heard very soft bubbling. I had no idea what would sound good or bad with fluid ventilation, I just had to trust things were good. I would have loved to have measured Babee's blood carbon dioxide levels but had no device to do that. I had to trust my best guess settings on the ventilator were broadly compatible with survival.

The next two weeks were very exhausting for me. I had to sleep in 2-hour sessions, at the longest as I really had to be attending to Babee all day, every day. I moved her around to prevent bedsores. I fed her via the stomach tube with reconstituted Soylent complete food mix. The food was meant to be drunk as full meal substitute, so it was perfect for tube feeding. It was good fortune, that we had a good supply of Soylent on the space-trip. When Babee's blood oxygen saturations reached 93% after a week she became restless, so I had to inject her sedation and relaxing medicines as well as her antibiotics.  I had no idea really how to handle the next steps or for how long to ventilate Babee. This was like flying an airplane by the seats of one's pants. I just made a guess that about 2 weeks would be good. By then, her saturations were 100%. I stopped the sedation and relaxing drugs. The next day Babee got very restless and actually pulled out her throat tubes with one hand. I thought "So be it", and flipped her onto her side slightly face down. She coughed and coughed and made a mess as the perfluorocarbon fluid came out of her lungs. She finally stopped coughing and lay peacefully on her side. I placed an oxygen tube to her nostrils. She had pulled out her feeding tube. Later I tried feeding her teaspoons of liquid food. She accepted it and got it down. Her saturations stayed 100%. Babee recovered with amazing speed over the next three days. She was at first confused and delirious. On the morning of the fourth-day after the ventilation was stopped and the tubes pulled out, Babee looked at Chris and asked what had happened.  He explained everything as best he could. In later days I explained in more detail. Babee had no memory of anything, although she had some partial confused recall of the four days from after she had pulled out her own throat tubes.

The Sphynx cat seemed to like Babee and wanted to sleep with her all the time. Babee needed a lot of strengthening exercise and the entire crew jumped to the task to help. The crew were relentless, and nearly cruel getting Babee moving nearly all day. Each day's physical levels for the exercises increased. Ten days after Babee became clear in her head, Chris invited her back to her roles in the mission. They now had a very busy schedule preparing for the ascent from Mars and for the return to Earth.

I was joyful about much. My joys included the fact that I could no longer do the planned experiments on the cat, as I had used up the supplies needed, on Babee. So Skabenga was going back to Earth. He was going to ask NASA to let me keep Skabenga as his pet, until Babee asked me if she could rather have Skabenga. Skabenga being on the flight, with cat lung research materials, had saved Babee's life.

The medical treatment of Babee and the perfect outcome, was in itself a very interesting medical report that could substitute for the missed cat experiment.

Isn't all of life one endless series of serendipity? Bad things befall you unexpectedly. Good things befall you unexpectedly. Then often those surprise events, have a strange series of connections making you be the one on the event. The serendipitous event that additionally made the entire crew happy, was that Skabenga, the unofficial mission mascot, was not going to be researched upon and euthanized anymore, because Babee, in her illness, had used up the research equipment. Skabenga was going home.

---

All the residual fuel in the two rockets staying behind on Mars, was transported and reloaded onto the ascent rocket. All leftover medical and nutritional supplies were loaded onto the ascent rocket. We Marsnauts took everything from all the experiments they had done. They also had two tons of Martian deep rock and soil samples. What was staying on Mars would be usable, by a future mission, if there ever was one.

Launch day hour and minute was set and under control of the onboard computers. There had never been one second of communication with the orbiting ship. If the launch was meticulous, and everything went as pre-calculated they would be in visual sight of the orbiting ship after one and a half orbits of Mars. Then we would dock and reassemble, and shuffle the various modules, to form our final return-to-Earth spaceship. They would leave the engine section of the orbiter behind to eventually crash down onto Martian soil, once its orbit decayed enough for high altitude gases to drag it down.

If we failed to find the space orbiter and the other two astronauts who stayed behind, it would be a monumental crisis. This crew had become very toughened. They did not dwell on the potential problem of failing to find the orbiter ship. They fully recognized the significance of that event. They just deferred chewing on problems until they became reality, and then dealt with it. Of course, if one can pre-act to divert or avoid a problem, one does. In life the only reality is today. Yesterday is a meaningless memory, and tomorrow is but a dream. Only today and this moment means anything, and is the only reality. That is why some philosophers have said; "Live for the moment."

I remembered his beloved wife's favorite thing when she was having a melt-down after a bad day at the office, was for me to walk up to her with a glass of French Rose wine for her, and say, "Here Honey! Have a glass of wine." I wondered what was it that settled her so well then. Was it the alcoholic-beverage? Or, was it the fact I was there with a smiling face and projecting my own relaxed aura onto her? She would possibly ever know; how therapeutic it actually was for me being there for her. I missed her a lot, on these last days on Mars.

---

Cecil, the computer voice spoke. "Final countdown ten seconds to ascent from Mars. Ten seconds, nine seconds, eight seconds, seven seconds, six seconds, five seconds, four seconds, three seconds, two seconds, one second, ignition, we have lift off. Goodbye Mr. Mars"

"Huh?" echoed everyone over their space-suit microphones. "Goodbye Mr. Mars?"

Babee spoke. "I persuaded Valborg to write that into the program. I am done with Mars. Skabenga and I just want to go home"

"Good one Cecil" spoke someone.

"Your welcome", I replied pretending to be Cecil, and imitating Cecil's computer Iowa-accent voice.

The space-ship's acceleration increased as the load to be lifted diminished by the weight of the fuel burned. Within an hour they were in Martian orbit. The computer managed flight should have placed them within half a mile behind the Mars-orbiter ship that had been up there on its own for an entire year. There was still no radio contact. Chris peered ahead out the rocket ship windows and saw nothing. The ascent rocket was still making small little thrust engine firings like it was adjusting our speed and altitude for some purpose. Those final adjustments would be based on a radar sensing of the other module to be joined to. Docking pilot role had been given to Judessa Weeks, or Dessie as they called her.

She said, "I have radar visual of something about 100 miles away, but it's not radio-talking to us. We have no identity-verification. Maybe the other crew have missed their docking process activation dead-line. They need to flip the switch".

Chris said, "Dessie us to 300 meters from that object."

"I hope everyone on board the orbiter is OK", said Marjena.

Chris spoke. "It is too dangerous to get too close without active flying, from their side. It has to be computer automatic or manual, but not nothing. Dessie when we hit 300 meters range switch to manual and do nothing. I think we must send an EVA (Extra-Vehicular Activity) person over to investigate the other ship."

Although they were now back in a ship that functioned at full atmospheric pressure, for less than two hours Captain Chris Bolder felt they still need to have at least a partial decompression routine. Valborg, will you go please. You are a second-tier engineer.

"Yes sir" said Valborg. As Valborg was already in his space suit for the launch, the preparations to do an EVA were mostly done. He loosened his seat straps and moved himself back down the ship to the EVA exit hatch in the next module downwards.

"Take a whiteboard and pen with you", added Chris.

A second Marsnaut accompanied him just to help with everything until Valborg was in the exit chamber and the exit hatch was closed.

It wasn't long before Valborg was in free space-walk mode with backpack mounted flight system. He just had to operate the joystick on the arm piece in front of him and he was jetting along towards the other spaceship. It took ten minutes to cross the distance. He moved around the orbiter-ship looking through the windows. He finally saw one of the two orbiting Marsnauts sleeping in his pod. Valborg banged on the window with his hand. He had to do it about ten times before Tyrone lifted his head. Tyrone was disorientated and took a few moments to realize the soft banging noise he heard came from a window. He drifted closer to look, after he got out of his sleeping bag. His paraplegic legs had shrunken back into more squatting type of natural position, since Valborg had last seen him a year ago. Tyrone seemed utterly startled to see a creature outside the spaceship window. He probably could not recognize who it was through the shaded poloid visor of the space-walk suit headpiece.

Valborg held up the white board with message.

"Switch on the docking system. Activate auto-pilot into A mode after 30 minutes."   Valborg pointed to the white board and then gave a thumbs up sign. Valborg was saying "Tyrone have you got it? Do you get the message? Do you understand?" He doubted Tyrone could hear him, but he hoped Tyrone got that exact message through the hand gestures.

Tyrone grinned and gave a double thumbs up sign. Valborg turned and jetted back to the ascent ship. As soon as he was out of the exit chamber and the air pressures equalized, he doffed his space suit. Everyone had done the same with their space-suits that they had worn during the launch off of Mars.

The ship in A-mode for docking would remain stationary and only adjust its alignment to have the docking hatch pointed laser-beam straight to the B-ship. Also, the A-mode ship would do the rotating actions to make that alignment component was perfect. The B-mode ship which was the ascent ship was the one that did the jet firing to approach. The Marsnauts knew that every time they hear a little mini roar, the ship would move and they themselves would not be moved as they floated. This meant they would suddenly drift a bit in some direction within the cabin, opposite to the direction that the ship had moved it. Most of them just got into their sleeping bags to avoid having to continuously hold on with hand to something. The docking took about an hour before the two ships were locked together. Then followed an hour of equalizing the gas pressure in the passage between the ships and verifying no leaks existed.

Soon both crews united and they caught up on all the news.

The orbiter guys had just settled into a sloppy life routine during the year they orbited Mars. They did complete their research projects. They apologized that they slept through the docking time that they should have awakened early for. They both knew the date it was to happen and that they had to flip a switch or two on that night. They had watched movies until late and had not set their wake-up alarms.

I said in an unemotional tone. "I guess the hardest part to take out of a human, is the human element. It doesn't make mistakes acceptable though. You have to spend your life checking to avoid the big mistakes." I had a lot of views on errors. Pilots make errors. The flying profession had done lot of studies into the factors contributing to human errors. Pilots then developed routines to avoid errors. That is why pilots are so famous for having checklists, with a second person to verify each item. Anesthesia professionals were also starting to embrace some aspects of pilot practices to avoid making drug errors in anesthesia practice. This was a topic I had lectured about for his entire academic career, and felt passionate about.

It transpired that, Tyrone and Larry did not set their wake-up alarms by accident, and nearly killed off the entire Mars mission's survival.

The orbit crew were shocked to hear of Russel's death. They were amazed that Babee had a medical crisis and survived on a cat-ventilator using techniques still in experimental phases. They thought that Vahini and Valborg getting engaged was a love story to be told over and over. The orbiter-Marsnauts told Valborg that they were going to be guests at the wedding whether they received invitations by post or not. Everyone laughed and Vahini assured them that the entire ship crew were going to be sitting at the main table with the bride and bridegroom, when the wedding finally happened.

The next space mission step was to reassemble the various modules into the return ship. Some fuel had to transferred. Just the orbiter's thrust engine module and one empty fuel tanker module would be discarded and left in space. All that rearranging took 24 hours. For the blast-off to escape Martian orbit and set out on their Earth return journey. That is call a Trans-Earth Injection (TEI) launch. We all had to be strapped in, but Space suits were not required. The cat and the baby however each had their own pressurized cot-container designed for cats.

Cecil the computer voice spoke. "Ten seconds to Mars-orbit escape blast-off. Ten seconds, nine seconds, eight seconds, seven seconds, six seconds, five seconds, four seconds, three seconds, two seconds, one second, ignite thrust engines"

"Go Cecil", said someone.

The rocket thrust made their arms feel heavy and soon these battle-weary Marsnauts could barely raise their arms off the arm rests of their reclined seats, in the crew capsule, that they were strapped into. Nothing phased these space-travelers any more. Most of them fell asleep.

Ares-1 was now on solar orbit at a speed and in a direction that would pull the spaceship closer to the orbit of planet-Earth. It would take Ares-1 nine months of flight to get as close as Earth's orbital plane around the Sun. The Mars escape launch was also timed so that when Ares1 reached Earth solar orbit level nine months later, it would arrive at that very point when the Earth arrived there, while on its own solar orbit. In fact, the spaceship would be so close to Earth that Earth's gravity would capture the spaceship and pull it into an orbit around the Earth. This was all worked out by computers, plotted. timed and controlled. About four times during the flight the spaceship would set itself up automatically to do some short blasts and thrusts to make minor corrections for any miscalculations. Some of the crew had developed the flight inter-planetary navigational programs for NASA and could easily work out flight adjustments of something odd happened or went wrong.

Ares-1 accelerated and drifted out of Martian orbit and the grip of the red planets gravitational hand. All of us space-travelers were convinced that we were to be the last life forms to ever visit that red dusty dry planet. We all felt that all the money that it cost to get us there could be vastly better invested in helping starving children in Africa. We strongly believed that the planet Earth was the natural beautiful and wonderful home of the human species. For Mars to become an alternative home for humans, Earth would have to first decay to being a worse hell to live in, that what Mars was. Earth only had one bad thing on it. Bad people. The question that then arose, is what do you do about the bad people on Earth. The Marsnauts would broadly agree on one answer. You first make *yourself,* as decent a human as best you can. The second thing to do is you treat the bad people as best you can. Pull them into the tent to share the food and wine on the table. The Ares-1 crew learned that. Some people re-phrase that wisdom as "Kill them with kindness".

## Chapter 17

## The dust storm, and fighting boredom. (week 70)

The routine of daily research became boring. A much as a crisis destroyed everyone souls for that moment of panic, as the Marsnauts found safe smooth routine times drove them to boredom. When they lived in fear for their lives, they came closer together. Boredom had potential to let depression and grumpiness appear.

The outside projects ram smoothly and producing results. We collected the deep soils and rock samples for investigations on Earth. The bacterial and chemical research on waste materials were productive. Plant growing in the second pressurized habitat flourished. Even the dead astronauts' projects were being done by others who made the time. No conflict existed between the crew.

The garden produced great red romaine leaves that the crew adored eating. It dramatically increased their stool production. Spaceship stored food was designed to produce minimal stools, which everyone liked a lot. After we started to notice once in three days became twice in day rectal-habits we thought twice before savoring crispy fresh green-leaf vegetables. The precious commodity of water dictated our lives. We could not shower twice daily or have deep soaking hot baths daily. Hygiene was limited to a moist-cloth wipe-down one per day. In the end we all agreed we would keep eating the fresh romaine lettuce. Also, the fresh potatoes tasted delicious. The only cooking option was to microwave. The most popular recipe was cooked potatoes, sliced, and mixed with mayonnaise and dried onion flakes. This poor man's potato-salad was the big treat of the day. One thing about being an astronaut was how a tiny-thing like these fresh food items could be such a massive treat.

Then the dust storm arrived. The dust was not overwhelming from up close up. We never saw much dust inside the habitat, due to its relative sparseness in the surrounding air. The biggest consequence of the dust storm, was that it reached twenty kilometers high in the sky, and how that cut sunlight intensity very much.   A typical Martian dust storm affects a small area for only two days, and happens twice a year. The horror storm envelops the entire planer for up to two months, occurring once every 10 years. They are unpredictable. In the past surface unmanned Mars rovers fully lost solar power, and after their batteries ran down, the unmanned Rover died becoming unresuscitatable.

When the dust storm arrived, it was a first-time experience for the Marsnauts. After four days we started to worry it could last a few months. Our battery supply of electric power would not last that long. Chris spoke at the evening conference.

"Everybody, we are going to immediately commence energy savings strategies. We have no way of knowing whether the dust storm will clear up tomorrow, or last maybe three months. So, I have developed a three-step energy savings protocol. We will stop all Rover trips related to the outside experiments. There can also be no EVA strolls for leisure or Rover rides for leisure. I have listed equipment in one of three tiers. We will cease use of all tier three equipment today. Each week longer that this dust storm lasts, we will cut use of another tier of equipment. The solar panels are presently producing power at about 10% of their maximum, capacity.  Our isotope generators, the Plutonium RTGs (Radio-isotope Thermo-Generators) will be unhooked from the Rovers and plugged into the habitat system, for the little extra help they will give."

RTGs are capable of powering low energy consuming satellites or slow creeping instrument surface-rovers for ten to twenty years, but their technology just cannot supply enough power on their own for manned habitats.

No one had any questions.

"One last thing please," added in Chris. "I want you to all wear your astronaut space suit hoods during the day and even when you are sleeping please. We need the physiology results for research".

No one questioned that, but it was a minor irritation. In fact, we had all been expecting to be asked to wear these hoods for the entire 3-year flight, so we had no complaints that this was starting a year and a half into the trip. Maybe Chris has had overlooked reminding us on this, for no special reason.

---

I wanted to work on my computer before going to sleep. Swiping my thumb-first finger webspace across my computer sensor opened the computer. I did not usually do this, as I preferred using my passwords, being old fashioned as I am. If I pinched the skin in the flesh web-space I could find the microchip. It was about the size of a grain of rice. Everyone had one on their right hand. It was like a chip-credit card. It opened computers, any secured electronic device, even safes, if you were cleared to be accessing the safe. These microchips had many functions like measuring our blood oxygen and contained a data base of our medical history and drug allergies. NASA made it mandatory to be microchipped, and in theory we all gave a signed consent. It was hinted refusal could cause exclusion from the mission. I felt bullied into accepting the implanted chips. The discomfort after insertion lasted two days.

The chip in his hand when it was inserted via an injection type of device. Inserting the ten scalp microchips hurt a lot more, because scalp skin is thick and firm. The space-surgeons had used local anesthetic injections first, before inserting the scalp micro-chips. I wondered whether if they had just inserting the chips without local anesthetic, whether it would have been no worse than the pain killer injections themselves. It all seemed not to make sense. Why hurt someone with one injection, just to take away the pain of a second injection? I was sure I could have done those injections myself, with far more skill than what those space surgeons had done. They seemed to have no clinical skills, nor any feelings for the astronauts. They seemed very clever however.

I had asked what purpose the scalp microchips served. The answers were very vague. The doctor inserting it just said it was for physiology experiments, and claimed ignorance of details. I underwent a lot of electroencephalogram tests before they tattooed my scalp where to inserted the ten scalp microchips. A week later when, supposedly, the skin was healed I had to undergo three days of tests reading books and texts with an electronic hood device over my head. The hood was the exact replica of the one with my astronaut space-suit inner garments. The cloth hood had sensors to communicate with the scalp microchips, and the sensors then communicated with the spaceship computers. The hoods were soft and comfortable. Even though I was the spaceship-surgeon, they said I had no role to play in the study. I should not be concerned nor, nor distracted from my other responsibilities, and this left me suspicious about these implanted scalp micro-chips. I forgotten I had imbedded microchips in my head until asked me to wear my hood for the first time. I planned to ask him for more information.

---

Because of the energy conserving modes, we had less day-time work to do and we decided to advance supper by an hour and have an extra hour for social time every day. This was my suggestion. Chris thought it was a great way to keep crew moral up during the dust storm. Normally crew social evenings were limited to Saturday and Sunday nights. Now it was to be every night.

Crew social time required we all had to be present and find ways to entertain ourselves as a group. Often, we watch movies on the big screen and listen to sound via the speakers like a cinema back home. It was a different experience watching movies together, than on one's computer with head phones. One could ask questions like, "Who is that actress with the blonde hair? I know her." Then someone would reply, "She is lieutenant Brady from Hollywood Cops", and a few others would add in a response. "Ah yes. I didn't recognize without her sunglasses." It added to the effect of feeling they were all on a mass-date together.

When we watched movies together someone would call a popcorn break and we would stop the movie and swop comments about the movie, while someone made the micro-wave packet-popcorn. The big idea was to share a presence with everyone. We, now having seven social nights per week, during the dust storm, each person got a turn to choose the format for the evening. A popular one was acting as DJ and selecting music for the evening. The ship had one hundred thousand songs in the music computer library, and five thousand movie options ranging from 1930's first black and white movies, to most recent ones up to the month of Earth launch.

One evening someone chose the soul music genre, and we then chose one song within the genre. I started with Ben E Kings "Stand by me". I said I just loved the background raspy percussion like scraping paper. The song took me back to memories of my youth putting a happy tear in my eye. Someone else chose Bobby Darin's "Splish splash" because he so longed to have a soaking deep hot bath. Everybody bopped sitting in their chairs, rocking their shoulders, and tilting their heads making movements as if they were drying themselves with towels. We felt so uninhibited during these relaxed evening hours. Some of the girls were super dancers to slower bop numbers. We would pick on any other crew member who was not bopping and say, "Come, let me coach you". Soon the two were getting their fingers snapping in synchronized rhythms, and others tapped their feet in time. What we lacked in not having alcoholic beverages to sweeten our smiles we, just found in passing little compliments around. "Hey man you've got the bounce there".

Laughter was contagious. If someone made a silly joke and someone else giggled, we would all giggle for ten minutes. Everyone wanted to be happy. We felt drunk on distraction, escaping our dire predicament. We were like lions to the last.

---

High on comradery, I felt comfortable to ask the question bugging me all night. Chris and I remained roommates and shared a two-bunk cabin in the surface habitat.

"Why did you ask us to keep our space-suit hoods on."

"In the ship-captains protocol, I am supposed to ask the crew to wear them whenever I worry about crew unrest or crew dysfunction developing. Each space-suit space hood is tailor-made for each Marsnaut. There are sensors in the hood, that read the implanted micro-chips in your scalp. The hood then communicates via Blue-Tooth radio with the ship computers. Originally, the hoods were meant to be worn for 24 hours every day, but I objected. With this dust storm potentially causing us to become very stressed, I decided to act and ask the crew to wear the hoods."

"So, what do you hope to learn, if those hoods only produce physiological data? Surely, I should be evaluating it. NASA command told me those implanted micro-chips just collected our heart rates and blood oxygen concentrations during rocket ascent or descent to and from the planets."

"I think I can trust you enough Rodney to tell you. Those things are mind-readers. The tests reading you did pre-launch helped the computers fine-calibrate their interpretation of the brain signals."

My jaw dropped.

"Wow! know about verbal and non-verbal speech in thinking processes. I think it may overlap with the concepts of vocalization and sub-vocalization of words. If one thinks out a word clearly in their head it is possible to measure electrical activities in their voice forming throat-muscles, even though they do not say any audible word. That is subvocalization. Scientists can measure matching electrical activity in the throat-muscle controlling part of your brain. It turns out it doesn't matter whether you say that word aloud or only silently within your thoughts, the brain or the muscle electrical changes can be measured. Researchers have calibrated and trained a computer through artificial intelligence processes, to recognize the words you say or think. They need to have electrical wires stuck into your scalp to do this. The first computers doing this got 60% of the words right. So, this space medicine research must be at a very advanced level and the computers read our thoughts 100% accurately via those implanted microchips."

"When crew members wear their space-hoods, I get a daily report on how often certain keys words entered their thoughts. There is a 100-word list, that gets reported back to me. It is things like; kill, murder, mutiny, assault punch, hit, kill, suicide etcetera."

"The thing that shocks me most is that we never consented to having our thoughts read. I think what goes on in the privacy of our minds is absolutely private. It is an extreme futuristic invasion of privacy. Chris, I am sorry but I am not going to wear my hood again."

Chris responded. "I cannot force you to wear your hood, however I wonder if I could have detected the mutiny early, if everyone was wearing theirs hoods at that time. I guess this confirms your opinion that the actual main experiment of this entire mission is us crew, and to see how far we survive."

By supper time the next night, I had a small cut in the first webspace of his right hand. It had one suture and some superglue over it to cover the wound. I was not wearing my hood.

"What did you do to your hand Rodney" asked Vicky.

I replied. "I cut my computer microchip out."

"Why? How do you open your computer?", asked Babee.

"I am old fashioned. I am happy to enter a password."

"But, why? What was wrong with your hand-microchip?"

I did not reply.

Chris, holding his own chin thinking, spoke up.

"Crew there is something I think I want to share with you. I don't feel I owe any special favors to NASA at this point. I am going to let you in on a secret. Your hand-microchips are a lot more than keys to unlock your computers. They register every-time you pass two sensors in every door or hatch, when you come within 20 centimeters of any locked storage shelf, electronic control board, or any mainframe computer. On my computer, I get a daily summary report of your movements. I can also set alarms to warn me instantly on my wrist computer if someone enters an area, I could have an interest in. I can also see when any two individuals are in close proximity to each other for any duration of time, and where they are, or where."

I decided to keep looking at Chris and not look around, in case anyone was blushing.

Chris continued, "The cotton white hoods have sensors sown into them to link with your scalp implanted micro-chips. That gets read anywhere within the spaceship and computer recorded. Those sensors, as well as actual words you speak. So, you have no privacy of thoughts. I can only access a list of 100 key words, that you might think. It was designed to help me recognize your potentials to act improperly even be criminally. NASA will get the full data base of every thought you ever had during the mission, once our mainframe computers get back to Earth. Your entire thoughts are recorded and stored for analysis when we get back to Earth.  Of course, no thought recordings can be made when you take your hoods off."

Babee ripped her hood off, and threw in onto the floor. I wondered what thoughts she wished to keep concealed. I guess I gave up my hood for similar thoughts. Everyone followed suit.

Babee asked, "Can we delete the computer records of all this......JUNK?"

"Yes. I can show you the drive that I know is the main storage drive. One of the IT guys will have to track down the backup files and delete them too. I am so sorry I never told you earlier about this.

I couldn't help myself. I shouted, "I TOLD YOU!!! We are the experiment!".

---

At the next social evening they decided to do improvise-acting. It was Vicky's idea. She said she would choose each pair or threesome of persons. They had to come stand in front. She would give each person a piece of paper, describing the character they had to act out. A mini script followed, while someone directed the story. No one was shy or had social fears, by this stage of the mission.

Applause was given for great acting, as well as poor acting and having just tried. Most importantly we all laughed our heads off. We enjoyed script development, trying out things. Some impromptu things didn't work too well. Some were phenomenal. Sometimes when a response was poor, someone would shout out. "That was no good. Try again". The person would then attempt an impromptu second take, as if we were directing and managing a multi-million-dollar movie set.

We rated this as some of the most fun we had had in our lives, again, surprisingly without alcohol. What made it unique was the trust they all felt in each other. How open and uninhibited we had become with each other. Maybe most, it was how we all accepted the others' particular personalities unconditionally, and problem solved as a team.

Three weeks later the dust storm cleared up.

.

# CHAPTER 18.

## You need an operation Doctor. (week 86)

Tyrone finally had woken up, and read the message on the white board Valborg carried. As instructed, Tyrone flipped the switch to activate for the autopilot docking computer-control. He waited an extra thirty minutes before activating the second switch, placing the Mars space-orbiter ship in the A-mode. Those thirty minutes gave Valborg enough time to return to and re-enter his ship.

Later, the crew, amused that a simple kid size white-board with an erasable black felt-tip pen, was the life-saving communications medium for part of this hundreds of billion-dollar Martian exploration project, joked how we were supposed to be the pinnacle of scientific and technology development. Not to mention, the space-walk between the two ships to tap on the window and initiate a neighborly discussion proved an <u>un</u>manned mission would have failed. On the other hand, automated and Houston ground-controlled unmanned missions don't have humans forgetting to set alarm clocks.

As Tyrone flipped the first switch of the two-ship auto-pilot computers starting communication and exchange of data on fuel reservoirs, ship orientation etcetera, once Valborg was back within his spaceship twenty minutes later. Tyrone opened his cell-phone and was able to speak to everyone on the launch ship. When Tyrone flipped the A-mode switch for his ship, it started making little jet thrusts. The system was for the A-mode ship to wait, and align itself correctly. The B-mode ship did the approach flying. Due to the mass of these ships measuring tons, but a thin structure, a crash into each other even at the slowest speeds would cause severe damage. Closing the last fifty meters took a few hours. Finally, the two docking-hatches latched onto each other, and the two ships computer and control system linked physically and the air pressures in the tunnel between the two docking doors increased. There was a drawn-out series of tests for everything before the astronauts performed a manual opening of the hatch doors.

Our hugs and heartfelt greetings exchanged by everyone was beyond the words of being joyous. Tyrone the genius paraplegic and Larry Rothman the one-legged engineer, who had survived twelve months in Martian orbit with just each other's company were best friends. Shocked to hear of the death of Russel Dunaszegi, their hearts warmed to hear how Russel sacrificed his life to give Vicky her chance to survive. The fact that help reached Vicky in probably her last twenty minutes of life was a chance event that some Marsnauts could only attribute to a Divine intervention. Of course, we couldn't take all the credit.

Babee's battle with ARDS in her lungs after aspirating on chlorine liquid, left the Tyrone and Larry open-mouthed and speechless. I did not want to talk about it, but all the girl-Marsnauts had machine-gun rapid stories to tell each, with another adding more when the one talking took a breath. They all acted like little school-kid best friends, enthusiastically telling stories and listened.

I watched and listened a lot. I thought our own inner child hidden deep inside every adult somewhere. Maybe it is one of the most beautiful things about adults, the child inside of them, and their innocence. The big question is then, where do all those mean and ugly-on-the inside adult behaviors come from? Maybe mean ugly-on-the-inside adults, become that way because their innocence was stolen from them by another mean and ugly-on-the-inside adult once. I recalled the many wonderful adults who retained a full child's innocence despite their high levels of education and functioning, become vulnerable in personal relationships, despite being effective high-level leaders and managers. I thought of my wife. Maybe it was that residual child's innocence in her that I loved most about her, and why I was deep inside, very protective of her. His wife was however not a total pushover. Despite her total lack of ugliness towards other people, spite or vengefulness, she was not scared to tell me when to shut up or inform me that she did not like something I said. I loved that straight-talking side of my wife. She was as harmless as a child in her demeanor, but as fierce as a tiger if someone she trusted sassed her too much. I wanted an equal life partner.

Our family of Marsnauts had been to a hellish place and back. We had lived in tiny spaces, nearly in the same beds, entering our third year together. We lived so close, we could identify each other's flatus. Secrets were very few. We had had some comrades die, and seen some more nearly die. We had become unified into a pride of lions. Many of us had shared with others our deepest and darkest innermost secrets of our souls. We found resilience. For each other, we would always fight like lions to the last. I could find some inner beauty within nearly everyone. The secret to seeing beauty in others was to be blind to yourself. Be looking outwards, not inwards.

The immediate priority for Tyrone and Larry, after completing post-docking checks, was to re-pack the two docked spaceships so that the return-to Earth ship could be prepared. The modules had to be in a certain order of front to back. All fuel had to be consolidated into one tanker module. There would be one more final re-arranging of modules in Mars orbit, to dump some more modules before exit the Mars orbit. Within two days, this task was done. We separated from one engine module, and one pressurized storage module. All the unpressurized modules had been left on the Mars surface. The ship was now less than half the size of the original.

In a computer calculated moment, correlated from the date, and celestial positions of the Sun, Earth and Mars, Cecil had a turn to speak again. Cecil was the metallic-like, but charming computer voice with an Iowa accent.

Everyone was strapped in their reclined flight seats, in the double tiered crew-capsule. The cat and baby Aresha were secured in their little pressurized containers. Space suites were only needed in case of sudden depressurization, when the ship entered the Earth or Martian atmosphere, or ascended from those planets. For this leaving-orbit rocket blast, it was considered safe enough to omit donning space suites. The cat and baby needed their pressurized boxes, however, mainly for the secure strapping and padding inside the boxes.

Cecil, the computer voice spoke, "Final ten-second count-down to launch from Mars orbit into a Trans-Earth Injection (TEI). Ten seconds, nine seconds, eight seconds, seven seconds, six seconds, five seconds, four seconds, three seconds, two seconds, one second. Ignition. We have blast-off."

"Go Cecil go!" said someone.

Our arms felt heavy, as we lay back in the reclined chairs, into which they were strapped. The crew cabin was at the apex of the spaceship. As fuel burned up, acceleration increased. We felt the 3G weigh on our arms. The engines reduced thrust automatically to limit the G-forces. This continued for many minutes, then silence as the thrust engines cut off. The ship achieved Mars-orbit escape velocity. No one moved. They were on our way back to planet Earth. We weren't in a rush. Nine months of flying ahead of us.

Chris eventually said "You can all unstrap and get up now. Head back to your stations. We will talk at supper conference."

I was glad to be back in my sick-bay module. I still shared it with Chris the captain. We once this small personal space and secrets. We never got so personal again, but we each had very strong respect and absolute trust in the other. If we survived this journey, we were an unlikely pair to transition to a frivolous hanging out with beer, kind of friendship. Our bond was on a higher plane. We would make it a life-long obligation to spend a week together once a year. I imagined us camping and trout fishing in remote Montana. We could include spouses on a trip to New York, visiting the tallest landmarks and taking in a Broadway musical. I realized that Chris and I were like two soldiers thrust into a trench in war, and who had survived. There was that survivor's bond.

At our supper conference Larry and Tyrone updated us on their accomplishment, while in orbit. They rebuilt noisy pumps. They changed filters. They fixed cooling devices, and heating devices. It was one endless home improvements project. They wanted the Orbiter-ship to be in even better condition than before the Earth launch.

And then came the big surprise. They checked out all the communications system and computer systems. They opened up every note book computer, totaling twenty. They opened every built in, desktop computer and tried to figure out each computer's primary function. Investigating the data backup systems revealed triple back-up systems, along with hundreds of thousands of digital files, taking a hard look at the files predating the communications breakdown.

Finally, they observed one motherboard component, attached to the communications control, that looked different to all the other mainframe computers. There was a single sub-board module plugged in, that had slightly different shade of green than the rest. Had they not looked at every single motherboard multiple times, they would never have noticed it. Larry spotted it first and called Tyrone to look at it. The knew the principle goal of the engineering, and even the hiring process, was to use overlapping qualifications. The objective being that items or people, could be poached and placed elsewhere for repairs or replacements.

Because of the off-coloring of this single component, they knew it did not belong. They attempted to determine its function and tried unplugging it. The whole ship power system shut down and they had to re-inserted it by touch in total darkness. They tried a variety of component arrangements but it was only when that one component was removed from that one computer that everything went wrong, and no component could substitute for it. Final investigations would have to take place back on Earth. This was a very different computer component.

Tyrone and Larry had a lot more to share. They found one digital file that was corrupted, while Ares-1 ship-modules were docked with the ISS in Earth Orbit. It coincided with the day of Vahini's assault. Making things extra interesting, they found another corrupted computer file with the exact date, hour, minutes and seconds that they had lost communications with Earth. The corrupted files were in the same folder, and in a communications systems directory.

After much discussion, Chris finally decided that we would not risk trying to repair the communications problems, and risk losing the entire mission. Tyrone and Larry had already tried, the best things. The rest of the crew agreed unanimously with Chris's decision. The suspicious module was one of the modules they would return to the Earth surface with, making it available for later for post-mission investigations.

Valborg had the last word. Remembering the Chinese astronauts company used green components, he deduced the anarchist swopped a good sub-board for a nearly identical virus laden sub-board module. The difference in color likely represented differences in shades of different batches at the Chines factory. He figured out that there were such complex and long supply chains for different computer components, that even though this was not as whole a Chinese computer, a single Chinese sourced component was not a surprise. Wei Zhang, the saboteur, however knew, of that single component and how to substitute it with a bad one.

-------------------------------------------------------------------------------------

------------------------------------

Chris Bolder, had been admiring Marjena Lubiski, the pilot-scientist, for some time. He felt as the Captain, he should keep away from flirtatious behavior, and lead by example from the front. But he could not help but notice her, how exemplary she could be, during the Mars landing. Even more attractive was how unassuming she acted afterwards. It was as if she had no idea how big her actions had been.

After that landing, he noticed her petit size, contrasting strong Celtic facial features, and especially her eyes. Chris' first wife personified passive-aggressive behavior. She played slow games, withdrawing tenderness and warmth when she was angered by him. Never speaking out about any irritations and grievances she had, Chris would have no clue something was wrong. Their relationship and its intimacy would incrementally deteriorate over, and finally Chris would confront her. After talking it out, the fell passionately back into their marital relationship. Then the downward cycle would start again. It took Chris decades to even see this pattern. It was only after she had divorced him that he came to learn about passive-aggressive personalities.

Now single, Chris was not actively seeking a new relationship. It's not like he could ask her out to dinner, and quite frankly he enjoyed the freedoms of bachelorhood without concerning anyone's feelings. It was not that Chris did not wish to share his home and life with a woman, it was just that he found bachelorhood a superb second best life style option, and one devoid of emotional risks and upheavals. He realized he appreciated woman, who were open about their feelings and thoughts in a relationship. The divorce process allowed Chris to discover himself, and understand his own personality quirks. Ultimately, he was to be a better person in himself.

Finally finding Marjena alone he approached her with a casual greeting. She looked directly at him and he held his breath.

"Do you want to have sex with me?" SHE asked the question. His heart stopped. That was like a dream come true, or had she thought he had been leering at her.

Marjena unblinkingly looked him in the face, and waited for his response. She had challenged him.

He got the words out, "Is that an offer, or an invitation?"

Marjena snapped back, "That is an unusual and rather unexpected answer. I think I am not sure about that. How do invitations and offers differ from each other?" She threw Chris' odd question straight back at him.

"I guess how they differ depends on what you exactly had in mind. An offer is more technical. It suggests you would make yourself a procedural partner to me, for me to carry out a technical exercise, as two consenting and equal adults. Nothing more than ten minutes of pleasure shared in privacy and confidentiality. There would be no after-event expectations or obligations of either party. The offer might actually be mighty fun. There is a big element of implicit trust in the other person, and I should be flattered to be made such an offer. I would predict that if the first encounter is generally satisfactory, it would have potential to be addictive and become a regular social engagement."

Softening his tone a bit, he continued, "An invitation is more humane. An invitation is the handing over of a business card, hinting at that there is a lot more on the plate being offered. An invitation proposes more humane interactions. If it was an invitation, it makes me wonder whether you like me in more ways. I wonder then, if you really want to test my feelings from close up."

"Oh my God! You so overthink things." She stood up and walked over to the gallery to make herself a mug-sized bag of coffee.

Chris was very surprised. He loved her cheek dimples when she smiled. During the last six months of the Earth-to-Mars journey,

Chris had stopped looking out of the ship's windows at the universe, Sun, stars and planets. Looking out the window made him feel like a meaningless speck of dust within the infinity of the Cosmos. When he confined his thoughts to only what happened in the ship, he felt more relevant. Her confrontation about sex reinvigorated his feelings he belonged, at least here in her eyes.

The biggest and maybe most meaningful experiments of the entire mission had been done during the Mars-surface phase of the mission. They were all wrapped up by this late time. Boredom is a terribly poison for astronauts. That free time lets their minds meander to dark places, or mischievous places. In Chris's case he had been thinking of befriending Marjena more. He has no specific romantic thought in the back of his head, and he hadn't even visualized what Marjena had offered him. He only created images of fun chats, and sitting close, and not about how woman and men can evolve in relationship beyond that.

Later at dinner, he seated himself near Marjena, but at a calculated safe distance.

"How are your bugs doing?" he asked about her laboratory work.

"Fine. Yours?"

"Fine too."

There followed a silence noticeable only to them. The rest of the crew paid no attention to Chris and Marjena. The silence did not seem uncomfortable. Chris thought Marjena had turned slightly towards him, and he had in response turned slightly towards her, before he even realized what he was doing. They seemed to both be aware of the other and be ready to talk to each other. Marjena sipped on her coffee and looked over the cup directly into Chris' eyes. She did not blink, but her eyes seemed friendly.

"Yes." Said Chris, as if affirming he was there to be with her and absorb her presence. His yes, did not have an upward end inflection, as if it was a question. He was answering a vastly bigger question, one felt instinctively, but not yet verbalized. Chris felt she had warmed to him when he said yes. He read it in her body language.

Marjena nodded her head slowly subtly forward, and looked away.

Chris wondered what that meant. Maybe she was saying she was hearing what he was thinking. Chris thought it was best not to say anything and leave Marjena to initiate a verbal conversation in any direction that she chose. He was intuitively feeling very comfortable. Fatalistic. What would be would be. All of his life he had never asked a girl out first. It was always the girl who asked him on a first date, or who asked him for a dance first. The one single girl he asked out first, was the one whom he had married, and she had divorced him twenty-years later.

Marjena looked at Chris, and asked, "Do you play chess?"

"Why, yes. I love chess."

"Great come to my cabin. I have a chess set. I have been playing computer chess for the whole trip. I am so excited to have my first human chess opponent on this trip."

"I must warn you. I am very good at chess psychology."

"Nonsense! Chess is purely intellectual."

"Just you wait," Chris grinned and laughed. "I will make a deal with you. I will give you a two pawn start over me."

"That's an insult. I'll give YOU a two pawn start and I'll whip you".

"You wish. I am not the whipping kind."

"What kind are you then?"

"Soft and gentle."

"You have potential, Captain Bolder," concluded Marjena, with teasing smile.

The two played chess nearly all night and conversed endlessly on a thousand topics. They won about equally, but Chris thought Marjena had actually let him win a few times. It did not take long for the rest of the crew long to realize that this was a new friendship. We were always to see crew members each find each other in friendship. It was great for mental health. Nobody studied them close enough to see more into the relationship than comradery. Chris had been a buddy to me, and remained that same buddy. Marjena was friends with all the girls, in a very general sense. Chris and Marjena after finally finding their way to each other's hearts spent at least an hour together every night.

---

Many weeks later I retched at breakfast time, and decided to discard the rest of the food I was eating. Marjena Lubiski did the exact same. Chris observed this and asked us if we were OK.

At lunch time I decided to drink as bland a drink as I could mix, but that was more than water. I did not eat, and I looked at Marjena who was also not eating. I quizzed her on what she had eaten over the preceding two days. I was wondering if we had each maybe eaten the same bad thing. There was nothing in common except for desert custard item on the second previous night. It was typical a space-meal of powder-in-a-bag that one dissolves with water, shakes the plastic bag to reconstitute it, and then squeezes it out like tooth paste to eat. Food poisoning in the spaceship is an extremely rare event, as the way all food is preserved, processed and prepared makes everything fresh, in a bacteriological sense, if not fresh tasting to the tongue. Still, I had to eliminate it. My stomach ached vaguely, while Marjena denied a tummy ache. I thought a liquid diet might be best for another day. I also recommended we each eat antacid chewable tablets to sooth things. Chris later asked Marjena twice if she was OK. The good ship-captain was caring for his crew.

The antacid medications did not alter my abdominal discomfort, and by evening, the pain was becoming sustained, had moved to my right side, and low down the abdomen. My fears were great. I placed myself on intravenous antibiotics, and managed with one hand to place an intravenous (IV) cannula into the back of my other hand. That was a lifetime first for me. By evening, I felt much worse and the pain was making me crouch up. I tried to conceal my discomfort, but Chris observed it. He asked how I was feeling, and I chose to deny my feeling unwell. I asked if Chris had seen Marjena, as she had missed supper. Chris assured me Marjena was fine, was nibling through the day, was drinking lots of fluid. She now craved chocolate, and sent him on a mission to find a candy bar. I did not analyze the special attention Chris gave Marjena. The cramp deep right groin nearly brought tears to my eyes. I had had kidney stones before, which I concealed from the NASA surgeons, because it was considered an illness to exclude someone from space travel. Being a civilian, the NASA officials could not access all my medical records; therefore, my lie escaped discovery. I knew this was not kidney stones. I was praying the antibiotics would help.

Early the next morning Marjena came to visit me before breakfast. She said her menstrual periods were late. I set up a table secured it to the floor and set up the ultrasound machine. Obviously, I had no pregnancy tests on board the ship, as all women astronauts were supposed to be sterilized.

I could barely stand straight, as I scanned Marjena's lower abdomen. Yes, there was a flickering little creature inside her womb which I showed her.

Marjena called out Chris' name very sweetly. She did not have to call very loud, as Chris immediately came in from behind the sheet curtain, like he was waiting to be called. He had heard all the dialogue, and floated next to Marjena, holding her hand in both his hands while smiling. He knew Marjena was pregnant.

"I presume I can congratulate this happy couple?"

Chris replied and said, "This event is a surprise to us. We were trying to follow Marjena's natural rhythms, to have her not fall pregnant."

I bent slightly forward, saying. "Marjena, I guess you falsified your medical certificate to NASA saying that you were sterilized. You wanted to keep your baby options open."

Marjena smiled, gave an affirmative head nod, and looked lovingly at Chris. After getting more information, I calculated that if this pregnancy went to term, Marjena's baby would be born in final Earth orbit.

Looking straight at Chris, squarely in the face, "Chris, I have acute appendicitis. I have to operate myself."

Chris was incredulous. "How can you do that? Are you sure?"

I replied, "I checked myself for rebound tenderness in my right fossa iliaca this morning. It is positive and very obvious. Also, the antibiotics I was gave myself have done nothing."

Chris asked. "What is the right fossa iliaca?"

I pointed to his abdomen, "It is over here, where the appendix usually sits".

Chris asked, "Did you not have it taken out before the mission. It was mandatory."

I replied, "I did not want to do that so close to flying and in the middle of my very intense and limited astronaut training. Remember, I was only called to this mission four weeks before launch. So, I just submitted a false sick note with no references to kidney stones, and it listed a date for my imaginary appendicectomy."

Chris mused, "We must have the world record amongst a crew for false sick-notes. How are you going to operate yourself?"

I sighed. "I have no Freaking idea. I'll just have to figure it out as we go along. This won't the first time in history that a doctor took out his own appendix, but unfortunately, I have never known how that Russian doctor in the Antarctic did it. Chris I will need you to be my assistant. Marjena will you help Chris? He will tell you how to pass him things. He is getting experienced at being a nurse."

I released Marjena's Velcro straps that secured her to the table, and mentally prepared to swop places with her.

It took me forty minutes to set up all the sterile equipment devices and drugs on the magnetic surgical tables. They were covered with sterile drapes and plenty of clear sterile plastic zipper bags all attached to the sterile cloth with Velcro. I had Marjena secure my chest and legs to the table with the straps, so that I could not float all over the show. I wore a sterile hat, mask, gloves, and a long-sleeved upper jacket. I used sterile wet swabs on sticks to disinfect my entire abdomen. I told Chris how to place the adhesive sterile drapes across my abdomen so as to cover all of my legs and most of my abdomen. Chris flexed the table slightly in its middle so that I was partially sitting. Marjena wedged some pillows behand my shoulders and neck to help me lean my head forward and see the operating field. I injected myself two different anti-emetic drugs beforehand to alleviate any nausea I might feel. I also injected myself ketorolac, an anti-inflammatory non-sedating pain killer, along with starting an infusion of acetaminophen, another non-sedating pain killer. Everything was ready now.

Taking a big breath, I injected a local anesthetic drug under the skin along the line where I intended to cut my skin. It burned more than I expected. I wished I could hypnotize himself. By having to focus on doing the injecting myself I likely increased the pain I may have felt, compared to what I would have felt with another doctor injecting me. The burning resolved very slowly. A minute later, I had the courage to inject deeper and deeper. I needed to inject down to the peritoneal lining of the abdominal wall, but I had no way to judge how deep to go. I did his best.

I waited about 10 minutes, then took the scalpel and cut through the skin. It felt like nails scratching and did not hurt. Next, Chris passed me the electro-cautery knife, and I cut with the electric arc deeper into the flesh, fat mainly that was 2-centimeter thick. Straining forward, I looked at the mirror Marjena held over the wound for me. It was very difficult, because Marjena could not hold the mirror at the exact angles that gave me best views. Between feeling with my fingers and interpreting the mirror glimpses, I decided that I had incised as far as the thick fascia covering the abdominal wall muscles. That was good. Next, I tried to grab the fascia with a pointed clamp device, designed to occlude small bleeding arteries, called a hemostat. Eventually after a few minutes I had a section of the muscle-covering fascia in the hemostat. I could lift it up and out of the wound, to see where it was pinching the fascia. With my other hand, I made a small incision into the fascia. Next, I placed one arm of the surgical scissors inside the opening on the fascia and the other hemostat limb outside the fascial opening. That let me snip and gradually extended the fascial incision with the scissors, to match the length of the twelve-centimeter skin incision. So far so good, and things were not hurting.

I had some memory of a technique of splitting the muscle fibers apart in their length, but it was forty years since had done an appendicectomy, and anyway I could not see deep enough into the wound to see the muscle layer. I decided to instead cut the muscle using the electrocautery. The muscles twitched violently when I did this, and it felt crazy as I cut, but it was tolerable. By making incremental steps I eventually penetrated the muscles and could place a finger right through the muscle layer, and onto the peritoneal fascia deep to the muscle layer. This gave me great relief.

I had worried about cutting too deep, and unknowingly cutting direct into a bowel. The toughest part of operating myself was that it was mostly a blind procedure. With one finger now inserted below the muscle and lifting it off the peritoneum, I was able to split the muscle to the same length as the skin wound without damaging the peritoneum. Finally, to open the peritoneum, I used a similar technique to that I had used to cut the first fascial layer. I hoisted a tiny piece of fascia to where I could see it and made a hole the same length of the skin incision.  The easy part of the surgery was complete.

Next, I squirted a large volume of local anesthetic drug into the wound and onto the bowels, using a syringe with no needle. Several to anesthetize the bowels, like a Coeliac plexus block, were not feasible for me, as they needed injections into the back. The only remaining option was to try to soak the intestinal bits I would be touching, with local anesthetic. It might help a bit, or maybe not at all. I waited just looking silently at the space module ceiling above me, thinking deeply. Marjena told me when ten minutes had passed.

Now I pushed my one index finger deep into my abdominal cavity. I hoped I would be able to feel the appendix. Fearing it was already so inflamed that it was stuck and buried in an inflammatory mass of bowels, would then be unable to remove it then, and if the antibiotic failed, I would most likely die. If the appendix ruptured it would cause diffuse peritonitis, and I would die. I also feared having a retrocecal appendix. Instead up pointing upwards and outwards, the appendix pointed backwards and the tip would be buried behind the Cecum of the large bowel. I was sure I would not be able to operate that one, without being able to look deep into my abdomen. I had operated a few retrocecal appendices years before, and I knew how to do a retrograde appendicectomy, but I doubted I could do it blind. I probed and gently explored inside my abdomen with my finger. I thought I felt a two-centimeter-wide firm twelve-centimeter-long sausage-like organ. The degree of adherence to the surroundings bowels seemed little enough, and with tenderness I was freeing it more and more. It was a bit slippery, so I used a small piece of dry absorbent gauze, to hold the appendix tip. Finally, I was able to drag the tip through the incision to where he should see it. A feeling of vertigo and nausea overwhelmed him. I lost my grip.

Things went dark a for a few moments. Next I heard Chris say, "Your rate is 65, it went to 50 for a moment." Bowel is a funny thing. It hurt severely when stretched, but cutting hardly caused pain. I had gotten a vasovagal effect when pulling on the appendix, slowing my heart rate enough to make me faint. The treatment for that is an injection of atropine, which I should have injected prophylactically beforehand, but I did not think of that. It would too complex now to try and get Marjena to find the ampule it and prepare it, so I just went ahead. I felt my forehead sweating heavily, and asked Marjena to wipe it dry. I could hear my heart rate speed up on the monitor, at 65 beats per minute now. I pulled on the appendix tip again but even more gentle this time too. Once I saw the appendix, I was more confident that I had pulled out the right organ. Looking at its swollen size and red color, I also felt the diagnosis of acute appendicitis was correct. I clipped a hemostat to its tip, so it could not slip back again. I pulled on it again very slowly and gently, until its base against the cecum became visible. Weirdly enough, it felt like a kidney stone passing. It ached where I was operating, and I also kept wanting to retch. I got two more hemostats applied close to the appendix base. The base of the appendix had a small mesenterium which I managed to clamp separately. Then I took scissors and cut above the mesenterial clamp, and tied a dissolving suture around the tissues within the mesentery clamp and removed the clamp. I could not see directly into the wound, but an absorbent-swab suggested there was no bleeding going on. Next, I cut between the two base hemostats cross clamped on the deep end of the appendix, and close to the cecum. That freed the appendix fully, which I lay it on my tummy and out of the way. Chris picked it up and placed on the operating tray. I finally believed my tentative diagnosis of me having acute appendicitis. That appendix was inflamed and swollen.

Finally, I tied a dissolving suture around the base of the appendix remnant, under the last hemostat. That knot had to hold well. If it slipped off later, the bowels would leak, and I would die. I tied it twice and firmly each time. The knots were in alternating directions so as not to form a hangman's noose knot which can slip. I finally swabbed the severed base of the appendix base remaining in the abdomen with an anti-septic soaked swab, and released the hemostat. The cecum and appendix base slid back deep into the abdomen. I lay my head back and just closed my eyes for a minute. I soon felt stronger. A clean swab from the peritoneal opening did not show any blood, which lowered my anxiety.

Suturing the appendicectomy abdominal wall incision, in three separate layers, took three quarters of an hour. I had to find the corners of each tissue group, like fascia, muscles, and subcutaneous fat, by blind touch, and then hoist it up to view using a hemostat clamp. He had to see where each first suture went. The rest I could do blind, aided by careful feeling with my fingertips. As a young family doctor operating on a real patient under general anesthesia, I could do this surgery skin-to-skin, as they say, in thirty minutes. The surgeons who are specialized in this field, and whom I admired and tried to emulate, could do it in fifteen minutes skin-to-skin. The current popular laparoscopic approach took good surgeons an hour.

There was in 1962 a Russian doctor on an Antarctic expedition, who in the middle of winter had to remove his own appendix. No airplane could fetch him. He was Dr. Leonid Rogozov and he was actually a surgeon. He took an hour and a half too. I was only an anesthesiologist, who had only been an operating family doctor, forty years prior, doing appendicectomies then as my biggest surgery.

Chris and Marjena knew how to mix and administer the antibiotics, as well as how to keep the intravenous fluids running. They nursed me after the surgery. I put my head back and slept like a log for ten hours. Chris and Marjena made sure that one of them was at my side at all times. After my first sleep, I was unsure if I was feeling better, but I was thirsty and successful retained a good volume of oral fluids. From that point on, things just went better at every step. I did not use pain killers and was obsessed with moving and getting about. I let himself eat liquid food after 24 hours, when I heard my bowels bubbling, using my stethoscope. When the liquid food stayed down, I took out my own IV.

Feeling conservative, I decided to leave my undissolving skin sutures in for ten days. I worried the wound had a low-grade of infection, enough to slow healing, but not enough to form pus. Taking out my own tummy sutures was the best thing I had ever done in my life. Chris laughed watching me do it, and when I made that comment, and responded in a growly tone, "Like a lion to the last".

## CHAPTER 19.

### Bullet damage and fire outside the spaceship. (Week 126)

The remaining months of the return-flight to Earth moved steadily onward. We enjoyed competing to see who had the most research data on anything. In respect, we even did the dead Marsnauts research projects as best we could.

Marjena's pregnancy went well and her initial morning sickness seemed to resolve at the same time her morning nausea-partner, recovered from my self-appendectomy.

There were computer managed flight trajectory corrections for the spaceship about every second month. Ares-1 Earth return ship was on a curving Sun gravitational orbit at a slower speed than Earth's Sun orbital speed, so that the ship was slowly pulled closer to the Sun. We expected to intersect with the Earth's orbit and be captured by Earth gravity into an Earth orbit. Once in Earth orbit we would abandon a few modules of the ship, and fire the rocket in reverse thrust to descend to the Earth surface. A water landing was planned. Marjena and Chris' unborn baby was thriving, kicking and growing. Marjena's rosy cheeks smiles detracted from my concerns about when the baby would be born. It seemed such a small problem considering all we had been through and survived. Marjena was just very happy and trusting in her obstetric fate. The last week of the mission was going to be immensely busy, with some unique challenges.

Having no contact with Earth, or Ground Control at Houston provided its own problems. The Marsnaut's Earth landing was originally going to be at sea, and with a large operation involving rescue ships that had to be ready at right times and at right places. Our other major hurdle in landing concerned the auto-communication beween the ship-navigational-computers and Earth computers. The Earth orbit might need modifications for axis. The timing of the descent had to be coordinated with the weather, and the site of landing could be varied a bit too, depending on the weather at the landing site. Captain Chris Bolder had a backup plan, though crude, but a plan.

---

Having no research of my own to do, I kept himself busy writing my diary, watching our blue planet get closer, and taking photographs. I wrote a lot of late night thoughts, mainly about very early-on events of the mission. I knew I had a potential book to write. Part of my mind doubted anyone would be interested in a doctor's experiences and perspectives. Some might cringe at any mention of blood, but maybe there were others who would enjoy the tale. Part of my mind said this trip was an incredible never-to-be repeated human adventure. How could it bore anyone?

Chris assigned Judessa Weeks to be first pilot for the landing, and Tyrone Wilson the IT expert to lead the calculations on navigation. Vicky Duploy was the backup IT support and Larry Rothman the back-up pilot. They had to work as a close foursome.

Doing a reverse thrust was likely not needed for this flight transition, but we had to be prepared to do it in a flash, for sudden speed adjustment while entering Earth orbit. We aligned the ship so that the engines were positioned to be reverse thrusters, on the advancing side of the spaceship. The ship's transition from Mars-to-Earth flight into Earth-Orbit should occur at a point where Earth's gravity effect upon the spaceship, exceeded that of the Sun.

If the ship reached Earth travelling too fast, two problems could arise. First, we might not get captured into orbit and would instead get a sling-shot off, away from Earth towards nowhere. We would all die of hunger and oxygen depletion. Second, if our speed was only slightly off, we would land up in a higher Earth orbit than what we needed, but that was correctable.

During our entrance in Earth orbit, we couldn't believe our luck. We experienced a perfect arrival in a 400-kilometer high orbit. It wasn't truly luck as the computer-autopilots got it right, or rather the computer programmers got it right. Judessa the pilot did not have to take over manual control.

Now came the mightiest navigation challenge any space venture ever experienced. We had no weather information. No satellite and Earth radio system to position us exactly, relative to Earth landmarks. Our biggest decision; when to fire reverse-thrust to slow us down enough to fall out of orbit and down to the surface. That chosen moment would determine whether we landed on land or sea and in which part of the world. The second part of the decision was for how long to fire reverse thrust. Beyond that, we had no other influence or control on the rest of our descent to the surface. There was no correcting for missing the sea. We would die upon impact with a ground landing. It had to be a water landing. The critical problem was that no one was expecting us, that we could tell. We could also land in a part of a sea that was very remote and had no sea traffic. We only had a 7-day food supply, as per the landing plan. The rest of the food, we left in the modules abandoned in Earth orbit. If our food ran out before we were discovered, we would all starve to death floating lost at sea. How ironic would that be? Fighting to return to Earth from outer space, only to ne lost at sea.

Tyrone was mighty clever. He said we should orbit Earth a few times and look down to the surface. We should choose an off-coastal area on either the East or the West side of the USA. Then we should aim to land about 20 kilometers out to sea. We could crudely guess that the sea section with the least clouds had the best weather and take a chance landing there.

Tyrone said we should rotate the ship in its axis so that one solar panel pointed to Earth. That would make its power generation suboptimal, but we still had a 30-hour battery life. There was an engineering camera at the base of the solar-panel to observe the solar-panel. We could use that camera view of the solar panel against the Earth view in the background. A measuring point would be when the solar panel edge crossed a land boundary. We knew the distance the spaceship would travel in descent. We would then calculate backwards from their target landing point to the spot above Earth, where in orbit we should start their reverse-thrust engines. Just to make the calculations really fun for Tyrone, each time crossed a land feature it was shifted s few degrees relative tour previous pass, but luckily a fixed amount. One full Earth orbit took be about ninety minutes. Tyrone was typing fast into the computer, doing calculations. For me this was crazy stuff, but all the engineers, pilots and IT persons on the crew grasped it well.

In the control cabin, we all heard a loud single banging twang sound like bullet ricochet sounded in old cowboy movies. They looked around puzzled.

"What was that?" asked Valborg?"

Suddenly alarms screamed like we had not ever heard before. All other technical problems became irrelevant. Control panels flashed red lights.

Cecil the automated voice said. "Emergency, pressure loss flight control module. Pressure loss flight control module" and kept repeating that message. Cecil also gave the pressure in the module between every warning message. The ship was damaged, and we were losing air via a hole.

"680 mmHg".

Pressure was supposed to be the same as one atmospheric Earth pressure at sea-level, being 760 mmHg, pronounced as 760 millimeters of Mercury.

Chris shouted "Everyone, evacuate control cabin. Tyrone and Valborg stay with me. Seal control cabin hatches. Guys, I think we have taken a space debris penetration. Find the hole or holes quick. Tyrone, check all systems. Tell me if there are any other problems"

Chris and Valborg started to examine the walls of the module.

"650mmHg." Cecil continued.

"640 mmHg."

"630 mmHg."

"I've got one," shouted Chris. "It's is about 3mm wide. I have my finger on it".

Val immediately started to look closer to the end of the ship module, where Chris was standing.

"620 mmHg."

"615 mmHg."

"I have the other one", shouted Valborg. It looks 5 mm across. I have my finger on it.

"610 mmHg."

Chris said. "It looks like whatever hit us had a clean trajectory through the module and never hit anything else. Tyrone any other problems?"

"610 mmHg."

"Whew", said Tyrone. "I think we have got it. No, all systems are normalizing."

"625 mmHg."

"Valborg, can you patch this. See if you have a screw the size of the holes. Screw them in with superglue. Tyrone take over Valborg's hole."

Valborg opened the module hatch, towards the direction of his sleep module. In a few minutes, he was back with a workman's tool box. He found a screw that was a perfect fit for each hole and had to turn them fairly hard to lock them in place on the final turns.

The superglue bulged slightly out the edge of the screws, as their wide heads crushed flush with the aluminum wall of the space-module.

"760 mm Hg. Pressures normal. Emergency over. Be cautious" said unemotional automaton voiced Cecil finally.

Tyrone is his ever-humorous style said back to the overhead computer voice, "Thank you Cecil, buddy!"

Protocols required us to do an outside inspection of the ship for other damage.

Chris said, "That was close. The debris trajectory through the ship suggest no vital structure outside the cabin could have been damaged. The big thing is I am sure our heat-shields will be unaffected. Let's just look out the windows, and inspect inside the cabin. I am happy to omit an inspection space-walk. What do you gentleman think?"

Valborg and Tyrone looked at each other and both nodded their heads.

"We agree with you Chris", answered Valborg." If we were in the middle of our 9-month flight from Mars, it would be no problem to do a space-walk inspection, as we would have had nothing else to do. Now in our Earth descent cycle, a space-walk with proper denitrogenation would throw us out by a day. The debris puncture holes don't align with the heat shields. We're safe for descent."

Tyrone nodded in affirmation.

"All systems fine."

Chris grabbed the microphone. "Crew. Emergency over. Continue with descent preparation countdown."

"Damn debris. The most dangerous part of trip to Mars and back, is being in Earth orbit. We come back home and get hit by a damned space-bullet. We in the orbital space-junk belt. Let's get out of it."

After 12 hours of orbiting Earth Tyrone had it figured out. Looking at the coast East of North Carolina the weather looked best. We would aim to land on sea 20 kilometers East of the Outer Banks land strip off North Carolina. The excitement of the crew was tangible. We donned our space suits. After Skabenga and baby Aresha were sealed in their space-boxes, we strapped into our crew-module seats. Getting Marjena and her unborn baby massive gravid tummy into a space suit was just another problem to be fixed. We had to bastardize and reassemble the largest spare space suit we had, with some smaller space-suit limb components. Protecting Marjena and her unborn baby from a sudden accidental cabin-depressurization during Earth descent reigned highest priority. Mobility in the space suit rated second.

Two hours later we hit Tyrone's mark and Dessie fired the reverse thrusters. We adjusted to the G-force on our very space-weary arms as the ship decelerated. Then the reverse-thrust engines went quiet. The Rocket-spaceship was flying backwards in order to decelerate. Next, the side-thrusters rotated the ship head over heels so that the ship descending in a sideway profile, like a sky-diver. The axial rotation of the ship also had to be perfect, so heat shield faced downwards. The side-thrusters intermittently fired the whole correcting the ship's falling position. Dessie had the option of taking manual control, but the autopilot control worked perfect.

As the atmospheric gasses started to drag on the falling spaceship, an orange-red glow appeared at the windows closest to the downside. The air friction caused enough heat to melt metal. The glow about the windows looked like fire yet wasn't fire. It was intriguing to those doing their first ever astronaut flights. I was wondering if we could catch fire, but seeing the more experienced Marsnauts being so relaxed made me relax too.

The rocket gave a little jerk and followed by another and another. The parachutes opening sequence deployed the first group to provide partial slowing, and another, then finally the main canopies.

It became serenely quiet. From my seat, I could see the sea and land far ahead. Just when I thought we looked spot-on target, informed us that it looked like our path drift was 30 kilometers further west than planned.

Tyrone shouted, "Dammit. I calculated for Zero winds. I should have factored in seasonal onshore winds. That is the factor I left out. The winds are blowing us too far west. We could land on land."

Although brilliant in our humanity, we were still always just human.

Dessie, with her amazing piloting instincts, "I see we are drifting across the North Carolina Outer Banks now, and quite high. I recognize Kitty Hawk down below, and even the Wright Brothers memorial on Devil Hills. There are the Albermarle Sound waters, between main land and the Outer banks. I am worried we will overfly the Sound. I can release a parachute or two to increase out descent speed. I think we will be better off hitting the sea too fast, than doing any land landing.

Chris said. "You are the pilot Dessie. We stand behind your call"

I wondered silently, if anyone down at Kitty Hawke was watching, as we passed overhead.

Dessie stared out of her closest window with unblinking eyes. As the Ares-1 Mars Mission final-Earth-landing-ship crossed the west land edge of the Outer Banks, she pushed a button on her controls. One canopy, of the group of canopies separated and flew up and away from the ship. We immediately felt the acceleration. It was nothing like an engine thrust, but more like amusement park ride. The spaceship descent flight path steepened.

We splashed down in Albermarle Sound, perfectly centered in between land to the East and land to the West. Hard and jarring does not begin to describe the feeling of impact. A giant spout of water splashed up and ascended twenty meters. I noticed water wash over all the crew cabin windows momentarily. I assumed we were under water for some moments.

Tyrone shouted. He always spoke loudly, with his very manly voice, "Whoah! I think I lost a tooth filling there." He paused, then added, "Just Joking!".

Then Cecil spoke, with its metallic computer-generated voice with an Iowa accent, "Welcome to planet Earth."

"I love you Cecil," shouted Tyrone.

"We love you, Tyrone," chorused a bunch of girls.

I started to sob, just loud enough for the others to hear. A moment later started sobbing softly, as if it was infectious. We all took off their helmets to be able to wipe their eyes and cheeks dry. I was amazing to feel ran to our chins, instead of floating off in the cabin, as it did in space.

We rocked gently in the small water waves.


We were home. We were home.


We doffed our space suits; the first ones out helped others, as it is usually a two-person job to put one on and take it off. It looked like a pajama party with everyone clothed in only their white long sleeve space-suit undergarments. We hugged ravenously, said, "I love you," in between words of amazement, disbelief, and also saying to everyone they hugged "I love you". Cheeks were wet, shirts were wet. Chris opened the two highest crew-module hatches to outside, that were above water.

In seconds people started to say.

"I smell Earth."

"I can smell it."

"I smell Earth too."

It was emotional catharsis after surviving a 3-year trip to hell and back.

Upon water contact an inflatable pontoon popped out on each side of every module, to stabilize the pipe-like round spaceship cum boat. The rocket-space-ship floated in its length on the water surface. A weighted keel-fin extended itself downwards into the water, from the most central module of the rocket-ship. This augmented the effect of the pontoons in stabilizing the long floating spaceship.

The Sun had set, and the early twilight sky was a rich, flawless color of azure blue.

Marjena said, "I think I am in labor."

# CHAPTER 20.

## BBC TV breaking news - The Martians are invading Earth.
## (week 126)

"Hello, I am Alice Banks, reporting for BBC TV World News – Our top story is this video, taken 30 minutes ago. It was filmed by a Bill Dicks, from the United States and posted immediately on YouTube and on Twitter, by his girl-friend, Sasha. The video titled, "The Martians are invading Earth," is breaking world records for being the fastest trending and most retweeted social media message in history. In these 30-minutes that it has also been in YouTube, it has had 50 million viewings and counting.

One of our staff managed to get Bill Dicks on a phone call, and he was breathless, barely able to speak coherently. He said that he and his girlfriend had sneaked onto the grounds of the Wright Brothers Airfield and Museum after closing time. This is near Kitty Hawk where the famous two Wright brothers took flight in their first ever powered manned fight. Bill and his girlfriend had walked up the Kill Devil Hills to sit at the Wright Brothers Monument and watch the sunset, over the Albermarle Sound West of these North Carolina Outer Banks.

Here is the video. You can see there was a Sun on the horizon and Bill Dicks and Sasha in the foreground."

---

Suddenly Bill screamed, "Oh my God what is that?"

The image moved and becomes crazy. "Sasha gimme the phone, gimme the phone!".

Next, the shaking camera image showed an azure blue sky and a full moon. As the image steadied, Sasha shouts "What's that, What's that!?"

Bill holding the phone a bit more steadily shouted, "It can't be from Earth, it can't be."

Into the film view, a massive object drifted across the face of the moon. It had five parachutes each about 100 meters across, all touching each other like a bunch of mushrooms. Suspended below the parachutes is a long round object, with a slightly tapered point.

Bill followed the object, filming it, as it moved directly overhead and Westwards. The moon shifted to the left, out of the camera image.

"That must be a Martian Spaceship. It's massive, it , it … it must be over one hundred feet long, maybe two hundred, maybe even more, I can't tell. I guess it is at 2000 feet above us."

Sasha screamed, "The Martians are coming, they're coming. We must run. Bill, we must run".

"Wait, wait", shouted Bill as he continued filming the monstrous object. The sky is cloudless, flawless and perfect. The peaceful beauty of the coastal sunset sky and the silence, was in total contrast to this monster strange object moving slowly, ominously and silently westward in the evening sky.

The spaceship got lower and lower, and dropped into the water of the Albermarle Sound, immediately West of this Outer Banks land strip, and East of the mainland coast of North Carolina. It slipped out of sight of the couple filming its journey. As it splashed into the waters of the Albermarle Sound, the giant parachutes collapsed. The orb of the setting Sun gently vanished below the horizon.

Bill lowered the phone and looked at Sasha silently. She looked at him wild eyed and blurted, "It is a Martian Spaceship. They coming to get us."

Bill stammered, "No that can't be. I don't know. I have never ever seen such a big thing in the sky. It was bigger than anything I have ever seen. Those parachutes could each have covered our whole little town in the Appalachian Mountains.   Why didn't it have wings like an airplane? I think you are right, Sasha. It must have come from outer space."

Sasha, "Gimme the phone, gimme the phone. I've gotta share this with all my friends. We have to warn people." She grabbed the phone back and started to operate its buttons at lightening-speed, using two thumbs.

Bill and Sasha grabbed hands and ran down the hill.

---------------------------------------------------------------------------------
------------------------------------------

"We have Oxford University Professor of Astronomy on the phone now. Hello Professor Ishmael Meredith. Welcome to BBC TV Breaking World News special."

"Hello Miss Banks," he replied sounding a bit nervous.

"Professor Meredith, thank you for being available for us at this time of night. You just saw this film.  Judging by the wild comments people are posting on social media, could this be the end of the world? Is this the first landing of an invader from outer space, possibly from Mars, as the filmers thought? This is the first UFO image in color HD film. Is these the first true UFO image ever?"

"Well, Alice. May I call you Alice?"

"Yes of course."

"Well, I have never seen such a structure in the air before. Long ago when the world still had space missions, most of them landed with a parachute or three, stretching about 100 feet across each. This is nothing like anything humans have ever done. After that tragic loss of the Ares-1 mission three years ago the space nations closed the International Space Station (ISS), and astronauts returned to Earth. All we have in space now are unmanned satellites for weather, research, communications, and likely some for military purposes".

"Professor Meredith, do you think this can be a Martian invader ship?"

"No. No. No. That is impossible, because we have never found life on Mars. The only other possible sophisticated life forms in the Cosmos would most likely exist outside of our solar system. Plus, the spaceship in the video looks different from the ones in movies. However, whom am I to know?" He had talked himself around in a circle, and out of his own good idea.

"Professor Meredith, if I can summarize? You believe the object that we saw in the video was probably a visitor from outer space, but unlikely one from Mars specifically"

"That is not exactly what I said, but . "

"Sorry, I must cut you off there. We have a reporter on the ground at the Wright Brothers Airfield, at Kitty Hawk."

"Hello Peter, did you hear Professor Meredith's opinion?"

"Yes, thank you Alice. This is Peter Jones reporting for the BBC from Kitty Hawk, USA".  It is now just short of an hour since that spaceship passed overhead, moving westwards. About a thousand people are already here now, and they forced their way through the locked airfield gates. They are all repeatedly viewing that amazing video of the spaceship floating into the sunset over

The Wright Brothers memorial. I heard Professor Meredith's opinion that it could actually be a visitor from further out in space and not from Mars. All the folks running around here are saying it's a Martian invader. The kids are all waving their illuminated toy space-swords in the dark. It is almost festive here.

I have tried to speak to the USA Coast Guard by phone about the flying object, and they know nothing at this point, or are not saying. We have citizen reports that the Coast Guard have sent several boats out. They headed to the believed water-landing point of the alien-ship, in Albermarle Sound west of the Outer Banks. We don't have more information at this point. I have a team trying to contact anyone to give us a statement."

"Thank you, Peter Jones. We might have more breaking news here. I have General Powowski in a New York studio on video link."

Hello General Powowski. We were lucky to get you into the studio. You, are Commander of the United States East Coast air security?"

"Yes, that is correct. I have just finished briefing the President about events."

"General, is this a security problem for the planet?"

"At this point, I can't say too much. The president may make a statement, later in the evening. I believe it is early morning in London, correct?"

"It is 3 AM in London. I am told no American news channel has yet picked up on this world wide panic about a space invasion."

"I don't know anything about that. I am busy dealing with this matter. I want to reassure all Americans watching the BBC News this evening at 8 PM New York time now, that we will have this situation under control. We have removed the Coast Guard from dealing with this. They are securing the far boundaries for us. The object is definitely in the water surface. We have secured the airspace and have strong water security very close by. We have contacted the local city Mayors and Police Captains in the region and cities, and instructed them to immediately evacuate all persons to inland beyond a 20-mile radius from Kitty Hawk. I am afraid I am not in a position to speak anymore at this minute, and all further information will come from the Oval Office."

"Thank you, General."

"This is Alice Banks reporting from BBC TV News International. We will be back after a short commercial break."

---

"Hello, this is Alice Banks from BBC international. We are back. An hour and a half ago, there was a most dramatic event off the East coast of the USA. An unidentified 300-foot long flying object landed by parachute in the Albermarle Sound just east of the Famous Kitty Hawk Wright brothers first flying field. You can see the monstrously large object drift below inconceivably large parachutes on the screen behind me." The studio recycled the video clip endlessly.

"We have a lot of experts assembled in the studio here."

"Professor Joseph Laur, you are from the Institute of International Security Studies, funded by the United Nations."

"Yes, Alice. Thank you for asking me to be here."

"Professor Laur, could this be an Earth-launched space vehicle?"

"I doubt it. There are no countries in the world who presently have rockets large enough."

"Professor Laur, we could not see much detail in this rather shaky video, but some say this looks like an entire space-rocket like we launched in the past."

"Alice, that is a good question, but it makes no sense. Most of those past massive launch rockets, like the Saturn-V or even the past Saturn-8 had serial stages, that had to separate before the next stage could be fired. This means an intact Saturn-V or a Saturn-8 rocket after launch is an impossible structure."

"Well, Professor Laur, there is another theory going around: this is an Earth-launched military object that was flown to Kitty Hawk and released for a parachute landing.  Could that be possible?"

"Hmmm! Alice, maybe. I guess a large enough helium balloon could have been used. I would need to estimate the weight and calculate the necessary helium balloon volume. It is beyond what I can visualize in my head. That theory seems impossible, as a snap thought"

"Professor," asked Alice Banks impatiently. "Presuming a foreign nation sent this object to America, could it be a nuclear device?"

"Alice, Alice, Alice, you are trying to create science fiction. A nuclear weapon of that size would contain more fission material than that of the entire world's known stores. It would probably be enough to disrupt the Earth's planetary crust and decimate all life forms in one blast. This could not be a nuclear bomb. That theory is even more ludicrous."

"Professor Laur," said Alice as she leaned forward towards him, "the most plausible explanation left, is that is a space-alien vehicle invading the planet".

Professor Laur's mouth open and closed a number of times as he raised his hand as if making a point. Finally, he said, "Alice, we have never ever seen scientifically plausible evidence of extra-terrestrial life forms. We have no idea what transport forms and types such creatures would use, if they even existed. When Hollywood shows a space, as a sort of flying saucer, it is pure folklore and fiction. I just can't answer that question confidently."

Alice Banks then turned to her left.

"Here we have Fryed Farsi. You are a student of flight history, have written books on the Wright brothers, and you lecture on Space exploration, is that correct?"

"Yes indeed. Thank you, Alice for bringing me here. My most recent book is called Is *Space Science Research is Dead. Space Militarization is the new Battlefront.* It is available on Amazon as an eBook and free press book. This viral video of this huge object is unreal."

Alice. "Fryed, can this massive parachuted vehicle be a remnant of past space activities from Earth. Maybe the International Space Station (ISS), finally falling to Earth?"

"Alice you have an imaginative mind indeed. Yes, it is true that the ISS, is the largest structure that ever was above the Earth atmosphere and in orbit. It is still orbital, and amateur space watchers have been reporting seeing it by telescope regularly. It is best visible when positioned as to reflect sunlight against a background of a darker sky, like at early evening and before dawn. But, I have never heard of the ISS having any parachute system designed, which would allow the ISS could land intact. Also, the ISS would need a rocket system to aim in reverse and slow it down substantially, creating a fall from orbit. When the ISS eventually falls to Earth, it will break into thousands of fragments most of which will burn up in in the air. So, this parachuting monstrosity, lying in the Albermarle Sound off Kitty Hawk is definitely not the ISS."

Alice responded, "Fryed, that brings us back to what the masses of people from around the planet are all tweeting, texting, and saying. This is an extra-terrestrial space vehicle."

"Alice, that would be thrilling. I cannot tell you how much that excites me. I think life on this planet as we know it is about to change. Can you imagine the exciting technologies they would bring us? I am assuming these alien-life forms will have a form we can identify and interact with. I have no ideas about how these space-life forms communicate. It can be via though brain waves, or retinal electrical signals, and not auditory air-carried mechanical waves like us Earthly mammals use. We have enough computer artificial intelligence to decode whatever signals the aliens send us. I predict we will be at the point of simple greetings and yes and no types of communication exchanges within 10 days. Alice, we need to be very broadminded about what sort of life forms these will be. They might not be like us, DNA-crafted, gravity-dependent, oxygen-consuming life forms. They can be any life form, beyond our limited imaginations. I am so excited!". No one saw the man take a breath or blink during this entire time.

Alice, unphased by his excitement said, "Fryed, thank you for your theories. My last question to you is, could this be the Ares-1 Mars Mission returning to Earth?"

A brief silence followed, then Fryed spoke tentatively. "Well, now Alice. That is a sadness no one has spoken about for nearly three years now. As you remember, after the explosion that was heard, and all communications broke down, we mourned our loss together as a nation." His energy had not depleted, but his body language showed he did not want to get seated on the wrong side of this discussion.

He continued, "I don't have to sound cavalier, but I want to be clear. The whole Ares-1 mission was a joke. They sent up a geriatric doctor who was retired, and not even licensed in the USA anymore, although licensed in a third world country. He only had 4-weeks astronaut training before launch.  There were so many astronauts who were trained for that mission as first team flyers, and as backup team flyers. Yet, in the end it was the most-odd mish-mash of misfits ever sent into space. One was even a paraplegic. They are all dead now. Fourteen useless deaths in one mission. No wonder all nations agreed to end human space-flight. It was widely opined that humans are not research rats. We can find out what ever we need to know about space with unmanned missions. No one talks about the Ares-1 mission disaster anymore. The whole world felt the horror of it and recognized the narcissism of political leaders seeking glory for their own countries and themselves. World politics changed with a domino effect. America's President resigned, because of the Ares-1 disaster. China got a new leader. Russia got a new leader. The United nations is different. Even the European Union has changed. Who knew fourteen lives lost could cause such a domino effect on world changes over the following 3 months after the mission failure?

Alice spoke. "Fryed . ."

Fryed cut her off.

"Sorry if I am monopolizing your time, but I am passionate about this. Please be respectful of those lost fourteen brave men and woman. We must not draw them into this commercial entertainment designed as news speculation. Whenever I look at the Stars at night, I think of them. Their dust is outside there somewhere. We should say a prayer for them."

Fryed lowered his head and wiped a tear from his cheek.

Silence followed.

Alice, touched her earpiece. "I have an announcement. We are about to cross to Washington DC. The President of the United States is about to make a statement."

"Good Evening citizens of the United States, and friends around the world. As we all know, a flying object descended from space, landing in the Albermarle Sound due West of Kitty Hawk at sunset this evening. We have secured the area, with a number of naval combat vessels surrounding the floating object, and holding a quarter mile back. Citizens have been evacuated to a safe distance of 20 miles from this object. We have full air space control with high altitude radar and bomber planes. We have a series of interception jet fighters in the air and will sustain continued air presence for as long as needed. The North Carolina National guard has been activated. We have Navy Seal and infantry units in close proximity, on all the surrounding land beaches.

We have tried all forms of radio communications with the object, to no avail yet. I have received personal communications from countries around the world, offering us any support we may need. I spoke to the leaders of Mexico, Canada, Britain, Germany, France, Russia, China, United Korea, and Australia. Many more leaders are scheduled to speak to me after this news cast. I am confident that we, as united members of the human community, can handle whatever emanates from out of this space object.

We are reviewing all our national security radar systems. It seems there was a brief dysfunction in the North Carolina coastal area, which we are investigating, in hope to determine where this object came from. We never saw the space-object and only heard of it first from BBC TV News.

There are as yet no signs of any chemical, or biological release from this object. We've detected no movements on it or about it. We have drones approaching with cameras, and flood lights to help in the approaching overnight hours.

We do not want to scare these possible space travelers. We want to seem friendly, but equally protective of our nation and our planet.

My chief communications officer will provide information updates as it comes in.

Thank you. God bless America."

The President went off camera, and Alice came back on.

"We will now take a brief commercial break. After that, we will return with updated news on this space invasion".

---

Hello. I am Alice Banks for BBC World News. We now have dramatic news about the origins of this vehicle. You see on screen here a video filmed from an American military drone. It is early nighttime in North Carolina. In the spotlight of the drone, you will clearly see numerous lettering on the side of the floating tube-like craft. It says NASA. We have a former NASA employee from Texas, Mr. Allister Black. Welcome Allister."

"Thank you, Alice."

"Allister, you used to work for NASA, and still live in Houston, correct?"

"Yes, I was director of the Ares-1 Manned Mars Mission. As you know, after we lost Ares-1, there was a severe political backlash, and Washington decided to defund NASA totally and disband it. We were forced to terminate all human space-missions and return the ISS astronauts to Earth. After the Ares-1 mission failure inquiry I was terminated."

Alice. "By terminated, you mean fired?"

"Yes. It is a very PC word that means nothing other than fired. The word protects the employer from being easily sued afterwards for unfair dismissal. It doesn't matter to me. The nation and the government just wanted to distance themselves as much as possible from the loss of the fourteen Ares-1 Marsnauts. We only learned later about the sabotage actions of the crazy Chinese astronaut, but by that time it didn't matter who was to blame. They had all been lost."

"Alister, the big question now is, what do the NASA logos on the side of this flying object floating in the water mean? Is this the Ares-1 Mars mission module?"

"Alice this can ONLY be the Ares-1 Mission. I cannot believe it. We have had no radio contact, of any form, with the mission for three years now."

Alice asked the question they were all thinking, "Do you think the Marsnauts are alive?"

"I always liked that term Marsnauts. It started as a joke, but soon became the official term in place of Mars-Astronauts. Alice, I just cannot say. In theory, the Mars spaceship was capable of automatic flight with navigation corrections. In theory it could fly from Earth to Mars, orbit Mars and return direct to Earth. We programmed in a number of different spaceship sub-module arrangements, all of which could return to Earth. It is a complex story. Based on the little I could see on these news videos suggest to me there was a crew descent cabin, a control module, a number of cargo modules, and a fuel and rocket-engine segment. That is correct for the Ares-1 returning manned Mars mission to have conjoined launch-landing modules, as seem to be parts of this object that came down presumably from space.

If this is simply an automated return of the original Mars fully flight-ship, it would be the greatest technical achievement ever done by man. I expect we will only find the bodies of the Marsnauts in the ship. It is hard to explain. We don't know what the explosion was about, what was damaged, or whether the Marsnauts survived. We don't know what was damaged and whether the Marsnauts survived it. I'm guess not.

Another mystery is that we sent a lot of modules off from ISS to Mars with the Ares-1 mission. Some of those modules were scheduled to be left on the surface of Mars. Some were scheduled to be abandoned, after entering Earth Orbit, and preceding Earth landing. I cannot tell what modules have been returned to Earth. If they are the correct ones, chosen for the return trip to Earth, it suggests some Marsnauts are alive and did the correct module re-arrangements in space flight. I need more information before I can comment more authoratively.

"Alister, now where does Chinese sabotage of the Mission come into the story"

"It is hard to say. I no longer work for NASA, but I would guess they may re-employ me to help with the scientific forensic investigation. This returned spaceship will give us so much information. I am sure some scientists and engineers will have their reputations restored, and possibly others will face criminal charges. The biggest question by far will be whether the allegation of Chinese sabotage can be validated or refuted".

Alice, "Thank you Alister for all of that information. I can't believe the next question I am going to ask you. Assuming we have live Marsnauts in that space vehicle, could they bring new disease back to Earth?"

"Correct. We once had a protocol in place for their return to Earth. They were to be transferred to a sealed airtight unit, for 10 days of observation and blood tests. The next 10 days, we would expose them to a variety, like parakeets, cats, dogs and monkeys. If no evidence arose suggesting an exotic disease from another planet, they would be allowed out of quarantine, and moved to an isolated open camp with spouses, nurses and doctors. Only after those 30 days would they be exposed on stage to the public. Of course, we don't have this isolation structure anymore. It got stripped down, after the Ares-1 loss disaster."

Alice, "Hold on. I have some breaking news. We are crossing to the US military control center set up in Elizabeth City, North Carolina. We will get our BBC reporter on the ground, Mary Johannsson. Hello Mary, can you hear me?"

"Hello Alice. I can hear you. I am standing in the main control room for the military control center, set up for this assumed alien invasion. We now know it is in fact a NASA vehicle, based on logos on the sides of the vehicle. Every breakthrough here is more fantastic than the other. We have had Navy Seal divers on top of the floating space vehicle. There is life inside the vehicle. There are people aboard. I have colleague, Missy Pace, with the divers. We will interview her via Skype."

---

"Alice, I have been given permission...."

The image blurred and the sound disappeared for a few seconds.

"Hello, Hello again. This is Missi Pace from BBC News; can you hear me?"

She sounded downright frantic. Was she in danger, or overly excited?

"Yes. Go ahead Missi" yelled Alice from the BBC desk.

The picture appeared, showing the journalist was wearing a scuba diver suit. Unbelievably she stood next the ship hatch and a Marsnaut wearing his white space-suit long-sleeve undergarments.

She held the phone as steadily as possible, realizing this was the moment of her career.

"I am Missy Pace, reporting for the BBC today. I work for ECTVK as a reporter. Can you introduce yourself?"

It was late twilight then and the camera flash-light was on.

"I am Valborg Schmidt, acting captain of the ship Ares-1 Mars Mission."

"Valborg, speaking to you is amazing. Are you OK?

"I think we are all doing well, thank you. This full gravity seems heavier than what we expected, so please excuse me resting on the hatch frame." He flashed a smile.

"We have so many questions Valborg. How many of you are in the module?"

"We are ten persons on board at this moment. Nine are astronauts and one is a baby."

"A baby?"

"Yes."

"A baby born and conceived in space?"

"Yes"

"Nine astronauts? Did five die?"

"No two died. Three have been transported to the Elizabeth City Hospital."

"I am confused. To a hospital? Is someone sick?"

"No. One lady Marsnaut was in labor with a baby, and we sent her, her partner, and the doctor"

Missy Pace, the wet-suited journalist, was clearly overwhelmed by all this unexpected and seemingly inexplicable news. "How did they get to the hospital?"

Valborg explained patiently, "A lobster fisherman came by the ship to investigate as soon as we were in the water, and the ship floatation tubes were out and the balance-rudder had dropped. We saw him when we opened the hatch and looked out. We called out for help. He took the three in his boat to Elizabeth City Hospital. It was a small boat, with an outboard motor. He said it would take 40 minutes to get to the harbor, and he could dock very close to his truck. He would drive them to the hospital that was only five minutes away. Doctor Rodney thought that was OK as Marjena, that is the pregnant lady, was only starting with labour. We haven't heard any news because our spaceship cellphones don't work that far apart."

---

Twenty minutes later. "Hello Alice. This is Mary Johannsson reporting from Elizabeth City. After hearing about the three remarkable Marsnauts who were brought here, we decided to reach out to them and ask if they were up to an interview. We received word they were willing to be on camera only. They will remain seated in semi reclining chairs, because they feel dizzy when they stand, and they are also very weak. From your left to your right we have Marjena Lubiski and her one-hour old baby son, with no name as yet. Next we have Ares-1 Mars-mission ship-captain Chris Bolder, and the ship-surgeon Doctor Rodney Powell. The three don't want to be interviewed today, but they do have one message to the world. Let me adjust my position so they are in good camera view."

The three Marsnauts were grinning massively, while Marjena cuddled her baby closer on her chest. Chris had his arm proudly around Marjena's shoulders. They raised their right hands and fist-punched the air, saying, "Like lions to the Last!"